Mom, Apple Pie, and Murder

Edited by Nancy Pickard

BERKLEY PRIME CRIME, NEW YORK

MOM, APPLE PIE, AND MURDER

A Berkley Prime Crime Book / published by agreement
with the editor

PRINTING HISTORY:
Berkley Prime Crime trade paperback edition / May 1999

All rights reserved.
Copyright © 1999 by Nancy Pickard and Tecno Books.
(For individual copyrights, see page iii.)

This book may not be reproduced in whole or in part,
by mimeograph or any other means, without permission.
For information address: The Berkley Publishing Group,
a division of Penguin Putnam Inc.,
375 Hudson Street
New York, New York 10014.

The Penguin Putnam Inc. World Wide Web site address is
http://www.penguinputnam.com

ISBN: 0-425-16890-5

Berkley Prime Crime Books are published by
The Berkley Publishing Group, a division of Penguin Putnam Inc.,
375 Hudson Street, New York, New York 10014.
The name BERKLEY PRIME CRIME and the
BERKLEY PRIME CRIME design are trademarks
belonging to the Penguin Putnam Inc.

PRINTED IN THE UNITED STATES OF AMERICA
10 9 8 7 6 5 4 3 2

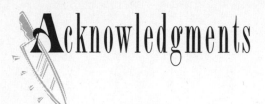

Acknowledgments

Contents

Introduction

Nancy Pickard

What could be more yummy than a good mystery and a delicious apple recipe? And who better to dedicate them to than Mom? That's the triple prize we've concocted for this collection of short stories by some of today's most talented mystery writers. The stories range from lighthearted and funny to dark and serious, but they all have two things in common: Every one features a "mom" someplace in the plot; and apple pie is mentioned, too, although you may have to search for it in some of the stories where it is most subtly, or devilishly, placed! In these pages, you'll find good moms, bad moms, hilarious moms, and tragic moms; you'll read some stories that revolve around murder, and others that hinge on crimes of the heart. But throughout, you'll find only the best writing and only the best apple recipes!

Now here's how to read this collection:

Grab a juicy round apple, or heat up the leftover apple pie.

Turn first to your favorite author, or anywhere else you wish. Start at the beginning, the back, or the middle. Feast on all of them at one sitting, or nibble on one story at a time. And enjoy!

These stories and recipes are dedicated to Mom . . . yours, mine, and ours.

Sincerely,
Nancy Pickard

A Worm in the Winesap

Susan Dunlap

One day, Susan Dunlap put aside the mystery novel she was reading and said to her husband, "I could write that." To which he replied, "I dare you." Never a woman to back down from a challenge, Sue is now the proud owner of not one, but three popular mystery series starring, in order of appearance, meter reader Veejay Haskell, Police Officer Jill Smith, and Private Investigator Kiernan O'Shaughnessy. They all live and work in California, as does their creator. Her husband is now very careful about what he dares her to do.

"Whopper Rooter: *We shoot your wad.* Good morning."

"It's afternoon, and hardly good."

"What's your problem, clogged pipe?" There was a sudden pause, then the dispatcher asked, "Is this Eve again?"

Eve groaned into the phone. It's never good, she knew, to be on a first-name basis with sewer rooter men. "Yes, it's Eve. The whole system's clogged. Send out the big truck."

"Eve in Eden Township, right?"

"Right. Your guys know the way. Hurry."

"We'll get someone out as soon as possible. At least now"—the dispatcher paused, and before he could control his snicker sufficiently to go on, she guessed what was coming—"at least you don't have to worry about a flood!"

She hung up. She would have slumped down on the couch if she hadn't already been sprawled there. She gazed at her Whopper Rooter Club card—all ten holes punched. Who would have thought she'd be eligible for her free root so soon?

Anyone who knew her sons, that's who.

This was a fine way to spend Mother's Day. All she'd ever wanted was to be respectable. With a sigh, she pushed herself up, stepped over a shepherd pup gnawing on the carpet, grabbed her eight-year-old son by the scruff of his decidedly scruffy neck, and shoved him into his bedroom. "You can stay there till you're ready to apologize to your older brother. If I were you, young man, I'd apologize sincerely enough to make him forgive you. You know your brother's temper." She shut the door with restraint—not, she knew, that that would make a difference. Both her sons could think till Christmas and the concept of personal responsibility wouldn't enter their cerebrums. They each had their own obsessions. They were, after all, their father's sons.

Their father, of course, was all too aware it was Mother's Day. He was presiding in the kitchen of his beloved restaurant, Adam's House of Ribs. From all over the state families came to claim their much-coveted reservations, and were now lining up in the lobby under the *Adam's, the Original Rib House* sign, eager to cram into the dining room and chow down in honor of Mom.

Adam's was always crowded. His ribs were known all over. He easily could have franchised, opened second, third, and fourth Houses of Ribs. His operation could have spread out like ribs from a breastbone, but, alas, he lacked the foresight. "Branch out, Adam," she had urged him time and again, "include pie, or cobbler, or pandowdy—we've got the apples." That, of course, was before one of the boys denuded the tree, flushed the apples, and the Whopper Rooter man punched hole number three. Still, with one phone call she could have bought apples—Golden Delicious, Red Delicious, Red Junes, Red Melbas, or Red Spies. A couple of E-mails would have scored her Jonathans, Kings, Pippins, even Newtown Pippins. For Cortlands or Arkansas Blacks. . . but it didn't matter. Adam had no head for apples. Adam was obsessed with ribs.

How had her life come to this—married to a man whose life was in ribs. Adam, alas, was the personification of stodgy. *Chances* were not items Adam took. To Adam, chances were slippery slopes. Twenty years ago when she stepped down off the bus in Eden Township she was too young to understand what stodgy meant. Twenty years ago when she stopped in the restaurant for takeout, she had been awed at Adam's renown, impressed by his status. And just about flattered out of her mind when Adam himself offered her one of his ribs.

Adam was looking for a hostess at the restaurant and she had beaten out nine other girls for the job. Then, she'd figured her victory was due to her chipper smile, her long blonde hair, her A in Algebra. It was only after she'd started at Adam's House of Ribs that the other waitresses kidded her about being chosen for her name. "Oh no," she'd assured them. "How silly. Adam is a businessman; he's tight with the guys in power—the mayor, the governor, and all. No way would he be so superficial as to pick a stranger off a Greyhound and install her as his hostess just because her name is Eve. He's a chef of renown, a force in the rib world. All over town, lips lick at the very thought of his barbecue sauce. No, no. He chose me because I'm a great hostess, not because I'm Eve."

She had been a great hostess, the best, Adam said. She had loved figuring out which table suited the mayor's party, and how to handle things when the governor came and the mayor was already ensconced at the best table. She knew what to do when the governor's wife and ex-wife arrived in separate parties and the governor was already there, eating with his girlfriend. She knew good and evil, and how to seat them at opposite ends of the room. Adam kept saying he didn't understand how she managed it. Of course he didn't—forethought and discrimination were not Adam's focus. Ribs were.

Adam may not have known how she managed to charm the customers, but her skill at it certainly charmed him. She was the only woman for him, he vowed; their's would be a marriage made in heaven. A rootless eighteen-year-old, she had been awed at the prospect of becoming the wife of such an important man, such an upstanding family man who would never humiliate her in public. She had had a father who philandered and a boyfriend who strayed; she knew all too well what it was like to have the neighbors uncover humiliating secrets and the whole family be disgraced. Never again would she hide behind closed doors while the neighbors smirked. But with a man like Adam such an abhorrent possibility was out of the question. Adam was everything good, trustworthy, and oh so respectable. For all that, stodgy was a small price to pay. And after the whirlwind trip to Reno and the Paradise Wedding Chapel (gown and tux provided) she had loved driving home into her garden in Eden and standing proudly at the gate with Adam. She loved walking through Eden with Adam; she loved it when Edenites greeted her smilingly because she was Adam's wife. The ridiculous idea that he might have been attracted by her name, she dismissed as easily as she brushed her blond hair away from her big blue eyes.

She had been wrong. How wrong, she didn't understand until the birth of their first child, Cain.

"Cain?" she had shrieked. "I thought we were going to call him Dwayne, or Derek, or Kyle. What about Cain for a *middle* name?"

But Adam would have none of it. Cain, just Cain, the boy was.

Adam adored him, adored his own status as a father and even more firmly settled pillar of the community. "We'll be having us another," he took to saying; "like with ribs from Adam's House of Ribs, you can't stop after just one."

Eve could have stopped. Cain was a fractious child. Eve's blond hair and blue eyes and experience at seating the governor's wives at opposite ends of the restaurant were not great preparation for child-rearing. She knew better than to repeat her mistake.

But Adam was adamant. "Little Cain needs a brother to rough-house with," he said night after night—*Monday* night after Monday night, when the House of Ribs was closed.

"Little Cain needs a brother," he insisted while the boy was battering at the sides of his ant farm.

"Little Cain needs a brother," he said as Cain pushed a play-mate off the jungle gym.

"Cain needs a brother," he intoned as they headed to Eden Acres Elementary School to get the boy reinstated after he backed up the plumbing and flooded the school.

"Cain is a natural-born farmer. What he needs is a little broth-er to help him out," he said as the boy worked off the debt to the school board cultivating Adam's oregano plants.

"Cain needs a little brother," Adam insisted as they got him from Juvenile Hall after the sheriff found Cain's own "oregano" patch.

How many times had she dreamed of leaving Adam? Lots more than she considered producing a second son. But leave him she could not. There was Cain. Cain was not an appealing child, an endearing adolescent, or an attractive teenager. Still, she was his mother and she couldn't abandon the boy. And she certainly wasn't about to leave and take the little ruffian with her.

Then, too, there was the restaurant, where she'd hostessed away her best years. After Cain's birth, she did all the ordering, threatening, permit-getting, inspector-bribing, and anything else not directly rib-connected. So there would be no danger of Adam's important friends wondering why he couldn't afford to hire an administrative assistant, she created that identity for herself. No supplier suspected that it was Eve ordering vinegar; no Health Department inspector guessed Eve was sending his payoff. As far as the neighbors, the mayor, the governor, and their wives knew, Eve was lounging in the garden with Cain. Between Cain and the restaurant work, however, she'd barely ever gotten *out* of the garden. If she left Adam, she'd never be recompensed for all her work. But she was Adam's wife, and she wanted her half.

Even so, she might have waited till Cain was collared again, then cut her losses and filed for divorce, but she had nowhere to go, and no friends in town to help her. "Family first," Adam always insisted. "When you've got a family you don't need friends coming by, filling your ears with gossip." With a respected man like Adam, what kind of case could she make for divorce? Inadequate, that's what. She could hardly protest that Adam was stodgy, boring, totally without imagination. Adultery was grounds for divorce; stodgy was not. And she had to admit, though it didn't make her think better of herself, that she did love being the respected wife of a pillar. She wasn't about to humiliate him, and herself, in public.

It had been too infuriating to think about, and so she hadn't.

She had no decent explanation why after ten years she'd let herself get pregnant again—maybe just the wish for a daughter. Adam was ecstatic. He created a new tomatoless sauce in honor of "Cain's impending brother." No amount of suggestion would convince him that babies come in two sexes, and by the time her due date arrived Eve knew within herself that he was right: Cain would have a brother. She did the only thing she could—bribed the birth certificate clerk, and named the baby Dominick. Adam, of course, was furious.

"You won't be happy till his brother kills him, will you, Adam?" she said.

But Adam's life was complete and he was happy. He built a gazebo and now on Monday evenings he sat there with Cain and Dominick watching *Monday Night Football*.

The rest of the time he was cooking ribs. Cain occupied himself by growing marijuana and picking on his brother; he didn't share his father's belief that he needed a little brother. Eve felt so guilty about poor little Dominick that when he asked for a dog she could not refuse him.

Not quickly enough did she realize the danger in giving the boy twenty dollars and sending him to the pound. By the time she remembered the pound's motto—"It is more blessed to give than to receive"—little Dominick's German shepherd had a litter of ten. Little Dominick petted them lovingly. Cain fingered them suspiciously. When Adam put his hands beneath the pup's ribs . . . well, it didn't make her think better of her husband.

How had her life gotten to this state? she asked herself as a brindle pup teethed on her hand. She would have washed off the slobber if she'd had more ambition, *and* if she'd had water. Where was the Whopper Rooter man? He knew the way here as clearly as to his own house. She thought longingly—

The knock on the door was so soft she almost missed it. The Whopper Rooter man? But no. Wayne, the Whopper Rooter man, used the front door. This knock was on the back door, the favored entry of Cain's "clients."

Only this morning she had walked in on Cain as he was packaging leaves and seeds and said, "One of these days, you're going to get yourself sent away for good."

"Nah, I won't." Cain twirled the pigtail left after he'd shaved his head. "Dad's got friends in high places."

"That's your father, not you. You don't make yourself likeable, Cain."

Cain had shrugged, and then spotting one of his brother's dogs, he'd kicked at it as he had a dozen times before.

"Hey, Crutch, lay off!" little Dominick had whined, knowing that the hated nickname would set his brother off as it always had. Then, as usual, Cain lunged, Dominick sidestepped and ran, furniture suffered.

But this morning when the scene replayed itself little Dominick had said nothing, just stalked out of the house. And it wasn't till the toilet backed up that Cain had realized his crop had gone downriver. Cain had screamed: "I'm going to kill you, you little bastard!" He'd uttered this same threat time and again without the interruption of originality—he was, after all, his father's son. But this time was different. This time Eve believed him.

Now Eve cocked an ear to hear what Cain was telling this disappointed customer. But before she could distinguish a word, the front doorbell rang. She pushed herself up, threaded through shepherds, and pulled the door open. Dog hair flew. The Whopper Rooter man would be a relief in more ways than one.

But when she opened the door there was no familiar brown-uniformed man holding a snake. On the stoop was a tall redhead wearing a boa, a feather boa.

"Adam here?" The woman was years older than she, but beautiful, voluptuous, and dressed like no one Eve had ever seen in the burg of Eden. Her flowing beige ensemble looked cool, comfortable, and likely to drive men wild. And her snakeskin boots were made for stomping. There was a jiggle to this woman, like she was an engine idling, an engine too busy to take time to stop and start again. This was a press-the-gas-and-go gal. "Adam? Is he here or what?"

"No, of course Adam's not here. It's Mother's Day. He's been at his ribs since four A.M."

"Oh, the rib thing," the woman said with a laugh. "You know, if we were talking anyone but Adam I'd give you my friend's card. My friend is a shrink in Vegas; deals with fetishes. But Adam—"

"Adam's *cooking* ribs, at his restaurant, Adam's House of Ribs. You must not be from around here if you don't know about Adam's House of Ribs. Who are you, anyway? And what do you want?"

The insistent woman shifted her weight on her stiletto heels and tossed her boa over her left shoulder. She was tapping her toe, ready to move on. "I used to live here. Just passing through on my way back to Vegas. Haven't heard from Adam in thirty years, not since I left. Just figured I'd stop in and see how the old bird was doing, you know?" She lifted her weight back, blinked her mascaraed eyes, and stared at Eve. "Who are *you?*"

"Me? I'm Adam's wife." She would have demanded an explanation from the woman but the woman was laughing too hard, her whole body shaking, her boa fluttering like a flock of flamingos. She was laughing so loud it set the dog barking, the pups whining.

"Adam scored another wife?" the woman managed to squeeze out between paroxysms.

"*Another* wife? What do you mean another wife? We've been married for twenty years. We've been together since the day I arrived in Eden. I've hostessed in his House of Ribs, I've borne his sons. . . . I am Adam's wife, his only wife. Adam and Eve. Our son is Cain," she added defensively. For the first time, she felt a pang of regret at not having named her younger son Abel, as if that would have clinched her argument and cemented her status as Adam's wife, a pillar-ette of the community. She glared up at the beautifully coiffed stranger. "Who the hell are *you?*"

The redhead swallowed hard. It took her three swallows and one more toss of the boa to get herself under control. Still she didn't answer.

"*Who are you?*"

"I'm Lilith, of course, Adam's first wife."

First wife! Eve stumbled back against the door. There were a hundred questions she could have asked, but she knew none of them would change anything. She wanted to scream at the woman, "Liar!" but she knew as sure as God made little green apples that this woman, this Lilith, was telling the truth. Lilith had been married to Adam.

Eve squeaked out the most pressing question: "Did you live here?"

Lilith shrugged, the kind of careless, offhand response more suited to a question like, "Do you want more peanuts?"

"Oh, yeah, I lived here, in this house, which I gotta say was in better shape back then. 'Course the town wasn't called Eden Township then, wasn't incorporated. I'll tell ya, hon, the burg was so dead back then that *Adam* looked good. The only time I wasn't bored was when I was pissed off."

"And so you got a divorce?" Eve asked hopefully.

"Divorce? Hell, no. One night I took a good look at Adam and what I saw was—well, you've put up with the guy for twenty years, you gotta know what he's like. Stodgy; everyone in town knew that. I'd had it, hon! Enough; you know what I mean? You don't live forever—just seems like it when you're in Eden and bored outta your skull. So, I up and lit out of here. Never looked back."

The damn woman was missing the point. "So Adam divorced you, then?"

"Never served me with papers. Coulda. I'm in the book in Vegas. Lilith's Realty." For the first time she stopped moving. Her alligator purse bounced against her hip and settled; the boa hung limp. She put an exquisitely manicured hand on Eve's shoulder. "Listen, kid, I'm sorry if I upset you. I'm sure your life is fine here in Eden. Excitement, independence, they're probably overrated anyway. A life of your own isn't for every woman. You got a nice house and garden, all those lovely apple trees. So what if Adam is stodgy—you hadda know that when you moved in with him, right? I mean everyone in town knows that. What do you care if all those dullards are laughing every time you're introduced as Adam's wife. But, listen, sweetie, forget all that. You just put me out of your mind. Here," she added, "for you."

Before Eve could open her drooping mouth, the boa was around her neck and the woman was climbing back into a white stretch limo Eve hadn't noticed before.

"First wife!" Eve stormed out of the house, jumped in the Adam's House of Ribs delivery truck, and headed for the restaurant, muttering as she went. "Damn you, Adam. I knew you were stodgy, but at least with stodgy you expect honest. But you, damn you, are stodgy and dishonest. Damn you."

Adam's House was built to resemble ribs: curved, red plaster cascading to the ground. She entered through the breastbone and stalked back to the heart of the operation. Adam was standing beside a huge stew pot he could almost have drowned in. Years ago he had succumbed to the occupational hazard of the chef and now for all Eve knew he might have given away all his own ribs. Certainly none of them showed. He was an apple of a man—red, round, and, with his clothes off, dead white underneath. Now he looked up at her furious face, smiled, and said, "I'm trying a new recipe, want to tas—"

"You were married before?" she demanded.

"Before what?" He gave the long wooden spoon a turn.

"Before me, that's what. You had a first wife!"

"Oh, that."

"That! Why didn't you tell me?"

"It was a long time ago. Before I met you. Before I even got the idea for Adam's House of Ribs." He stirred the pot twice around. "Lilith wasn't into ribs." He stirred a third time. "This sauce, I'm using flax powder and cardamon, see, and—"

She yanked the spoon out of his hand and slammed it to the floor. "So Lilith just left, right? Did she divorce you?"

Adam stopped the spoon. "I don't know."

"How can you not know?"

"I don't know. Gone is gone. I didn't have time to worry about her. I had ribs to cook, sauce to stir," he said, pulling himself up righteously to his full five and a half feet.

"I could go, too, just like she did."

Adam fished another ladle out of a drawer. Then he laughed. "You? You, Eve? Where would you go? You haven't spent a night out of Eden since we've been married. And how would you support yourself? The only work you ever did was hostessing here, and surely you don't expect a reference from me."

"I could get a different kind of job."

"What, Eve? As a housekeeper? *Our* house looks like a kennel. Or maybe you could apply as a governess. Tell them what a great job you did with Cain."

"Cain is your son, too." But she knew that this argument would change not one mind. For once Adam had thought more clearly than she. Of course, he'd had years to prepare for this moment, ever since he'd spotted a potential second wife.

Questions and accusations lined up in her brain, but she didn't bother to voice them. She was too depressed. She drove slowly home, suddenly seeing every corner as Lilith must have, as a spot with four roads leading out. This is what her life had come to— married to a stodge, laughed at all over town—and what was the best she could hope for? That the Whopper Rooter man had arrived at the house and cleared her pipes.

But he hadn't. When she pulled into the driveway she saw not the hoped-for rooter truck, but three motorcycles, and the front door ajar. In the house deep-voiced men were swearing, dogs barking, howling, and whining, and little Dominick screaming as if his life depended on it.

"Cain!" Eve yelled as she flew through the door. "Cain, don't you slay your brother!"

But Cain was nowhere to be found. The three hulking muscle-shirted men whom she recognized as Cain's customers were stalking from room to room. Little Dominick was howling. Three little shepherds had knocked over the cookie jar and one was regurgitating on the sofa, while the rest of the dogs ran in circles, kicking up fur. The only word she could make out in the melee was "kill."

"I'll kill him. Where is the bastard?" one of the men demanded.

"Out!" she commanded. "Out of. . ." But it wasn't her house, was it? It wasn't her furniture. Outside, it wasn't her garden. The clothes she was wearing. . . legally, were they even hers? She fingered the only thing that was unquestionably hers—the feather boa. Cain's three enormous and irate customers stalked toward the door. One of them was holding a Gravestein. *Her* apple? Without thinking she grabbed it out of the man's hand. The behemoth scowled, did a double take, and kept moving.

Eve held the Gravestein in her hand and stared at the light shining off its shiny red skin. Now, she realized the truth in Cain's customer's question: *Where is the bastard?* Cain was, indeed, a bastard, spiritually and genetically. Cain was a total bastard. Adam, whose interests spread no farther than the rib cage, had, of course, never bothered to divorce his first wife. Not his *first* wife; his *wife, period.* And she, Eve, what did that make her? She was not his wife at all. She was his concubine, his mistress, his woman of the night, his whore, and his dupe. She was astonished, furious, and most of all humiliated. How could she ever again stand at her garden gate and face the upright people of Eden? She felt totally exposed—in fact, naked. The Gravestein was still in her hand. Without thinking, she took a bite.

Before she could swallow, little Dominick raced up to her, squeaking, "Crummy Cain tried to poison my dogs. Mama Dog, she went after him and he ran. That way!"

Calming herself, she said, "Dominick dear, where is the poison?"

"In the dog food, Mother."

"How do you know it's poison, dear?"

"Because crummy Cain poured it from the bottle with the skull and crossbones," he said, nodding his little head sincerely. "I always watch over the dog's food. Sometimes I even taste it. Cain doesn't like my shepherds and he might—"

"But you're not sick, are you Dominick? If there was poison—"

"The black puppy got to the bowl before I could get there. I grabbed him around the middle and made him throw up."

She glanced at the small shaking dog and the mess around him. He was an empty dog, and she could tell he would survive, though the couch would not. She took a necessarily shallow breath to calm herself and asked little Dominick, "Does your brother know you taste the dog food?"

"Of course, Mother. I made sure of that. So he knows he can't kill my dogs, see?"

She grabbed the phone and dialed Adam.

"Adam's House of—"

"Put Adam on." The fury that filled her like extra hot sauce must have steamed out of her mouth. The present hostess at the House of Ribs didn't ask who she was or what she thought was important enough to interrupt the chef in the act of creation. She must have run for the kitchen. In less than a minute Adam was at the phone. "Eve? What do you—"

"Cain tried to kill Dominick."

"How could—"

"He put poison in the dog food he knew Dominick would eat." She could hear the horror in Adam's thick intake of breath.

She'd never heard such outrage from him. Perhaps she had misjudged him as a father. He took another labored breath before he could speak. "My son eats dog food?" Adam croaked out. "*My* son eats dog food? I'll be laughed out of the barbecue business. How could you let this happen? You have no responsibilities, Eve, except to maintain our place in Eden, and you can't even do that. Every chef in town is going to be laughing in his sauce. Eve, you've got to hush this up. You've got to—"

She slammed down the phone and turned to little Dominick. "Pack your dogs, dear." Grabbing the poisoned dog food, she herded little Dominick and the shepherds into the restaurant truck and drove to the House of Ribs, to the back door. She left the engine running.

For once the kitchen was empty. Adam was nowhere in sight. She looked at the great steel pots. She stared at the kitchen of this restaurant to which she had tied her security, for which she had endured two decades of boredom, with neighbors nodding knowingly behind her back, for which she had endangered the life of her younger son, not to mention his shepherds. This kitchen was not half hers. It would never be half hers. The new sauce boiled, sauce that was not hers. This sauce was Adam's alone, and when he died it would be the sauce of his legal wife and his sons, plural, if Dominick evaded his brother that long. Never would it be hers. Fans rattled, sauce boiled. She looked at the sauce. She looked down at the dog food in her hands. She poured.

Evelyn, as she is known now, sat on the veranda of her new home. It was a rental, but Lilith had gotten her a good deal on it. "Here, Spot. Here, Blackie. Here, Whitey, Here, Tan-o." (Dominick was a nice child, but not a whiz at names.) She smiled as the dogs dropped the *Eden Township Sentinel*, the *Tribune*, the *Wall Street Journal*, the *New York Times*, and the *Washington Post* at her feet. Front page of all five. She picked up the *Sentinel* and smiled at the headline: "Local chef poisoned by own sauce. Scads of Edenites get the runs." The *Tribune*, after insisting it was not its policy to speculate, noted that Adam's wife—or more accurately, long-term mistress—and younger son were missing and that some of the ribs in Adam's House were of questionable origin. The *Times*, after insisting it was not its policy to speculate, alluded to Adam's notorious first wife, and to his infamous son Cain. The *Wall Street Journal*, after insisting it was not its policy to speculate, commented that while Adam had been beyond reproach, the same was not likely to be said of his beneficiary, his remaining son, Cain. And the *Washington Post* noted that Cain had fled the saucy scene of the crime and had been spotted in Nod, a sleepy village east of Eden, before vanishing. But authorities had distributed flyers with his picture and insisted they expected little difficulty in capturing him. Cain was, after all, marked.

The other dogs arrived, papers in mouths, but Evelyn had to put off reading them. She was in a new town, in a new state, and this was her first day as pastry chef down at the New Jerusalem Pie Shoppe.

She planned to make a name for herself with apples.

Coin of the Realm

Pamela J. Fesler

Pam Fesler is a new and talented kid on the mystery block, but she's hardly new to professional writing. She's a former advertising copywriter and magazine editor whose fiction has appeared in Mystery Scene *magazine,* Rosebud, *and* Mystery Forum *magazine. Her short fiction is also featured in the anthology* Marilyn: Shades of Blonde. *Pam lives in the Kansas City area.*

I sat on the second step of the marble stairs leading to the fountain across the road from City Centre Mall. Cal sat on the third step, his legs splayed, his arms encircled around my neck. Two women, blonde, tanned, and be-diamonded at ear, neck, and wrist, walked in front of us and ran their eyes up Cal's thirty-six-inch inseam. One squinched her overpainted, inflated lips at me. I blocked their view of better things.

"This is apple pie in name only," Cal said as he unwrapped a lump from our sack o' lunch. It was Sunday and people from all over metropolitan Kansas City were at places like Fedora having fluffy omelets and thick-sliced bacon washed down with mimosas. I was dining out of a paper bag. Again.

I reached back and patted his cheek. One of the women said

something to the other and they snickered. I ran a hand over Cal's knee and grinned at them. They took their tennis-tanned act on down the sidewalk.

Cal sucked hard on the straw in his iced tea and drained the forty-four-ounce paper cup. His right hand moved closer to the armhole of my sleeveless denim blouse. My cell phone vibrated.

"Maddy's ready to open the store. Tell Cal to keep his hands to himself."

"Yes, Mother." I turned the phone off and tossed it into my straw bag.

"Time to go shopping." I dropped my half-finished soda into the trash and waited for Cal. He stood and dusted off his rear.

"Other than determining that many of these women wear far too much makeup, what have we learned?" Cal asked.

"We've learned that there might be good reason why Maddy Carlisle needs our help. Whispers of a Baby Bubbies shipment can draw a crowd faster than rumors of free Kansas City Chiefs tickets."

Cal picked me up with one arm and swung me around.

"Give the little lady a big hand." He put me down.

"Cal, don't do that."

"Just keeping up the image, Cassandra. We're supposed to be a couple. By the way, your roots could use a touch-up."

It's comments like that one that keep me from being attracted to Cal. Oh, I'd be lying if I said I found Cal Belmont unappealing. He's taller than I am, intelligent, athletic, quick-witted, and often kind. He's also a smart-ass, at twenty-five too young for my thirty—and our employee.

Still, after several stakeouts with my mother, Lacey, with whom I'm in partnership at Fairchild & Fairchild Investigations, I can tell you I have been on worse assignments, than in the park in front of the mall. Who'd suspect a love-struck couple of being on the lookout for the person who sent a note threatening to swipe a shipment of society's latest coin of the realm, Baby Bubbies, from my mother's best friend's store?

I've been peed on by a dog while hiding in a bush to see if a husband and his private parts were where they weren't supposed to be. I've been scratched by the three-inch carmine nails of a woman in a bar who turned out to be a man who thought I was hitting on her date, a suspect in an embezzlement investigation. I've had my foot run over by a car driven by a ten-year-old boy who thought he was smarter than the world and could get away with murder.

But when it came time to choose who would be working inside Madeline's keeping an eye on Madeline "Maddy" Carlisle and her expected shipment and who'd be outside watching, I begged to be outside, and it wasn't because of Cal.

It's because I hate, loathe, despise, abominate, and abhor Baby Bubbies.

Mrs. Eleanor Weaver, who runs M&W Cleaning Services from the office next to Mom's and mine, has four complete sets of all of the little stuffed-with-Lord-knows-what creatures. She hunts you down to brag about it. I know this because once she stuck her permed red hair under the bathroom stall door to tell me about them.

"One set's for my son, one set's for my daughter, one's for me, and one's in case we need cash right away. There's no way they can do anything but increase in value. Look at all the Baby Bubbies that are retired." At that point, her eyes glazed over with the certainty that she'd made a sound investment.

It's a bull market for Baby Bubbies right now and I'm sure she thinks I'm a fool because I don't know the bull's birth name and date as shown on the tag in his ear.

I do know that, according to reliable gossip, Mrs. Weaver is behind on her house and car payments. Last month her husband began running around with a kindergarten teacher half his age because his wife's entire life is now centered on what started out as a children's toy and has become a marketer's dream.

The latest by-product of the toy craze was what had brought Fairchild & Fairchild into the madness. Six shipments of Baby Bubbies had gone missing within the space of a month. The owners of each of the stores that lost shipments had received notes before the fact informing them—in rhyme—that they'd be the next store hit. Mom's best friend, Madeline Carlisle, had received note number seven.

This is to inform you, you're lucky number seven.
Let the Bubbies go unprotected, or be on the road to Heaven.

It wasn't Emily Dickinson, but it was enough to send Maddy to our office.

"I'm worried, Lacey," she said to my mother. "When that shipment was stolen in St. Louis, the note threatened a kidnapping. When the assistant manager didn't show up for work, someone from the mall office called to tell the owner her store hadn't opened. Then a raspy voice phoned, telling the owner to stay where she was, that someone would sign for her shipment at the store and the assistant manager wouldn't be hurt if she didn't call the police, and that he'd be released when the Bubbies were collected."

"So someone signed for the boxes?" Mom asked.

"The deliveryman said it was a woman in a hat and sunglasses. She was taking out the trash."

"Name?"

"Jane Smith."

"And the assistant manager?"

"Had two flat tires when he went out to start his car. Who carries two spare tires around with him?"

Mom arched her left eyebrow. "Convenient."

"I'm expecting a shipment, Lacey. I'm paying extra for Sunday delivery. Please be here," Maddy had said. Her hands shook as she pulled a stick of cinnamon gum from the pack. A fingernail caught in the foil and she shook it loose. The pack and the nail sailed across the store. Maddy had been trying to stop biting her nails and covers them with fakes, layered by coats of red, green, or purple enamel.

"They cost too much to gnaw on," Maddy said of her nails.

"Maddy?"

"No, Lacey, I haven't called the police."

"Is there anything unusual about this shipment, Maddy?" Mom asked.

Maddy nodded.

"It contains Algernon the Albino Alligator."

Cal, who'd been looking out the window watching the women come out of the fitness center, spoke up.

"That's the newest Bubby. Supposed to be worth a thou off the bat." He resumed his inventory.

"A thousand?" Mother looked even paler than usual. "That's insane!"

"I agree. That's why I want you there to protect my investment."

"And you, Maddy. We need to protect you," I said.

"And me," she said softly. "The last time we got Baby Bubbies, collectors lined up in the wee hours of the morning. Security goes off duty at midnight and the mall manager was furious with me for 'disturbing the peace.' So this time I arranged Sunday delivery to fool the public. Not that I have a lot of hope it will."

It hadn't, not for the smallest fraction of time. Word had leaked out, the way it always does when greed puts its big foot down.

Now, on Sunday, a line snaked from the front of the store down past Sweet Stuff, A Confectionery Shoppe and ended at Blitzen, a store that carried a bit of everything—mostly the owner's ego, according to Maddy.

Cal and I walked hand-in-hand across the street. I fought the urge to skip.

"We're not the only ones on watch, Cassandra. Look."

Framed in two windows were two scowling faces.

"Unhappy store owners?" Cal guessed.

We settled on the bench closest to Maddy's and Cal threw his arm around my shoulders.

I leaned over to Cal's ear. "May I tell you about my top two pet peeves? People who spell perfectly good words like shop as shoppe." I pronounced it with two syllables. "And babes who don't know how to walk in high heels."

To complement the look of her three-and-a-half-inch open-toed slingbacks, she wore a skinny black silk suit. Her steps sounded like dueling castanets. She swept past the line and pounded on the door of Madeline's. Mom opened the door and a crush of people moved forward.

"Hey, lady, get in the damn line," a frizzy-headed man yelled at the woman in black.

She wheeled around and hissed at him.

"I'm Rosemary Barron and I manage this mall. I can have you out of here so fast it will make you unsure that you were even here."

The line recoiled.

"We'll be open at noon," Mom said. Before Miss Stiletto could say anything, Maddy appeared.

"What is it, Rosemary?"

"People are complaining, Madeline. They're lined up outside my office telling me about the chaos in front of your store. You don't see Boyson McGee running a shop like this." She whined in a cadence that accented every third word.

"Oh, Rosemary," Maddy said, hand to heart. "You'd better run right back there and see that no one starts a fight. I know how it is when people bother you when you're trying to open up. Excuse me. We open in fifteen minutes." Maddy shut the door, maybe grazing Rosemary's toes. Oh, well, she needed a pedicure anyway. The crowd applauded.

Rosemary Barron stepped back from the door, turning her head, then her back to the line of people, and marched off. I wanted to know how she did that. No one in line saw her face. I did, and it was not a pretty sight. Her body was stiff as a stick, but her face quivered with rage.

I sucked in my breath.

"I agree," Cal whispered in my ear. "If we were looking for a crime of hate, I'd vote for her."

Mother opened the door of Madeline's.

"Ladies and gentlemen, we've just found out the shipment of Baby Bubbies we were to receive this morning has been delayed." A buzz of outrage went up from the crowd. "To compensate you for your time, you'll be given a number. When the shipment comes in tomorrow, that will be your place in line. This number will be good for tomorrow only. We're sorry for the inconvenience."

Just as they do when boarding for an airplane is called, people surged forward, hoping to get a better spot in line.

"Please hold your place. No rain checks will be given to crashers." Mom smiled, but she said it in the same voice that kept my brother and me from picking fights in the car.

"Who are you?" a man with love handles and a cigar stuck in his mouth wanted to know. I'm sure he left out "the hell" only because his share of Baby Bubbies was at stake.

"I'm the woman handing out the cards that determine whether you have a shot at Algernon the Alligator." The line snapped as straight and smooth as the hem of a dress sewn by Great-

Grandmother Lindquist, the state fair's best homemaker six years in a row.

The crowd was quiet as Mom passed out hot pink, numbered plastic cards. Mouthy Guy got number 11. He beamed. The reptile was as good as his.

"Psssst."

"I'm sitting right next to you, Cal, why are you hissing at me?"

"Just quoting her." Cal inclined his head to the south. It was Mrs. Weaver, Our Lady of Perpetual Bubbies, the woman from our office building. I motioned her over because I knew she'd come anyway.

"Hello, dear. Could you put in a good word for me with your mother?" She waved card number 25 at me. "I just don't know her as well as I know you." Meaning she wouldn't have nerve enough to trap Mom and her reserved manner in the bathroom. Me she followed in to comment on the skimpiness of my underwear.

"I'll pass the word along."

"I have other outlets, but we have to cover all the bases."

"Absolutely, Mrs. Weaver."

She giggled and stuck her pudgy left index finger in her mouth.

"I have contacts all over the world. Networking makes my mission so much easier." Her eyes burned with the zeal of the committed and flakes of red glistened from her gum line.

Networking? Mission? I shivered as I always do when I feel nauseous.

Mrs. Weaver removed her finger from her mouth.

"I know you consider this foolishness, Cassandra, but many of us don't. I'm taking care of myself and my children, which is a damn sight more than my husband's doing."

"I'll see what I can do."

"Thank you." Mrs. Weaver scuttled away.

"I've wondered," Cal said. "What does she think we do?"

The sign on our office door just says Fairchild & Fairchild. Going to an investigator's a lot like going to a therapist. People don't want to advertise that they go to either.

"I've been told she thinks Mother and I run an escort service."

"And me? Does she think I'm one of the escorts?"

"Oh, yes. Actually, her words were 'He's the big blond hunk who keeps that operation afloat.'"

"Mrs. Weaver is not as flaky as she looks." Cal stood up and offered me his hand. "Come on, love biscuit."

I took his hand and we walked into Madeline's.

"May I help you?" A curly-haired woman with a workout body, black eyeliner drawn to the sides of her temples, and a name tag that read Marcia spoke to Cal's midriff.

"We're here to see Aunt Maddy," I said, and hugged Cal's arm to my side. Mop Top's eyes followed the hug.

"She's rather busy right now. I'm the assistant manager, may I help you?"

"You must be new, I'm—"

"Cassandra, darling. I'm so glad you're here." Maddy swept— no other word for it—from the back of the store. We air-kissed.

"And Calvin. So happy you both could come." Maddy moved to Mother's side. "Well, I have an announcement to make. You two remember Lacey Fairchild? If things go the way I hope, she'll be my partner." Marcia's mouth opened wide enough for me to count her fillings.

Still, she recovered nicely, I thought, considering she'd have another boss to answer to. Marcia offered Mother her hand.

"Welcome to Madeline's."

I noticed that Mom shook from the top instead of the side just in case Marcia decided to pump a little power into the handshake.

"Thank you, Marcia."

Silence draped itself around the room. I'd started to say something when the door opened and a woman with a chin like an ax and a bosom wide as the ax handle came in. A tall man with a rear that should have had a wide-load sign hung from it rolled after her.

"Madeline, we have to talk," the woman said through her nose. The man waddled toward Maddy's office and the rest of us followed.

"Marcia, could you watch the front of the store?" Maddy said. "Thank you."

Maddy shut the door. Her office looked small with six people in it.

"Who are all these people?"

"They're no doubt wondering the same about you, Boyson. Lacey, these people are Boyson McGee, owner of Sweet Stuff: A Confectionery Shoppe and Amalee Blakely, who has Blitzen. This is Lacey Fairchild, who's buying part of Madeline's, and my niece, Cassandra, and her fiancé, Cal."

Neither said they were pleased to meet us, although Boyson McGee did nod to Mother's and my chests before he continued. His inventory did not go unnoticed by Amalee Blakely, who curled her lips in disgust.

"Madeline," he said. "You've repeatedly ignored Rosemary's efforts to maintain order. We're sick of your unruly crowds blocking our doors to customers. Get out of this center. Now."

Amalee Blakely sniffed and looked at us as if we'd neglected to wear deodorant and change clothes for several weeks.

"And, Madeline, we know you've been threatened. It's just a matter of time until someone gets hurt by your greed." A bit of spit fell out of Amalee Blakely's mouth. She pulled a tissue from her cuff and touched it to her thin lips.

"How did you know Ms. Carlisle had been threatened?" Mom asked.

"Use what brain you have, lady—it was her turn," McGee said.

"Turn?"

"Yes. All the stores that get the big shipments are being hit."

"Have you been threatened also?" Mother asked.

"No!" they shouted together.

"I wonder why not."

"Like Boyson said, the volume stores are the only ones worth the effort."

"Amalee, you know we get the same amount. Everybody does," Maddy said.

"Madeline, I do not know whom you're sleeping with or paying off, but you're getting twice the supply we are. Last week you got fifteen Reginald the Reticulating Pythons. We each got eight. Explain that," Amalee said.

Maddy is rarely at a loss for words. She was now.

"I'll say it again. Get out or we'll have you thrown out." Boyson McGee pulled the door open and it banged against Maddy's desk. He and Amalee marched out of the store. Marcia and the handful of early Sunday afternoon customers were half-gawking in the way you do when it would be politer not to look but too interesting not to peek.

"Well, that was fun," Mother said.

Maddy sighed.

"Lacey, could you and Marcia hold down the fort today? I'm going home."

Mom nodded.

"Maddy, take tomorrow off. I'll open the store in the morning."

Marcia's jaw jutted into fifth gear, advertising what she thought about Mom's plan, but she walked over to a woman fingering the Bubbies display and asked if she needed help. Maddy, Cal, and I left by the back door. When we got outside, Maddy leaned against me. I put my arm around her.

"I'm tired, Cassie."

"I know, Maddy. Has anyone else complained to you about the crowds?"

"No, Cassie. Oh, I'm not the most beloved tenant out here— you know I speak my mind. But this . . . "

Maddy's left eye drooped, a sign I've recognized since my childhood that she's reached her limit. I hugged her and Cal and I looked at each other over her head.

"We'll take care of it. You know Mom. She'll make it okay."

We can talk ourselves into believing almost anything, can't we?

The phone at the office rang the next morning at eight-thirty.

"Cassie, I think you and Cal had better get over to Madeline's now. I just found Rosemary Barron dead on the floor of Madeline's office."

"What?"

"It's hard to tell from where I'm standing, but I think there's a python wrapped around her throat."

"She was snake-bit?"

"Cassie, a panel's been removed from the ceiling in the bathroom. I think I've found where the missing shipments of Baby Bubbies are hidden. You know the white alligators that were stolen? They're here, along with a whole menagerie of other animals. I'll say this, Cassie, Baby Bubbies are more absorbent than cat litter. There's not nearly as much blood as I'd expect on this floor."

"Wait a minute. Wait a minute! Blood? Absorbent? You said she had a snake around her neck."

"Cassie, I think her throat's been cut. I'm guessing the snake went around her throat first and stanched that initial gush of blood after her killer used the utility knife."

"Utility knife?"

"You know, that retractable knife Maddy uses to open boxes. It's right next to Rosemary."

Oh, that knife. The one that makes your spine clinch when you snick it open.

"We're on our way." Just as soon, I thought, as I rest my head between my legs.

Mom and I have worked hard from our little suburban office to have a good relationship with the police. So I wasn't unhappy when Cal and I got there and found Lt. Mike MacIlheney in charge.

And Maddy? Well, she went into overdrive when she arrived and saw him.

"What are you doing here?" she said through clenched teeth.

"Just doing my job, Ms. Carlisle."

"Like you did when I was robbed? At gunpoint?" Maddy's robber was never caught, and she blames the ineptitude of the "small-town, small-minded police" rather than their having about zero clues to go on.

We love Maddy; we don't pretend she's always reasonable.

"Well, maybe since it's murder, you'll give this a little more attention. How was she killed, or haven't you had time to figure it out?"

"We have some thoughts on that, Ms. Carlisle. I'd like to hear yours. Perhaps we could sit down out front and talk about it? That Stickley sofa looks comfortable."

Maddy's lips moved.

"Excuse me, did you say you want to call a lawyer?"

"Do I need one?"

"Do you?"

"No."

"Miss Carlisle, you want us to talk with everyone, don't you?"

"What I said was 'Oh, Lord, he actually knows who Gustav Stickley is.'"

I heard Mom give a little groan.

From a law enforcement standpoint I'd want to talk with Maddy, too. Maddy's store. Maddy's enemy dead on a pile of contraband Baby Bubbies. Maddy's fingerprints undoubtedly on the knife. Maddy's feud with other store owners.

Other than that, Mrs. Lincoln, how was the play?

After an officer with far too many teeth for his own good got through questioning me about what I knew, I called Maddy's lawyer and told him to stand by if we needed him.

I'd just hung up the phone when an angry buzz rose in front of the store. I looked out the window and saw Mrs. Weaver, and the lippy guy waving his stogie and number 11, and a bunch of people hell-bent on getting their Baby Bubbies. Today. I wondered if they'd still want Algernon if they could see him now. I figured they would.

What next?

Boyson McGee, pounding on the glass, flanked by Marcia and Amalee Blakely.

"Madeline, what the hell is going on now!" Boyson yelled when an officer opened the door to tell them the store was closed.

"Rosemary's dead. Someone cut her throat," Madeline blurted. Amalee and Boyson looked at each other and their lips pursed back the urge to chant, "*We told you so, we told you so.*"

Shock swung in the air and crashed.

"What!" Boyson.

"You are truly sick, Madeline. I know you didn't like Rosemary, but that was no reason to kill her." Amalee.

"So does that mean we won't be open today?" Marcia.

Different people have different reactions to tragedy.

Maddy got up from the sofa. "Lacey, Lieutenant MacIlheney says we can go now." She looked at the three at the door. "But I think he'd like to speak to you."

Mom, Cal, and I filed out the front door. Mom turned right

and we turned left. The crowd had been dispersed, but I expected to find Mrs. Weaver on our office doorstep soon. She'd probably want to know if any Baby Bubbies were injured. I fantasized about going into graphic detail with her.

"Cassie, wait for me," Maddy called as she ran-walked on the high heels she thinks make her look taller.

"I called your attorney, Maddy." She hugged me.

"And he'll make cleanup arrangements when the police say it's okay."

"Thanks, honey."

We walked toward the mom-mobile, the minivan that lets us spy in the guise of a suburban soccer mom. "I didn't do it, Lacey," Maddy said as Mom reached for the car door. Mom patted her hand.

"Maddy, we know you didn't."

"That damned detective thinks I did."

We couldn't tell her she was wrong.

"Maddy," I said, "who has keys to your store?"

"I do. Marcia. The mall office. The cleaning service."

"Cleaning service? Who?"

"M&W. They're bonded. I've used them for years."

Mom and I looked at each other.

"We're familiar with them, Maddy."

"The keys can't be duplicated." I could almost see Maddy's mind turning over, frantically hunting for answers. Mine was jogging right alongside hers.

"I don't think the murderer had to, Maddy—I think he or she already had one," Mom said. "I wonder if Rosemary's key was on her."

We learned that it was when Lieutenant MeIlheney stopped by our office the next morning. He said it had been in her suit pocket.

"Whose prints were on the knife? Besides Maddy's. And

Marcia's," I asked.

Mother cleared her throat. "And mine."

Lieutenant McIlheney shrugged. "And the woman who owns the cleaning service."

I ran a scene through my head. Mrs. Weaver moving that pesky knife so she could dust under it. Mrs. Weaver picking the knife up from the floor where it had fallen so she could vacuum under it.

"I really stopped by to see if you could tell me where Maddy Carlisle is."

"Detective McIlheney," Mom said with her soft voice/fixed stare combination. "Did you lose track of her?"

He stared right back.

"Ms. Fairchild, we weren't following her." He had a half-smile that made him look younger and sort of innocent. If I were choosing sides for a lying contest I'd want first dibs on him.

"When can she reopen?"

"Soon. Probably tomorrow afternoon." Mom walked him out the office door.

"So how old is he?" I asked when she came back.

"Forty-one."

"Just made the limit."

Cal looked from Mom to me. "What are you talking about?"

"Just a theory Mom has. No man is really worth a damn until he's forty."

"There are, of course, exceptions to every rule," Mom said. Cal beamed. He also believes that, unlike me, she's a natural blonde. I can't tell him that she showed me how to color my hair the same time she taught me how to shoot. Everyone deserves to have some illusions.

Mom and I spent most of the night and the next morning playing "what if." We got back into Madeline's in the afternoon. Cal dropped us off and went to retrieve Maddy from the day spa where she'd sequestered herself. No jokes, please, about women and what they do in crises. It's why we live longer.

The two of us stood in the center of the back room. I don't know how many times we'd been there in the twenty years that Maddy's owned Madeline's. Mom and I looked at the floor. I was seeing Rosemary Barron surrounded by blood and Baby Bubbies. I shook my head to clear the image.

"They did a good job," Mom said.

The floor was as clean as you could get a piece of linoleum that had played host to hundreds of dragged boxes, numerous penetrating spills, and, finally, a bloody murder.

In the bathroom, the ceiling panel was back in place. I looked for the stepladder and couldn't find it, so I stood on the rim of the toilet and pushed upward. The tile moved but didn't fall. I jockeyed the panel back and forth and it came about halfway out.

"Cassandra, hand me the kit."

I got down and found Mom on the floor on her hands and knees, nose close to the ground. I gave her a black leather bag that's togged out with everything from a magnifying glass to several individually wrapped funnels that make a female investigator's stakeout as effortless as a male with an empty milk carton.

Mom took the glass out of its leather case. She peered through it.

"Look at this, Cassie."

"Blood?"

"Yes. You have to expect some seepage—it's an old floor and linoleum has ground cork in it. But this is different."

Mom dug out a one-sided razor blade and scraped a tiny bit from the floor. "I think it's nail polish. One of those blue reds. Look here. And here." She pointed to two faint lines about a foot apart.

They were there. Fainter than praise for a bistate tax hike, but there. They looked like they'd been scraped already. The police no doubt had a sample in a bag at a lab at this moment.

Mom and I sat back on our heels and looked at each other.

"Rosemary Barron was wearing kind of a maroon polish, wasn't she?" I asked.

"It's called Strike Me Red," Marcia said from the doorway. She held a 9mm Glock. Since when did assistant store managers start carrying firearms? "I was at the beauty shop when she was having a pedicure. Don't bother to get up."

Marcia took a flip phone out of her pocket, hit a single number, and said, "Get over here now." She listened for a minute.

"Because I just walked in on two new problems. And bring my black leather briefcase." Marcia flipped the phone shut.

Mom and I swiveled our eyes around, trying to figure a way out.

"Don't even think about it," Marcia said. She tightened her grip on the gun.

"May I guess what happened, Marcia?" Mom said. "I don't think you set out to kill Rosemary." Marcia looked at me.

"I agree. If you had, you'd have used the gun."

"We think Rosemary Barron had a crush on Boyson McGee. She held him up to Maddy as an example of how Maddy should act. Since two examples are better than one, we wondered why she didn't mention Amalee Blakely," Mom said.

Marcia's lips twitched.

"I thought you looked smart. That's why we had to get the Bubbies out of here. Before you tried to put your stamp on things like all new owners do and redecorated the bathroom or something."

"Why use Madeline's instead of Sweet Stuff for storage?" I said. Marcia shot me an "are you really that stupid" look.

"Rosemary wanted to be around Boyson. She was in and out of his place all the time."

"So he played along with her?" Mom asked.

"He took her out whenever I stored a shipment. The bitch practically never went home, so we had to get her out of the way. I picked up shipments on my days off and we hid them in the ceiling here when Maddy was gone."

"Jane Smith, I presume?" I said, and shifted positions on the floor. My left leg had gone to sleep.

"In the flesh."

"Seems like a lot of work to skim a few Bubbies off the top to fatten up the shipments to some of the stores," I said.

"Wrong!" Marcia looked delighted. "Our contacts took complete shipments. It was Boyson's idea to seed your friend's supply with some, ah. . . appropriated Bubbies. It kept old Amalee focused on Madeline."

"Did Rosemary walk in on you and Boyson?" Mom asked.

"Oh, yeah. We were taking a shipment out of the ceiling. I couldn't find the stupid stepladder so he was holding on to me by the waist. The next thing we knew she was screaming at us."

"Because he was holding on to you?"

"Because, Lacey, she heard me say something like, 'Hold me tighter, Boyson. We're almost there. Just a couple more minutes.' Damn stuck ceiling tile."

"And then you killed her?"

"No, then Boyson shook her, trying to shut her up. He dragged her around the floor. That must have been when she smeared her new polish job. She crashed into me and the Baby Bubbies fell out of the ceiling. I grabbed a snake and wound it around her throat." Marcia moved from one foot to the other.

"She kept struggling, didn't she, Marcia." Keep them talking.

"She just wouldn't quit. The snake wasn't long enough to strangle her with, but it was long enough to grip both ends. I had the knife in my pocket. We'd opened all those boxes from Italy in the afternoon and I just stuck it in my jacket so it'd be handy."

Marcia looked at her watch. I could see sweat around the band.

Where was Boyson?

"So you clicked open the knife and. . ."

Marcia was silent.

All three of us jumped at the knock on the door.

"Answer it," Marcia said, pointing at Mom and stepping into the bathroom. Mom got up off the floor and opened the door. From the floor I had a spectacular view of the muscular legs of the delivery service driver. I knew they were his because Maddy had described his dimpled knees often.

"Hey, how's it going? This is what the boss is waiting for. Sorry it got routed wrong. Hope you didn't have a bunch of unhappy people." He set two good-size boxes on the floor, took a clipboard from the top box, and handed it to Mom.

"Sign on line seven."

Mom signed.

"Take care," he said, and bounded out the door.

"I hope you didn't do anything stupid like write 'Call the police,'" Marcia said. "But just in case, I think we'd better get out of here. Move. We're going to go get your car. Don't be silly and try anything. It's a long walk."

She was right—it was a long walk. You'd think that because mall employees get there early they snag the best parking spots. Wrong. Some malls even have shuttles to ferry employees to work. This one owned a lot that faced the shopping center. If you worked there, you parked across the street or you got a hefty ticket and a reprimanding letter.

We went out the back, strolled around to the front just like three girlfriends on our way to a margarita-laced dinner, and were greeted with shouts from Mrs. Weaver, Number 11, and a gaggle of other Baby Bubbies seekers.

"Yoo-hoo, Cassandra! We saw the deliveryman. Did *it* come? Did you get *it*?" Mrs. Weaver no doubt thought she was talking in code, the better to fool a line crasher.

"Hey, toots, we're talkin' to you," Number 11 yelled at Mom as he stabbed in her direction with his cigar. He had his number and could afford to be a smart-ass.

"Uh, Marcia, I don't think your associate or your money will be joining us."

I pointed across the street at Boyson McGee, attaché case in hand, getting into his tuna boat of a car. Large and environmentally incorrect, it had the roomy front seat that he no doubt needed for his wide butt to make a comfortable getaway.

"Son of a . . ." Marcia looked at us, then at Boyson, and ran toward him.

McGee went into a swivet, his head shaking like a tambourine and his right hand waving her out of the way while his left steered the ship.

Marcia fired at the car. He veered right. Marcia fired again. He steered left and ran over her foot. She dropped the gun and fell to the ground, screaming.

"Been there, done that, know it hurts," I said to Mom as the sirens got closer.

"We messed up big time, Mom." I put my arm around her shoulder.

"How?"

I gestured to the crowd of people who until a couple of minutes ago were gathered in front of Madeline's. The shooting was over and curiosity was pulling them closer.

"We should have handed the whole damn thing over to them from the beginning. They would have solved it in a New York minute."

Mom and Dad at Home

Ed Gorman

Kirkus recently called Ed Gorman "one of the most original crime writers around," and anyone who has followed his work knows that to be wonderfully true. He's the author of twelve novels, including Black River Falls *and* Cold Blue Midnight, *and four collections of short stories. This Edgar nominee and Shamus Award winner lives in Iowa, a state known for growing good writers.*

Dad always called the night before he came home.

Sometimes he was in Kansas City, sometimes he was in Peoria, sometimes he was in St. Louis. He was a salesman, sold barber supplies, and sometimes he traveled as much as two weeks of the month. Usually, though, it was eight, nine days. He had a big territory because he was the owner and sole employee of his company. He said hiring salespeople was a pain. You always had to stand over them and make sure they were doing what they should. Plus they always wanted big monthly draws and full health insurance and a new car and insurance for the car and even then they were always griping about something the boss did or didn't do. So Sam worked alone and made out just fine.

Young Sam Culver never got much sleep the night before his

daddy got home. Much as eleven-year-old Sam loved his mom, it was his father he adored. His dad was cool. And this wasn't just his opinion. All the kids in the Riverside Apartments said so, said they wished their dads were cool like Sam's. He was full of jokes, Sam Culver was, and he listened to a lot of the same rock and roll songs they did and when a kid used a dirty word he'd just grin and say, "You give me a buck, I won't tell your mom you said that." And then he'd wink at the kid and all the other kids would laugh. Cool.

Young Sam wasn't pure of heart, of course; nobody is. Another reason he couldn't sleep was he'd lie awake wondering what kind of gift his dad was going to bring him this time. Dad was great for gifts. A real nice one for Mom, a real nice one for Sam. He never forgot. The last few times, Sam had gotten a guitar, a CD player, a football helmet and new football, and a gift certificate to Blockbuster good for any five CDs Sam wanted.

He was usually sleepy, Sam, the day Daddy came home. Not that this slowed him down or dulled his excitement.

As now.

He came into the kitchen and Mom said, "You finish your comic book already?" She was at the sink, washing off dishes and putting them in the dishwasher. She wore tight jeans and an electric-blue blouse. She was pretty but she looked a lot older than Dad. Sam had heard her arguing with her sister once, Aunt Kathy, and Aunt Kathy said, "Good-looking man on the road all the time like that, you're just not looking at the facts, Mary Jo. I told you when you married him, a good-looking man twelve years younger than you, it's going to be trouble. But you know how you are about not looking at the facts."

Sam had never understood what "facts" Aunt Kathy was talking about. He just knew that after Aunt Kathy left that time, Mom collapsed on her bed and cried and cried and cried. Sam lay down next to her for a while and then she all of a sudden took him in her arms, her warm face against his neck, and he could smell her tears. It was so funny that tears had a *smell*.

"Yeah. I only had one comic anyway. 'Spawn.'"

"There aren't any cartoons on?"

"I tried to watch 'em. But I've seen all 'em already."

She looked down at him and smiled. It was kind of funny, how Mom's face was so wrinkled up and old already and Dad still looked so young and handsome. Sometimes he felt sorry for his mom and he'd go right up and hug her and he wouldn't even know why.

"Can you smell what I'm baking?"

He sniffed the air. "Great! Apple pie."

"With the crust crisscrossed on the top the way Dad likes it."

She put a soapy hand on his shoulder. "He'll be along, hon. He said when he called last night that it'd probably be around supper time. And that's not for another hour yet. So why don't you go play with some of your friends."

The Riverside Apartments was four large native stone buildings set up on a prairie hill on the west edge of the city. Almost all the couples who lived there had kids and all the women worked as well as the men and when they'd cook burgers on the outside grills, they'd sit around and drink beer and swat mosquitoes and talk about how nice it'd be when they could finally afford a house of their own. Every once in a while there'd be a fight between two of the men who'd had too much to drink, or between a man and his woman, the man usually accusing her of flirting with somebody. Dad always knew how to handle these situations. Everybody always said that nobody could calm people down like Dad. He just had the knack was all.

Sam went and played ball around the back of building four. It was a warm June and the late afternoon was sweet with a soft breeze and the smell of newly mown grass and the deep shifting shadows of oncoming dusk.

He told the kids that his dad was coming home and so what they wanted to know was what he figured his gift would be this time and he could see how envious they were. Birthdays and Christmas was when they got gifts. They didn't have dads who traveled and brought gifts home once a month.

He played until the mothers started coming home in their dusty cars. Even the new cars were dusty. The workday was so long there wasn't time for washing the car except once a month or so on Saturday mornings down at the do-it-yourself wash where the grit never quite got washed away. The mothers all took turns coming to the back of building four and calling for their kids. There was something melancholy about it, the sound of those female voices, something timeless too, mothers calling their children home in the gathering dusk as they had for thousands and thousands of years. The girls were usually more obedient, and headed home right away. The boys stalled for a while. Sam was always curious about the young-looking mothers. Some of them still looked like they were in high school, still sweet and fresh. Sometimes for a week or two at a time, Sam would get a crush on one of these mothers. He always saved them from fires or burglars or dope addicts. He'd lie in bed and have these heroic daydreams and his crotch would feel funny and he would love these women so much and so truly at these moments that it was painful. Literally painful. The other mothers looked old, like his mom, old and wrinkled and worn, though you could see that they actually weren't all that much older than the young mothers. Time isn't always nice to some women, his mom had said one day.

Around six, Sam's mom was there, calling him in. He ran over to her and said, "Dad home?" Her smile gave her away.

He ran all the way to the back of their building and then up two steep flights of carpeted steps. The carpet still smelled kind of spicy from a recent shampooing.

He hit the door running. Dad sat inside on the edge of the

couch. He had a beer in the hand that was resting on the arm of the couch. He wore a white shirt with the sleeves rolled up to the elbows and a pair of blue slacks. His sun-blond hair was movie-star long, curled slightly at the collar line. He had a smile that brought back a lot of Sam's loneliness and occasional resentment. And he smiled that smile now.

Sam ran over to him like a little kid. Dad stood up and got Sam under the shoulders and then started swinging him around. Sam giggled. "How's that boy of mine?"

"G-g-g-o-o-o-d!" Sam said, giggling so hard that the word was broken up.

"Don't swing him too hard," Mom said from the doorway. "We're going to eat in just a little while."

It was one of those things that moms said that didn't make any sense when you thought about it. What did swinging him too hard have to do with eating dinner? But that's the way moms were.

Dad put Sam on the couch next to him. "Bring this young man a martini, miss, and put it on my tab."

Sam giggled some more.

"I'll martini you two all right," Mom said, smiling as she went to check on the roast in the oven. That was Dad's favorite meal. Pot roast with potatoes and onions and carrots fixed in right with the meat. You put a piece of fresh apple pie with that and you had Dad's favorite meal. Mom fixed it just about every time Dad came home.

Dad had kind of a semiformal interrogation that he wove into his dinner conversation. He said to Sam:

"You been good to your mom?"

"Uh-huh."

"You make your bed every morning?"

"Uh-huh."

"You take out the garbage?"

"Uh-huh."

"You help your mom carry the groceries upstairs?"

"Uh-huh."

"You say your Our Father and Hail Mary and Glory Be every night before you go to sleep?"

"Uh-huh."

Then Dad would look slyly at Mom and say, "Well, honey, sounds like this is a boy who deserves a present."

Dad reached below the table to his lap and brought up a small gift-wrapped box and handed it to Sam.

Sam set a couple of world records getting the box open. Then he said, in order, "Oh, man!" followed by, "Fantastic, Dad!" And finally: "Cool!" Three new computer game CDs, three exclamations. Sam knew how expensive these CDs were. Once the word got out—and there is no faster form of communication than that of kids in an apartment complex—everybody would be stopping by the apartment and driving Mom crazy.

Mom got perfume and hand lotion. She threw her arms around her husband and held him tight. Sam looked at her hands behind Dad's neck. They were starting to wrinkle, too.

While they were having the apple pie, Dad said, "How about helping me clean out my car tomorrow. Then we'll go wash it and stop by the ole DQ." That's how Dad always referred to the Dairy Queen. The ole DQ.

"Sure," Sam said. Dad always let him buy the most expensive stuff on the menu.

After dinner, Sam went immediately to the living room, where he rigged everything up so he could play one of his new computer games on the television. He chose "Space Harlots." The girls on it were cool.

Mom and Dad were in the bedroom with the door closed. She always gave him a back rub so he could go to sleep faster. After his trips, Dad would usually sack out about seven o'clock and sleep till eight, nine the next morning. He was a hard worker.

About an hour later Mom came out, closing the bedroom door very, very quietly, meaning that Dad was asleep.

"It's so good to have him home," she said, and yet she sounded somehow sad about it, too. Maybe you got that way, sad all the time, Sam reasoned, when you got older. Maybe your sadness defenses didn't work as well as when you were young. Sam was rarely sad.

She sat on the edge of the couch and watched him play. He had everything set up on the coffee table. A couple of times he said "Shit!" when he made a mistake but Mom didn't say anything.

After a while, she said, "You know what'd be nice?"

"What?"

"You could go down and clean Dad's car out now."

"Now?"

"Umm-hmm. So that when he goes down in the morning and sees his car, all the junk'll be hauled out of it."

He looked longingly at the computer in front of him. "Well—"

"C'mon, while you've still got some light left. Just take a plastic bag from under the sink and throw everything in there and just throw the plastic bag in the Dumpster when you're done."

Five minutes later, he was down in the parking lot. In the dusk he could see fireflies. And hear Jenny Akins. Jenny was his one true love. She was twelve and had no idea that he even existed. But someday she would. Someday he'd save her from a burning building or an alien attack and then she'd know he existed all right.

Dad was a self-described "muncher." Which was weird, because he never gained any weight. All the time he was driving and selling barber supplies, he was eating Baby Ruths and Almond Joys and Lay's salsa potato chips and Hostess pies (he was partial to blueberry) and Snickers. And drinking Diet Pepsi. Dad was a Diet Pepsi fiend. Cleaning out Dad's car meant gathering up all the candy wrappers that cluttered up the front and back seats and the floors as well. Dad was kind of an in-car litterer. He had one of those cheap little plastic waste dealies you hung off the radio knob, but that was always full. So Dad just pitched things where they landed. There were magazines, too, mostly *Time* and *Newsweek* and *U.S. News & World Report*. Dad was a Republican. He liked to read articles that made the Democrats look bad. He'd always say, "Just listen to this one, honey." And then he'd read it out loud to Mom.

Sam spent maybe ten, twelve minutes cleaning out the car. He stuffed everything into the small plastic bag and carried the bag to the Dumpster. He hated opening the Dumpster lid. It smelled like a grave inside and there were always flies buzzing around it and he always wanted to wash his hands right away because he felt dirty all of a sudden.

He was in a hurry to get back to "Space Harlots." He was almost to the stairs when he felt Dad's car keys in his pocket bumping against his leg. He'd forgotten: Mom had asked him to bring up Dad's sample case from the trunk of the car. Dad always forgot to bring it up.

Sam went over to the car and opened up the trunk. The car was still new enough to smell new but now there was a different, sour scent, too. For some reason, he thought of the Dumpster and how it smelled like a grave.

The case was a black leather attaché case. It sat next to the spare tire and the jack. The trunk was very neat and organized. He lifted the case up—it wasn't heavy at all—and then he saw the newspapers. He wondered why Dad would have newspapers in the trunk.

He took the newspapers out to look at them in the starry dusk light of the dying day. There were four of them and they were all front sections of newspapers from the towns where Dad traveled.

There were smudges on the newspaper, too. Dark stains that looked faintly red in the dusk light. He thought of the time Jimmy Naylor had taken his pocketknife and stabbed a hamster in its bloated belly and how the blood had looked smeared on the newspaper in the bottom of the hamster cage. Smeared. Like this.

He looked at the headlines:

(St. Louis)
BEAUTICIAN SLAIN—INTENSE POLICE SEARCH

(Peoria)
POLICE HUNT KILLER OF XXX-DANCER

(Kansas City)
SUBURBAN HOUSEWIFE "BUTCHERED"

(Des Moines)
SPINSTER FOUND WITH THROAT SLASHED

And on each front page appeared the dark but somehow red stain. Holding these, he felt the way he did when he opened up the Dumpster. Dirty. Wanting to wash his hands.

He tried not to think about what it could mean. He'd seen a show once where this young boy was the only one who knew his older brother was a serial killer.

Sam shrugged. Dad probably had some good reason for saving the papers. He'd have to ask him, if he remembered to do it. With school out and "Space Harlot" on the screen, Sam would be likely to forget.

He went upstairs. Mom had an extra slice of apple pie waiting for him. He thought of how he'd come home from school sometimes and find her sitting at the kitchen table with tears in her eyes. He wondered if this was because of what Aunt Kathy had said about handsome younger men, or maybe because Mom knew about the stuff in the trunk.

"This is when I like it," she said, mussing his hair as he shoveled the pie into his mouth. "When it's late in the day and everybody's relaxed and I've got both of my men home with me."

She looked so tired now, even when she was smiling. So tired and so sad and it made him wonder if she knew about the newspapers and the blood in the trunk. He was trying hard not to think about these things but it was difficult. Very difficult.

After he finished his pie, he carried his dishes to the sink and then walked over to where his mom still sat at the kitchen table. He slid his arms around her and held her tight. He could *feel* the loose flesh in her neck. She loved Dad so much. So much.

Sam played "Space Harlots" until the ten o'clock news came on. Then he went in and brushed his teeth and kissed Mom good night and went into his own small bedroom and crawled into bed. He started thinking about the car trunk again but stopped himself. It was a lot better thinking about Jenny Akins. He loved her even more than he loved some of the young moms he had crushes on. He yawned. He was sleepy.

He fell asleep almost right away, even before he had time to save Jenny Akins from drowning or from being eaten by the escaped black bear. He always slept better for some reason when Dad was home.

The Second-Oldest Profession

Linda Grant

It's a wonder that a woman who lives right on top of a fault line in Berkeley, California, can concentrate on writing, but Linda Grant does, to the great pleasure of her many fans. She's the creator of the popular and critically acclaimed Catherine Sayler mystery series, and a former president of Sisters in Crime.

N*o one in their right mind goes to the market at five o'clock,* Bianca Diamante thought as she surveyed the crowded parking lot. *Unless, of course, they've spent the entire day waiting for the repairman to come fix the dishwasher.*

At four-thirty she had called Angeli's Appliances for the third time to check on Mario's progress toward her home.

"Oh, Mrs. Diamante," an apologetic female voice had said, "he's so sorry. He was really trying to get to you, but this last job has just lasted much longer than he expected. He said to tell you he'd be at your house first thing tomorrow."

I've heard that before, Bianca had thought. Yesterday, in fact. Mario himself had promised to be there "first thing."

She'd felt genuine sympathy for the young woman at the other end of the phone. They both knew that in all likelihood Mario's last job had been performed in the bedroom of some bored house-wife. It was too much to wish that the cuckolded husband might arrive home early and armed, but the possibility cheered Bianca.

She knew the repairman well enough to recognize how he pri-oritized his work orders. Attractive, horny women first, less attractive, horny women second, old ladies last. If she didn't keep after him, it could take weeks to get her dishwasher fixed.

In the parking lot ahead of her a tan station wagon was back-ing out, but before she could pull forward, a red Miata zipped around her, pulled in front, and took the place.

Bianca honked, then pulled up behind the Miata and got out. "I beg your pardon," she said, "that was my parking place."

A young woman with a shaved skull and a skirt up to her crotch stepped out of the Miata with a snippy smile on her face. "Too bad, Grandma," she said. "Slow folks suck."

The girl turned and headed for the store, and Bianca steamed. She allowed herself a moment to visualize the back of the shaved head in the sights of a rifle, then climbed into her car. The world was producing far too many overindulged, undersocialized young people these days.

It took several turns through the parking lot to find a place, and Bianca had thought of at least three nasty ways that the shaved one might meet an early end by the time she pulled her Plymouth into a slot made too narrow by the monstrous sports utility vehicle hulking over the white line. SUV drivers were another category of people the world could do without.

The light on the supermarket's glass door had turned it into a mirror. As she approached it, an old woman walked to meet her. Bianca studied the image with satisfaction. Gray hair framed a wrinkled face, a shapeless dark dress shrouded a short, plump body. Up close she could even see the dark eyebrow pencil that stood in for thinning brows and the lipstick that went slightly outside the line of the lips. The eternal grandma. Harmless and invisible.

Another woman might have regretted the signs of age, maybe considered a visit to the hairdresser or a trip to the mall. Not Bianca. She'd worked hard for that look, plucked her luxurious brows down to next to nothing and fought off every suggestion of a tint or a more modern hairstyle. No actor had spent more time perfecting the stooped posture and halting movements of old age than Bianca had.

But today she had no need for the stoop or shuffling walk as she pushed the door open and hurried inside. Today, she wasn't working.

The store was as crowded as the parking lot, and half the women had small, whiny children attached to their legs. Bianca was glad she didn't have a lot to buy, just a few things for dinner and apples for the pie.

She headed for the meat counter to get some lamb chops. As she was reaching for the only package that had two chops, a woman in a charcoal power suit stepped forward and grabbed it. She bumped Bianca's arm as she did and gave her a quick look, mumbled "Sorry," and hustled off.

You would be sorry if you knew who you were pushing, Bianca thought. That was the downside of being invisible: You had to put up with people treating you poorly. And you never got the satisfaction of seeing the look on their faces when they realized they'd just insulted someone who killed people for a living.

But it was worth it. Being a harmless old woman was the best possible cover for a hit person. Who else could get close to a powerful Mafia leader without being noticed, or remembered? No man certainly, even an old one. And a young woman would attract notice. But an old woman could go anywhere, and even the most alert bodyguard wouldn't push her out of the way if she passed too close and stumbled.

That's how she'd gotten Johnny the Clam, number three man in the Detroit family. She'd devised a special ring, a gaudy stone on the top, a sharp tack on the back of the band. A tack that she'd dipped in a poison that certain primitive people used on the tips of their arrows. Then it had been a matter of finding the right time and place where she could pass Johnny close enough to grasp his hand when she stumbled. He'd winced when she cut him, but a man like Johnny didn't make a fuss over a cut. In fact, Johnny never made a fuss again.

She'd used a sharp-tipped umbrella with the same poison, and it might have become her favorite weapon if the Bulgarians hadn't used it to assassinate a mark in England and botched the hit. Now everyone knew about umbrellas.

She picked up a quart of milk, a loaf of bread, two tomatoes, and some green beans for dinner, then remembered she'd come for apples.

As she surveyed the neatly stacked pyramids of bright green to deep red apples, a familiar, too-loud voice said, "McIntoshes are the best for pies."

It was Isabel Brasi, she who knew all and couldn't wait to share it. Bianca sighed, then came as close to a smile as she could manage as she turned to greet her neighbor.

Isabel was a constant trial. A bird fanatic, she called at least once a day to complain that Bianca's cats were stalking the birds at her feeders, digging in her garden, or doing something "nasty" in her yard. When she wasn't fussing over the cats, she was gossiping about the other neighbors. Her nosiness knew no bounds, and while Bianca was careful never to have clients come to her house, she didn't like the idea that someone was watching her every move.

Bianca's husband, Tony, had taught her that the first rule of a professional was never to let your personal feelings get involved. "We're probably the world's second-oldest profession," he'd said with a smile. "And we follow the same rules as the oldest profession. Never give it away." No whacking your enemies or those you found intolerably annoying. Isabel was a real test of Bianca's professionalism.

"Of course, the Gravesteins are very nice, too," Isabel said in her annoyingly chirpy voice, "but you can always count on the McIntoshes for flavor. My apple pie has won first place at the church bazaar for the last four years."

Bianca's smile was genuine as she congratulated Isabel; she was thinking of the apple pie she was going to bake. It was a safe bet no one had ever paid $10,000 for one of Isabel's pies.

"The children coming for Mother's Day?" Isabel asked.

Mother's Day! Bianca stared at Isabel in horror. "Mother's Day?" she said. "This Sunday is Mother's Day?"

Sympathy pulled Isabel's face into a somber expression. Poor Bianca. Obviously her children had forgotten all about Mother's Day.

Jesus, Mary, and Joseph, Bianca thought, *how could I miss that? I must be slipping.* She prided herself on her attention to detail, never leaving any loose ends, and here she was three days from the job and she'd missed completely that Sunday was Mother's Day.

"They get so busy," Isabel was saying. "So many things to remember when you're young. They don't realize how we look forward to their visits."

Speak for yourself, Bianca thought. Cara and Sophia visited quite often enough, thank you. She loved them dearly, but they fussed over her like mother hens. Lately Cara'd started interrogating her about whether she was taking her medicine, how well she was eating, every little thing. You'd think she was an errant teenager the way her daughter fussed. Even her social life was an object of scrutiny. She should get out more, join the bridge club or the garden society, maybe think of moving into one of those nice adult communities.

And Sophia had suggested on two occasions that her friendship with certain members of the Gianni family should be terminated.

"You don't know what kind of people they are," she'd said, her lips stretched tight with disapproval.

Bianca knew exactly what kind of people they were. They were the kind of people whose money had bought shoes and put food on the table. Her husband Tony had never been a member of the Gianni family, but favors had been exchanged from time to time, and the Don had been particularly helpful after Tony's cancer had left her a widow with children to support. It was Gianni money that had sent Cara, Sophia, and their brother Robert to college. And her family's connection to the Gianni family had meant that the wild boys stayed away from Cara and Sophia and never challenged Robert.

She and Tony had been careful to shield the children from the realities of Tony's profession. They thought he worked for a company that sold office machines and that his frequent trips were to distant business sites. You couldn't have your kid bringing his father's gun to show-and-tell.

"Maybe Cara's planning to surprise you?" Isabel said, trying to put a good face on things.

Bianca hated surprises, always had. Especially now.

She'd told the client the hit was scheduled for Sunday so that he could arrange an airtight alibi, and she was always careful to deliver exactly what she promised. It hadn't been easy making it as a woman in this field, even with Tony's training and his contacts. Clients were hesitant to trust a woman. For years after Tony's death she'd maintained the fiction that she was just a go-between who set things up with his "brother." At least half her clients still believed that. A hit man could reschedule; a hit woman could not.

She made as quick an escape as possible from Isabel, who was anxious to discuss at length her own children's plans for Mother's Day, and hurried to the checkout counter. There were only four registers open, and long lines of carts were stacked up at each one.

The line at the nine-items-or-less counter was the shortest of the four, an encouraging bit of luck until she realized that the man at the head of it had piled at least twice that many items on the belt. The clerk rolled his eyes at the pile but rang up the goods. It was only as he announced the total that the man pulled out his checkbook.

A ripple of irritation ran up the line. "I could kill him," the woman in front of Bianca muttered.

Bianca nodded agreement. Lucky for him she was a professional.

The checker was pleasant and efficient. The bagger looked to be about fourteen and dropped the tomatoes into the bag first, where they would have been smashed by the milk if Bianca hadn't made him retrieve them.

I'd be doing the world a favor to take that one out of the gene pool, Bianca thought.

"Would you like help to the car with that, ma'am," the kid asked, indicating the small bag of groceries. She detected a slight smirk on his face.

"I think I can manage, thank you," she said.

Sunday's target was a sleazy lawyer who'd cheated the wrong person once too often. Bianca demanded a fair amount of background on her jobs. She'd developed her own rather quirky code. Abusive husbands were fair game; inconvenient witnesses were not. She needed to know about the marks so she could devise an appropriate exit strategy for them.

You didn't need to know a lot about a guy's habits if you were going to pick him off with a rifle, but Bianca specialized in deaths from natural causes, and for that, you needed background. Sometimes the client supplied it; sometimes she did the research herself. Always, there was a premium for a method that wouldn't attract police attention.

The roads were crammed with cranky drivers working themselves into a frenzy to get home quickly so they could relax. Bianca was deep in thought as she stopped at a traffic light and didn't notice when it changed to green. A loud horn blasted her awake, and a man's angry voice yelled, "Get a move on, Granny. We don't have all day."

At home, she decided the best solution to her problem was to find out what, if anything, her daughters had in mind for Sunday. She called Cara, who was more likely to be home than her sister.

"Mother, I'm so glad you called," Cara said. She sounded a bit guilty, Bianca thought. "I've been meaning to call you, but things have been crazy at the office."

"How's your wrist?" Bianca asked. Cara had sprained her wrist when she tripped on the stairs.

"Much better, thanks," Cara said, then launched into a long description of a problem involving a secretary at her office. Bianca made comforting sounds. There was always some problem at the office; she could never keep all the players straight. It was enough to make her glad she worked alone.

"So how are you doing?" Cara asked as she finished her lament.

"The dishwasher's broken," Bianca said. "It stopped midway through the cycle last night. I've been waiting for Mario to come fix it."

"Mario? Is he still fixing appliances? He's such a creep." Cara had gone to school with Mario. They had even dated briefly, until Cara found out he was also dating one of her close friends. No one had ever accused Mario of being long on brains.

"He fixes appliances when he gets around to it," Bianca said. "He's not very reliable."

"Never was," Cara said. "He still have an eye for the ladies?"

"More than an eye," Bianca said. "He's married, but he hasn't let that slow him down."

"He's a creep," Cara repeated. "I don't think he even lives with Sarah—that's his wife. I heard he has a place on Rose Street."

"You mean he's divorced?"

"Oh, no. Mario doesn't believe in divorce; that'd mean child support, and he's not big on sharing his money with his wife and children. Sarah had to take a job, just to get by."

"Why doesn't she file for divorce? She certainly has grounds."

"She won't talk about it," Cara said. "I don't know if she's scared of him or still hopes he'll come back. She just refuses to discuss it. She's one of those women who can't stand up for herself."

Cara told her about another friend who'd filed for divorce only to end up with crushing legal bills and no way to collect child support, then about a colleague who was continuing to date a man who broke her nose. It was all very depressing. Finally, just when Bianca had decided she'd have to bring up the issue of Mother's Day herself, Cara said, "Oh, Sophia and I would like to take you to dinner on Sunday."

"How sweet of you," Bianca said, then added quickly, "How about four o'clock?"

"Uh, fine, four o'clock would be fine."

"Would you like to meet somewhere?"

"No, no. We'll pick you up at the house," Cara said.

As she hung up, Bianca realized they hadn't discussed where they'd go. That meant the girls had already chosen a place, no doubt one that prided itself on combining unlikely ingredients into miniscule servings on gigantic plates. You couldn't even trust the pasta in such places.

But at least she'd gotten the time schedule right. That meant she would be able to use the poisoned pie.

The lawyer was the perfect candidate for a pie. There weren't that many people who were. First off, you couldn't give a poisoned pie to a family man—too much chance of unintended victims. And you couldn't give it to someone who'd take it to a sick friend or ask a buddy over for dinner. Or a gentleman of the old school who'd feel obliged to invite her to have a piece. No, a pie only worked with the selfish loner, the kind of guy who as a kid would have rather eaten lunch by himself than risk having to share his dessert.

The lawyer was just such a guy. Bianca could count on him to keep every bite for himself.

She could drop by with the pie around eleven. She'd already introduced herself as a new neighbor and told him she'd just moved in with her daughter up the block. As she'd expected, he wasn't interested enough to ask the name of her "daughter." He probably didn't know his neighbors' names.

She'd played the lonely widow checking out the prospects. He wasn't bad-looking and had plenty of money, so he'd probably been through that routine before. Sunday, she'd pay a second visit and give him the pie, then scurry off shyly. Just after dark she'd come back to check on him. If the car was there and the lights were out, she'd know she'd succeeded. A call from a phone booth late that night would confirm it.

Bianca made the apple pie Saturday morning so she could cook it before the day heated up. If she'd believed Mario's promise to come by "first thing," she'd have waited, but she knew better than that. In fact, she didn't expect him until Monday. He only worked a half-day on Saturday, and she figured it'd take more than four hours for him to get around to her, so she was surprised when the doorbell rang at eleven o'clock, just as she was taking the pie from the oven.

"Hear the dishwasher's on the fritz," he said. "I got a cancellation so I hurried right over."

"I thought you were coming yesterday," Bianca said sternly.

"I got held up. It's not like a busted dishwasher is an emergency," he said in a tone that suggested *he* was the wronged party.

"No, not like a freezer that's not working," Bianca said,

remembering the time she'd had to throw everything out because he'd been "held up."

"Right," he said, no memory of the freezer incident clouding his smile.

Mario spotted the pie as soon as he entered the kitchen. "Boy, that pie sure smells good," he said. "I love apple pie."

"I baked that one for a friend," Bianca said, knowing that Mario was on his way to asking for a piece.

"Aren't I your friend? Come out on a Saturday to fix your dishwasher?"

Bianca smiled thinly and resisted mentioning that he wouldn't have been there at all if he'd come when he was supposed to. Instead, she explained what was wrong with the dishwasher.

Mario dumped his tools on her clean floor and studied the appliance.

"Aw, you got a KitchenAid. I tried to warn you about them. You shoulda bought the GE I tried to sell you. It was a good machine."

Bianca was fairly sure that the "good machine" had fallen off a truck somewhere. Mario had been much too anxious to sell it. "Yes, well, this is the machine I have, so it's the one you'll have to fix."

Mario bent down to pry the front off the dishwasher and continued his complaints about it.

Bianca decided it was time to find something to do in another room before she gave in to the temptation to tap Mario on the head with a cast-iron skillet. "Don't you touch that pie, Mario Angeli," she ordered.

"No need to get overheated," Mario said. He said something else as she was leaving, but he lowered his voice so she couldn't hear it.

When she came back to the kitchen fifteen minutes later, Mario had parts of the motor spread all over the floor and was talking on her phone.

"Tell him you're going to a movie with a girlfriend," he said in a wheedling tone. "Come on, just a couple of hours."

"Mario," Bianca said sternly. "I'm not paying you to arrange your social calendar."

"Gotta go," he said. "Meet me at eight at Phinny's." He gave her his best aw-shucks smile and said, "Sorry, Mrs. D. I won't charge you for the time I was on the phone."

"Very generous of you," Bianca said.

"Speaking of generous, how about a piece of that pie?" Mario moved toward the counter where the pie was cooling.

"No," Bianca said, loudly enough to stop him in his tracks. "Stay away from that pie."

"Just one piece. Your friend wouldn't miss one piece."

Only Mario would imagine it was proper to give a friend a pie with one piece missing. She almost wished she could give it to him, but she was a professional and Tony's second cardinal rule of professionalism was: You never hit someone you know. Tony used to say that anger was one emotion a pro couldn't afford.

"I said no," Bianca said sternly, "and I meant it. You are to stay away from that pie. Do you understand?"

But of course, he didn't. He only understood what he wanted to understand. Bianca put on the oven mitts, picked up the still-hot pie, and carried it into the study where she could keep an eye on it.

She was going over her plans for Sunday a second time when the phone rang. It was Cara.

"Sophia can't make it at four," she said. "So we had this great idea. She'll take you to brunch at around ten or so, and I'll take you to dinner at four. How's that?"

Dreadful, Bianca thought. *It's just dreadful.* It was hard to imagine a worse schedule.

"Oh, now, you're making much too much of a fuss over me,"

she said. "Why don't we all just go to brunch?"

"We *want* to make a fuss," Cara said. "We want your Mother's Day to be special."

"Just being with you will be special," Bianca said. "I'd really rather just do the brunch. After all, I get tired easily these days."

"Is something wrong?" Cara asked anxiously. "Aren't you feeling well?"

"I'm fine," Bianca said quickly. "Really. It's just that you don't have as much energy at my age."

"Maybe you should see the doctor."

"Cara, don't be such a worrywart. I'm in excellent health."

"How's your shoulder? Is it still bothering you?"

"It's much better." Bianca had hurt her shoulder six months ago when she'd had to rearrange the body of a minor mob figure who'd lurched the wrong way in his final moments. Cara and Sophia had assumed it was arthritis.

"I really think you should see the doctor. Fatigue can be a symptom of more serious problems."

Bianca sighed. She should have known better than to plead anything remotely connected to poor health. Now she'd have to prove how fit she was or they'd drive her crazy with their fussing. "I'm fine," she said. "And your plans for Mother's Day sound lovely."

"You're sure? We don't want to tire you."

"I'm sure," Bianca said.

As she hung up the phone, she could hear Mario whistling tunelessly in the kitchen. She looked at her watch. He'd been at work for over an hour. At this rate she could have bought a new dishwasher and saved herself a lot of aggravation.

She couldn't use the pie. The timing was too tight. She'd just have to find another way. Aggravating, but not too difficult. Still, it was a shame she'd gone to the work of baking the pie.

For just a moment, she considered offering the pie to Mario.

There was no danger of him sharing it with anyone—he was self-ish enough to keep it all for himself. She doubted that the woman he'd been cajoling on the phone would go looking for him when he stood her up, and the poison she'd carefully mixed into the pie filling produced symptoms close enough to food poisoning to confuse all but the most sophisticated autopsy.

She could get away with it, and no one would be the wiser, but it violated the code. No personal hits. It was an indulgence she couldn't afford. Whack Mario and next week it'd be Isabel or the bimbo with the shaved head. One simply had to have standards in this business.

The whole problem with Sunday's job was the deadline. She hated deadlines; they made things so much more difficult. Poisons acted differently on different bodies, even when you tried to adjust the dose to size.

With enough time, she could always come up with a means that would slip by most coroners. The trick was to give them a set of symptoms that looked like a natural cause they recognized. As long as you weren't dealing with a high-profile mark and didn't leave any glaring evidence, you could rely on them to see what they expected.

To insure that the lawyer was dead by Sunday night, she'd need a fairly fast-acting poison. The ring with the spring-loaded injector was the best bet for a delivery device. She was particularly proud of her latest invention; it was a big step beyond the old ring with the tack on the back. That had been a crude device with no way to measure the dose and too much risk of nicking herself.

She'd found the injector in a medical supply book, another benefit of her volunteer work for the Poison Control Center, and designed the device herself. A hollow glass stone served as the reservoir for the poison; the injector extended down from it, fitting between her fingers. It remained safely sheathed until triggered by the pressure of her hand against a solid surface.

She glanced in the kitchen on her way upstairs to get the ring. Mario seemed to be finishing up—at least there were fewer tools on the floor.

In her bedroom, she carefully removed the ring from its hiding place in the lovely antique bureau with the secret drawer. A note on a yellow Post-it in the box reminded her that it still contained a deadly dose of brown recluse spider venom.

It was a nearly ideal weapon for a local hit. The spider was indigenous to this area, and the venom caused so little pain on injection that by the time the first symptoms appeared a couple of hours later, the victim might not even remember being stuck.

But would it do for this job? She decided it wouldn't. Death usually took more than a day, and the victim could sometimes be saved if he got to a doctor in time.

She slipped the ring on her finger. The safest means to release the venom was to shoot it into an apple or an orange. That wouldn't damage the needle, and the flesh of the fruit would absorb the poison.

As she headed down to the kitchen, the phone summoned her back.

"Mrs. D? This is Jason." Jason, her "social secretary."

"Hello, Jason. How's your daughter?" The question was her signal that it was all right to talk.

"She's fine, thank you. I just learned that my client would like to reschedule the package you were to deliver tomorrow. If you could take care of it today, there'd be a twenty percent bonus."

Bianca considered. She hated changes in plan, but this time it worked to her advantage. She checked her watch. There was still time to deliver the pie.

"I think that would be possible," she said. She didn't ask why the change in plans. She didn't care.

"Excellent. I'll inform my client."

Bianca replaced the receiver and smiled. Everything was working out after all. Now all she had to do was get Mario out of her kitchen, put on her old-lady clothes, and drive the pie across town.

She hurried to the kitchen to tell Mario he had fifteen minutes to finish fixing her dishwasher, but the room was empty. The dishwasher had been reassembled and the tools were back in their box, but the repairman was nowhere to be seen.

Bianca rushed to the study. There, she found Mario by the desk, carefully lifting a fat piece of pie from the pan. She dashed across the room and smacked his hand, knocking the pie from it.

The pie landed with a splat on the blotter, spewing crust and filling across the desk. Mario yelped. "Jeeze, Mrs. Diamante," he protested, "don't get so excited. I didn't mean no harm."

He launched into a string of excuses, while Bianca stared at the tiny bright red spot of blood on his hand.

Rotten to the Core

Jeremiah Healy

While a professor for eighteen years at the New England School of Law, Jeremiah Healy managed to turn out eleven private eye novels in his spare time, all of them starring Boston private investigator John Francis Cuddy. He is also the author of the legal thriller The Stalking of Sheilah Quinn, *and a past president of the Private Eye Writers of America. He is currently vice president of the International Association of Crime Writers. Now that he's writing full-time, what will he do in his spare time?*

Thirty-three years old, and I'm still working for my mother.

Life can really suck, you know it?

I mean, if we're still turning a profit growing apples, that'd be one thing. But ever since the old man bit the big one five years ago and the land came to be all hers, Ma's been getting fat around the middle and thin around the business.

Not that it's all her fault, mind. We ain't got but a hundred acres of trees, which used to be enough to compete, long as you had two strong backs to help out most of the year. Come picking season, we hire another twenty, plus enough grading ladies on the packing line to tell the good apples from the ones bound for cider.

Only now, it ain't enough to know how to *grow* good product. No, these days, the fruit's in oversupply. Washington State is killing us, and China is killing them.

Ma says to me, "Orrin, I don't know how they can do it. I mean, whoever heard of *Chinese* apples?"

And I says to her, "Ma, how they can do it is if everybody in that country plants just one miserable tree, they've got four billion of them."

And she says to me, "Oh, I don't think there are that many people in China, do you?"

You see what I'm up against, a woman who can't keep her facts straight?

And, even without the overseas competition, the regional wholesaler here can play one of us little growers against the rest, which means we got to give away another dollar a box to keep that wholesaler's business. Only way to make a go of it at all is to build a pissy little retail store on the country road next to our packing barn, with apple jelly, apple potpourri, apple everything for sale to the dumbos up from the city, driving past and making believe they're some kind of country gentry by buying our stuff for twice what it'd cost in any supermarket worth its name.

Except that Ma don't believe in having a retail store. No sir, not Mrs. Jeannette T. Weems.

She believes in baking apple pies. With her little "JTW" initials as a "mark of quality" in the center of the crust. But without preservatives or anything else "unnatural." And guess what that means.

Right the first time. It means I got to be on the road pretty near every day, driving this old panel truck with shelves in it that the Nissen Bread folks pitched away. One pie to a box, nine boxes to a bread rack, thirty racks to the truck. And drive that sucker I do, fifty, sixty hours a week, delivering Ma's fresh, unpreserved apple pies to gourmet shops and fancy restaurants. Even a few of the big estates, too, think it's cool to have a local peasant drive up to the servants' entrance with the "fruit of the land," as I heard one of the whales in a whale-patterned shirt and tweed skirt say once.

Goldarnit, but I do hate the smell of apples.

You'd think working in a fish market or a slaughterhouse'd be worse, the stench of death all around you, getting into your clothes, your hair, even your skin. But nothing's worse than apples when you can't get away from them, especially if one's rotten to the core. It's a stink that. . . penetrates, that's what it does. Goes *past* your skin, all the way to the bone. And it festers there, like some kind of infection, till it drives you near crazy.

As you drive over half the county in that goldarn panel truck with those goldarn racks of pies in the back.

I says to her, "Ma, you should just sell the farm for real estate development."

"Now, Orrin, your father wouldn't like that."

"Ma, the old man's got his own land. Measures about eight by three and six feet under."

Which naturally made Mrs. Jeannette T. Weems cry, to hear me bring up the truth.

Even so, though, I thought I had her leaning—I *know* I did—until that Earle Shay showed up two months ago.

We'd lost the other fella working the orchard with us to a selling job at the Wal-Mart, so Ma put an ad in the county weekly for "Hired Help, No Room or Board, Must Be Clean and Polite and Willing to Work Hard."

And, wouldn't you know it, Earle had to be all three?

He's also black as coal, with a chest like a pickle barrel and a shaved head so shiny you dast not look at him on a sunny day without a good pair of dark glasses on you. I think Earle's around Ma's age—I can't never tell how old black people are, at least until they hit seventy or so, when their skin just seems to go into raisin mode and they start shuffling instead of walking right. But Earle's a long way from shuffling. He can work all day and keep Ma laughing in her kitchen half the night. She's been laughing so hard, Ma's dropped about ten pounds or so of that weight around her middle, and she's even taken to going to Bessie's Hair-a-Dome again, first time since the old man went in the ground.

But that's not the worst part.

No, the worst part is, Earle's got Ma believing we—and "we" don't mean just me and her—can run the farm at a profit again.

In that deep, booming voice he has, Earle says to Ma, "Why, Jeannette, all we have to do is put in a retail store and devote a couple of acres to speciality veggies for the gourmet shops and restaurants."

"But Earle, who would tend this store and garden?"

"I've got relatives aplenty in the city who'd love to come up here, stay in the county for a time. Clean air, no crime. And Orrin's already visiting most of the places we'd sell the veggies to with his panel truck and your pies."

"Well," Ma says to him, "it might work."

Might work. And if it did, I'd be stuck in the goldarn panel truck for the rest of my natural life. Only then I'd have goldarn garden dirt under my fingernails to go with the goldarn apple stench in my bones.

In fact, I couldn't hardly see a light at the end of the tunnel.

Until I finally got The Idea.

It happened on a cold, rainy day in late October, maybe a month after Earle'd used the John Deere forklift to stack the bins of McIntosh eight tiers high in our C.A. room. The "C.A." stands for "controlled atmosphere." Basically, if you've got a hundred acres of apples, a lot of them are gonna get ripe in the same two-week stretch, so you bring in the pickers and box the fruit quick as you can. Unless you want the product breaking down and getting soft, though, you got to seal it up in C.A. storage. Where the air's maybe 90 percent nitrogen—like they must have on the planet Mars? Put in a refrigeration unit to cool and blow that Martian air around the apples, and they'll keep preserved for a good five months.

I'd already parked the panel truck outside the packing barn, between the John Deere tractor that tows our AgTec crop sprayer—a big white thing, looks a little like a ten-foot dog kennel with tubes and nozzles at the back—and the Agway rototiller—which, long as I'm describing things, looks a lot like a gasoline-powered wheelbarrow with little propellers that dig into the ground. I walked past the brush chopper—this heavy flail mower that rolls behind the tractor, too, only it can chop-and-chip pieces of junk timber two inches thick. In the barn, I was on my way to the little fridge where I keep some cold beers when I realized the packing line looked a little longer than the day before.

Jesus God, I remember thinking. They've gone and done it.

Earle'd been after Ma for weeks to spring for a waxing machine. Even she thought seventeen thousand dollars—seventeen *thousand!*—was kind of steep, but Earle kept pressing her and teasing her with that Darth Vader voice. His idea was that we—"we" as in "three" again—could sell to the wholesalers who supply the big supermarkets that want their apples to sparkle like fire trucks. Takes another six hundred dollars of wax to polish fifteen thousand bushels of apples, but they come out looking better than the one Eve must have flashed at Adam back in their garden.

I had to sit down hard, on an old slatted crate in the packing barn.

Ain't no grower in this whole county—or, hell, even over there in *China*—that's gonna burn the price of a new pickup truck for her one and only son if she's really leaning towards selling the land for development. As apple orchard, our land wasn't worth spit, and we didn't have the kind of houses around us that'd let us carve off a small building lot here and there at the edges. But I knew we could divide the whole shebang up into "mini-estates," and get a fortune for every five-acre chunk. Sure, we'd have to put in a road and run the electric and arrange for probably half a dozen other things, but I knew it'd all work from the numbers side.

Only right then, sitting on that packing crate, I couldn't see it working at all, not with Ma doing whatever Earle told her he thought it was made sense. Next thing'd be the designer veggies and a retail store, with even more "employees"—dark in color—on our land.

Or Ma's land, I guessed. At least until . . . .

I jumped back up and ran outside. Our crop sprayer looked mean enough, but I didn't see how showering Mrs. Jeannette T. Weems with pesticide would solve my problem. The rototiller had those little prop blades, but at best they'd take off some toes or maybe a finger, you got careless clearing a jam. Then I stared—long and hard—at our brush chopper. It'd do the job all right, but despite what Ma was doing to me, I couldn't quite stomach her being spritzed like hamburger spread over a row of our trees.

Scuffing my boots in the dust, I went back inside the packing barn.

And saw . . . the packing line?

No. No, even with the new waxing machine, the equipment at most might mangle an arm. And, anyway, with the crop already in storage, there'd be no reason to run the line, nor for Ma to be fiddling with the different stages, not with Earle around.

But that's when I heard it. A simple little noise, though maybe more beautiful than any country tune Garth Brooks ever wailed.

The noise was coming from our C.A. room. That metal-on-metal shear of a bearing going bad in the refrigeration unit's blower.

I went over to the big steel door we have bolted on the storage. You got to keep the room sealed absolute tight, otherwise the nitrogen air inside would seep out, rotting the apples and maybe killing you, you breathed deep enough close enough. Of course, nobody could predict when something might go wrong with the refrigeration unit either, so we had a little kitty-cat trap-door on the bottom of the steel one. The little door was hinged on top and bolted at the corners, too. But it'd give you a way in and out of the C.A. room in case some kinda repair was necessary. And we even had an old airpac Ma bought off the Volunteer Fire—the kind that rides on your back, like the tanks in this scuba-diving flick I saw one time? Our tank's yellow, with a hose running to the nose-and-mouth cover that you strap on over your head, the way fighter pilots do in those old war movies.

Right then, though, I pushed all the Hollywood stuff out of my head. Sitting down on that packing crate again, I closed my eyes to recollect the inside of our C.A. storage. Solid cement floor, ceiling twenty feet high, walls made from white insulated foam. Over the years, we'd spackled food-grade tar here and there to patch leaks, so the whole room'd look to you like the hide of a pinto pony. And most of the space was filled with those eight tiers of weathered-wood bins with the McIntosh in them.

But every other cubic foot was 90 percent nitrogen. That only a Martian could breathe without an airpac.

I took The Idea as an omen. Especially since that same night—after driving my old pickup over to Clete's Tap to celebrate—I met Honey.

Clete's ain't nothing more than a taproom, one of maybe ten in the county. It's about the only place where the races mix much,

though, and so I wouldn't go there but for it's the closest by far
to the farm, and I don't fancy getting stopped by a sheriff's
deputy for Driving Under the Influence account of I'm already
Driving Without a License from another such encounter.

Anyway, I go into Clete's that night, and the crowd—fortu-
nately—is mostly white. Oh, there're a couple of big young
bucks bellied up to the bar, but I move over to a table by itself
and tell Amy the airhead waitress to bring me a bottle of champagne, they had one cold. She asks me if I was sure I wanted that
and not a Miller High Life, "the champagne of bottled beers." I
say I'm sure, and as Amy turns away, airhead shaking like one of
those ballplayer dolls on the TV, the stunner standing at my end
of the bar turns a little.

The girl was black, technically, but her skin really glowed the
color of honey, her hair maybe two shades darker. About five-five
or so in jeans and a pair of those spiky cowboy boots, she was all
legs and had just the cutest little rump I ever did see. She seemed
to know she'd caught my eye, too, because before I could even get
up, the girl'd click-clacked over to my table, asking if she could
sit.

I says to her, "Honey, you can sit on anything you'd like."

All of a sudden, she looks sorta funny, like maybe I offended
her kinda.

But all she says to me is, "How'd you, like, know that's my
name?"

And I says to her, "What is?"

"'Honey.'"

"Only on account of that's what you remind me of, girl. A gorgeous itty-bitty thing just spun out of honey."

Which made her smile, and as Amy finally arrived with my
champagne—in this spittoon with ice—I knew the chair across
from me in Clete's Tap wasn't the only thing Honey'd be sitting
on that night.

* * *

Honey says to me, "So, you're gonna kill your mama?"

It was afterwards, and now she's towards the passenger's side of my pickup, still at the turnaround off the dirt road we'd parked at beforehand. To this moment, I can't remember how The Idea'd come up in our conversation. But it seemed natural enough, telling her about it. Especially since Honey'd already told me she was up from the city for just the weekend, visiting relatives until she had to get away from all the "My, child, how you have growed up" talk.

I says to Honey, "Well, yeah, I have to kill her. But like I said, I couldn't feature Ma scattered over half an acre by the brush chopper like so much ground chuck."

Honey looked a little funny again, but this time more like she might urp up. All she says to me, though, is "How you gonna use that storage room?"

I told her about the bearing in the refrigeration unit, how I could hear it was going, and why we'd have to replace it or risk losing the fruit to a system failure.

"And your mama's just gonna, like, walk in there through that little trapdoor you have?"

I says to her, "No, Honey. All's I have to do is *tell* her about it when Earle ain't around. Then she'll have to go out to the packing barn with me and stand a ways off, because the safety rule is, nobody goes into C.A. storage without somebody else being on the outside."

"Like Lassie."

"Huh?"

"Like Lassie," Honey says to me. "That dog who'd go get help when some person was in trouble."

I shake my head, but I says to her, "Yeah, like that. Only I'm not going in there myself."

"What are you gonna do?"

"I'm gonna wear that airpac, and use a wrench on the trapdoor, and then say to Ma, 'Come over closer, I need help with this last bolt.' And when she's close enough, I'm gonna rap her upside the head with that wrench. Once Mrs. Jeannette T. Weems is for sure out cold, I'm gonna open the kitty-cat door on its hinge, push her in through it, and close the door again."

"I don't, like, get it."

I close my eyes. She might have a body like spun honey, but the brain was more like spun cotton. "I wait maybe two minutes, just to be sure Ma's a goner. Then I bleed out all that's left in the airpac, and I slide it off me. I take a deep breath, open the trapdoor again, and push the airpac inside. After that, I toss the wrench in, too."

Honey looked kind of sick again, but she says to me, "Oh, so everybody will think your mama was, like, trying to fix the bearing thing and ran out of good air."

"Right the first time. And, once the lawyers get through with doing her estate, I'm rich as that Trump fella."

Honey puts on a smile, a cousin to the last one she gave me at Clete's Tap. "You know, Orrin, I probably don't have to be back to my relatives for, like, another hour or so."

Omens. I'm telling you, they were everywhere for me, that afternoon and night.

Next morning in the kitchen, I says to Ma, "Where's Earle?"

Mrs. Jeannette T. Weems looks up from a pie she's making her little "mark of quality" in the crust of. "He said he had to run into town for something."

"Well, maybe Earle oughta spend a little less time running to town and a little more time checking the barn."

"Why, what do you mean, Orrin?"

"I mean, I was in there yesterday after I broke my back delivering all your pies, and I could hear this bearing starting to go on the C.A. blower."

"Oh, my goodness, no."

"Oh, my goodness, yes," I says to her. "I think you and me ought to go over there, quick as we can."

"Of course, Orrin. Let me just get this last batch out of the oven."

Last batch. I especially liked the sound of that first part.

"Ma," I says to her, over my shoulder and casual as can be, considering how the nose-and-mouth cover of the airpac's muffling my voice. "I'm having a little trouble with this last bolt."

Her voice comes from a corner of the packing barn. "Is it safe for me to join you there?"

"Sure it's safe. The room's still sealed. I just need a little help with the wrench is all."

"Well, if you really can't do it without me . . ."

"No, Ma," I says to her, my face against the trapdoor so she won't see me grinning ear-to-ear. "Take my word on this. I can't make it work without you."

I hear footsteps, only there're sounding heavy, like Ma was before Earle answered her ad in the weekly. I get ready anyway, figuring to just stand up a little and—

—I wake up in the dark, lying on my right side.

My head hurts behind my left ear. When I reach back there, I can feel a lump the size of a small hen's first egg.

I also feel the strap of the nose-and-mouth cover of the airpac.

I try to sit up, but when I do, the yellow tank part makes a scraping noise on the cold cement floor.

Cold? Cement?

"Orrin?" Ma yells to me from outside somewheres. "Can you hear me, Orrin?"

"Yeah," I says to her, muffled by the cover, but . . . echoing, too.

Like I'm in a room with twenty-foot walls.

"Orrin, I never believed you would consider doing such a thing to your own mother."

"What such a thing?"

"Murder for profit," booms Earle's voice, and I have a pretty good idea whose footsteps I heard coming up behind me on the other side of the kitty-cat door.

I says to him, "I don't know what you're talking about."

He booms to me, "Lucky thing that when I was in town this morning, my niece up from the city told me what you laid out for her last night."

"Laid" was the only word I really focused on.

Ma yells to me, "Orrin, how could you even have *contemplated* that?"

I says to her, "Ma, she's the one picked *me* up in Clete's."

"That's not what I mean, young man. I'm talking about killing your own mother."

I didn't like the way my air from the yellow tank was tasting. "Let me out of here."

"No, Orrin," Ma yells. "Earle believes Honey, and I believe Earle. What I don't believe is that you haven't even the decency to own up to the things they've said."

"Ma?"

"What?"

"Let . . . me . . . out . . . of . . . here."

Her voice goes different. "I couldn't bear to have Earle kill you the way he wanted to, after you'd planned to kill his beloved."

His "beloved"? Things were just getting better and better.

"So we compromised," Ma yells to me now. "We slid you in there with the airpac on and rebolted the trap here. I don't know how much time you have left, but at least you'll go quickly after reflecting on the horrible deed you intended."

"Ma—"

She yells this time till her voice about cracks. "And then we'll take a page from your book, Orrin. Earle will unbolt the trap again and toss in the wrench, so everyone will think the same tragic accident that you so diabolically aimed at me simply befell you instead."

"Ma, listen—"

Earle booms to me, "Poetic justice for a boy that just went rotten, rotten to the core."

I started saying a whole string of words Ma never liked to hear. When I'm done, neither of them's yelling or booming to me anymore.

So here I sit, in the dark and the cold. I really don't like the taste of my air from the yellow tank at all now. It's sour, like everything's going stale, and I practically have to whistle in reverse to feel anything reach down towards my lungs.

Then I remember something else from that scuba-diving flick I saw. One of the jerks you know is going to die anyway runs out of air when he's maybe three hundred feet down. Even though he knows it's stupid, he pulls off the mouthpiece from under his mask and starts breathing in water.

I guess it's like a reflex or something. Which means that, pretty soon, I'll probably be doing the same thing.

Which oughta bother me a lot, but somehow it don't. No, what does bother me is something else.

I'm in a controlled atmosphere storage room. When I take off the nose-and-mouth cover and draw in that first—and last— breath of Martian air, I'm also gonna smell . . . *them*.

The last goldarn thing on God's green earth I'll ever experience is the goldarn stench of goldarn apples.

Didn't I tell you that life can really suck?

The Maggody Files: Death in Bloom

Joan Hess

Joan Hess does not speak with a discernible Southern accent, but her wickedly funny mysteries do. From her home in Fayetteville, Arkansas, Joan creates both the Arly Hanks and the Claire Malloy mystery series. She has won the Agatha, Macavity, and American Mystery Awards, and she is the president of the Arkansas Mystery Writers Alliance, a past president of the American Crime Writers League, and a former national board member of the Mystery Writers of America.

"The thing is," Ruby Bee announced before Estelle could once again start in squawking like a bluejay, which, for the record, she'd been doing for the last ten minutes, give or take, "Beryl makes superior apple pies. I'm thinking she might be inclined to share her secret. That's why we're doing this."

Estelle adjusted the rearview mirror and made sure her beehive of red hair was securely pinned and ready to withstand anything short of hurricane-strength winds. "I still don't see why the both of us should close up shop and go over to drink coffee, eat a piece of pie, and be so bored we're gonna wish we'd joined a book club. Beryl's pies take the blue ribbon every year at the county fair. That doesn't mean I want to spend an hour admiring her begonias and zucchinis."

Ruby Bee sighed as she drove up County 103. "Did you hear what I said, Estelle? Beryl's apple pies have a certain something. I've been trying to figure out for most of thirty years what her secret is. Times I think it's an extra dash of nutmeg or cinnamon, and then I think it must be ginger. I realize this sounds odd, but there are nights I toss and turn until dawn."

"Odd," Estelle echoed in a voice meant to irritate Ruby Bee, which it most certainly did. "You're saying you can't sleep on account of Beryl Blanchard winning the blue ribbon at the county fair every year on account of ginger? I spend a lot more hours worrying if the IRS will come after me—or if a slobbering serial killer will bust into my house."

Ruby Bee turned up the gravel driveway to Beryl's house. "I suspect you're losing sleep over something less likely than Idalupino Buchanon's face appearing on the cover of *People* magazine. We're gonna have pie and coffee, spend a few minutes with Buck, and dutifully admire the garden. If Beryl wants to give me her secret recipe, so be it. If not, no one has yet dared to criticize the apple pie I serve at the bar and grill."

"Not if they want to live to see the dawning of another day," Estelle muttered, then looked at the weedy pasture as Ruby Bee's car bounced up the rutted driveway. The house was, at best, serviceable. The garden, on the other hand, was enough to suck the breath out of any soul's body. Yellows and reds and fuchsias and oranges and pinks and purples—every glorious color on the spectrum—exploded from all sides. Blooms stretched to meet the sun; others cascaded like iridescent waterfalls.

"You got to admit," Ruby Bee said solemnly, "that this is

something. Beryl may not be on the top of my list of favorite people, but you'd almost think she gets seed catalogs direct from the Garden of Eden."

"Then we'd better keep an eye out for the serpent," Estelle said as she unbuckled her seat belt.

Ruby Bee frowned but held her peace as they got out of the car. Maggody was a quiet little town most of the time, although things seemed to keep happening. Today, however, held no undertones of menace. Arly, who just happened to be the chief of police as well as Ruby Bee's daughter, had last been seen napping at her desk at the two-room police department, most likely dreaming of an escape to a somewhat more invigorating lifestyle that precluded moonshiners and dim-witted locals. There were no banks in Maggody, so the odds of a robbery-in-progress were limited. Anyone who imprudently ran the sole stoplight was in luck for the next hour or so.

"Ruby Bee, Estelle!" shrieked Beryl as she arose from a bed of exceedingly tall purple perennials. "I am delighted that you came! This is such a treat for me. So few people drop by these days. Buck and Sylvie are as excited as I am."

Ruby Bee pasted on a smile. "You know I'm always in the mood for pie and coffee. How's Buck doing?"

Beryl, whose gray hair held a tint of the same purple as the flowers surrounding her, wiped her face on her shirt cuff, leaving a smudge of dirt on her otherwise properly schoolmarmish features. "The wheelchair's not been easy for him, but he knows he has to be careful. He gets all these crazy ideas about European tours and African safaris and how we can travel to all these places like he never had the heart surgery. Sylvie's forever bringing home brochures about cruises and the like. Silliness! You name another place on earth more beautiful than where we're standing." She spread her arms as if embracing nature in its entirety. "What more could anyone want?"

"Something more exciting than Maggody," Buck said as he wheeled onto the porch. "I just want to go while we can. A few years from now, maybe I'll be content to sit here, watching the turkey vultures circle in on me. I was in the United States Navy, as you ladies must know. We had shore leave in Athens and Naples and a whole lot of fascinating places. I keep trying to persuade Beryl here to take a gander at them while we can. I drank a little ouzo in my time, I did, and climbed to the very rim of Vesuvius. One night when I was on the Isle of Capri—"

"We don't have any reason to travel," Beryl cut in. "We've got a vegetable garden, an orchard ripe with peaches and apples, and flowers that could dazzle a blind man. Why would I want to go to some foreign place where I'm likely to get a disease? Home is where you get meat loaf, mashed potatoes, and apple pie."

Buck made a gesture that indicated he'd heard the argument more times than he could count. "Just thought I'd mention it," he said darkly as he spun around and went inside.

"He doing okay otherwise?" asked Ruby Bee.

Beryl shrugged as she picked up a muddy trowel and stacked together several empty plastic pots. "He'd do better if he did away with all his foolish ideas about traveling. Taking care of the property is a full-time job, what with planting in the spring, tending in the summer, harvesting in the fall, and pruning and planning in the winter. It's not like Sylvie could step in for even a week or two. I'd be terrified that she'd make such a mess of everything that it'd take me two or three years to recover."

"I just love your hollyhocks," Estelle said tactfully.

"Me, too," Beryl said. "Now let's go inside for pie and coffee, and then we'll have a nice stroll. I'm particularly pleased with the dianthus along the back fence. It has a wonderful cinnamon scent."

Ruby Bee smiled with all the subtlety of a fox teetering on the henhouse roof. "Speaking of cinnamon, Beryl . . ."

They went into the house. The living room was dark and sparse, what with the drapes drawn and the wood floor unadorned. The obligatory crocheted doilies were spread across the arms of the sofa. Photographs of dyspeptic ancestors glowered from the walls. Tables that might have held vases of nature's glories were bare, with the exception of the odd crystal dish that most likely had arrived as a wedding present and had never since held so much as a mint. The only book in sight was a family Bible.

"Sylvie!" Beryl called as they went down the hall. "We have company. I hope you're not sulking in your room." She lowered her voice and looked back at Ruby Bee and Estelle. "Sylvie's not always fit for company. She did insist on baking the apple pie this morning, though."

The baker under discussion trudged into the kitchen. She was thick, pale, somewhat sallow, and clearly unhappy. "You didn't mention company, Ma."

Ruby Bee managed a smile. "And how are you doing these days, Sylvie? Still attending the community college in Farberville?"

"No," Sylvie muttered. "I did for a year, but now I'm here, taking care of things. Maybe down the road I can get some kind of degree." She put on an apron and began to shove pots and pans into the gray dishwasher in the sink. "How's Arly doing?"

"Real fine," Ruby Bee said, looking at Estelle for help. A bullfrog caught in a spotlight might have appeared less panicky.

"Yeah, real fine," said Estelle. "Why, Arly's just happy as a hog in a wallow. I'm sure she'd like to be out and about with men of an acceptable persuasion, but she's willing to settle for a grilled cheese sandwich and happy hour at the bar and grill. How about you, Sylvie? You ever think about coming by for a beer? Things start jumping on Friday afternoons."

Rather than responding, Sylvie grimly set a pie on the dinette. "Coffee'll be ready in a minute," she said, then disappeared down the hallway.

Beryl sighed. "I just don't know what to do with that girl. I've made it clear she can take a class or two at the community college, as long as she can work around Buck's needs. I'm just not strong enough to deal with him. I can't help him in or out of his chair, or see to his basic needs in certain matters. I want you to know I've tried, Ruby Bee and Estelle; the spirit is willing, but . . ."

"How about I pour the coffee?" Ruby Bee said. She waited until Beryl nodded, then found cups and saucers in a cabinet and filled each cup. "Shall I cut the pie?"

Beryl sighed. "These days, the complaints are enough to wear me out. Sylvie acts like we should find a way to pay a private nurse to see to Buck, but we can't. He spends his days whining about trips to foreign places. He needs the wheelchair, for pity's sake. I can't see myself lugging it up the gangplank of a ship or through the streets of some nasty place like Rome. I've been told that men"—her voice dropped to a whisper—"urinate in the streets. Can you imagine?"

"What about a cruise?" said Estelle as she accepted a plate from Ruby Bee. "Seems like there'd be one that caters to folks with disabilities. If Sylvie went along, you could visit some exotic ports and Buck might feel better."

"Some of the brochures say they do," Beryl said, "but most likely all they offer is wide bathroom doors. Besides, who'd look after my hybrid tea roses and prune the flowering crab apples? My garden means everything to me. I can't leave it to amateurs."

Ruby Bee was trying to come up with a rebuttal as she took a bite of the blue-ribbon pie. It was not easy to swallow. "A bit tart," she mumbled.

"I'd say so!" Beryl banged down her fork. "Sylvie! You march yourself in here right now, young lady. Here I invited guests for a nice dessert! This pie could pucker a face inside out. I'm so embarrassed I could just crawl under the table. I would never have served this if . . ."

Sylvie came into the kitchen. "Sorry, Mother. We ran out of sugar, and I thought I could adjust the recipe with honey. We've got some oatmeal cookies in the freezer. Maybe I can—"

Beryl rose with the menace of a summer squall. "That's quite enough, Sylvie. Give your father his bath, then remain in your room until I call for you."

"Now, Beryl," said Estelle, "it isn't like this was submitted to the committee at the county fair. All of us have substituted ingredients on occasion, although I can tell you molasses and Karo syrup just don't—"

"Shall we go outside?" Beryl said coldly.

Ruby Bee could tell it was not the moment to broach the most delicate topic of ginger versus an extra pinch of cinnamon. "It isn't that bad," she said to Sylvie, who was hovering in the doorway with a very peculiar look on her face. "The crust is very flaky and light, and nicely browned. Sometimes, mine are so soggy I feel like I plucked 'em out of a swamp."

Sylvie stared at her mother. "If I'd known we were expecting company, I would have tried more honey."

"Be sure to give your father's back a good scrub," Beryl said. She went across the kitchen, picked up a plastic bottle, and squirted cream into her palm. "I never go outside without a good slathering of sunscreen. We can't be too careful about skin cancer, can we?" Without waiting for a response, she began to apply it to her face, neck, and bare forearms.

Ruby Bee gave Estelle a hard look, then said, "We can't stay for long, Beryl. I'm supposed to be open for lunch, and I believe Estelle has an appointment before too long."

"That's right," Estelle said brightly. "Elsie McMay gets mighty testy if I keep her waiting for so much as a butterfly's flitter. We'll just take a quick gander at your garden and be on our way."

Beryl finished rubbing the lotion onto her skin. "Sylvie, you get busy with your duties. Tell your father I'll be in to see to his lunch after I've cut back the verbena. There are times when it feels like I'm the only person in this family able to take responsibility. You might as well have made that pie with green persimmons."

Ruby Bee gazed longingly at her car as they went outside. In a few minutes, she assured herself, she and Estelle could bounce down the driveway and turn on County 103. Not even the most delectable apple pie this side of heaven could warrant putting up with Beryl Blanchard and her mean-spirited tongue. The pie might have needed more honey, but Beryl needed an infusion.

Buck was seated in his wheelchair on the far corner of the porch. "Leaving so soon?" he called.

Ruby Bee sat down on a wicker chair beside him. "I was thinking how much I'd like to hear about your adventures in Naples and Athens," she said, wishing she had the gumption to grab his hand but keenly aware of Beryl's glare. "I'll bet you have all sorts of souvenirs and trinkets from your Navy days. Would you mind if I came by at another time?"

"If it works out," said Buck. "I may be gone."

She couldn't stop herself from clasping his bony arm. "Now, Buck, it can't be that bad. Beryl's feeding you a healthy diet of fresh fruits and vegetables. You're as nice and pink as"—she waved vaguely at the yard—"those blossoms over by the gate. Once you get back your strength, why, you might just be arm-wrasslin' at the bar and grill come Friday night. I seem to recollect you were pretty darn good at it once upon a time."

Beryl loomed over them. "Before he got sick, there was a lot of things he could do. Now all he's good for is sitting and complaining. Estelle's around back, looking at the dianthus. You want to see them?"

Sylvie came out of the front door. "There's something I should tell you, Ma."

"I don't want to hear one more word from you, young lady," said Beryl. "You just take your father in and see to him, then go to your room and read your Bible until I call you. See if you can find any recipes using milk and honey."

"I'm warning you—you should hear me out."

Beryl's cheeks turned red. "Maybe I'll hear you out of house and home if you don't obey me. If I find so much as a single travel brochure on the table when I come back inside, I'll pack your bags myself and throw them at the end of the driveway. As for your father, he can learn to wear diapers and suck soup through a straw. Do you understand?"

Sylvie grabbed the handles of Buck's wheelchair and took him into the house. Ruby Bee was too appalled to do more than follow Beryl down the steps to the yard.

Beryl stopped at a trellis covered with sweet-scented, creamy blossoms. "This is an antique variety of honeysuckle called Serotina that blooms all summer. In the fall, it will be laden with lovely red berries that draw in our feathered friends. We are all nature's guardians, are we not? As opposed as I am to disorganization, I allow the butterfly weed just beyond the fence to thrive in order to nurture our winged visitors."

Ruby Bee was steeling herself to make a remark about nurturing those a mite closer to home when she saw a yellow jacket light on Beryl's arm. "You got another friend," she said, pointing.

Beryl flicked it off. "They never bother me. Out here in the splendors of . . ." She stopped to flick off another one. "Why, I haven't been stung since . . ."

"Take it easy," advised Ruby Bee, backing away. "Don't slap at 'em."

Beryl was staring in horror as several more yellow jackets began to crawl up her arm. "I'm allergic to them. Up until three years ago, I didn't know I was, but then I got stung and had to be taken to the emergency room. Why are they doing this? Make them go away!" She gasped as one lit on her cheek. "Away!"

Ruby Bee had no idea what she was supposed to do. "Don't make any sudden moves. They're just—"

"What?" shrieked Beryl as several more alit.

Estelle came dashing around the corner. "What in tarnation's wrong?"

"She must have disturbed a nest," Ruby Bee said, still not willing to move in any closer. "All they're doing is investigating thus far. As long as she doesn't . . ."

Beryl began to slap at her arms. "What are they doing? Why won't they leave me alone?" She ducked her head and stumbled backward. "Make them go away! Oh my Gawd! I've been stung! Get these things off me!"

"What should I do?" demanded Ruby Bee. "Call for an ambulance?"

"Do you have one of those kits?" Estelle said, grabbing Beryl's arm despite the yellow jackets descending like ants at a picnic. "Can you give yourself a shot?"

Beryl fell onto the grass. "Kit's in the refrigerator." Her voice thickened. "Need it now."

Estelle nodded. "I'll get it right away. You just rest easy for a minute."

"I can barely breathe," Beryl gasped. She rolled over and weakly attempted to brush the yellow jackets off her face and arms. "Help me!"

Estelle ran into the kitchen and jerked open the refrigerator door. A carton of milk, a covered dish with leftover pot roast, a bowl of green beans. "Sylvie!" she called as she pawed through bowls. "Where's the kit?"

"Kit?" said Sylvie as she came into the kitchen, rubbing her eyes and yawning.

"Your mother has been stung!"

Sylvie paused. "Oh, dear."

"She says there's a kit in the refrigerator!"

"Then let's have a look, shall we?" Sylvie opened the refrigerator door, pondered the contents, and then closed it. "No, I don't see any kit. Why don't you ask Mother which shelf she put it on?"

Estelle went back to the yard, where she found Ruby Bee twisting her hands. Beryl was still, white, and to be real blunt, as dead as a doornail. "I don't know if this so-called kit might have helped, but I feel like we should have done something," she said as she stared down at Beryl's body. Yellow jackets seemed to be feasting on her as if she were a crumb of cake at a Sunday school picnic. "You'd almost think . . ."

"When they collect the body," Ruby Bee mused, "ain't nobody going to test her skin. She was allergic to bee stings. She went into shock, and she died before she could give herself a shot. Yellow jackets are nasty critters. When riled, they attack. They're a sight smaller than hornets, but they're meaner and more willing to attack."

"Why did they?" asked Sylvie as she sank down on the grass.

"I reckon you know," Ruby Bee said as she folded Beryl's hands over her chest. "You and Buck are gonna have to live with it. I won't say anything. You'll have to decide if a Caribbean cruise is enough to wash away your sins. You have to live with what happened, not me. If the sugar that was meant for the pie ended up in the sunblock lotion, that's not up to me."

"You won't say anything?" said Sylvie.

Ruby Bee gazed at Estelle. "We need to go. If I don't put an apple pie in the oven before long, the truckers will be squawking like jays long about noon. Maybe I'll try an extra pinch of ginger."

"Do that," murmured Sylvia as she went inside the house and closed the door.

The Gift

Gregory Janicke

Gregory Janicke is an award-winning short story writer, a playwright, Young Adult novelist, and artist. In addition to writing funny melodramas and serious newspaper columns, he creates educational stories and games for children.

Now *I remember:* The dog died first, and then my grandmother.

I am looking out of one of a thousand restaurants in one of a thousand towns that all sprawl with car lots and gas stations and convenience stores and motels with letters missing from their names like the rotted mouth of a dying old man.

"There lives an old lady——" I say this, aloud, to the watery reflections of a young woman in the window.

"Excuse me?" the waitress says, her voice candy pink.

"She's—with something."

The girl leans. She smells of perfume and cigarettes. "Oh. She's walking her dog."

"Dog."

In a breath, I've frightened the girl. "Uh, more coffee, sir?" She is not looking at me.

"What? Why, yes. Guess it won't kill me."

She pours the coffee, black as old oil, into my chipped mug.

What will kill me is her calling me "sir." I am anything but a "sir." Yes, I am fifty, but don't feel it, don't feel the age or failure or implosion. I see a faint image of myself in the window, but it has to be another man gray-streaked with the sorrows of age. I am alive.

The waitress wanders to fill other cups. I shake two bags of sugar, peel them open, dump them into the cup. Sugar granules spill onto the table. They seem disturbing, like beach sand.

The waitress returns. "Pie?" she asks.

"What?"

"Would you like some pie?"

The question echoes from somewhere far beyond the back of her blonde head.

"Uh, yes," I say, mostly to end the conversation.

"What kind?"

"How's that?"

"What kind of pie would you like, sir?"

"The regular kind."

She sniffs sharply. "We have blueberry, rhubarb, cherry, and apple."

"Did you say apple?"

"Yep. Homemade."

"I'll have the cherry."

"Fine. Be right back."

A car door opens across the street, the reflected light from its window searing my eyes. I am blind.

"Wait," I say, dazzled.

Amazingly, the waitress waits.

"I'll take it," I say.

"Take what?"

"The apple. Apple pie."

"Whatever."

While I'm blinded, she is a voice, only a voice, that trails off.

My sight returns. I sip sugared coffee. I take my finger and assemble the granules on the table into a column. I look outside again. The old woman plays with the dog, slowly leaning to pet it. The dog has slick black fur, like a raven transmuted into a four-legged beast.

Why is she playing with a dog?

The waitress returns, deposits the pie in front of me, rips the check from her pad of paper, and slaps it on the table. This is her ritual. She is done with me.

This is not apple pie but a wedge, a triangle, a thorn. It is stuck deeply in me.

How long has it been—thirty-five years, since I've had apple pie?

I turn the pie so that the tip of it faces me. It is an angle of pie opening outward to infinity. I raise my weapon, the fork. It hovers over the wedge of apple pie. Which corner to cut? The tip? The crust? The decision is crucial. People eat without thinking, ignoring the bitter poetry.

Look at the crust, flaky, golden; the prong marks that let the pie breathe; the light dusting of sugar. The crust bulges with chunks of brightly sliced and baked apple. I feel my mouth watering.

The fork descends, guillotine that it is, and slices the tip. The pie bleeds apple filling. The apple and crust slides onto the fork. I slowly raise the fork to my mouth but feel I'm raising a knife to my throat.

The dog outside starts barking. I jam the pie into my mouth.

Flavors burst, sweet apple flavors, a green fruit sliced white, carved of seeds. It is, as I feared, delicious. I take another bite. A third.

I nearly swoon from the bittersweet taste. It is overwhelming. This food becomes an explanation of heaven. Why have I waited so long to enjoy it?

I am dizzy. The room crushes around me, liquefies, stirs into a mushy pulp. Sugar drizzles from the skies, the earth is all crust.

I am lost. Years fall like apple tree leaves. In a blink, I am young again, fifteen, climbing, rising from our mottled, weed-beaten backyard on a rickety ladder, armed with a rake, about to smack silly the ripe green fruit. . . .

I stagger out of the restaurant into the blinding light and drive through the impossibly gentle weather of May. The car leads me to a place I've never seen.

My visit is long overdue. After all, it has taken me thirty-five years to eat a piece of apple pie again.

I drive from the restaurant to an unfamiliar part of town, where ancient oaks bow in homage over quiet streets. There are gaps between the homes, vast sprawling lawns, pristine and emerald. Some lawns look as severe as a crew cut. Not a weed, not a leaf, not a dry bald patch.

Eden. Of course.

There it is, around the bend, hidden in spruce and elm. Lawn soft and flowing as hair, soft enough to stroke.

The car stops. It seems to know. Something tight as a fist squeezes my chest. I gasp for air.

The grass is perfect. It doesn't seem to reflect sun as much as it radiates its own green light.

It isn't at all like—

Like—

Now I remember: the house in which I grew up, on the far side of town, the aging, rotted, eastern edge of town, first founded when Kingsford, Kansas, was a child, first abandoned when it grew into a city.

We lived in a small white frame house that groaned at night like an old woman with brittle bones. There was no *lawn,* no *grass,* only yard, a bad blanket of grass, weed, and waste. There was something Grandma hated about the yard—no, not the yard itself, but something in the yard. There was something in the yard—

A dog. An oily black dog. A black moving mass of muscle, fang, and fur—

The dog. I remember now. Looking into the past is like rebuilding a shattered pane of glass. It is excruciating for me. But something deep in my soul keeps whispering, "Now."

The hateful man Carver, who lived down the street from us in East Kingsford, let his dog do whatever it wanted to on our yard. Once, when I was young, Grandma demanded I go outside and chase the beast from our yard. I was terrified. Grandma pushed me out the front door with a rake. I carried the rake across my small pounding chest, fear gnawing at me head to foot. The dog looked up, its black oily fur standing on end. It growled at me, and all the world was loud and growling, and I was frightened beyond comprehension, and the dog lunged. I shoved the rake at it, and its teeth sank into the wooden handle, which could have been my arm, and I ran back up the porch and slammed the door and ran to my little room and slammed that door too.

I heard barking and snarling, I heard Carver shouting obscenities in the thin, dizzy, afternoon air, I heard Grandma shouting something back in a foreign tongue. I huddled in a ball on the floor behind my bed and covered my ears, and the world rang with rage. . . .

I now hoist myself from the car, using all my strength, fighting the knot in my chest. I shut the car door, walk past the perfect green lawn, and ring the doorbell on the towering white house. I immediately regret pressing the small white button. Ringing a doorbell means someone might answer. The back of my shirt is already wringing wet with sweat. I have remembered my childhood house and the yard and the dog and the fact that the dog and my grandmother had died. What more can I do?

There is not a single sign of life through the white gauze of curtains draped on the windows. The knot in my chest eases. No one is home.

I turn and take three steps toward the car when the front door slowly opens. Something thin, white and vaporous as a ghost, stands in the crack of the opening.

It speaks.

"Andrew?"

It knows my name.

I want to go back to the car, the town, the highway, my distant home, but the voice has me paralyzed.

"Andrew."

A wild thought knifes through me—if I turn around and gaze at the ghost, I will become a pillar of salt and will fall to the perfect lawn in a white puff.

"Is it you?"

I have a moment to lie, to say I am confused and in the wrong place.

"Yes. Mother."

A wispy woman in white sweater and slacks steps into the light. She does not vanish, as ghosts do. She stands like a white wire, primed with an electric charge. She looks exactly like my grandmother now, not the young mother I remembered from years ago. She has to be in her seventies.

A lightning crack of silence races between us.

I look down, as I always had. I struggle for words.

"Nice—lawn," I finally said.

My mother raises a hand as if about to cast seed. "It's perfect. The way Ma always wanted it. Remember—"

"Yes," I say.

"It was disgusting. That awful man—"

"Carver—"

"And that filthy dog soiling our yard. That man and his dog

killed your poor grandmother."

"Did they?"

My mother squints. Her eyes, twin slits in a cracked field of flesh, scan my face.

"You look so old," she says to me.

"So do you."

Another lightning-slash of silence.

"Why are you here, Andrew?"

I consider the question. Why exactly have I come home, on today of all days, after all this time?

"I had some apple pie," I conclude.

Her eyes widen. "Really? Was it good?"

"It—reminded me."

"Don't let apple pie bother you."

"Too late."

"Well," Mother says, her mind reaching for a thought. "Come in."

I enter the house I have never seen before. I had known one home, the small frame house in East Kingsford, where I had lived with my mother and my grandmother. That place had been as dark and damp as the grip of an old man's hand. This place is light and airy. Lace curtains lift in the soft springtime breeze.

There is a couch the color of spilled red wine, a huge Oriental rug at its feet. There are smartly polished end tables and tall lamps and a towering bookcase and a mantel adorned with silver-framed photos.

There is something in the air, cologne, the scent of a man.

Reading my mind, Mother speaks. "Carl's out picking up a few groceries. He should be right back. Soon. I want you to meet him. You'd like him."

I have no idea who Carl is. A husband? A boyfriend? A hired hand?

"Sit," mother orders, and I do so, in a corner of the wine-colored couch. She drifts like a stranger through the room, unsure where to land. She leans on the mantel; the framed photos look over her shoulder. A photo of Grandma shows her gazing with pain at a distant place.

"So," my mother says, as if beginning—or ending—our meeting.

"So," I respond, stroking the arm of the sofa. It is soft to the touch.

"What brings you here, Andrew?"

I do not answer.

"Is there something you want?"

I stare at the Oriental rug. "You tell me."

"You haven't visited since—"

"Since—"

"I hope this isn't a joke, Andrew."

"Nothing is."

"Your pants are shiny. You must want money from me."

"I'm not poor," I counter.

Mother draws a breath, and releases. "I have everything now. Ma wanted me to have everything."

"I'm sure she did."

"Come see. I'll show you everything."

Mother leads me through the soft flow of curtains, soft as angel wings, through the dining room impossibly set for six people, through the shadows of the kitchen. A door glows like something from a dream, a passage to something never clearly remembered.

But I do remember. The moment Mother throws open the back door and shows me the softly undulating yard and the unmistakable growth that could only be an apple tree, I feel the past strike with a vengeance. Sharp and piercing as a hound's teeth.

I hear Grandma's voice asking: "Would you like some pie?"

I hear my fifteen-year-old voice answering: "Uh, yes."

"Then take the rake and ladder and go knock some apples

down from the tree. I'll bake us a special pie."

I stand outside with my mother in the here and now looking at her beautiful back yard but see our old yard. In mind and memory I see Grandma's apple tree. The apples are as big as fists, dripping with summer light . . .

Back then, I could never carry the rake without noticing the dog's toothmarks on it. The animal's teeth had punctured the wood, forever scarring it. Carver was a menace and his dog was a monster. In my deep and fearful dreams, I had wished the dog would die. I couldn't step outside of the house without a jolt of fear coursing through me. I never knew when the dog would spring from its deep shadows and attack me. Whenever I saw it relieving itself on our grass, I froze. The dog glared defiantly at me until it had finished its business. Left its filth. Carver always laughed.

In my dreams, the rake became a sword, sharp and swift.

All Grandma had wanted was a nice lawn, a clean house, a stronge apple tree. She periodically applied a white powdery fertilizer to help the lawn grow. I remember thinking once that it had snowed in July. She had talked to Carver, had insisted that he keep the dog away from her precious yard, but Carver only responded with a twisted grin and said, "My doggie will give ya plenty of his own fertilizer, old lady."

That one summer when I was fifteen, I carried the wooden ladder to the apple tree. I grabbed my rake and climbed the ladder. I swatted apples from the tree. They fell with a pulpy thud on the ground. As I gathered the apples in a basket, I smelled something foul and furious in the warm summer air. The smell was coming from the alley, which made sense. The intensity overwhelmed me.

I wandered like a sleepwalker toward the alley, toward the fallen fence and powdered grass along the fence, toward the black mass immobile in the cinders. Flies buzzed around the mass. I moved forward, driven by sick curiosity. I stopped when I recognized the dog. It wasn't moving, but it wasn't asleep, either.

I stepped forward, extending the handle of the rake. The smell was unbearable. My eyes watered. I poked the dog. It was limp, a pile of oily rags. There was white powder around its nose.

The dog was dead.

Carver was very much alive after that, cursing our names, threatening to kill us all, throwing rocks through our windows. He tried suing Grandma, claiming that she had poisoned his poor little pet. He got another dog, bigger and meaner, but it never came near our house.

I remember it all now, as I stand with Mother in her clean backyard.

We had won long ago, but after the battle with Carver, Grandma moved sluggishly and ate little. Stopped speaking.

I never believed that she had poisoned the dog until the day I found four unmarked paper sacks hidden behind a box in the basement. My mind raged. *Fertilizer or poison? Was there a difference?*

I later determined that the four sacks contained: flour, sugar, fertilizer, and poison.

Grandma was mean at times—everyone had to be in our world—but not enough to poison the black dog. It had to have been a terrible mistake. People in East Kingsford had two essential household items: guns and poison. We'd had rats in the basement. Grandma must have grabbed the poison instead of fertilizer for the lawn. An easy mistake. The basement was always so dark. Grandma's vision had been bad.

Besides, I'd found the dog in the back alley, not in the front yard.

Still, she'd said often enough, I'd like to kill that creature. . . .

The dog could have wandered into the alley with a stomachful of poison. . . .

Carver harassed us relentlessly. Finally, I got up the courage to stuff an anonymous note in his mailbox. In bloodred letters I wrote: YOU'RE NEXT.

Carver left us alone. It was as if he had died and turned to dust.

"Enough," I say in the here and now as I stand with Mother on the sun-washed shore of her perfect green yard. Her apple tree seems small and distant compared with the one I had climbed and swatted with a dog-bitten rake so long ago.

"Is my property too nice for you?" Mother challenges.

"It may be too nice for *you*."

"I deserve this, Andrew. After all I put up with, I deserve this."

"What did you put up with, Mother?"

"Your grandmother. And you. And that filthy man and his stinking dog. And that rotten little house with no yard and a scrawny apple tree."

"It was our home."

Mother turns on me. She pinches my shoulder. She is seventy, I am fifty, and she still pinches my shoulder. "Why are you here? For my money? I'll give you my money. After I die."

"The way you got Grandma's money."

Mother gives me a scathing glare. "So. That's why you're here. You can't let it rest. Ma got sick. I didn't take her to the hospital or put her in a home, and everybody says I killed her."

"Everybody? Nobody ever talked to us."

"But they talked *about* us. The newspaper?"

"I remember the newspaper. Someone taped the report about you to my locker at school."

Mother fusses with a thread on a sleeve of her white sweater. "They don't know. No one knows what it's like to live with a sick old woman, day in and day out. I couldn't do anything right."

"Did Grandma poison the black dog?"

"What? Who told you that?"

"Did she?"

"I—"

"You—"

She squints. "I don't recall."

"We're not in court, Mother."

"Oh, no?"

"I'm your son."

"You can't prove that by me. I haven't seen you in—"

"In a long time. I know."

Mother's wrinkled face looks like a riverbed baked in the sun. Her steel eyes mist. Her voice cracks. "I wonder where Carl is. I sent him for ice cream. He should have been back by now."

"I'll look for Carl. Where did he go?"

"The store."

"Which one?"

"I don't know. The ice cream store."

"I'll be back."

I leave my mother in the backyard. I circle the house and return to the car. I drive off in search of a man I've never met.

I stop in two nearby grocery stores and look for a man I suspect might be Carl. No luck.

Maybe there is no Carl.

I sit in the car. It is stifling. I roll down the window and gasp for air. The pain in my chest is now attacking my lungs. It feels as if I have swallowed a sliver of glass. I can't breathe.

Why have I come here? I could have left the past in a tangled ball of black yarn, in a lump of coal, lost. Instead, something in me claws toward the light. A mad dog of truth that feels its day in the sun is long overdue.

Haven't I recalled enough? The home, the yard, the tree, the dog, the man? Can't I look at the past in safe angles, instead of directly?

No. Not anymore. I have weakened. My defenses are as thin and pointless as the handle of a rake.

I have to see this through to the end.

I drive east. To the end.

It is there, beaten and battered. The front yard, once a battle-ground with a black dog, is now bald and slick as oil. The porch steps sink at an angle like a sneer. Weeds coil from the cracks. The torn screen door hangs on a hinge.

The house seems as if it has exhaled.

I sit in the car, clutching the steering wheel. It is still hard to breathe. I am old, but frightened as if I were still a little boy. I fear that at any moment my heart will burst from my chest and fall to the ground like a rotten apple.

What do I fear worse than any hellish dog?

The facts.

The fact that maybe someone had poisoned the black dog.

Grandma.

She had gotten so sick. A healthy woman had fallen ill. No one knew what it was like to live with a sick old woman, day in and day out.

With the dog dead, with Carver gone, with Grandma mute, a dark shroud of silence had fallen over the world. I lived in utter silence, my own voices of fear screaming inside me.

As I now sit in the warm, dry silence of the car, I look across the street at a window, closed. It had been the window to Grandma's room. In an insane flash, I think she might be there in bed, waiting for me.

Waiting for me, as she had when I was fifteen . . .

I had drifted by her room one day. I was more afraid of her than the black dog. She waved her hand as if tossing seed in the air and said something.

"Make a pie," I thought she had said.

Like a creature hypnotized, I did as she had ordered. I dutiful-ly got out the dog-chewed rake, the rickety ladder, and I climbed up the ladder and swatted down apples. I put them into the basket and carried them to the house.

"What are you doing?" my mother had demanded.

"Grandma wants a pie."

"Oh, she does."

"She said so."

"Right."

My mother grabbed me by the hand, and we went back to Grandma's room.

"Andrew says you want a pie."

Grandma shook her head. She said something.

What?

I now clutch the steering wheel in the car and shut my eyes and concentrate, sweat streaming down my face. What had Grandma said to us?

No—

Not "make a pie."

I focus the pain in my chest and use it to knife through the time and tide of thirty-five years, through the doubt and denial hard as carbon, through the layers of life that hid horrid truths.

Grandma had said, "Don't let me die."

"So. You came back."

I nod.

"I thought you'd gone for good."

"Maybe I have."

Mother sits at the dinner table. We have finished eating dinner. "Sorry you missed Carl again. He got the wrong ice cream. I sent him back to the store."

"Does he even exist? Do I?"

"He's a good man. Does what I tell him to do."

"I went to East Kingsford," I say.

Mother flinches. "To that rat trap? Why on earth would you waste any time there?"

"To remember."

"Remember what?"

"To remember what happened. First the dog died, then Grandma."

Mother stands from the table.

"You made pie for her," I insist.

"I made lots of things."

"You fed her apple pie. She died that night."

"She was so weak."

"She was strong."

"I wanted things perfect for Grandma, but I was never good enough," my mother says. She grabs our dishes and goes into the kitchen. There is the rattling of plates and silverware in the sink, the thud of cabinet doors opening and closing.

Mother returns with two pieces of apple pie. She sets one in front of me and gives me a clean fork.

"You know what day today is, don't you?" she asks.

"Mother's Day. That's why I'm here."

"To celebrate?"

"To remember."

"That's not much of a gift."

"I do have a gift for you," I say.

"Fine. Have some pie first. I dare you."

I had eaten pie at the restaurant without a problem. I can't stand the mocking look in her eyes now. She's never had faith in anything but herself.

"I don't know about Carver's dog," I say as I lower the fork onto the tip of the pie.

"I hope Carl gets back soon with the right ice cream. This would be perfect with ice cream. I almost can't eat this yet. Then again, neither can you."

Nothing is more powerful than a mother's taunting remarks. I cut into the tip of the pie, scoop it on the fork, lift it to my mouth, chew the piece of pie, and swallow.

"I don't know about the dog," I repeat, "but I know about you."

"What about me?"

"About you and Grandma and the apple pie and the four paper sacks from the basement."

"You need rest. You're old and tired."

I grin, probably for the first time in thirty-five years. "I remember now. I know all about you."

"You don't know anything."

"My gift to you is that I'm not going to say anything about what you did."

Mother also grins. It is the perfect image of a goblin. "Of course you won't. You know who carried those sacks up from the basement for me. Eat your pie, son."

I pause, fork hovering in the air.

I obey my mother.

Sex, Lies, and Apple Pie

Janet LaPierre

Janet LePierre conducts her writing life the way other writers only wish they could: Along with her husband, their Labrador retriever, and their elderly Manx cat, she researches her stories from a twenty-five-foot travel trailer which they park in campgrounds throughout northern California. Janet is a Macavity and Anthony Award nominee who sets most of her stories on the foggy, austerely beautiful north coast of California. Her newest work, Baby Mine, *will appear in mid-1999, and she is currently at work on a novel set in Trinity County, California.*

"I'm sorry, but I don't involve myself in cases the police are actively investigating," Patience told the well-dressed but twitchy woman seated across the desk from her.

"But Captain Svoboda has no objections," Jeanette Carter said eagerly. "My father particularly liked your ad in the phone book—Patience Smith Investigations: Licensed, Experienced, Quiet. So I called Captain Svoboda and asked him about you, and he gave you a strong personal recommendation."

And who better? thought Patience, mildly amused. "Mrs. Carter,

I'm not quite clear on what it is you want from me. Are you looking for evidence that this young woman *did* rob your father, or
that she didn't?"

"Well, you see, that's the problem. I'm not sure."

"I beg your pardon?"

"The police have not found sufficient evidence for bringing
charges against her," Jeanette Carter said.

"Then I think you'd be wasting your time and money hiring
me. Port Silva has a highly capable police force."

"But my father *insists* he saw her!" the other woman said in a
voice that trembled. "The thing is, that may be just illusion, or
stubbornness, because he was so furious with her. And that's part-
ly my fault, you see, because I never approved of that relationship, and may even have said something like, you know, 'I told
you so,' when she broke it off."

"Mrs. Carter, I don't think—"

Jeanette Carter didn't hear her. "But whatever the truth, you
just have to help me find it, because if he continues this vendet-
ta, he's going to get himself in terrible trouble."

"Tell me about . . . the new case." Verity, just in from a late-
afternoon run, was moving her tall body through her chosen
cooldown of yoga Sun Salutations. Patience, much shorter and
rounder, sat at the kitchen table sipping wine and admiring her
daughter's energy as well as her figure.

"The client is the daughter of Tom Gunderson, the retired
contractor who was assaulted and robbed in his home two weeks
ago. I have an appointment with him tomorrow."

Verity did her last stretch, paused with hands palm to palm
before her face, then dropped into a chair. "I remember. He
accused his nurse?"

"His trainer at the Y. He had a heart attack last spring, and his
doctor advised strength training as a follow-up. Mr. Gunderson is

seventy-five, Darcy Kelly is thirty-three."

"Do I hear a note of disapproval?" asked Verity.

"Jeanette Gunderson Carter's, not mine. She says her father, a longtime widower, went totally out of his aged mind over Ms. Kelly. She and her husband were afraid he was going to marry her."

"Aha. As I recall the story, Mr. Gunderson is a well-known and by inference well-off local citizen."

"And accustomed to being the boss, according to his daughter. She says she doesn't know the details, but suspects his habit of giving orders and expecting instant obedience finally caused Darcy Kelly to break off what Mrs. Carter called 'that relationship.'"

"I bet that cheered the Carters right up," said Verity.

"I think they were greatly relieved," Patience admitted as she got up and went to the refrigerator. "For a short while. Would you like some chardonnay? Or a beer?"

"Beer, please."

Patience brought her daughter a brown bottle and an opener, then topped off her own glass of wine.

"But one night two weeks ago," she went on, "according to Mr. Gunderson, he was awakened by a noise around eleven-thirty, got up, and went downstairs to look. Someone hit him and knocked him out, then took ten thousand dollars from his safe. He told the police that the robber was Darcy Kelly.

"However, it turned out to be he-said, she-said. No one else saw anything, and Darcy Kelly has witnesses to her being somewhere else at the time. The police think the robbery was committed by a gang, probably some young locals who they believe have pulled off several household burglaries recently."

"Let me guess. Mr. Gunderson is unhappy."

"Mr. Gunderson is convinced he's being ignored or lied to, and his daughter is afraid he's going to work himself into another heart attack or maybe even a harassment suit." Patience paused for a sip of wine. "So I agreed to give it a look. Are you free tomorrow?"

Verity, thirty-year-old refugee from a bad marriage and a power-suit-and-briefcase position in San Francisco, now worked several part-time jobs in the little north-coast town of Port Silva, one of them for her mother's detective agency. "Friday? I'm busy in the morning, but the afternoon is all yours."

"Good. Now, who's cooking tonight?"

Thomas Gunderson lived at the north end of town, where lumber barons had built themselves family homes around the turn of the century. His house was one of the largest, a two-story, brown-shingled structure with deep eaves and many windows. Patience rang the bell and was admiring what was surely the original door, with an oval panel of etched glass set in a brass frame, when it swung wide; the tall old man standing there had a cane in his hand but was making an effort not to lean on it.

"Patience Smith. You look like a sensible woman," he said, eyeing her gray hair and nice wool skirt and jacket before stepping aside to admit her. She moved through the flagstone entry hall into a spacious room with a high, beamed ceiling, dark wood, and an enormous fireplace.

As Gunderson closed the door, Patience took note of heavy mission-style furniture, most of it leather-upholstered and patterned deep-toned rugs. An antlered head looked down from the wall to the right of the fireplace; on the left, racks held three long guns. The room was polished and orderly and gave Patience an uncharacteristic longing for pink ruffled curtains.

Gunderson gestured her forward through an archway into what had probably been a dining room but was now clearly an office. "Sit down, sit down. My daughter tells me you can help me out."

"I agreed to try." Patience took the seat he indicated and pulled pad and pen from her handbag. Gunderson settled into a big leather chair and fixed her with a stern gaze. The chair belonged to a monster of an antique rolltop desk; next to that was a table with a computer and its peripherals. Across the room, two filing cabinets framed a wall safe.

Gunderson had followed her gaze. "This is where it happened," he said. "I came down in the middle of the night and found Darcy Kelly here with my safe open, and she hit me with something I didn't see." He lifted a hand to his head, where a shaved patch still bore a small bandage. "And left me bleeding there on the floor and robbed me."

"Was Ms. Kelly living here at the time?"

"No!" Gunderson's weathered face, pale from winter or illness, now reddened. "I'd asked her to move in. Didn't see any reason to keep paying rent on that dump she lived in and pay a housekeeper here, too. She wouldn't do it, said she was grateful for my help but she needed to keep her own place."

Patience waited.

"'Help,' she called it! I bought her a car, dressed her like a lady, took her places. Paid to send her foulmouthed bastard to private school up in Trinity County, get him off the streets and teach him some discipline.

"So I told her, okay, I wouldn't be paying any more of her bills. I figured she'd think that over, and come around," he added in plaintive tones; for a moment he looked not angry, but confused. "I sure didn't expect her to turn on me the way she did."

"I haven't spoken with the police yet," said Patience. "But Mrs. Carter told me that they'd not found sufficient evidence to charge Ms. Kelly."

"Lady, I'll tell you like I told the cops, there's not a goddamned thing wrong with my mind or my eyesight!" Age and illness had melted flesh from Tom Gunderson's big frame, but his long jaw was firm, his ice-blue eyes piercing. "Streetlight's right outside the window—I saw that slut clear as I'm seeing you. Smelled her, too, the perfume *I* bought her. She's taking the cops in, same as she did me."

"Did she have keys to this house?"

"Damn right she did! She told me she'd lost 'em, but it's obvious that was a lie."

"Did she know the combination to your safe?"

"She knew where to find it, right there under the desk pad. I sometimes had her fetch stuff from the safe, and she had no head for remembering numbers. And she knew I always had cash on hand!" Gunderson slashed the air with his cane for emphasis.

"Do you know, Mr. Gunderson, whether Ms. Kelly had any kind of criminal record?"

"The cops say she didn't," he said, sullenly. "But I don't know how hard they looked." He took a deep breath and faced her squarely. "Fact is, I figure I pissed the cops off, gave them the idea that I'm some rich old fart demanding special service. But what I really am is a sick old man who got taken advantage of."

What you are is an old man who wants to have it both ways, Patience thought. "The money hasn't turned up?" she asked.

He shook his head.

"What do you think became of it?"

Rage splotched his face with red, put a quaver in his voice— even, it seemed to Patience, made his thin gray hair bristle. "I figure she had her boyfriend waiting, and gave it to him."

"Name?" asked Patience, pen poised over her notebook.

"Maybe Doolittle, who runs the rehab program for the Y. I saw her rubbing up against him one time when I first started going there. Or the guy who teaches tennis at the community college. Or one of the other coaches in the soccer league; she wouldn't give that up even when I said it was taking too much of her time."

Patience jotted down a few words. "Did you suspect Ms. Kelly of having other relationships *before* the robbery?"

"No, because I was a fool. All I know for sure is, she's the one hit me and robbed me."

"Mr. Gunderson . . ."

"Now you get out there and find out who's lying for her. Because I want to see her"—the cane slashed the air twice in a giant *X*—"punished."

"We believe Gunderson's mistaken." Hank Svoboda, Port Silva police captain and Patience's good friend, leaned back in his desk chair and shook his burr-cut gray head. Patience thought she heard a faint hesitation before the word "mistaken" and put that interesting possibility aside to pursue later.

"That Saturday night," Hank went on, "Darcy Kelly was at the monthly dinner meeting of county-league soccer coaches, at the Carson Hotel in Ukiah. Finished around nine, then she and two of the guys from the coast division drank coffee at Denny's until after ten-thirty."

"Sixty or seventy hard nighttime driving miles from here," noted Patience.

"Right. With the help of God and a strong tailwind, she might just have made it. But. No evidence. No prints on the door or the safe; no money on her or in her car or house. No keys; she'd told him weeks earlier that she'd lost them. No criminal record in Fresno, where she lived until two years ago."

"Mr. Gunderson seemed so *sure*."

"He's pissed. Maybe at being robbed, maybe because he thinks his paid-for woman was shortchanging him."

"Was she?"

Hank shrugged. "She knew a lot of guys, but the ones we talked to say they saw her as a buddy, a tennis or racquetball pal. A woman who works with Kelly says she's a real pushover for a sad story, and that old man put the moves on her so fast and hard, he was running her life before she knew it."

"Then who? This local gang?"

"Good possibility; there was a hit in that neighborhood just a week earlier. We've got our eye on one kid maybe involved who's younger than the rest and real nervous."

"Mr. Gunderson feels he may have offended you—the police, that is—by acting as though he deserved special treatment."

"Mr. Gunderson doesn't know how hard it is to offend cops used to facing down loggers and university professors. He send you in here to make an apology for him?"

"That's probably what he thought he was doing," she said with a grin. "But I have a question instead."

He raised his eyebrows.

"How do you feel about Gunderson himself?"

He let the silence stretch, and finally shrugged. "Nobody on the street heard or saw anything that night until the police arrived. Kelly's friends—and she has quite a few—say he'd been bad-mouthing her publicly from the time she broke off with him."

Patience waited.

"According to the doc, the rap Gunderson took on the head was real, and hard. Its position was such that it could have been self-inflicted, but he thought probably not by a seventy-five-year-old man with a damaged heart."

Damaged in more ways than one, thought Patience. "Well. I have a few more people to talk to if I'm going to earn my fee. I thank you for the recommendation, I think."

"I couldn't stop them from hiring an investigator, and I figured you'd handle Gunderson—and that poor girl, too—without raising many hackles."

"Poor girl?"

He brushed a hand over his hair. "Oops. Maybe the old guy

did piss me off."

"He's not a nice man," said Patience as she got to her feet. "But I think he's sad as well as angry."

Svoboda got up, too. "I'd tell you to be careful with him, if I didn't know you'd spit in my eye. Patience, if you find something I've missed . . ."

"I know the rules, Captain Svoboda."

"Yes ma'am."

"And I'll see you tonight."

"Probably around seven, if that's okay. Our reservation at Mary's is for eight."

At noon on a chilly, drizzly March Friday, Verity slid into investigator's mode and headed for the Port Silva YMCA, to find it crowded and noisy. She buttonholed any employee she could pry loose for a minute or two, and got a breakdown of four in Darcy's corner to one vehemently not. ("What do you expect from sports-trash?")

Number six was Jill, who led the aerobics class Verity attended when she had time. "Poor kid. She cut her hours here way back and then finally quit, because that old goat insisted. She came in last week and asked about working again, but the manager had already replaced her."

"Maybe he believed she committed that robbery," suggested Verity.

"No way; not Darcy. She's a sweetie—never loses her temper with even the worst whiners, wouldn't hurt a fly. Well, except in a contest. On the tennis court she's a killer."

An hour later, after sharing a deli-sandwich lunch with her mother at the downtown office, Verity pulled to the curb in front of a ratty little stucco bungalow set close among others of its kind. It struck her as just the kind of place where an undereducated single mother given to bad luck might wind up. And commit robbery to escape?

Her knock on the door was answered by a willowy six-footer with boyishly short fair hair, tired brown eyes, and glorious cheekbones. Darcy Kelly took Verity's card, listened to the explanation of her presence, and said, "Shit, I knew I shouldn't answer the damned door. I don't have to talk to you."

"True," said Verity.

"Oh, hell, you might as well come in out of the rain. But you'll have to grill me while I work." She closed the door and led the way across a small, low-ceilinged living room, through a narrow hall, and into a kitchen just big enough for its appliances, a rectangular pine table, and two chairs.

"This is all crazy," she said, and bent over something on the table. "I spent months working with Tom Gunderson to make him stronger; I wouldn't hurt him."

"I'm told he's absolutely sure it was you," said Verity.

"But that's just Tom, he's mad because I wouldn't . . . Damn! I'm never going to get this right!"

In the center of the floury table lay a sorry-looking piece of pastry, its edges split and its surface uneven. Darcy dropped her rolling pin, scrunched the dough into a lump, and flung it into a nearby garbage bin. Where others had preceded it, Verity noted.

Darcy sank into a chair and rubbed her hands together, scattering dried flakes of pastry. "My kid is coming home tomorrow, just for the weekend."

"Oh?" Verity pulled out the other chair and sat.

"Yup, first time since Christmas." Her mouth curved briefly in a sad-edged little smile. "He's in this school up in Trinity County that Tom thought would be good for him."

"What's the name of the school?"

"Why would you need to know that?" Darcy demanded.

Oho. Sweetie Darcy had her tiger-mom side. "A friend of mine is looking for a good boarding school for her son."

"Well, this isn't it. Aaron hates the place, but the tuition is paid through the semester and it's not refundable, and I'm so broke I just told him he had to tough it out till June. But I really miss him, so I scraped together a few bucks for a bus ticket.

"Anyway, apple pie's his favorite thing, and I was trying to make him one," Darcy went on. "But the store was out of those ready-to-bake crusts, so I decided to try from scratch." She gestured sadly toward a cluttered sink counter, where everything, including a bag of apples, was dusted with flour.

Verity had been cooking since childhood, when her policeman father had received the injury that put him in a wheelchair and sent her mother to work. "Tell you what," she said, getting to her feet. "I'll make the piecrust, you tell the story."

"Could you make enough for two?"

"I can." As Verity wiped out a big metal bowl, scooped flour into it, and added a dash of salt, Darcy set her feet neatly together and folded her hands in her lap, like a good child ready to recite.

"Okay. I was in a real bad place when Tom met me. My kid was giving me trouble, the landlord raised the rent on this dump, my old car died. So what looks now like sex for money, I saw as two people helping each other out."

Verity said nothing, and Darcy flushed. "So okay, I guess it was sex for money. But I'd been looking around for a second job, any job, to try to get things together. I'm not real smart, but I'm not a tramp."

Verity added a big lump of shortening to the flour and decided that anyone who'd buy piecrusts would not own a pastry blender; knives and fingers would have to serve. "Weren't there any other men in your life?"

"Nope, I've been pretty gun-shy the last few years. Well, except for a bunch of fifteen-year-olds," she said, a momentary note of cheer in her voice. "I started coaching soccer a while back, because Aaron was playing. He lost interest when he got tall enough for basketball, but I didn't."

Verity kept her eyes on her work and her fingers busy; disarm your subject by doing her housework. "Where's Aaron's father?"

"God knows. I've got a history of real bad luck with men, starting with the guy who got me pregnant when I was sixteen and right away left town. And *boy* do nice guys not have time for a woman who's got a kid. But I kept my kid, and finished high school and worked at whatever I could find. Even got in some community college courses; I figured that once Aaron was through high school, I could go full-time. I'd really like to be a junior high P.E. teacher."

Verity looked up, to see the sad brown eyes staring past her. "Then last summer the balancing act fell apart, like I said."

The tiny freezer compartment in the old refrigerator contained no ice trays, only a package of frozen hamburger. Verity let the tap water run as cold as it would, then filled a cup and sprinkled some of it into the pastry bowl. "I believe Mr. Gunderson paid the rent here?"

"Yeah."

"And did he buy that little Honda in your driveway?"

"That, and clothes, and, oh, stuff. A couple rings and a neck-lace—I gave those back. Oh, and Aaron's school."

Verity turned to face her. "Darcy, suppose Tom Gunderson had presented you with a bill for all he'd spent on you. What would you have done?"

"What I actually did when we split. I promised to pay him back, over time."

Verity didn't think ten thou would have covered it. "Suppose he didn't find that satisfactory?"

The tired face split into a real grin. "Hey, he's gonna put me in debtors prison? I don't think so. If you've got nothing," she said, waving a hand around her, "you got nothing to lose."

Except your name, credit rating if any, friends, future jobs, maybe even your son. Verity found a nailbrush beside the sink and concentrated on scrubbing her hands. "My boss says he appears to be absolutely convinced you're the one who hit him and robbed him."

"God, if he'd just let me *talk* to him . . . !"

"Not a good idea," said Verity, remembering Patience's description of an angry old man. "There's your piecrust. Wrap it up and refrigerate it for a while. Then make your pies and enjoy your son's visit."

Darcy stood up, a look of panic on her face. "Don't you believe me either?"

Verity quelled her urge to hug this woman, to reassure her. Maybe, she thought, she should go back to banking for a while, to restore her armor. "Darcy, you have my card. Call me if you remember anything you think might help."

Saturday morning was gray and cold, yesterday's drizzle replaced by a wet fog. Verity woke early in her chilly studio, gulped a can of grapefruit juice and went out to run five miles, came back for a long, hot shower. When she let herself in the kitchen door of the main house, Patience was just emerging sleepy-eyed from her bedroom.

"Late night, huh?"

"Coffee," croaked Patience.

Verity filled the kettle and set it over a flame. "And how's Hank?" She was mostly amused, and only occasionally irritated, by the fact that her fifty-five-year-old mother had a life while she did not.

"He's fine. How are you?"

"I think I spent the night with Darcy Kelly."

"Oh dear. I'm sorry." Patience sat down at the table and

watched Verity set up coffee cups and filters.

"I worried about my identification with her: another woman who made bad choices when it came to men. But I've decided I believe her. If she bashed that old guy, she's the most convincing liar I ever came across, including bankers."

The kettle shrieked; Verity made two cups of coffee and set them on the table.

Patience inhaled the fragrant steam, took a tiny sip, murmured, "Lovely. Well, Darcy's near-alibi checks out. The men she drank coffee with that night say they left Denny's before she did and did not see her pass them. They know the road, drove well over the limit, got into town at fifteen minutes past midnight; Mr. Gunderson had already called the police by then."

"Okay." Verity found a banana in the fruit bowl and peeled it.

Patience took another sip of coffee. "Her reputation with her male acquaintances is good pal, terrific athlete, no sexual signals. With the women, it's good friend, good mom, clueless about men but doesn't poach. So I think we'll close this out, and present a bill for one and a half person-days."

"Do you think Gunderson is lying?"

"Maybe. And maybe he woke from a dream, went downstairs still bemused, and saw someone who was there only in his head. And promptly got bashed by the real robber."

"That makes sense." Verity finished her banana, and poured herself a glass of milk. "What did Hank Svoboda say about Darcy's kid?"

"Just that he was in bed in his dorm that night—at Trinity Academy for Boys, a few miles north of Weaverville. Why?"

"I don't know. Just something I want to check." She gulped the milk and poured her coffee into a travel cup. "I'll probably be back before you finish breakfast."

Patience, at the table with her laptop computer, her notes, and a third cup of coffee, glanced up briefly as Verity came in the door. "Already?" When there was no response, she looked up again, hit "Save," and said, "Verity, what is it?"

"Here, you have a look." She handed her mother a folder and waited until Patience had cleared space for it on the table. "I went to the *Sentinel* office, to see some of the back issues on our people. That's the first story on the robbery, with a picture of Gunderson that makes him look like a mean old bastard."

"Fair enough."

"Then there's the follow-up story, for which Darcy ought to be able to sue him."

Patience scanned the first paragraphs. "Nasty, but not all untrue."

"Oops. Right you are. Okay, here's the Winter Ball, six weeks ago." The photo showed a gaunt but almost-smiling Gunderson, leaning on a cane. Close beside him was a striking woman in a narrow black gown, thick fair hair waving loosely to her shoulders.

"Darcy Kelly," said Verity.

"Handsome."

"Right. And here's soccer coach Kelly, with the Sharks." A ragged line of teenaged boys grinned or scowled at the camera, Darcy looking like a taller boy behind them.

"Ah. She wears a wig for dress-up," said Patience.

"So it appears. And her's last year's team." Darcy Kelly in another line of boys, the lanky, sober-faced one next to her clearly her son. Aaron Kelly had inherited a masculine version of his mother's elegant bone structure. "I think we might have an *Oh shit* here, Mom."

"Interesting." The telephone at Patience's elbow rang; she picked it up, said hello, and Verity saw her mother's face freeze, eyes wide.

"What?" she demanded as Patience put the phone down.

"There's been a shooting at Tom Gunderson's."

"That *stupid* woman!" Verity pulled from driveway to road, shifted up and then again too soon, nearly stalling the Alfa's engine. "I told her to stay away from that old man!"

"Apparently she didn't listen. There's a lumber truck," Patience pointed out.

Verity whipped past the truck. "Stupid! If she's gotten herself killed, what's going to happen to the kid?"

"Officer Coates didn't say anyone was dead—yet. Just that it was a shooting and Captain Svoboda wanted us there." They roared across a humpbacked bridge, and Patience put a bracing hand against the dash as the little car went briefly airborne. "Sorry," Verity said, and settled into a just-over-the-limit pace for the remainder of the five-mile trip.

A red Honda Civic occupied Gunderson's driveway. Two black-and-white Port Silva Police Department cars stood nose to nose at the curb, a uniformed cop beside one of them talking into a microphone or maybe a cell phone. As the two women climbed out of their low-slung car, the cop raised his free hand in their direction, and Verity sent Patience a glance of guilty relief. "You go ahead. I'll talk to Johnny for a minute."

Patience hurried up the walk to a front door that stood wide, revealing flagstones marked with footprints and the tracks of narrow tires: a wheeled stretcher, she thought, from an ambulance that had come and gone. Hank Svoboda's bulk loomed against the wall near the fireplace, where a rug Patience remembered as patterned was now rucked up and wetly red; she had a disoriented sense of steam rising from it. "How bad?" she asked Hank.

"Heavy blood loss, big exit wound. How really bad we'll know when they find out what got torn up inside. Then we'll see whether we've got a murder charge," he said, his voice heavy and his face sad. Patience knew he was seeing disaster on all sides, misery he could perhaps have prevented had he only tried harder.

"I just wanted to talk to him." Darcy Kelly huddled in a big wood-and-leather chair with her hands cuffed behind her and a uniformed cop standing close by. One of the gun racks by the fireplace was now empty.

"Please. See, I brought him an apple pie," she said, nodding toward the sticky mess on the fireplace hearth. "I wanted to tell him I was sorry I'd hurt him, that I'd pay him back what I owed him.

"But he threw the pie on the floor and grabbed one of those guns—he always kept them loaded. I tried to take it away from him, and it went off."

The three others stood silent, watching her. Unable to raise an arm to wipe away tears, she settled for a sniff. "I didn't mean it to happen," she whispered.

Patience called up an image of Tom Gunderson: tall, gaunt, unable to rise from a chair without the help of his cane. Unable to walk more than a step or two without it. Darcy Kelly, also tall, weighed probably 135 very well-conditioned pounds. The woman was an athlete.

Patience was grateful that working out the probabilities would be Hank's department. "Sorry you'd hurt him? You mean when you knocked him out and robbed him two weeks ago?"

"No way!" She hitched herself up in the chair and lifted her chin. "I mean I was sorry I'd hurt his feelings, made him look foolish. I would *never* have . . ."

Low voices came from the direction of the front door, followed by footsteps on the flagstones. Patience turned to see Verity enter, closely followed by Sgt. Johnny Hebert. Darcy Kelly sat straighter and said "Verity!" her hopeful expression fading as she registered the other woman's bleak face. Verity gave Darcy only a brief glance before stepping aside to give Johnny Hebert the floor.

"Aaron Kelly decided to cooperate, Captain," Hebert said. "He admits he borrowed a buddy's car two weeks ago, drove down here and assaulted and robbed Mr. Gunderson, then drove back before anyone missed him."

"No," said Darcy.

"A Trinity County deputy is getting ready to bring him down."

"That's bullshit!" Darcy planted her feet as if to rise, but subsided at Hank Svoboda's gesture. "*I'm* the one who came here to rob Tom Gunderson that night. I needed the money and figured he owed it to me, after the stuff he'd been saying about me all over town." Her voice was firm, her back as straight as she could manage with her arms behind her. "My son is just trying to protect me."

"Where's the money now?" asked Hank.

She blinked slowly once, and again. "You aren't going to believe this, but there wasn't any money in that safe. Now I want to see a lawyer. And my son is a minor—I forbid you to talk any more to him until I've seen him and *he* has a lawyer."

Hank Svoboda stared at her for a long moment. "Okay. Hebert, let's put Ms. Kelly in your car, and you and Coates can take her downtown. I'll be along later."

Patience and Verity trailed the policeman and their silent, unresisting prisoner outside and watched Hebert and Coates tuck Darcy Kelly, still cuffed, into the backseat of a black-and-white while Svoboda leaned into the front to use the radio.

"So," said Patience softly when he rejoined them.

"What do you mean, 'So'?" Verity's voice was sharp. "That woman lied and backed off and lied again."

"So which were real lies?" asked Patience, and Hank Svoboda snorted.

"Well, the money. I bet it'll turn up—big surprise all

around. And the robbery; Aaron puts his mother's wig on and guess who Mr. Gunderson sees."

"She did shoot Mr. Gunderson," Patience acknowledged.

"She'll claim self-defense, or accident," said Svoboda. "He's still alive, and has a fair chance of staying that way, the hospital says."

"Oh, well, that's all right, then," snapped Verity. She turned to glare after the departing police car, gritting her teeth against the fact that she'd been conned. She'd provided the crust for what looked to her like an implement in a crime. She was practically an accessory.

The pure silliness of this notion revived Verity. Darcy Kelly had a son and little else. Maybe it wasn't a matter of lies or truth, but of lightning reflexes. Maybe Darcy was simply being tiger-mom.

Growth Marks

Margaret Maron

When Margaret Maron is not playing with her granddaughter or birdwatching from her gazebo, she may be found creating her acclaimed Deborah Knott mystery series. For Bootlegger's Daughter, *Margaret won an unprecedented four major awards for best novel of the year, including the Anthony, Agatha, Macavity, and Edgar awards. Margaret and her artist husband Joe live near Raleigh, North Carolina.*

Sun., Feb. 7th—Ted & Abby have finally left. It's 90 min. by the interstate back to Winston & I persuaded them to leave early so I wouldn't worry about them slipping & sliding on dark icy roads.

Not that they would, thought Grace Currin as she reread what she had just written in her journal. Ted approached driving like everything else in life: safely, cautiously. That was a terrible thing to say about one's son and Grace knew she should be down on her knees giving thanks for his thoughtfulness. On the other hand, he didn't have to come running over here today as if one day without hot water would trigger a massive heart attack or something.

Just because her heart had started giving a couple of irregular stutters in the last year didn't mean she wasn't perfectly capable of managing till tomorrow when her usual fixit man could come. Nevertheless, as soon as Ted called that morning and she mentioned the problem, nothing would do but that he and Abby had to drive down with his plumbing tools and spend the afternoon tearing out the innards of her water heater.

Just like Hank used to be, she thought. Couldn't stand to let things go unfixed five minutes.

Abby didn't seem to mind helping him either. Grace *knew* she should be grateful for their solicitude, but it had meant running out in the rain to the grocery store so her refrigerator wouldn't look as if she didn't eat properly and then hurrying back to freshen up the whole downstairs so they wouldn't know that she spent most of these short winter days either in the kitchen or holed up in her bedroom.

So of course that had left her a little breathless, which meant she'd had to listen to yet another round of how the house was too much work and much too big for one woman alone. Never did have an ounce of imagination, Ted. Not like Will, who—

"Oh no you don't, Grace Currin!" she scolded herself out loud. "Stop whining for what you've lost and be grateful for what you still have."

Quickly, almost superstitiously, she counted her blessings: a sensible solid son and pleasant daughter-in-law who seemed to love each other, adequate income, good friends—though Sally was remarried and involved with stepgrandchildren and Jan had moved to Florida—and, above everything else, reasonably good health (if you don't count the arrhythmia, and I don't, thought Grace) which allowed her to continue living on her own.

So the house calls up lonesome memories sometimes, she thought. So what? "You should be glad you've had people, things, a whole *life* worth feeling lonesome for," she told herself sternly.

When she and Hank first moved in and began restoring the house themselves, the inside was scarcely habitable: crumbling plaster, rotten roof, bare lightbulbs dangling at the end of frayed cords—what the classifieds used to call a real handyman's special. Will was three, Ted eighteen months, and she was blissfully pregnant again. (Even though they'd gotten a late start, she and Hank were going for four.)

Hank always blamed the paint-remover fumes for her miscarriage and it nearly broke their hearts at first when the doctor said there would be no more babies, but Will and Ted kept them hopping: Cub Scouts, Little League, swimming lessons, the big house filled with friends and family.

Even now, all these years later, when she wandered through the wide halls and spacious rooms, she could still hear echoes of running sneakers, doors slamming, boyish laughter. She could pass the scarred newel post and remember how Will's baseball bat always banged it as he swung around the corner and took the stairs two at a time. Forever in a hurry. As if he'd known that he—

"There you go again!" Grace fumed, annoyed that she was letting old memories overwhelm her. "If you can't write a journal entry without turning into Poor Pitiful Pearl, then you should clean up the kitchen, read a book, or go watch a rerun of *Murder, She Wrote* up in your bedroom."

Sat. March 6th—I could absolutely spit! That mouthy Sally Massengill. Spends so much time minding Martin's puling grandbabies that her brain's turned to mush. After I specifically swore her to secrecy, what's the first thing she says to Ted when she sees him out pruning the shrubs that have overgrown my driveway?

(I'd come back in to stir up a Brunswick stew so Abby won't have to cook tomorrow. She didn't feel well enough to come this morning. Nothing serious, T. says; just that she's been working hard lately & can't seem to catch up on her sleep.)

Anyhow, soon as S. got through breaking her solemn word & had pushed that baby stroller on down the sidewalk, T. burst into the kitchen, all excited because some idiot with more money than brains made that ridiculous offer for my house last week. Now that this neighborhood's been designated a historical section, we get more sightseers driving through & the minute that man saw the eight-sided corner turret, the porch & eaves dripping with gingerbread, & the leaded glass windows on either side of the front door, he'd slammed on his brakes & marched right up to ring my bell.

"Did he really offer you that much money?" asked Ted.

"What price dreams?" Grace asked tartly, adding a dash of red pepper to the savory stew.

Ted looked puzzled.

"He said when he was a poor boy growing up in Buffalo, there was an old Victorian house near his school and he promised himself he'd have one just like it someday."

Despite barging in on her like that, the man from Buffalo had been charming. She'd given him a cup of coffee, a slice of her apple pie, and, because his story had disarmed her, a tour of the house.

"Great!" said Ted. "I was afraid this place might be a white elephant."

No imagination at all, thought Grace. Ted and Abby and their friends moaned about mortgages, but they really did think suburban new was worth more than restored urban old. Against her better judgment, she told him what Jan and Bill got for their 1922 brick house on its quarter-acre corner lot when they moved to Florida last August.

Ted's first reaction was shock; his second was to ask how soon her lawyer could draw up the papers.

"You forget," Grace said crisply. "When your father and I were living over our first store in Boylan Heights, this was *our* dream house, too."

* * *

Tues. March 23rd—Like it or not, it seems I'm going to give the man
from Buffalo exactly what he wants.

After Hank's death, Grace had resumed her girlhood habit of
keeping a journal. It was company somehow, a way of coping
with loss and a hedge against loneliness now that the last store
was sold and she was officially retired these past two years. She
didn't write in it every day, only as the mood took her, which was
usually of an evening after looking back over the last few days or
week. But today, she was still so shaken that as soon as Abby left,
she found herself needing to set down the words that had flown
between them.

Abby had taken off from work at lunch for a doctor's appointment and afterward had driven straight over to tell what Grace
knew she probably should have guessed two weeks ago—finally
there was to be a baby.

Abby blurted it out as soon as Grace opened the door.
Downstairs was so chilly that Grace had bundled her right up to
the bedroom and tucked her into a blue velvet chaise lounge with
the fleecy white afghan Hank's mother had crocheted many long
Christmases ago. With hot water bubbling over an old-fashioned
spirit lamp, Grace soon had her daughter-in-law's hands around a
steaming cup of tea.

Abby had never been inside that room unannounced and Grace
was embarrassed by its untidiness: the heaped-up pillows on the
bed, her robe draped across the foot; newspapers and murder mysteries piled on the nightstand; yarn spilling around the rocking
chair before the fireplace, where gas logs flamed warmly beneath
a mantel cluttered with family pictures. (Grace hadn't the
patience to become an expert knitter, but it seemed to keep the
arthritis in her fingers at bay so she made herself do it while she
watched the evening news every night.) On a tray beside the door,
used teacups waited to be carried back to the kitchen. A jug of

spent pussy willows dropped pollen on the wide window ledge, but she'd always had good luck forcing spring bulbs so crocuses bloomed brightly in their shallow bowls and a dozen hyacinths made the room smell like springtime.

Abby took it all in with interest and before Grace could apologize for the mess, she snuggled deeper into the woolly afghan. "What a cozy hobbit-hole. I don't blame you for wanting to stay."

Grace smiled warily, pushed the knitting out of the rocker, and sat down with her own cup of milky tea. "Maybe now that Ted's going to have you and a baby to worry about, he'll quit trying to make me leave."

"If you really think that, then you don't know Ted very well," Abby said, more bluntly than she'd ever spoken to Grace in the six years she and Ted had been married.

It was good to discover Abby had some backbone, but Grace was so surprised to have it jabbed at her that she could only stare at the younger woman with her mouth open.

"Ted's afraid that your heart—"

"My heart's perfectly fine," Grace said stiffly. "Dr. Lemmon says as long as I take my pills and don't overdo, I can live with it stuttering along like this for another twenty years. Ted knows that."

"Just the same, he feels responsible for taking care of you," Abby said.

"Nobody asked him to," she snapped impatiently.

"Hank did." Abby's voice was quiet. "A month before he died."

I should have known, thought Grace, and abruptly lifted the cup to her lips to mask her sudden emotion.

Dear steady Hank! Hers might have been the flair and imagination that attracted customers to their three office supply stores, but his was the service and reliability that kept them coming back. And Ted was his child, just as Will was always hers; so of course he'd absorbed that sense of responsibility. As a child, Will was totally enchanted by helium balloons and sparklers, but ephemeral wonders brought Ted little joy. He was usually so worried that the string might break or that a hot wire might burn someone that he seldom lost himself in rapture.

"Poor Ted," she said with a sigh.

"I know you think he's dull and stodgy—"

"I've never said that!" Grace protested, guilt sharpening her tone. "I adore Ted."

"Not as much as you adored Will." Abby set her empty cup down on the low table between them so hard that her teaspoon rattled on the saucer.

"That's not true!" Rattled herself, Grace filled the teapot with more hot water, but Abby waved away her offer of another cup.

"You never met Will," Grace said defensively. "I didn't love him more. Just differently."

"Ted thinks you wish he'd died instead of Will."

Grace was so stricken by the accusation that she couldn't reply.

At least, Grace acknowledged to herself, Abby was perceptive enough to recognize genuine shock. She reached across the table and, in a rare gesture between them, clasped her mother-in-law's hand. "I *thought* he was wrong," she said. "I told him he was, but he's always blamed himself, you know."

"Yes." Being Ted, how could he not? Grace thought, anguished. It was never Ted's fault, though. Will was older and should have realized the danger. Diving into the moon, he called it, forgetting how dry the summer had been, not noticing in the moonlight how low the lake level had fallen beneath the rock they used for a diving platform.

"Anyhow," said Abby, "Ted worries about you. Your heart, this house. That's not going to change, Grace. And I don't want him to change," she added fiercely.

"No," Grace agreed, still shaken.

"So it looks like we have two options." She spoke bravely enough, but Grace could hear the tremor beneath her bravado. "Ted and I can give up our jobs in Winston and move here near you, or you can sell this place and move to Winston, because once the baby comes, I'm not going to watch Ted keep tearing himself apart racing back and forth on the interstate every weekend and feeling guilty because he can't give his mother and his child equal time."

"My dear, don't give it another thought," Grace told her briskly. "Of *course* I'll sell now that there's a real reason to. I wouldn't miss the opportunity to baby-sit with my very first grandchild for all the houses in the world. Now, what are you hoping for? A boy or a girl?"

Grace knew that, perceptive though she might be, Abby was too newly pregnant not to be diverted by her questions; and if Abby were a little puzzled by her easy victory, she wouldn't risk losing it by asking any questions.

Numbly, Grace uncapped her pen and continued writing.

Part of me dies every time I think of what I've agreed to, but fair is fair. I owe Ted this, if nothing else, if I really did let him see—Not that I ever thought it again after that first wild grief. I didn't. I swear I didn't.

Mon. Apr. 19th—We signed the papers this morning. I've agreed to vacate by the first of June. My last spring to see in bloom the dogwoods & azaleas we planted, the drift of daffodils on the west lawn, Aunt E.'s yellow jasmine twining through the pines at the back of the lot. I'll be gone before my hydrangea blooms beside the kitchen door.

Will and Ted had given it to her for Mother's Day the year they were ten and eight, proudly lugging it up to her bedroom in a foil-wrapped pot that was top-heavy with two huge blue pompons.

"Will says they're the same color as your eyes," said Ted as he'd crawled into bed with Hank and Grace and put his solemn little face up to hers for a closer look.

"Why, so they are," Hank had said, looking from the flowers to her eyes to confirm the claim.

But Will had known without needing to compare, thought Grace, and her heart was sliced anew by his senseless death.

Fri. May 14th—For a while there, began to think I'd have to put everything in storage & camp in on Ted & Abby.

With the first of June hurtling down on them, Grace had diligently read the classifieds, listed herself with two different real estate agencies and trotted in and out of dozens of condos, town houses, and duplexes without finding anything remotely suitable until three days ago. The ad appeared in a biweekly newspaper published in a small town outside Winston, only seven minutes by back roads from Ted and Abby.

Starter home. 2 bdrms, 1 bath, din.rm, fireplc, mod.kit, nice garden, many extras. Reasonably priced.

Their idea of reasonable certainly wasn't Grace's and the many extras seemed to include a quick-stop convenience store at one end of the street and a volunteer fire department at the other. The floors needed refinishing, the master bedroom was currently papered in nursery rhymes, and Ted thought both the roof and the heating system would probably have to be replaced in the next three or four years; but after some of the places Grace had seen those past few weeks, this "starter home" was a house she felt she could end in, and she had signed the papers that day.

Anyhow, it's a location I've bought, she wrote in her journal, *not a home, so what difference does it make?*

At least Ted was pleased.

Sun. May 30th—The movers will come on Tues. Ted & Abby both volunteered to come back & help pack the smaller, special things tomorrow, but Sally & I did most of them today. They seem a little shocked by how much I'm willing to part with.

After Grace had tagged all the furniture she planned to take with her and told the children to keep or sell whatever was left, she realized that Ted had begun to feel guilty because she wouldn't be able to fit ten rooms of furnishings into the new house. As if that mattered! Thirty years old, she thought impatiently, and he still didn't understand that things in and of themselves had never meant much to her.

Silver, crystal, porcelain, even the few valuable antiques that had come to her through the years had always been treasured more or less in direct proportion of their personal associations. The cane-bottom rocking chair her grandfather made with his own two hands was infinitely dearer than a period Sheraton drop-leaf table bought to fill a troublesome space in the front parlor, so the rocker would go in her new bedroom while Abby and Ted were given the table. Her nieces were delighted to get the Bavarian crystal chandelier and the mahogany breakfront they'd always admired; but Grace kept the ceramic lamp her sister Meg had made in her first pottery class.

"Oh, Grace, are you sure?" squealed Sally when Grace brought over a dozen brass candlesticks to add to Sally's collection.

"We use things, we enjoy them, and then we let them go," Grace told her. "Why make complications out of something so simple?"

What wasn't simple were the things she could neither keep nor give away, the instances where she had no choice. She would not let herself get morbid about it, but there was a certain slant of light across her bedroom ceiling that always woke her early on summer mornings, the satin smoothness of the banister as she pulled herself around the top step, an autumnal winelike fragrance that drifted over from Sally and Martin's yard when their scuppernongs ripened, those patterns cast by the full moon when she visited her hibernating garden on a chill winter night.

Dry-eyed, she watched the Goodwill people cart away Hank's den: the old rug worn threadbare beneath his desk, the rump-sprung leather couch where he used to stretch out to watch ball games, the boys piled on top of him like two puppies. The man from Buffalo had four young children and she did not flinch when they pulled from the garage outgrown bicycles, skateboards with missing wheels, and other relics of her sons' separate pasts. Those were only things.

The only time it got really tricky was when Abby and Ted were helping her clear the kitchen and she opened the pantry door and saw the growth marks. She wondered if many houses still had them? Her grandparents' house had, and all her aunts and uncles'. "Oh my! Look how you've grown!" they'd exclaim; and before the visit was over, they would make her pull off her shoes and stand up as straight as she could while someone laid a pencil on her head, drew a short line on the inside jamb of the pantry door, then labeled it *Grace, 5½; Grace, 14 years.*

The lowest mark on her own pantry doorjamb belonged to her brother's first grandchild, just five months old at the time. (The last time they measured him, he was still a fraction under six feet.) The oldest mark, though, was Will's, caught in mid-flight as he darted through the unfamiliar rooms joyfully exploring every new cubbyhole. It was neatly labeled the day they moved in. Next day, feeling vaguely historical, she and Hank solemnly measured each other and Ted, too.

Through the years it became almost a logbook as visiting relatives, close friends, the boys' first girlfriends removed their shoes and stood up tall to be measured, each mark identified by name and date. Tipsy with New Year's Eve champagne, someone would herd the whole party out to the kitchen. "Let's see if anybody's grown this year!"

Abby's mark was dated the night she and Ted announced their engagement.

No matter how many times she and Hank redecorated, that inner doorjamb was left unpainted, and part of each birthday celebration was the ritual measuring: Will at 9, Ted at 7; Will at 14, Ted 12; Will at 19—after that, Ted's marks went on alone, passing Will's, passing his father. Grace remembered how proud he was the day he caught up to Hank. Proud and yet a little anxious, too, not to hurt Hank's own pride.

Soon the man from Buffalo would send the painters through, she thought. Two layers of fresh white enamel and it would be as if none of them had ever stood there, flushed with laughter, self-conscious, barefooted.

Ted paused behind her on his way out to the hall with a carton of dishes. "Something wrong, Mom?"

"No, no," she said brightly. "Why in the world do you suppose I accumulated so many cans of mushroom soup? Packing canned goods is such a bore. Why don't we just leave this pantry for the movers."

Sat. Aug. 21st—While looking through my knitting bag for some patterns (I'm going to try my hand at a fancy crib blanket for the baby as soon as the weather turns cooler), I unearthed this journal. Couldn't think where in the world I'd stuck it in all the last-minute confusion of packing.

To catch up: The man we'd hired to paint & repaper here at the new house turned out to be slower than molasses & it took an extra week before the place was ready.

Grace leaned back in her chair, remembering how the movers had agreed to hold the furniture and how, rather than make a further nuisance of herself with Ted and Abby, she had decided it'd be just as easy for her to drive down to Wilmington with the things she wanted her sister to have as it would be to box and ship them.

Her brother's wife said she'd drive up from Charleston and at that point two Atlanta cousins said well, if it was a party, they'd come, too. There were things Grace wanted each of them to have, so in the end she'd driven off into the sunrise feeling like a gypsy peddler with her car jammed full and a small rental trailer tagging along behind.

That week at the beach was just exactly what she'd needed. The five women had known each other since infancy, through childbirths and deaths, and now with sagging breasts, flat-heeled shoes, hearing aids, and the first walking cane. They talked and laughed and talked and cried and then talked some more until Grace finally felt that she was in control of her life again.

The movers had already delivered her things under Ted and Abby's supervision the Saturday morning that she returned, and Abby had gone out for sandwiches, so that Ted was there alone when she pulled into the drive.

The first thing she noticed as she went up the walk to the open front door was her hydrangea bush, drastically pruned and a little wilted around the edges, but not bad, she thought, considering all it must have gone through.

"I know June's a bad month to transplant things," said Ted from the doorway, "but I think I cut it back enough to make up for root loss and I've watered it every night. We can plant it somewhere else if you'd rather."

"No, this is perfect," Grace said, absurdly pleased to see that scraggly bush again and picturing how pretty it'd look once it regained its full spread. "How on earth did you sweet-talk the man from Buffalo . . .?"

"Mr. Heit," said Ted, looking almost as happy as the day he'd helped Will lug that pot of blue flowers up to her bedroom. "He's going to build a brick terrace at the kitchen door, so he was glad for me to take it."

Her old furniture looked strange in their new positions but as

Grace walked through the little house, she knew time would soon make everything familiar.

Ted followed her out to the kitchen, where he and Abby had been unpacking pots and pans and all those cans of mushroom soup. Without a pantry, the new cabinets were going to be hopelessly crammed, but Grace assured Ted that everything was fine, just fine.

"We did your bedroom first," he told her, "so if you'd like to lie down for a few minutes—"

Grace sharply reminded him that she was only sixty-four, not ninety-four, and certainly not in need of a morning nap after a mere three-hour drive.

The cheerfulness faded from his face. "Okay," he said, and went back to unpacking dishes while she stepped into the bathroom to freshen up and give herself a good scolding in the mirror.

She decided it was all the newness that had set her nerves on edge. Everything sparkled and gleamed and the very air smelled of new paint, new paper, new grout. Once she'd been eager for new experiences, but this house had no history, this house—

It's because Hank was never here, Grace told herself bleakly. And there was no mark on any ceiling where Will once bounced a ball too hard, no chip missing from the sink where he dropped his first bottle of aftershave lotion, no lingering echo of his excited "Hey, Mom! Guess what?"

She splashed cold water on her face, took a deep breath, and opened the door in time to see Ted shut the closet at the end of the hall. He had a guilty expression on his face.

"I wondered if you were all right," he said.

Will could always look her in the eye and spin the most outrageous and totally believable lies. Poor Ted couldn't shade the truth by a hair without giving himself away.

Grace walked down the hall. For such a small house, the closet was rather large: four feet deep with wide shelves above the clothes pole and narrow shelves running from floor to ceiling on the left wall. Two storage bags hung from the pole and boxes of Christmas ornaments had been stacked above. Nothing to make a grown man apprehensive.

Puzzled, she started to close the door, and then she saw the marks penciled on the freshly painted inner jamb, marks that began less than two feet from the floor and stair-stepped up past six feet, each neatly labeled with a familiar name and a date.

"I traced them off on tissue paper," Ted said. "You don't mind, do you? I know you're not sentimental, but with the baby coming, I thought it'd be fun to watch—" He hesitated. "And besides, it was like bringing along something of Will."

Even as a small boy, he'd always saved the real truth for last.

"Mom?"

Blindly she turned to him—the sturdy son she had loved yet never properly valued—and at the sight of her face, his crumpled, too.

They held each other wordlessly for a long moment, then Grace heard Ted's choked voice say, "I *did* try to stop him, Mom. Honest I did."

"Shh, honey," she murmured brokenly. "I know you did. It wasn't your fault, Ted. I've never blamed you for Will's death. Never."

She looked him straight in the eyes and said it again and this time, unlike thirteen years ago, she saw that he finally believed her.

How stupid and selfish of me, she thought, and, yes, how unimaginative, too, to think I was the only one with grief still green after all these years.

Well, that was June and this is August. I won't say there aren't things I still miss but the library's within walking distance, the fire engines add excitement, & now that I'm practically living in his pocket, Ted's quit worrying about me so much & spends more time worrying about Abby. He'll always be a worrier, I guess. "Just like his father," I tell Abby.

"If I'm as lucky as you," she says.

With Thanks to Agatha Christie

Sarah J. Mason

Sarah J. Mason was born in England, lived in Scotland, sojourned in New Zealand, and came back to settle where she started. She has a husband, two dogs, and an ex-lawyer sister who lives in Texas, collects books, and is a licensed private investigator. Sound familiar? It will, once you read her story. Sarah writes the Trewley & Stone cozy police procedural mysteries. As Hamilton Crane she continues the Miss Seeton series created by the late Heron Carvic.

First, I carried my groceries through to the kitchen, where I unpacked them and set the kettle on the boil. Then I went back for my luggage—one small, half-empty case and a large bag of grubby clothes—and dropped it on the hall floor: it could wait. I was just going out again to put the car in the garage when the telephone started to ring.

My immediate response was to curse: I'd had a long day. I wondered about letting the answering machine take the strain, but then curiosity got the better of me. I picked up the receiver to interrupt the after-the-tone message; an anguished wail burst upon my ears before I'd done more than say hello. "Mother? Oh, thank goodness you're back! I've been so worried. . . ."

The wail made it easy. "Deborah," I said. My twenty-three-year-old twins aren't identical—except for their voices, which even a devoted mother can confuse in normal speech; but only Deborah wails. On the (rare) occasions when she loses control of her emotions, Melissa will throw herself into a full-bodied tantrum and throw breakables at the wall. "Deborah, stop wailing and tell me what's wrong." There had to be something wrong. Deb would never phone before the cheap rate unless it was an emergency. Money had been short while I was raising the twins, and old habits—reinforced by Deb's marriage to a skinflint—die hard.

"Oh, Mother . . ." At least she'd stopped wailing. "Oh, Mother—he's going to kill me! You're my only hope!"

"He's going to kill you," I echoed. "You mean Alec, of course." Perhaps it was a little tactless to add 'of course,' but I'd never really taken to my son-in-law.

"You've never really taken to Alec," said Deb.

I kept quiet. Her voice had steadied; it could have been Melissa speaking as she went on:

"You never wanted me to marry him—of course." I gave the telephone a sharp look. Deborah—and sarcasm? "Other people's mothers cry at their daughters' weddings. *You* just drowned your sorrows in champagne."

A half-share in her father's insurance, which I had reinvested on the twins' behalf after his sudden death, had paid for that wedding. I'd seen no good reason why his widow shouldn't raise a glass, or maybe two, in his memory. I didn't say any of this to Deborah: The twins' birth had not been easy, and Deb, small and weak, had stayed in the incubator long after the livelier Mel had come home. Deb was hardly a fool, but even a devoted mother could see that of the pair she was the twin more likely to be fooled by a glib tongue and a handsome face.

But now I wondered if her words held some hint that she might be less of a fool than I thought; that she'd found him out, at last, and was worried by what he might do.

Yet I would have said Alec was the type to charm, rather than murder, his way out of any little difficulty, such as a betrayed wife. He relied—too much, in my view—on the theory that love is blind. I didn't forget the postwedding party, when he'd backed me—forty-five-year-old mother of the bride—into a corner and tried the old "Without your glasses you'd be beautiful" routine before lunging at me in a way I couldn't blame on the champagne. The voice he'd used had *not* been a jokey Jimmy Stewart imitation, and he wasn't (at that stage) drunk. And he'd still seemed sober later, when I saw him attempting a quick cuddle with the chief bridesmaid in the shadow of a potted palm. Melissa's shoes had higher, sharper heels than mine; I'd had to stifle a shriek of maternal triumph when she hacked his shins with even greater force than I had done.

Melissa was always the practical twin: She takes after me, though *my* practical skills are self-taught. I tried to teach both girls alike, but Deb had been a sickly child, with so many lengthy spells in bed that she learned nothing except to read faster than her sister. Mel, of course, soon caught up, and they raced through the children's section of the library in alphabetical order, one starting at *A* and the other at *Z*, seeing who could first reach *M*. Once the overlap was passed and they had exhausted the juvenile stock, their tastes were pretty well defined. Mel went on to devour science fiction, mysteries, and straight history; Deb wallowed in romance (which goes some way to explaining Alec) and historical sagas. Perhaps I should have stopped them from borrowing all those books on my adult ticket when they were so young: A senior librarian (even part-time) should set a good example, but our town is small, and funds are limited. We couldn't afford to buy every new book that was published, and the twins were beginning to suffer withdrawal symptoms. What else could a devoted mother do but allow herself to be coaxed?

"He's going to kill me as soon as he walks through the door," enlarged Deborah, as at my end of the telephone I remained quiet.

But I was curious, naturally. "Why is he going to kill you?" I asked. "And what do you want me to do about it—witness your dying words?"

"Agatha Christie," said Deb. "And I do think you ought to be more sympathetic, Mother. Grannie's far more maternal than you are—"

"Then why not phone Grannie? Why me?" But I could hazard a guess. "She lives miles away, and I'm just the other side of town. Convenient for witness purposes—right?"

"Sort of," said Deb. "But it's not funny, Mother. It's all Agatha Christie's fault—well, nearly all; the rest is Mel's—and I phoned you because if we can't sort something out before he comes home, Alec will murder me!"

"So you keep saying," I reminded her. "What you don't say is why—or what it has to do with Dame Agatha. She can hardly have done anything to you personally—she died years ago. Do you suspect him of wanting to polish you off using some devious method learned from one of her books?"

"Oh, Mother!"

I ignored the renewed wailing. "And what has Mel to do with all this? When I went on holiday she was finalizing her plans to emigrate to the United States to specialize in divorce law." A faint light dawned. "Are you saying she's started early and tipped you the wink that Alec is about to bump you off, to save money?" But it seemed unlikely. Alec would begrudge the loss of a cheap housekeeper even more than the cost of his defense—or his divorce.

"Oh, Mother!"

"So I guessed wrong," I said. "So, tell me."

"Mel's not going to be a lawyer anymore," said Deb.

This was something of a shock. "Do you mean she's been . . . struck off? How? Why?"

"She hasn't been struck," said Deb. "She's struck herself. She said she was bored. She said she wanted . . . more from life—variety, excitement, a chance to see the world before she gets into a rut. Like you."

I ground my teeth. I'd hitherto thought I had made a decent job of raising the twins after their father died and I'd had to learn (and had tried to teach them) to be independent. "Librarians," I informed my younger daughter, "are in no more of a rut than anyone else, unless they choose to be. You may tell your sister I don't care for having my profession disparaged by someone who should know better—"

"Like you *now,*" broke in Deb as I drew breath, "is what she meant. You aren't stuck in a boring office, you pick and choose your hours, you jet off on package tours, you go to evening classes, you have a wild social life."

"Wilder than yours," I conceded. How Deb had been content to settle as a housewife I never really understood; all I could get out of her was that Alec preferred her to stay at home than to work. My suspicion was he hoped that if she rusted inside the house she was less likely to step outside and see him with an illicit blonde on his arm. "But not too wild," I added, in case my daughter got the wrong idea. Parents are supposed to set the examples for their children to ignore or profit by, as they please.

"Wild enough to make Melissa jealous," said Melissa's twin. "She says she'll go mad if she stays another week in that office— any office. She's sick of paperwork. She says now she's going to

America to train as a private eye!"

"Oh," I said. "Really?" A devoted mother supports her children in every endeavor, no matter how bizarre. "Well, the legal background should give her a head start, even if the system is different over there." Mel was a bright girl: I knew she could cope. "Did Agatha Christie," I inquired, "use this situation in any of her books? I don't remember this plot, but—"

"Mother!" cried Deborah. "Will you please just listen? Mel is going to America. She is selling her flat. She is leaving all her furniture behind, and—she's offered me . . ." If she wailed again, I would scream.

She didn't. "She said," said Deb, "she couldn't afford to take them with her, and she knew they'd be going to a good home, and she—she's giving me her complete set!"

"Her complete . . . you mean her Agatha Christie?"

"The whole hardback set—in the matching bindings!" cried Deb; I would swear she was wringing her hands as she spoke. "Alec was furious when she bought them, you know." I hadn't known. I could guess a lot, but Deb didn't confide everything about her marriage, by any means. "He said," she said, "that if he ever caught me spending so much money on—on book club editions that weren't even a good investment, he'd kill me!"

"If Mel is *giving* you the books, I don't think you need worry about being killed," I soothed her. "She wants to educate your reading palate, that's all." Mel often teased her twin about her liking for three-generation costume sagas with a birth, a marriage, or a death in every chapter. Then another—glaring—light dawned. "Hardback," I echoed. "The whole set . . ."

"Mother, have you *any idea* how many detective stories Agatha Christie wrote?"

I took a quick mental look at the assorted bookshelves in Mel's flat, then for accurate comparison ran along the shelves, and through the fiction catalog, in the town library. "Seventy or eighty," I said.

Deborah uttered a hollow laugh. "There's no 'or' about it," she said. "Mel dumped eighty hardback books all over my sitting room floor—and if you want to tell me they'll save wear and tear on the carpet, please don't. I'm in no mood for jokes about economy drives. And if I can't get them out of the way before Alec—"

"Yes," I broke in, before she could babble again about being killed. "Wait. You mean you have the books there *now?*"

"Mel brought them round an hour ago. She made me help her unload the boxes, but she couldn't stay to help me tidy because she was delivering some other bits and pieces to her friends, and setting up last-drinks parties, and—"

"And do you want me to take the books into protective custody until you've broken the news to Alec?"

"Oh, no," said Deb. "Mel's sure to drop in again before she goes, and she'd want to see them on display. And I want them, Mother. They'd be such fun on the shelf, except . . ."

"Except," I supplied, "you haven't got a shelf." Any librarian, even one whose daughters *don't* collect authors in complete sets, knows about shortage of space; and eighty hardback books, whether the bindings match or not, take up several valuable yards. If you haven't several yards to spare, when the books arrive by the boxload you are in big trouble. . . .

Such as husbands-coming-home-from-trips-abroad trouble. Alec was always taking business trips somewhere, mostly in foreign parts but occasionally in Britain. The suspicious (meaning me) might wonder how often a secretary went with him. Deb, bless her trusting heart, didn't wonder. Or hadn't, in the past. Now, perhaps, with a complete set of Christie at her disposal . . .

I was theorizing without proper data. "Then how can I help you?" I prompted.

"Help me find a bookcase before Alec gets back," came Deb's quick reply. "If I present him with a . . . with a fait accompli, he won't be able to moan—at least, not so much. He's never liked

Mel, I know, but that's silly. Sisters are supposed to be close, and twins—"

"Yes," I interrupted, before she could reach the shaky ground of what happened at the wedding reception, and what might have been happening at other venues since. "When's he coming home?"

"His plane lands at half past ten, and with only hand luggage—it was an overnight trip to Belgium—he won't have to wait. He'll clear Customs in—"

"Ten-thirty *tonight?*" Now I really did scream.

"Oh, I've solved it, if you'll only help," she said as I prepared to launch into Stern Mother mode. "I can't drive, but you can— and the do-it-yourself place on the industrial estate stays open until eight. And they sell self-assembly furniture in flatpacks. . . ."

A devoted mother knows the workings of her children's minds. "You've already phoned," I said, "to check there's something suitable in stock. You want me to drop everything I had planned for this evening—washing my hair, sherry and biscuits in front of an old movie while a fortnight's laundry goes round in the machine—and go waltzing off to the do-it-yourself, where, I've no doubt, there is a flat-pack waiting to be collected and taken back to your house, where, again, I've no further doubt that you want me to put it together for you—don't you?"

There was a guilty silence on the other end of the telephone. "Mother," said Deborah, mouse-meek, "Alec will kill me if they're still all over the floor when he comes home. And you're a librarian—you understand these things—and, well, you *are* my mother. . . ."

I'd spent most of the day behind the wheel—but what else could a mother do? "Let's have the details," I said, seizing a pencil and pad. "Give me the order number, the price, the name of the person you spoke to. . . ."

* * *

By the time I arrived at Deborah's house she had moved both furniture and books as close as she could to the sitting room walls so that there was a clear space in which we—meaning I—could work. Dame Agatha was out of her assorted cardboard boxes: Deborah had clearly been savoring her new treasures even as she bewailed their bulk and (irresistible librarian pun) volume. "You owe me," I told her as between us we hefted the flat-pack from the boot of my car. "Start by making a cup of tea—a plate of biscuits wouldn't hurt—and don't talk to me until I've read these instructions through. Twice."

"Tea? Twice?"

"Exactly. Off you go." I waved her into the kitchen, dropped on a chair, and opened the instruction leaflet I'd been given by the young assistant (male) who'd found it hard to suppress the sneer with which he contemplated a middle-aged woman's proposal to assemble one of his company's brainchildren without masculine supervision.

I had not sneered back: I had even smiled as he loaded the flat-pack into the car. He might *not've known it*, but Deb had been right to ask for my help. I'm not the world's best handywoman, but I get things done. I can fix a broken fuse, change a plug, even carry out routine maintenance on my car. Deb's telephone informant had assured her that in addition to the flat-pack only a hammer, a screwdriver, a bradawl, and a sharp knife would be needed. I had these in my toolbox—and knew how to use them.

"Unpack the carton," I muttered, writing this on the lined pad Deb had produced at my request. "Check contents—use flattened carton as a mat for the floor—sides, back, base, four shelves, eight cross-axial screws, eight cover-caps . . ." I went on counting, checking off my handwritten list against the printed version and, when she returned with my tea, making Deb double-check as I recounted. "Right," I told her at last. "Let's get cracking."

It takes time, patience, and an organized mind to build a flat-pack bookcase from scratch. I have patience, and I am organized, but I am not encouraged when I have the eventual owner of the bookcase hovering at my elbow displaying her wristwatch at regular intervals. At least she didn't offer to help. I told her that classical music would soothe the nerves—I didn't say whose—and she tuned to the channel with hourly news and weather reports. Learning that flights to Heathrow were being diverted, because of fog, to Gatwick had her shouting with glee as she estimated that the delay would give us another hour, at least.

"We didn't need that extra hour," I told her with pride as I handed her the hammer to let her tap the last cover-cap in place. "Go ahead, hit it. My treat—and then you can treat me. Once you've shelved those books we'll go out for pizza, and you're paying. And we'll have a glass or two of plonk by way of celebration—we can wet Dame Agatha's head in proper . . . styles."

"Mother!" Deborah's groan showed that my pun had found a ready victim. She wagged the hammer under my nose before applying it to the cover-cap, and then—there stood the finished bookcase in all its veneered chipboard glory. "If you were me," said my daughter, "would you file them by publication date, or with Poirots and Marples and—and the others all together? Just look at the short story collections. I had no idea how many—"

From my mental review of the catalog, I had. And I could guess how long it would take to arrange the books in proper order; and I was hungry. "If I were you," I said, "I'd shove them on the shelves any old how to get them off the floor—and Alec, once he's home, off your back until you can sort them properly. By which I mean the way that suits you best—they're your books, after all. You're the one who's going to read them."

After my flat-pack exertions I was happy to sit and supervise as Deborah moved handfuls of dark blue leatherette from the carpet to the shelves. "Alphabetically by title?" she murmured, as she found *Appointment with Death* straight after *Witness for the Prosecution*.

"Not yet," I warned. "I've earned that drink, and I see no reason to wait. I'm starving. Tea and biscuits don't go far when you've been rushing around all day and you're working overtime on an empty stomach."

Deb apologized at once, and with my maternal nagging to spur her on shelved the last of her trophies in record time. I made her help me squash the cardboard, polystyrene, and plastic wrap of the discarded flat-pack and cart it outside for the dustmen, who were due next day.

"Right," I said as I washed my hands at the kitchen sink. "Food. And remember you're paying, my child."

I drove, of course: Deb can't. Alec had convinced her that her mechanical ineptitude would ruin either the clutch, the gears, or the engine; and for once he had a degree of truth on his side. But my suspicious mind had always felt that his wife's lack of personal transport meant that she couldn't, no matter what she might suspect, follow him when he set off on any of his jolly mainland jaunts. And to ask anyone else to follow him to obtain the evidence she might need for a no-contest divorce . . .

My next remark was logical enough, given the recent revelation. "So Mel's giving up divorce work in favor of the mean streets," I said as I turned the car into one of our not-so-mean Home Counties streets. "She could start by staking out a few houses around here, to catch our local burglar and earn herself some brownie points before she leaves—I assume he's still in business?"

"I locked both the doors," said Deborah, "and all the windows were shut. We can't stay at home forever, can we?"

She sounded rather wistful. The twins had never been inseparable, but they had always been close, and I knew she was thinking of Mel.

She was. "She's running round to all her friends every night this week with keepsakes," Deb went on, with a sigh; I couldn't tell whether it was for Dame Agatha's prolific output or for Melissa's imminent departure.

"I'm sure they'll be pleased to have them," I said. "My share of the loot hasn't been delivered yet." Not that I'd really had time to notice anything extra in the knickknack, souvenir, or furniture line before being diverted by Deb's cry for help. "I wonder," I said, "what she'll—Deb! If you've lured me out for the evening so that Mel can sneak in something horrible, I'll—"

"Oh, Mother!" cried Deb. Her indignation sounded almost real; but I couldn't help wondering if it had been such a good idea for us all to have keys to one another's homes in case of emergency.

Oh well, too late now. We were at the famously best pizza place in town, where the toppings are lavish and the prices suitably steep. Deb owed me a decent meal—and if she was indeed fronting for Melissa, I'd need my strength built up before I went home to face whatever horrors were in store. When Deb frowned at my request for double cheese, I resolved that dessert would be apple pie with whipped as well as ice cream. Cholesterol be bothered. A glass or two of red wine would compensate for that.

We weren't far into our first glass when we were greeted by a cheerful group in dark suits, men and women alike. They were Melissa's soon-to-be-former colleagues, legal minds who had been hard at work all day and wanted to relax over food that was good, but didn't need gourmet appreciation. They were full of Mel's change of plan, and wanted to know more; though I had nothing to tell them, Deb had a few details she hadn't imparted to me. Our quiet mother-and-daughter table turned into a jolly party, and Deb roused herself to become the center of attention. We bought another bottle, or two. We toasted the immortal memory of Agatha Christie, we toasted Melissa's new career, we toasted my brilliance as a bookcase builder, and I crossed mental fingers

I'd earned the compliment.

It was closer to midnight than eleven when we reached Deborah's house again.

"I'll come in with you," I offered. With burglars on the loose, what else would a devoted mother do? And if the bookcase had fallen to pieces, I wanted to know.

"It won't have," said my loyal daughter, who can sometimes read my mind. "You did a splendid job, Mother."

"Praise indeed," I murmured as she fumbled in her pocket for her keys. Perhaps I should have hinted that a third glass of wine wasn't such a good idea; but a mother knows how far she can go with offering advice to her children. Deb had been in top form, and enjoying herself. Who was I to spoil her fun, with Alec due home that night?

She found the keys, and dropped them. I picked them up and opened the door for her. "You ought," I said, "to have two locks, these days. One by itself is hardly adequate, especially when it's not even a deadlock."

"Alec says it would cost too much to replace the spare keys," said Deb. "Of course," she added, "if he didn't spend half our hard-earned cash on his extramarital fun and games, we could probably afford it. . . ."

In vino veritas. So she *did* know—or at least strongly suspected—that Alec played the field. I wondered when and how the scales had fallen from her eyes.

"Right," I said as I pushed the door open. The hall was dark: Alec disapproved of wasting electricity by leaving a light on in an empty house. "Where's the switch?"

Deb started fumbling again. Yes, that third glass had been a mistake—but then there was a click, and we were both blinking on the threshold. I may be her mother, but my eyes are better than Deb's. I moved in front of her almost without thinking.

Which is why it wasn't Deb but I who opened the door of the

sitting room and found Alec's body on the floor.

"Stay where you are," I said in my best Bossy Mother voice. "Don't come in here. There's been a—an accident, Deborah. Alec. He . . ."

"He's tripped over Agatha Christie and broken his neck," Deb finished for me, with a giggle. "The bookcase fell to pieces after all, Mother—you fraud!"

She was stepping blithely toward the sitting room door, convinced I was joking. But I wasn't. Alec lay on the Christie-free carpet with his eyes wide open, staring at the ceiling. His eyes wide in a face as white as his shirt. . .

Except in those patches where the shirt was red.

"You'd better call the police," I said, pushing Deb—Alec's wife. . . Alec's widow—out of the room. But I'd been too slow. My daughter had already seen the staring eyes and the shirt with its white—and its red. Its brownish red. Sticky brownish red. Bloody red . . .

The police came, and were very busy. They took photographs, asked questions, tried to find the right thing to say when it was obvious they harbored the darkest suspicions of the not-so-grieving relict. I stayed with her as they asked their questions: What else could a mother do? And I learned I hadn't been wrong: Deborah had indeed known more about Alec's charming little ways than she ever admitted to anyone—especially her mother. And while she might be given to romance and drama, she was no actress, even stone-cold sober and unshocked, which on this occasion was far from the case. With strong, sweet coffee inside her and me ready to jog her elbow if she seemed on the point of saying the wrong thing, she still couldn't hide her true feelings from the skilled interrogators, who probed as firmly as they could while yet being gentle with their chief suspect, the widow.

The widow of Alec, who—as I overheard the woman plainclothes officer saying—was infamous for his philandering. "Nobody could blame her if she did," said this kindred spirit cheerfully. "He had it coming to him. Her sister's a solicitor— she'll advise her to plead undue provocation, and no jury on earth would convict her."

Another plainclothes officer (a man) muttered something about girls ganging up on helpless males, but someone else pointed out:

"She may not need a solicitor. The mother says they were together the whole evening."

"It's a poor mother," said the kindred-spirit, "who wouldn't perjure herself for her daughter."

"Probably both in it together," said her male colleague. "When we check out the crowd they say they met at the pizza place they'll give them the perfect alibi, mark my words."

"Before we jump to conclusions," said the kindred spirit in a more somber voice, "who's to say that he *didn't* disturb a burglar, the way it looks as if he did? If they hadn't left the toolbox so conveniently to hand he would probably have been brained with the poker instead of getting a bradawl through the heart."

"There have," conceded her colleague, "been a number of break-ins around here recently—not that Chummie's used violence in the past."

"But the husband was home earlier than anyone expected, to a house unexpectedly empty. Or not, depending on your point of view. It's typical of the man to have cadged a lift rather than wait and pay for a taxi. Chummie could have seen the house in darkness, rung the doorbell while mother and daughter were whooping it up over red wine and pizza and apple pie with cream, and when nobody answered broke that window round the back. Then along comes the husband, Chummie panics, and—bingo."

"Bingo?" The cynical voice of masculine logic wasn't giving in without a struggle. "Let's try talking to the pizza crowd before we jump to any more conclusions . . ."

They talked; they listened; and they gave up jumping, because everything we'd told them was corroborated in every detail. Deborah and I had arrived together, had sat—with a gaggle of Melissa's cronies—together, had drunk wine and eaten pizza together, and apart from natural breaks in the festivities had left together. Deb was in the clear.

And so, by association, was I.

The police filed the case under *Unsolved,* and the burglar was never caught. Alec had no immediate family, and few friends. As nobody seems to care anymore I doubt whether the mystery of who killed him will ever be satisfactorily explained. Deb was, after some argument, paid a comfortable sum by the insurance people, and I persuaded her to buy a small car and take driving lessons. It's all very well to enjoy Agatha Christie, but you can't live that life anymore. Things have moved on since the 1930s. Women are liberated. Independent. They drive cars, buses, trains. They pilot planes like the one that took Melissa to America and her new job. . . .

Deb didn't insist, as I had worried that she might, on having her twin come home to investigate Alec's death in the manner of classic mystery fiction, the mean-streets private eye stumbling against all the odds across the one vital clue the thickheaded cops have missed. As a family, we know each other very well. Deb's favorite reading right now is Dame Agatha: She's working her way along the shelves in order, just as she did when she and Melissa were children, using my library ticket.

I bought myself a new bradawl. The image of the old one plunged into Alec's chest was impossible to shake off. I didn't grudge the cost of another—no mother would.

I didn't like my daughter's staying alone in that house, unprotected against any casual marauder. I talked her into spending some more of the insurance on double glazing with security locks on every window—and on every door. Too many members of the family, plus assorted friends, turned out to have spare keys in case Deborah accidentally locked herself out during one of Alec's adulterous absences. Too many people could have let themselves in without the effort of breaking a window round the back. . . .

But it confused the trail, and that was enough. Nobody was to know, nobody could prove whether the window had been broken before or after Alec came home to find someone studying the brand-new bookcase full of seventy-nine Agatha Christie titles in matching blue bindings—someone about to add the one title, the *Autobiography,* she had forgotten to bring with her earlier because it wasn't a mystery and she'd had it on another shelf in another room.

Melissa had never cared for Alec.

She cared still less when he tried a good-bye grope with her, his wife's sister, in his wife's absence, and wouldn't take no for an answer. The only answer he understood was the desperate bradawl snatched up from my open toolbox nearby. Giving my daughter the benefit of the doubt, I'd say she meant to do no more than frighten him off.

But with a devious legal mind like hers, you can never be sure. As I said, I'm glad Deb didn't ask her sister to help solve the puzzle of Alec's death. It would have been embarrassing to watch Melissa's dilemma: A private detective, like a librarian, must have her professional pride. It's not that she would have detected herself as the guilty party, I'm sure, but she's becoming a success in her new career; she would have hated to admit defeat. She might even, at the worst, have been prepared to accuse me of the crime, reasoning that a mother will sacrifice a lot for her children and I would be unlikely to argue with her proof that I had been back to the house that fateful night. . . .

Because a private eye isn't the only one who knows how to

cover her tracks. Melissa's friends had been in a superjovial mood, full of admiration for Melissa's new plans and hanging on Deb's every word. They had ignored me, so that when I slipped away with a murmured excuse, nobody noticed that I was gone for a little longer than all but the most desperate bodily needs would have required.

But a librarian doesn't just catalog and stamp and shelve the books in her care: She reads them, too. You don't have to be the dedicated mystery reader Mel has taught Deb to be to pick up a few tips. I had been anxious about that bookcase: I didn't want Alec to come home and blame Deb, or me, if my workmanship had failed and those seventy-nine blue leatherette volumes were scattered all over his precious carpet.

Seventy-nine. I had automatically counted them as Deb arranged them on the shelves, even though she carried two or three or four at a time; professional habits die hard. I lazed on my chair, watching my daughter work, and I counted seventy-nine. And when I slipped away from the pizza place to check the bookcase again, I recounted them—and made eighty. Counting them had managed to divert my thoughts for a few moments from the horrid sight of Alec lying dead on the floor with my bradawl through his heart. . . .

That's how I know it must have been Melissa. Only a librarian would have spotted it; and only someone with the instincts of a private eye could have covered it up so well.

I'm glad Melissa didn't come back to investigate Alec's death on her sister's behalf. When she finished her training course—she passed out top of her class, naturally—I sent her a congratulations card. I wrote inside that her mother was proud of her. . . .

I didn't go into detail. As a family, we know each other very well. I'm sure she understood.

Out of Africa

Nancy Pickard

Soccer mom and mystery writer Nancy Pickard practices both skills in the number one youth soccer state in the nation, Kansas. When she's not car-pooling, she writes the Jenny Cain and Eugenia Potter mystery series and edits anthologies like this one. A former president of Sisters in Crime, she has won the Anthony, Agatha, Macavity, and Shamus Awards for her novels and short stories.

Theme music swelled, and a golden meadow in Kenya appeared on the television screen in Room 312. On top of the TV set, a bolted-down VCR unrolled *Out of Africa*, a movie that was made in 1985 but which was set back in 1913. It was a story based on truth and real people, and it told of a time when the skies above East Africa were blue and beautiful, and still empty of anything but clouds, spears, arrows, insects, and birds. The first airplane had not yet appeared to swoop around the hills, or to fly low and scatter the herds on the ground. No smell of gasoline or of diesel touched the senses of people accustomed to breathing dust raised by wind, by running feet and galloping hooves. Great numbers of animals ran free. Fabulous flocks of white birds took wing, as from an unfenced Eden. Hills rose all around, as if to protect and hold in their embrace all manner of species who didn't know that their millions of years of freedom were drawing to a close.

In Room 312, Ward C, of the Heartlines Nursing Home, nurse's aide Susan Stefano stared at the screen. She listened to the movie for a moment, and then she looked at the resident in the wheelchair.

"You really love this movie, Mrs. Golden," she said, quietly.

Maude Golden's gaze remained fixed on the screen.

"I like it, too." Susan placed her right hand on the bony, veined left hand that rested unmoving on the arm of the wheelchair. She might have spoken louder, as she usually did with elderly residents who were hard of hearing. But she didn't know how much this patient could hear, or what she understood. Susan felt that she and Mrs. Golden communicated mostly in unspoken ways.

"You hear the music, though, don't you?" she asked.

Susan thought this movie's music was beautiful, but it was so sad she couldn't hear it without feeling as if she wanted to cry. Sometimes, she actually did shed a few tears, especially if she happened to be in the room during certain scenes. Such as when Robert Redford first took Meryl Streep up in his new airplane, and you just knew he was going to crash one day, and die, and leave her all alone. That scene always got to Susan, and she could hardly bear the one where Meryl Streep boarded the train to leave Africa forever. She just wanted to sob like a baby when she caught that one. The sad music got to her, every time.

But this afternoon, Susan had purposely come in at the start of the movie. Now she watched Mrs. Golden, and waited to see if something happened which she had seen happen once before.

In the movie, Meryl Streep said, "I had a farm in Africa."

And sure enough, Susan saw Mrs. Golden's lips move in sync with the words: "*I had a farm.*" There was no sound, but Susan was sure that's what she saw. There was the definite *f* when Mrs. Golden touched her teeth to her lower lip, and the *m* when her lips closed at the end of the phrase.

"Mrs. Golden! You said something!"

There was no response from the old woman, who just kept on staring at the television screen without any expression in her eyes, and without moving her lips again. But that was all right with Susan, for now. At least it meant there still might be a bit of a person alive inside Mrs. Golden. Maybe with a little extra work, Susan could tease her out again. She knew that was unlikely, as Mrs. Golden had a diagnosis of dementia, but Susan never liked to give up on any of her patients. It was probably the TV that Mrs. Golden was talking to, and not to her. But still, she could hope. She could try. Heartened by the tiny clue, Susan gently squeezed Maude Golden's hand, and settled in to steal a little time to watch some of the rest of the movie with her.

Meryl Streep was playing a woman who had actually lived, and who became famous as the writer Isak Dinesen. However, at the time portrayed in the movie about her, she was still known by her married name, Karen Blixen. Again, in the movie, she said, ". . . I had a farm . . ." It was the most oft-repeated line of dialogue in the movie.

And again, Mrs. Golden's lips moved to the words.

Susan Stefano, kneeling beside the wheelchair, thought it was an amazing thing, how Mrs. Golden couldn't seem to register anything else in her poor demented brain, but could watch this movie, *Out of Africa,* over and over and over, and even mouth those words. To Susan's knowledge, they were the first ones anybody in the nursing home had ever known her to say that made any sense at all.

"I had a farm."

It was another aide who had discovered that watching this movie seemed to calm this patient. While removing it from the VCR one day, the aide had witnessed Mrs. Golden becoming extremely agitated; on inspiration, the aide put the movie back on, and the patient immediately quieted down. After that, it played almost constantly in Room 312. When it was on, she was no trouble at all; when it was off, she moaned and groaned and jerked her limbs, and tried to talk to the invisible people who haunted her hallucinations.

It seemed a mercy to leave it on.

In the movie, Karen Blixen was telling the truth when she uttered those words about her life in Africa. But Mrs. Golden's daughter and son-in-law had told the staff of Heartlines that Mrs. Golden had always lived in the city.

As the music played, Susan gazed at the face of her favorite patient. There was something about Mrs. Golden that Susan loved, in spite of the fact that there was never really any true response from her, and that she was really hard work to take care of, since she could do practically nothing for herself. "Might be Alzheimer's," the nursing home doctor had said, pursing his lips in the baffled way he had of demonstrating the mystery of dementia. "Might be the result of a stroke, or a lot of little strokes. Could be any number of things, and we probably won't know exactly what unless the family wants an autopsy after she dies."

"No autopsy," her daughter had said, looking horrified. "Mother's been Christian Science all her life!"

"What good would that do anyway?" the son-in-law had objected.

The doctor had cast a tactful glance at Mrs. Golden's daughter before saying, "Sometimes people like to know, since some of these things run in families."

"I don't want to know," the daughter had said, with a shudder.

"No autopsy," her husband had stated, with feeling.

"Whatever you wish," the doctor had agreed.

It didn't matter to him, Susan had thought, overhearing it all. He wasn't the one who might have inherited the terrible gene.

"You make me want to cry," she thought as she gazed up at Mrs. Golden.

None of the other patients, pitiful though some of them were, made her feel like that. She didn't know why this one old woman affected her so strongly. She didn't know what it was about silent, passive Mrs. Golden that tugged at her heart as if this were her own grandmother sitting day after day in a wheelchair staring over and over at the same movie . . . hearing day after day the same heartbreaking music and the same tragic words. Seeing Robert Redford's character love Meryl Streep's character. Laughing as the monkeys listened to Mozart. Helplessly watching Denys Finch-Hatton fly off to his death. Half-dreading, half-anticipating the unbearable moment when Karen Blixen received the news. Seeing her packing to leave Africa. Watching her smile one last time at the wonderful African man who had served her so faithfully. Hearing him utter her given name, for the first and only time. *"I want to hear you say my name." "You are Karen, M'msah'b."* And, at the end of the movie, seeing the great herds move across the plains, without Karen Blixen or Denys Fitch-Hatton to watch them ever again.

"I had a farm in Africa."

At least three times, Meryl Streep said those words.

And now Susan knew for sure that Mrs. Golden said them, too.

Susan had never known an Alzheimer's patient to be able to concentrate on a television show, which was one of the signs that raised her hopes for Mrs. Golden. Plus, Susan thought it was nice that Mrs. Golden had this, at least, to keep her company and to comfort her.

"Oops. Let me fix that for you."

She reached up to readjust Mrs. Golden's robe where it had slipped off her left shoulder, revealing a big, ugly, old-fashioned smallpox vaccination scar, and skin of a much paler hue below her age-spotted face and neck. Susan gently tucked the robe around her patient, allowing for modesty and comfort.

Each room on every wing at the Heartlines Nursing Home was an outside room, having its own large picture window in the very center of its exterior wall. From inside Room 312, looking out, it appeared that the scene was framed by a single tall cottonwood tree, rising up the right side of the picture, extending its leaves and branches over the top. And stretching beyond it, as on an African veldt, there was only the prairie, golden in the summer, rusty in the autumn, white and sere in winter, green in spring. And the sky, blue and cloudless, or black with Kansas thunderstorms, white with blowing snow, or gray with endless days of hazy drizzle or rain. Nothing moved in that picture, unless a hawk flew by a long way up, or an airplane. No streets or highways crossed it, no pedestrian path. There was no patio out there on that side, and the parking lots lay on the other side of the building. There was only the cottonwood tree, framing the tallgrass prairie. In spring, rain hit the window screen; in summer, bugs buzzed against it; in fall, leaves brushed past; and in the winter, hail and snow pinged against the storm window.

Maude Golden had lived there one full year.

When Mrs. Golden wasn't in her wheelchair, but sitting up in her single bed, she usually turned her face toward the window, as if it were a television screen, as if the Kansas prairie were the African plain from *Out of Africa,* as if she were watching lions in the grass, or waiting for the elephants to walk by, or perhaps a band of Masai warriors, holding their spears high, utterly self-contained, trotting across the desert just as they did in the movie.

"I'm sick of this damned movie!"

"What?" Mamie Golden Threlkeld nearly spilled her homemade chicken broth from the thermos out of which she was pouring it into a cup for her mother. Annoyed that he had startled her, she glared at her husband. "Look what you almost did. You almost made me burn my hand."

"You make sure she drinks all that."

"She always does," Mamie said, in an exasperated tone.

He stood over his mother-in-law, his hands in his pants pockets, frowning first at the white head below him, then at the television screen. "She never does anything but watch this damned movie," he announced. "She ought to be doing something else. It's not like she knows what she's looking at, anyway. She could be watching the damned wall, for all she knows."

"John!" His wife remonstrated. "Don't say things like that."

On the screen, Meryl Streep was kneeling on the ground in front of the newly appointed governor of Kenya, begging him to provide land where the tribe who had worked for her could live, now that she was bankrupt and leaving Africa. Her long white skirt would be ruined; the spectators were shocked and disapproving. The governor tried to get her to stand up again. The governor's wife appeared to be the only white person there who understood the rightness and pitiful justice of Karen Blixen's plea.

In the nursing home, John Threlkeld thrust out his jaw. "It's all she does."

"Well, what do you think she should be doing, John? You think she should read a good book? Take dancing lessons? Maybe a little basket-weaving? It's all she can do, John. For heaven's sake."

"It's always on, every time we come."

"So?" Mamie blew on the broth to cool it, before she placed a straw in it and held it to her mother's lips.

"Stupid movie."

"It's not! I love Robert Redford."

"It's sappy."

He reached over and pushed the "Stop" button on the VCR.

Almost immediately, a network soap opera came onto the screen.

In the wheelchair, Mrs. Golden's mouth opened, her fingers trembled on the chair arms, her eyes widened slightly. For a moment, she didn't suck when her daughter put the straw between her lips.

"John! Put that back on—that's cruel! What else has she got!"

But he wouldn't turn it back on, and Mamie didn't do it, so it stayed off during the remainder of their visit that Sunday, which took only as long as it took the old woman to swallow all of the chicken broth. On their way out, John made a detour toward the nursing desk, to say, "I don't want my mother-in-law listening to that same damn movie all the time. You're supposed to give her something to do. That's what you get paid for. She shouldn't be sitting in front of a television set twenty-four hours a day."

As soon as Susan saw the Threlkelds' car pull out of the parking lot, she hurried back to Ward C, and into Room 312, to start up Mrs. Golden's movie again. She was rewarded in a way that thrilled her: For the first time, Mrs. Golden raised her eyes to look at Susan. The nurse's aide could have sworn she saw a hint of a smile around her patient's lips.

"Mrs. Golden!" she breathed, as if she were saying, "You're home!"

But the pale blue gaze shifted away from her face, and slid back to the television screen. Susan wasn't sure if it had really happened, or if Mrs. Golden had just happened to turn her head that way for a moment and it didn't actually mean anything at all.

The movie started up again right at the point where Robert Redford, playing Denys Finch-Hatton, strode in all dusty and gorgeous to raise Karen Blixen to her feet again and to remove her from the scene with dignity. "I didn't hear about it until I got to the border," he said, referring to the fire that had destroyed her coffee farm, resulting in her bankruptcy.

Susan took a moment to sit on the carpet at Mrs. Golden's feet, hold one of her hands, and watch her movie with her. The moment turned into many minutes. When Meryl Streep turned to board the train that would take her away from Africa forever, Susan felt Mrs. Golden's fingers tremble in her hand. She gently squeezed the thin fingers, and glanced up at the face of the woman above her.

"Oh, Mrs. Golden!" the tenderhearted aide murmured.

Tears were streaming down her patient's face.

Susan dabbed them away with a tissue and then, acting on impulse, reached up and kissed Mrs. Golden on her forehead.

"Do you want me to start your movie for you again?"

"I had a farm," the old woman whispered, and this time, Susan even heard the words. Susan felt her hand being turned over so that it was held instead of doing the holding; she sensed the effort the old woman was putting into trying to grasp it tightly. Mrs. Golden's whisper grew strained, as if she were attempting to shout. *"I had a farm! I had a farm. I had a farm."* The last words were only mouthed, with no sound coming out. She became more agitated, making unintelligible sounds and acting as though she were trying to get up from her wheelchair.

The young nurse's aide felt shaken, as if she had done something wrong.

But she removed herself from Mrs. Golden's clutches, and rewound the movie for her, and pushed "Start" again. As the lovely music began to play, the old woman sank back into her wheelchair.

"Mrs. Golden?"

Her patient heaved a little sigh and stared at her movie.

"Mrs. Golden?"

Susan left Room 312, feeling disturbed and troubled in her heart. It was so strange, what demented patients could do and say. They could confuse strangers with their own children, believe they were being persecuted by the cops, think they were going to trial, see hallucinations, talk to thin air, become passionately convinced of something ridiculous. Like Mrs. Golden, who thought she had a farm, when she had lived in a city all her life.

"Mrs. Golden upset again?" her supervisor asked. "I swear, sometimes I hate it when the relatives come. It just upsets them. They can be calm as anything, and let a relative visit them and suddenly we've got tears and tantrums on our hands. I hate to say this, because they're good about coming to see her, but Mrs. Golden is always worse after her daughter leaves."

Susan performed the rest of her job quietly that day.

She had little to say to her children and husband when she reached home. She felt exhausted, but she had a hard time falling asleep that night, for thinking about Mrs. Golden in Room 312. When she finally did sleep, she dreamed of monkeys running over cars, of giraffes eating leaves at the top of impossibly high trees, and of lions tearing horribly into the flesh of a living antelope.

The next afternoon when Susan walked into her favorite patient's room to see if she needed to start the movie going, she discovered that it was missing.

"Mrs. Golden! Where's your movie?"

Mrs. Golden was sitting in her wheelchair in front of the television set, as usual, but she wasn't watching the game show that was playing on it. Her head was bent, her eyes were open, and she appeared to be staring at her lap, or at nothing.

"Did somebody take your movie?"

Susan was indignant. "I'll be right back, Mrs. Golden."

At the nurses' desk, she said, "Who took Mrs. Golden's movie away?"

"I did," one of the registered nurses informed her. "Family's orders."

"But it's not fair! She loves that movie—it's all she has!"

"Can't be helped, Susan," she was chided. "We have to be able to tell her family we did what they wanted us to do."

"What's she supposed to do now?"

The nurse looked at her sympathetically, and shrugged.

Susan felt like bursting into tears. "Where is it?"

"The movie?" The nurse smiled a little. "I don't think I'd better tell you, Sue. Anyway, you know you're not supposed to get so personally involved with the patients. It's not professional." Trying to be comforting, she added, "Mrs. Golden probably doesn't even know it's gone."

But even as she turned away with tears of frustration in her eyes, Susan thought, "Oh, yes she does too know."

That evening, when the residents were wheeled into the dining room, Mrs. Golden refused to eat her dinner. Nothing Susan could do or say persuaded the old woman to open her mouth, or to admit even a morsel of nourishment, not even a forkful of warm apple pie.

"Please, Mrs. Golden," Susan urged her. "Please, for me?"

When Susan reported to her supervisor that Mrs. Golden wouldn't eat, the woman remarked, "Really? She didn't eat any lunch, either. You know what this probably means, don't you, Susan?"

"She wants to die," the nurse's aide said bitterly.

"She knows that it's her time to die," the supervisor corrected her.

It was well-known among medical and hospice personnel that dying people had a sense of their bodies shutting down. Left alone to do what came naturally, they would speed up the process themselves by refusing food and drink. If nothing was done to interfere, death came soon.

"Can we give her a feeding tube?" Susan asked.

"No," the supervisor said. "We've got a directive."

Which meant the nursing home had a form saying the patient was not to be force-fed in order to be kept alive. Susan had a desperate feeling of events snowballing; of bad things happening that she couldn't stop.

"Mrs. Golden signed a directive?"

The supervisor shook her head, and smiled tolerantly. "Oh, no, of course not. But she's Christian Science, you know. And her daughter has power of attorney. Her daughter and her son-in-law took care of everything."

This time, when Susan turned away from her supervisor, she was thinking bitterly, "I'll *bet* they did." But then she turned back, making one last try to convince somebody with the power to do something. "The only reason she wants to die is because we took her movie away! She doesn't have anything to live for anymore!"

"Oh, Susan," the supervisor said, indulgently. "A movie can't keep somebody alive. It's sad, I know, but it's just Mrs. Golden's time, that's all. Would you really want to keep her alive in the condition she's in? She can't move by herself, she can't talk; we don't really even know how much she sees or hears. Susan, she can't even think anymore. Do you really want to keep that poor woman alive just so you can keep watching a motion picture?"

"Yes!" thought Susan, who only the day before had felt Mrs. Golden attempt to squeeze her hand, and had seen Mrs. Golden cry, and even thought she had looked at Susan with gratitude in her eyes. If Mrs. Golden really wants to die, she could have stopped eating anytime before this, Susan thought, but it was only now, after her movie was taken away from her, that she suddenly started refusing food. That was too much of a coincidence for Susan to dismiss. She believed she had seen too much life, too much emotion in the old woman to let her go so easily now.

"Can we try an experiment?" Susan pleaded.

"What?" Her supervisor was starting to sound and look exasperated.

"Let her have her movie back tonight? And see if she eats then? If she does, wouldn't that mean she still wants to stay alive?"

The supervisor heaved a put-upon sigh, but she said, "Oh, okay, I guess you're right, it wouldn't hurt to see what happens. But, Susan, if she refuses to eat—"

"I know, I know, I'll let her alone."

"All right, then." And she told Susan where to find the movie cartridge.

Two and a half hours later, as the final credits rolled, Mrs. Golden was eating the piece of warm apple pie that Susan had put back for her in the kitchen.

On Tuesday, all three of Susan's small children came down with an intestinal bug within a half hour of each other, so that she had to stay home with them that day, as there was "too much throwing up for one husband to manage alone," as she told her supervisor.

That same day, Mrs. Golden's son-in-law had a fit when he and his wife walked into Room 312 and found "that movie" still playing. This time, no longer trusting the staff to obey his instructions, Mrs. Golden's son-in-law ejected the movie cartridge from the VCR and took it away with him.

Wednesday and Thursday were Susan's scheduled days off that week.

It was Friday before she returned to Heartlines.

Mrs. Golden had not eaten or had anything to drink for two days, except for the little bit of broth her daughter brought on Thursday.

"Not even any water?" Susan exclaimed to another nurse's aide.

"No, she clamps her teeth together and won't take anything."

"But that's because she wants her movie!"

"Well, he took it."

"Why did they let him do that?"

"Susan, calm down, it's not like they had a choice. You weren't here—you don't know how it was. You should have seen him. He was yelling at us, and waving that movie in the air like he was going to throw it at somebody. What were we supposed to do, tackle him and make him give it back?"

"I would have!"

The other aide shook her head. "I believe it."

"He stole it. That movie belongs to the nursing home."

"So, they'll bill him for it." The nurse's aide was busy, and harried, and ran out of patience suddenly. "Susan, leave poor Mrs. Golden alone. She's pitiful, and now she wants to die. It's not the movie. It's just her time to go."

Filled with distress and with the urgency of good intentions, Susan sneaked a peak into Mrs. Golden's patient file when nobody was looking. Then she waited for a chance to use a telephone when there wasn't anybody around to overhear her. As soon as a woman's voice answered, Susan rushed to ask, "Mrs. Threlkeld? This is Susan, from the nursing home? Excuse me for calling you, but I just have to ask you if you can bring your mom's movie back? I think it would be really good for her—"

"What? Who did you say this is?" Mamie Golden Threlkeld sounded confused, annoyed. "What is it you want? Her movie?"

"Yes, ma'am. You see, I've noticed—"

"That damned movie has caused me nothing but trouble!"

"I'm sorry. But if you could bring—"

"We tossed it in the trash."

Susan's heart plunged. "Can you get it out?"

"Out of the trash?" The daughter's voice rose as if in disbelief at what she had heard Susan say. "Not unless I want to plow through an entire landfill I can't. Who'd you say you are? One of the nurses?"

"No, I'm just an aide."

"Well, we don't have that movie anymore, and I wouldn't return it if we did. It would just upset my husband."

"But your mom—"

"Let my mother alone, okay? It's her time to go. She's suffered enough. And I've got to deal with my grief, and this doesn't help me at all."

"I'm sorry, but—"

Mrs. Golden's daughter hung up.

Susan turned around, and found her supervisor staring at her.

"Who was that, Sue?"

"Mrs. Threlkeld. Mrs. Golden's daughter. I was trying—"

"You called a patient's family? Without permission?"

"But . . . yes."

"Why?"

"Because . . . I thought they could bring her movie back, and that would help her feel better."

"Susan, is this job too emotionally difficult for you?"

"No!"

"Do you think you get too personally involved?"

Susan shook her head, wanting to defend herself, but she felt too frightened to speak up. This was a small town, and there weren't many jobs. She had a high school diploma and three little kids.

"I'm taking you off Mrs. Golden's room for the rest of the day, Susan. It'll be better for you to stay away from her."

Susan nodded obediently, not trusting herself to speak for fear she would burst out in anger, or in tears. Her supervisor dismissed her to her other duties, and Susan hurried away, with her head bowed. Her face felt so hot that she touched her cheeks, just to feel them. For a few moments, she could hardly walk straight; her whole body felt weak with the relief that she hadn't been fired on the spot. But when she discovered her equilibrium, she found her resolve, too.

Every time she hurried past Mrs. Golden's open door that day, she sent out a thought to the old woman who lay gaunt and pale in the bed in the room: "I'm here! I'll get it back for you. I promise."

That evening, Susan got on the phone at home, determined to call every video store in Kansas if she had to. The only place in which videos were rented and sold in her own town were a couple of grocery stores and a gas station, but there were other outlets, fifty and a hundred fifty miles away in the bigger cities of Emporia and Wichita. Susan swore she'd go all the way to Kansas City, or south to Tulsa, if she had to.

A clerk at a movie store in Emporia said they had one copy of the movie, but it was checked out and wasn't due back for five days.

"She could die by then," Susan told her husband.

At a store in Wichita, she finally located a copy for sale.

"I'm going to get it," she announced to him.

"Now? Right now?"

"Yeah."

"Susan, that's nuts." Her husband had been understanding up to this point, but now he said, "Do you realize its already eight o'clock? It'll take you hours to get there. And then you've got to find the store, and buy the tape, and drive home. It'll be well after midnight, Susan! I don't like this. I don't see why you think you have to do this for one old lady who just wants to die."

"She doesn't want to die!" Susan yelled at her husband.

And then, horror-stricken at treating him like that, she threw her arms around him and said, "I'm sorry, I'm sorry—it's just that nobody seems to understand what's happening here. We're going to let somebody die because it's easier, but she wouldn't die if she had just this one thing to live for."

"You don't know that, Sue."

"I know how I'll feel if I don't try!"

"Well, just be careful, all right?"

"I promise."

As she began the long, late drive to Wichita, Susan was aware that she was making a lot of promises to people, and she didn't know if she'd be able to keep a single one of them. The truth was, she was scared to drive to Wichita alone at night, scared she'd get lost, or drive off the road, or get hit by somebody. Mostly, she was scared they wouldn't really have the movie for her when she got there, and she was scared that then Mrs. Golden would die.

On the drive down, she thought about the movie.

She thought about how in the movie Karen Blixen kept trying to get the men in her life—or any white man in the whole country—to listen to her, and to stick around long enough to really hear her and to help her. But the only men who would stay still long enough to do that were the Africans she paid to work for her. Not even the first man who loved her was willing to lend a hand, even if he was the one who got her into her jam. And practically the only way she kept Denys Finch-Hatton around for any longer than a day was to entrance him by telling him stories that she made up just for him.

"How'd she get herself in a fix like that?" Susan wondered.

She finally decided it was because Karen Blixen had made a pact with the devil: At the start of the movie, she had persuaded a man to marry her and take her to Africa with him. He had lost all his money, and so with marriage to her he would get access to all of hers; for her part, she got to be a married woman with the title of baroness.

"Bad bargain," Susan pronounced, on the outskirts of Wichita.

But she wondered if she might not have done the same thing, in those times, in those circumstances.

She'd read one time that the reason different people react to motion pictures in different ways had to do with something the movies touched way deep inside them, or did not. *Out of Africa* always made her cry; but it left some people cold, which she didn't understand. Mrs. Golden was passionately attached to it. Susan thought it didn't take a college degree to see that Mrs. Golden probably felt just like Karen Blixen: She needed help, and nobody heard her.

"Except me," Susan whispered, feeling frightened and over-whelmed by a responsibility she sensed but couldn't define. Well, there was one thing she could do, and that was find the movie and take it back to Mrs. Golden. If it saved her life for a few days, if it gave an old woman a few more hours of pleasure, it was well worth it, as far as Susan was concerned.

Just as the clerk at the video store had promised her, the copy of *Out of Africa* was there. But when she got home again, she found her husband waiting up for her.

"The nursing home called," he said. "They thought you'd want to know—"

"No!" Susan cried. "She didn't die!"

"No, but they think it's really close now, and maybe you want a chance to tell her good-bye." He added, pointedly, "In the morning."

Of course, she didn't—couldn't—wait until then.

Fifteen minutes after midnight, Mrs. Golden was propped up on pillows in her bed. Susan had awakened her, and even slipped her dentures into her mouth. Now she was staring at her movie on the screen, while she sipped warm chicken broth through a straw in the cup that Susan held for her. It wasn't the homemade kind her daughter brought to her once a week, but it was warm and nourishing all the same, Susan hoped.

When the time came for Meryl Streep to say the familiar

words for the first time in the movie, Susan held her breath. Mrs. Golden backed weakly away from the straw. Susan held the cup still. Mrs. Golden looked into Susan's eyes as on the screen the actress said, "I had a farm."

Mrs. Golden's eyes filled with tears.

Susan gently returned the straw to her mouth, and said, "You have to get your strength back. Eat this broth. Watch your movie. I won't let anybody take it away from you again. I promise."

Like the heroine of the movie, Mrs. Golden was asking for help, Susan believed, and nobody but Susan was listening. And suddenly, just by having that single thought, several disparate facts clicked into place in Susan's mind, leaving her breathless and frightened. She stared at her patient and whispered again, "I promise."

On Saturday, Susan was mopping Mrs. Golden's bathroom when her patient's daughter and son-in-law arrived for their every-other-day visit. A few moments after Susan heard them enter the room, she propped her mop against the wall and stepped out of the bathroom.

"Excuse me," she said to the Threlkelds. "I'll leave and give you all some privacy. I'll just pick up my cleaning supplies." She walked over to the chair where Mrs. Golden's daughter had flung her coat and put down her purse and the thermos in which she carried the chicken soup she made each week for her mother. Susan bent to retrieve a bag of her cleaning supplies, then swept the thermos up with her and hurried out of the room with it.

Susan walked as fast as she could down the hall and into the tiny galley off the ward dining room, where she had saved a pitcher of chicken broth she'd made in the nursing home's kitchen. She set the thermos on a counter and unscrewed its lid and stopper, and placed them quietly on the counter, too. She poured the contents of the thermos into a container she had brought for the purpose, and then quickly sealed it with a lid. Finally, she began to empty the broth she had made into the thermos, with the idea of filling it so that no one could tell she'd replaced its original contents.

She'd almost accomplished her mission when a hand suddenly clamped down on her mouth.

"You little bitch," John Threlkeld whispered. "What do you think you're doing with our thermos? You want some of that broth my wife makes? Is that it? It's a whole lot more powerful than she knows, but I guess you figured that out, didn't you? Here! You try it."

He turned her around to face him, pressing himself against her and her against the wall, with his right hand still over her mouth, so that she was pinioned. She watched him grab the thermos with his left hand and bring it toward her mouth.

A vision from the movie flashed through her mind: of the heroine confronted with a lion who was about to charge and kill her. Of the hero saying urgently, *"Don't move."*

Under the man's body, Susan made herself go limp.

It surprised him enough that he briefly lost his grip on her, long enough for Susan to begin to scream and to kick and struggle. The thermos flew out of his hands and broth flew everywhere, but it didn't matter, because the evidence Susan had collected still lay safely in the sealed container she had brought from home.

"Tranquilizers and hallucinogens," the county sheriff told the staff at the nursing home when the police laboratory report came in. "That's the devil's broth they fed her to keep her demented."

Susan's supervisor asked, "Why didn't they just kill her and be done with it?"

"Because," the sheriff explained, "then they would have had to pay huge estate taxes. This way, they kept her alive while they lived off her money and gradually transferred her assets over to themselves. It was an attempt at tax fraud. Once she was penniless, they would have got Medicaid to pick up the bill for her nursing care."

"Or killed her"

"Or just let her die."

"But he told Susan his wife didn't know about the broth."

"It's the only thing she didn't know. She thought her mother really did have Alzheimer's. She went along with the tax fraud, but she didn't know the worst of it. She didn't know that her husband had purposely incapacitated her mother in order to get his hands on her assets. It was his idea to claim that medical treatment was against her religion, so that nobody could run blood or urine tests on her and there would never be an autopsy. The daughter let her husband convince her that it would be cruel to try to prolong her mother's life. He said that if they lied about her religion, no doctor would argue about it, not for an old woman."

Somebody who hadn't already heard the whole story asked the young aide: "How'd you figure it out, Susan?"

Shyly, she said, "She was supposedly a Christian Scientist, but she had a smallpox vaccination and dentures. And every time her daughter came to visit her, she got worse afterward. And she had skin like you wouldn't expect a city woman to have, with color and sunspots on her face and neck and hands, but the rest of her so pale. And . . . and . . ." Susan felt at a loss to explain something so mysterious as the unspoken bond between her and her patient. How could she make them understand something so fragile, so eerie? "I just felt like she was trying to tell me something, with that movie."

Maude Golden stepped out of Susan's car without assistance.

She was considerably stronger now, returning to her former state of physical and mental well-being, that of a healthy seventy-two-year-old woman who had worked hard outdoors for most of her life.

"Come look, Susan."

The young aide ran up to the side of her former patient, who put an arm around her affectionately and then pointed with her free hand. Both women wore jeans, boots, and long-sleeved shirts. "You can see almost my entire property from here—that's why I wanted you to drive up here first. See? There's the house; we'll go down there in a minute, and I'll fix us some tea. And there's the lake beyond. I want you to bring your husband and your children out here, all right? You come anytime you like. They can swim, and take the canoe out, and go fishing. Do you think they'd come?"

"Yes, Maude," Susan breathed, overcome by the beauty of the vista.

In front of them, the prairie stretched out like an African veldt.

But fence lines intersected these many acres, and crops grew in rich green rows. There were thousands of acres and a lot of work. Sensing her encroaching age, Maude had asked her daughter and son-in-law to come live with her, and to share in the work and the profits. In Susan's view, Maude had made a pact with the devil, just as Karen Blixen in the movie had.

Gently, Susan asked her friend the question she hadn't had the courage to ask until now. "Maude? Did you know what he was doing to you?"

The older woman shook her head. "Not really, Susan—I was too confused for that—but I knew I had to hang on somehow. And when I watched that movie, it wasn't as if I was sitting there having logical thoughts that I couldn't express. It was more like it set up in me a longing . . . a terrible longing, Susan, for something I couldn't quite remember, but which I wanted with all my heart."

"When he took the movie away . . ."

"I lost all hope. I'm ashamed to say, I gave up."

"Don't be ashamed! You were so brave, like Karen Blixen."

"And you, my dear—you are my hero."

"It was those words. . . ."

"Yes." Maude Golden gazed out over her acreage, and she said quietly, gratefully, "I have a farm."

Clear Sailing

Gillian Roberts

Like her mystery series heroine Amanda Pepper, Gillian Roberts is probably from Philadelphia, but nobody really knows for sure. She might just as easily be from northern California, where she sets her other mystery series starring Emma Howe and Billie August. The reason for the confusion is that Gillian Roberts is, in real life, the mainstream novelist Judith Greber, who definitely is from Philadelphia and definitely does live in northern California. One, or possibly both, of them won an Anthony Award for Best First Mystery Novel, for Caught Dead in Philadelphia.

Mr. Hackett stood at the entrance to the terrace, straining to hear beyond the cocktail chatter and shush of the palm fronds, out to the ocean. It was music to him—the sound of silent power, stealth, deceptive surface calm. He listened, inhaled deeply, and felt ready to take on the night.

The group of executives—his team, his people—were backlit by the sunset over the ocean. They looked elegant in their tropical finery ("resort casual," the agenda had suggested). Dressed for success, even at play, with their wives as their most spectacular accessories.

As the company's annual profits rose, the annual retreats had been set at ever more opulent, spectacular, and exotic resorts. As if to keep up with the scenery, the wives were likewise upgraded, becoming ever younger and more aesthetically pleasing.

A quick check by Mr. Hackett failed to reveal his own, unupgraded wife, so, he decided, he was free to openly appreciate the flowerlike beauties as they posed, laughing excessively at whatever anyone said. Honing their wife acts, Mrs. Hackett would say. She, the queen of fake laughter, made fun of newcomers who copied her act. She didn't like the ingenues, as she called them, the ever-younger wives, and she nastily suggested that they were evidence of some failing on their husbands' part. Some childish belief that a spouse could turn back the clock. "They confuse women and mirrors," she'd murmured—Hannah Hackett lacked the oomph to even raise her voice—"as if what they see is their own reflection, their own youth. Their wives are their very own portraits of Dora Ann Gray."

He had no idea what she was talking about, except that it was more proof of her menopausal jealousy. He smiled with pleasure at the young woman's animation, their overlarge gestures, their bright laughter. Their great legs. Their great tans. Their everything.

He was starved for such views. The sight of Mrs. Hackett across a patio, let alone a marital bed, had long since lost its charm. And his short-term changes of scene were no longer enough. Why should he have to sneak a few hours of pleasure? He was the boss. The number one man. Look what his underlings had! It was time for a major revision of his landscape. He deserved it. He'd earned it.

Hannah Hackett had been a ball of fire when they met, but the sad truth was, she was down to cool embers now. Whatever had once been had melted into a lump, with all the beauty and interest lumps had. His wife, as they said, hadn't grown. Except in the hips. And waist. And thighs and upper arms. And her mind and interests were so narrowly focused on him, his career, his children, his home, he felt as if he were in a straitjacket.

The young women gazed adoringly at their men. They knew on which side their bread was buttered. And their men's jowls almost jiggled with smug contentment, as well they might. They'd made it, and they had the wives to prove it.

A person of consequence attracted the best of breed. It was nature's way, survival of the fittest, nothing more, nothing less. Made the struggling and scrimping and clawing your way up worthwhile. To the victor goes the spoils.

Speaking of something spoiled, where was Hannah? The least she could do was be here, do her one and only job.

He frowned as a deafening buzz obliterated the sound of the ocean. A helicopter, he realized, circling the darkening sea. Jesus! Hannah was out sailing. Was she still out there, and in trouble? Sailing was Hannah's one remaining passion, if the word "passion" could be applied to something basically dull. Hannah-like: quiet, solitary, and interminable.

So she could be out there, in trouble. His mind raced around that possibility until he realized he'd seen her in the lobby an hour ago, back from the day's sail. The helicopters weren't searching for Hannah.

His regret was nothing like a twinge. It was more like a heart attack.

What was he going to do about that woman? He wanted her away. Permanently. Out of his sight. Didn't want to start a mess, but somehow . . . . Then again, he mused, she'd probably be relieved to be retired from being the CEO's wife; even phlegmatic Hannah must be bored with her do-nothing life.

Problem was, judges tended to be overgenerous to long-term first wives who had no life or income of their own. He'd have to get the accountant on it immediately, move funds, take care of things before he said a word to Hannah.

It wasn't as if Hannah cared about him. If she did, she'd notice him, including noticing where he went, with whom he spent time. Wonder where he was when he wasn't home. But she had no idea, zero, about his extracurricular activities. Didn't that mean she didn't care? That he was below her notice? That she had no interest in him? Given that, there was no reason for him to feel guilty, when his own wife didn't notice and didn't mind his playing around.

He was tethered to the most overly domesticated woman on God's green earth—if it didn't have to do with recipes, child-rearing, or gardening, she wasn't interested.

She did have a little stubborn streak, though. Might not leave quietly. It would be about money. His money. The woman had been an economics major, after all, and she knew things. All through their marriage, she'd invested and rolled over and planted whatever portion of his income she could in places where it was almost sure to grow. Not just the stocks and real estate, but even the art she'd selected—he'd definitely have to work on getting that all in his own name—had appreciated to the point where it was worth a small fortune. She had the touch. He just didn't want her touch in his wallet.

Besides, it was high time she did something for herself, quit the pro-wifing circuit. She should be grateful to him, he reflected, if he terminated the marriage. Thank him for setting her free so she'd finally be able to find out what it was she'd rather do. Lord knows that once upon a time she'd muttered about lost options. Of course, he blamed that on the damned women's movement that had to come along during their marriage. No man in history had ever had to listen to his wife demand "more" or "it all," whatever that meant. Why, then, all of a sudden, when it was Richard Hackett's turn, did everything have to change? But even that was long ago, and Hannah hadn't wanted anything since. He'd jog her memory, remind her about wanting more, wanting it all.

His reverie was interrupted by Susie Waters, the newest of the new crop of wives. She was smiling at him, and not with your basic cocktail hour smile, or the warm but respectful one given the boss. Susie was making major eye contact. Massaging him with her eyes.

Her husband, Sam, was talking to someone else about golf. The man should keep a better eye on his little woman, he thought. His job wasn't good enough, high up enough, to allow for an acting-out wife. She was not an asset to the corporation.

As for being a private asset, one he might enjoy, well, that was different.

Besides, whatever happened was Hannah's fault. She should be here if she didn't want this to happen. In return for the easiest life on the planet, the very least she could do for him was show up when she was expected to. If ever he'd needed proof that Hannah was tired of this life and its duties, would be glad to be rid of it, this was it.

Setting her free would be doing her a favor.

He walked over to where Susie Waters was accepting a fresh martini from the waiter. She took a second one off the serving tray and held it out to him.

He accepted her offer. All her offers.

"You know, science has proven it is humanly possible for a person to survive twenty-four hours without talking to her mother," Jared Tomkins said.

Betsy Hackett Tomkins screwed her face into a mock-pout. "Mom's the exception to the rule. Her family's her entire life. She'll be upset if I don't tell her right away."

"Is this worth interrupting her vacation for? She's in the Caribbean, for God's sake. Tell her when she gets back."

Betsy shook her head with loving exasperation. "She isn't like us, hon," she said. "She doesn't have anything to interrupt. A vacation's *from* something. What would that mean to her? She's there because Daddy's there. She's Mrs. Richard Hackett here, and Mrs. Richard Hackett there. On the job. I feel sorry for her."

"She'd be *Hannah* Hackett if it didn't sound like a coughing disease," Jared said.

Betsy mock-scowled again and dialed the long-distance number her mother had left with her. Jared didn't really mind the call; he couldn't afford to. Her mother, whispering "Don't tell Daddy—if he knew I was managing the money this well, he'd reduce my allowance," had been astoundingly generous to the two of them and to all her children and grandchildren.

"Besides," Betsy said, covering the mouthpiece, "they'll be out for the evening, and I'll leave a message. Won't actually have to talk." The truth was, her mother had nothing to say, but said it at length.

The phone rang only once in the faraway hotel room before she heard her mother's eager "Hello? Yes?"

"Mom! I'm—you okay?"

"Of course—who is—Betsy? What's wrong?"

"Nothing, Mom. It's just—what are you doing in your room at this hour?"

"Waiting for your call, obviously. What is it, darling? What's wrong?"

"Mom? Cara took her first step today."

"The dear! She didn't! But she's so young!"

"We were shocked, too."

"A prodigy. An athlete. She'll be an Olympic star."

Her mother always spun the simplest achievements into signs of stratospheric triumphs where her children, and now her grandchildren, were concerned. Never did she do this, however, where she herself was concerned. She was not an achiever beyond the kitchen.

A month earlier, at a conference—she was a lawyer, working part-time on the Mommy track with a large firm—Betsy had been introduced to a guest speaker, a Superior Court judge, who, it turned out, had gone to college with her mother. "And how is Hannah?" the woman had asked. "What's she running? We voted her most likely to be the first woman president. Haven't seen her name in the White House, so where is she?"

It was embarrassing answering that, no matter how many euphemisms she used. Her mother wasn't running the world or running for office. Her mother was running a household. Housewife, plain and simple, emphasis on simple. "But she's the happiest person I know," Betsy had said in her defense, and unbelievable as it was, it seemed true. Hannah Hackett always seemed contented, although her daughter couldn't imagine why. Devoting your life and energies to a selfish, cold man didn't seem the world's most gratifying job. But for reasons unknown, her mother had settled down and hunkered in and never looked back or out.

"Excuse me? What's that?" Her mother's telephone chatter apparently required a response.

"I can barely hear myself thinking—there's a helicopter over the ocean. Wait, there's actually two—no, three of them. Searchlights on the water. Oh, dear."

"I'm glad you're safely back on shore," Betsy said.

"You worry too much! I had a lovely long sail today, and I expect to have an even lovelier, longer one tomorrow. The men will be playing golf for most of the day, so I am free of wifely duties and I can be out on the ocean forever. And I am a very, very cautious woman."

"Know what?" Betsy said. "It's probably not a rescue at all. It's a drug bust. To add a little excitement to your trip." She chuckled.

"Betsy! This is a respectable—anyway, I'm late for cocktails.

Daddy will be looking for me."

"I didn't mean to make you uncomfortable," Betsy said. "Sorry. I was joking because you get so uppity when we suggest water safety. So be careful, okay? The water looks calm, but things happen, as you can hear."

"Stop worrying. I'm an excellent sailor, and you know it. After all, Daddy trained me."

That wasn't true. Betsy's parents had taken lessons together, and Hannah had excelled, had been a natural. Betsy's father hated it, could never figure out which direction the wind came from. He wanted motors and noise and gave up on sailing almost instantly. But as always, Hannah deferred to her husband, insisted he was the best, asked him for help when none was needed. It wasn't worth mentioning. Hannah Hackett wore rose-colored blinders. Always had and always would.

After again marveling at the baby's amazing agility, mother and daughter promised to talk the next day and said good night, with hugs and kisses to all and sundry.

"I'm sure they'll find the sailor," Betsy said by way of closing. "Don't worry, Mom, and be sure and wear your life jacket all day tomorrow."

"I always do," Hannah Hackett said. "Daddy would be upset otherwise."

Liz Evans was about to go stark raving mad listening to these insane, politicking, stupid women! She would have said you could rip her tongue out before she'd trash her sisters, but she didn't want these women as siblings! She wanted . . . wanted what she and her husband, David, were supposedly having. A vacation. Piña coladas and margaritas beneath beach umbrellas. Romance, soft breezes. Tropical paradise. Dancing under the stars.

Not this. This was work. Except that she liked her work, and hated this.

Liz felt her chin push out like a pouting child's until she realized it and realigned her face.

Ungrateful bitch, she told herself. Half the world's starving to death, living in hovels, and even most of the lucky ones are enduring winter, while you're in paradise, compliments of your husband's employer.

But she knew that wasn't true. A nice stage, yes, but she was working on it, performing in a play set in paradise. It was all an act—the setting, the lush room, the complimentary bathrobes and breakfasts and all her lines. Her gestures, her moves. Not even improv—all pre-scripted. This is how a junior executive's wife acts. This is what she wears. Drinks. Laughs at. Discusses. And worst of all, the play was a farce. Was Liz actually supposed to care about Mitzi's remodeling job and precisely how long and tedious her extravagances could be, let alone the exact shade of tile she picked for the guest bath after an agonizing, heartbreaking hunt? Did Liz need to care about how magnificent Violet's son had been as Hamlet in his ninth-grade production of same? Thank God her corporate wifely duties hadn't included attending the show.

On the edge of the patio, Susie Waters was ignoring the script, writing her own. Where had the woman left her brains? Liz wondered. Maybe they were down in her cleavage, where her spandex dress had squeezed them to death.

In any case, Susie wasn't playing her part as written by Hannah Hackett, the perfect corporate wife.

The two women on the other side of Liz were doing their bit. Their jobs, like Liz's, were to look good, admire anyone who worked for the company, and demonstrate the worth of the company's paychecks by becoming expert consumers. The two wives sounded in ecstasy because designer wear was less expensive on the island, and they breathlessly described every name-brand piece of attire they hoped to find the next day. "The Calvin Klein that—" floated across the terrace. "Manolo—" "Prada . . . ." " . . . tiny purse shaped like a peacock, that—"

Women were supposed to be part of the greater world now, not standing in separate clumps talking about kids and bathroom tile and how most efficiently to spend money somebody else earned. Women weren't supposed to be parlaying their bodies, climbing the corporate ladder via new mates. Women had evolved. At least half the women on this patio had jobs, but it was company policy to treat such activities as time-fillers, inconsequential and somewhat embarrassing hobbies.

Liz kept her daily activities almost a dirty secret at company events. She wanted to fit in, for David's sake. Not that she could understand why a wife who wasn't a clone of the CEO's other half made a man unfit to construct engineering projects, but so it seemed. This was supposedly one big family and "Dad," the CEO himself, didn't like his female kids to be distracted by their own concerns.

So far, she and David were successfully faking compliance. David was the official whiz kid, the youngest senior executive in the firm. Soon enough, he'd be able to either break from here or take it over. It was in her own interests to help him reach that goal. To play the game, no matter how she felt about it.

And, damn, there she was. Hannah Hackett, looking flushed. What on earth had penetrated the fog bank she lived inside? Hannah spent a whole lot of time out at sea, both figuratively and literally. "Mrs. H.," Liz said warmly. "You look like you got some sun today. Your cheeks are pink."

Hannah put a fingertip to her face, as if testing its color in Braille. "I was out for a long time, but I thought I used enough sunblock, but . . . you know, I'm just excited, is all."

"About the drug bust?" a red-haired woman asked.

Mrs. Hackett looked confused. "The what?"

"Didn't you hear it? Helicopters all over the ocean. A policeman told me they were tipped off that smugglers were dropping drugs off this beach, this hotel."

"For heaven's sake—my daughter made a joke and I—but—are you saying they're doing this now? While we're here?" Mrs. Hackett said.

The woman could be amusing, Liz decided. The dimwit thought Colombian drug dealers should check Hannah Hackett's travel plans before making their own.

"The policeman said the beach might be closed tomorrow if it isn't all wrapped up tonight."

The redhead shivered. "He had this enormous gun or rifle or bazooka, I don't know what it was, but I wasn't about to protest!"

"But since it's new to you, Mrs. H., that obviously wasn't what had you excited," another gushing middle-management wife said. "So what was it?"

Hannah Hackett smiled. "You'll think it silly after news of a drug bust, but my daughter phoned to say our youngest grandchild just took her first step."

Liz smiled, as if this were the biggest news she'd heard in years. The other women cooed and aahed. Astounding that a human child had decided to walk.

Another five minutes of this and she'd run screaming into the sea, helicopters or no helicopters.

The hypocrites asked if Hannah had any photos, knowing full well that Hannah always carried gigantic handbags, bags large enough to contain a bulging photo album. "This is Jason in his kindergarten Halloween parade. He was dressed as a clown—isn't that dear? I just love old-fashioned costumes. Actually, I sewed it up for him. Such fun! And this is Terry when he lost those teeth—"

"Haven't they grown, though," the women murmured. As if that were surprising.

"Looks like he's going to be a basketball player!"

Liz knew she ought to come up with her own inanity, but her mind was blank, which in turn produced panic. Your mind wasn't allowed to go blank until you were the CEO's wife. Until you were Hannah Hackett.

Which meant, perhaps, that it was an inevitable transition, which was terrifying in itself because Liz had noticed a Phi Beta Kappa key on Hannah Hackett's charm bracelet. "Oh, that," Hannah had said when Liz commented. "That was long ago. You know, I earned my M.R.S. degree and that was that. Not that I'm saying it was a waste. Not at all. My major in college, economics, has helped me be a better wife, better at managing a household." And then she laughed, dismissing her past achievements, dismissing herself.

"But don't you—did you—do you ever think about—" Liz was a partner in a landscape design firm. If David said she had to give it up—well, that was unthinkable. He wouldn't, and if he did for some sick reason, she'd refuse.

"We decided that one career was all this family could handle, and I agreed," Hannah had said, not noticing her choice of words. "We" decided, but then "she" agreed? Who was the "we" then? Liz was sure that was the way Richard Hackett practiced domestic democracy. He was the majority, and that was that.

"You know, we moved seven times," Hannah had continued. "How could I have any kind of job? Moving, plus taking care of the house and the family—and doing it right—was my job, and it was more than full-time."

Liz understood this as a warning and polite rebuke, but something in her insisted on following the thought through. "Even now that the children are grown-up and you're in one place?" she asked. She smiled, as if all this talk was inconsequential chitchat, not at all disapproving, not at all real.

"Who has the time?" Hannah asked lightly, all wide-eyed innocence. "My calendar's full, between the household maintenance, our social obligations, the grandchildren, the dogs, and volunteering for the Foundation."

Ah, the Foundation. Second only to the grandchildren as a topic of staggeringly boring conversation. Not that it wasn't worthy—just achingly uninteresting. Trust Hannah to have found The Shadow Foundation, a hands-on, unglamorous aggregate, Liz assumed, of professional mommies like Hannah who volunteered their time cooking and reading and sewing and tutoring. Extremely worthy, extremely dull listening. Very Hannah.

"Several years ago, I committed to provide three dozen apple pies a month," Hannah said. "Two for the homeless outreach program, and one for the women's shelter. That's a lot of baking, but how could I give it up? I hope I don't sound like I'm bragging, but I've been told my apple pie is their most popular dessert. They've put my recipe in the volunteer newsletter this month. I didn't want my name involved, so I asked them to call it 'A Nonna's Apple Pie.' Nonna's Italian for grandmother, did you know that? I liked how it sounded—almost like 'anonymous,' get it? I'm not Italian and neither is apple pie, so it makes it funnier, I think. Maybe now, with the recipe in print, maybe some other people will help with the baking. Which would give me more time for the grandchildren."

Liz gave up. Anonymous's apple pies, which Liz had to admit were exceptional, went out in miniature versions in homemade Christmas baskets to all employees each year. Plus tiny tarts, miniature loaves of tea breads, and intricately designed and decorated cookies. Liz was grateful for small mercies—Hannah didn't weave the baskets herself.

Liz watched as Hannah's glance floated toward the edge of the patio, where Susie Waters and Richard Hackett appeared to be having an intense conversation. Except that Liz had spoken with Susie long enough to know that the woman couldn't spell "conversation," let alone make it. But whatever the words were that passed between the two of them, Susie Waters and Richard Hackett's body language was as easy to read as if it had Supertitles translating it in enormous print.

Hannah's glance floated on without pause, as if all she'd seen was another piece of the landscape. She was one oblivious woman. You could hardly blame Richard Hackett for seeking stimulation elsewhere, although the sort of stimulation Susie Waters could provide was not what Liz meant. But even a woman as dull as Hannah should feel a spark of indignation, Liz told herself. Or maybe Susie was welcome—a relief shift to take care of an onerous wifely duty and give Hannah more time for baking for the homeless and playing with the grandchildren.

Liz's husband flashed her a private smile that heated the air between them, and she remembered again why she was here and why it was worth playing her role. As long as she knew he was playing along with her, that they were a team and that both of them recognized the game for all it could yield and what it was, this was a beautiful island and life was fine.

Liz turned her smile on Hannah, with honest gratitude. She was glad to have been presented with this woman early on as an example of everything to be avoided. A woman who had devoted all her talents to fostering her ungrateful, philandering, negligent husband's career, a woman without an interest of her own—except for sailing, and how often did she get to do that, except on corporate getaways?—a woman whose entire life revolved around others.

I will never give up my identity the way you have, Liz silently vowed. I will never be completely dependent on my husband's earnings and my husband's pleasure in me. I will never let my interests and life and ambitions be squeezed away by meaningless corporate pleasures. Thank you, Saint Hannah, for showing me precisely how not to be.

* * *

"I am so very sorry, madam," the man in white said.

"Excuse me?" The woman stopped sharply, as if he'd accosted her. She stood still, seemingly confused and overburdened, her flowered duffel bag clutched to her chest. "I was just going to—"

"But you see, the marina is closed," the man said.

"It can't be—I have a boat reserved."

He shook his head. There were notices posted every five feet. Stupid Americans can't read, he thought. Won't. Kings of the world. Rules didn't apply to them. Signs didn't apply to them. First, the bikini girlies who didn't care what the signs said, they wanted their time on the sand. This precise stretch of sand, because it was near their overpriced rooms. But this dowdy one wasn't a bikini girlie, for sure. Dressed in baggy pants and shirt, clutching her enormous pink-flowered old-lady bag. But not old enough to be this confused, and if she was this easily muddled, if she ignored signs so completely, she shouldn't be thinking of sailing out there by herself.

"I took a boat out yesterday, too," she added as if she'd read his mind. "Right here. From this very spot."

"Yes, madam. We're so very sorry for the inconvenience, but it is forbidden for you to go on this beach today. However, there is—"

"But we—my husband's company—this is our annual—our people are entitled to all the amenities of this—"

"Madam, please. There are police all over this beach, and they're armed. You don't want to be shot, do you?"

"*Shot?* This is a resort, not a . . . . why on earth would anybody shoot me? I wouldn't even be on the beach. I'd be sailing. And why are those policemen out there now? This is a terrible time to have a practice drill."

"Madam, this is real. The authorities believe that drug smugglers have targeted this beach as a rendezvous point where they transport the stuff. A drop-off."

"I heard that last night—but that was last night!"

"Yes, madam. And this is the morning. And they are still not yet here."

"And they won't be. In broad daylight? At a resort? That's ridiculous!"

"That's all I know. Hide in clear sight, maybe. I'm not a security guard working with the police to protect you." Goddam rich bitch thinks she owns the island, owns me, he thought. He couldn't stand how he had to smile and keep the polite patter up while she told him how *her* people have these rights on *his* island.

"Now you listen here," she said. "This foolishness is making me waste a perfectly beautiful morning. I'd like to register a complaint. Not against you—you're just doing your job. If my husband had known such things happened here, we would have never—"

"Yes, madam. This is very unusual, I assure you. But it is also very regrettable." Go ahead, he said to himself. Complain because our crystal ball didn't work, so we didn't know when something was going to happen for the first time. Complain as if drug smugglers have schedules, predictable drop-off points, the way trains do. And because it's your ocean. You're paying for it, drug drop or not. "Best talk to the person at the main desk," he said.

She sighed, and then she nodded, the way maybe a queen would, and huffed off.

And here came another one with her rear hanging out in a thong and her chest barely covered at all. And all of it inside a transparent so-called jacket. He stood straighter, smoothed his mustache, and smiled. "Beach is closed today, madam," he said. "We have transportation to the neighboring beach just beyond the jetty, however, if you will go up to the main house."

She looked startled, then pouty, then shrugged and agreed. Good. He got to watch that thonged backside all the way up the hill to the main house.

She couldn't believe how easy it was. Like blowing magic powder in everybody's eyes, making them see only what you wanted them to.

The breeze fluttered Hannah Hackett's hair. She lay back, her head cushioned by her pink-flowered beach bag as she sunbathed in the late afternoon heat, eyes closed in a blissful half-daze. Arturo the sailor was as excellent as Arturo the lover. She let her mind drift back to the past several hours alone with him, in a private, hidden cove. Lovely. She was still slightly breathless. Arturo did everything brilliantly.

Even bake apple pies. Three dozen of them at a clip. And how their scent filled the house while the two of them filled the baking time.

She was free. Nobody would connect Hannah Hackett, Richard's wife, fuddy-duddy complainer at the resort's beach, with the lady who'd hired a man to sail her out of a marina halfway across the island.

Let Arturo steer the boat. Let him run the business from now on. She trusted him at the helm of anything; she didn't need to be captain of anything anymore. She was happily retiring.

There was nothing like the sea, and nothing like making sure that the island's woefully inadequate police force would be massed elsewhere. She'd done this before, on other islands and on the coasts of several small countries. That's what set her operation apart. She wasn't as greedy as her competitors, many of whom were now either dead or in some country's jail. But marriage and motherhood teaches many valuable lessons—how to make sacrifices, to defer and distract, and give a little up. She'd transferred those skills to her business and sacrificed a part of the whole. A small part.

That set them apart. That diverted the local constables. That avoided notice. That, and the fact they used sailboats midway, had no set routes, no set country, no pattern any official body could fathom. Everything depended on where Mr. Hackett's boondoggle business trips took them. Once she knew the next destination, she and Arturo worked out the logistics, part of which was sacrificing a bit of the haul to put the police on alert at the wrong place, waiting for the rest of the drop to float in while she and Arturo carried on business—and carried on—elsewhere. From their first job on, the idea worked, and it was all, always, clear sailing ahead.

She wasn't the sort to arouse suspicions. For all the years she'd run her business from exotic ports of call taking major risks, using ever-changing ruses and plans—all anybody saw was a dithering, boring middle-aged woman. Their radar was shut down, their suspicions nonexistent.

At Customs, too. Not once since her first hot flash had she been stopped or inspected. She was that most respectable and least feared of creatures—a middle-aged, middle-class woman. They waved her through.

At first it had annoyed her. She felt stripped of her power as a woman. But then she realized she could use her invisibility to her advantage, amass power through the gift of not mattering.

"You seem quiet today, my love," Arturo said. "Are you sad about giving up the business?"

"Not at all," she said. "It's time. It's your turn. And it's not like I'm giving up you."

He smiled and blew her a kiss. She wondered how long they'd last as lovers once she was no longer captain. Days? Weeks? Well, for however long. He'd set the stage for his departure by turning over the apple-pie duties to a small bakery that promised to follow his recipe. She'd known it was a gallant, quiet, first step out the door. But it had been splendid for a long time now, and all things change and move on. He'd been a particularly apt and willing learner, and not only about business. He was an elegant man, and she'd miss him.

But with or without him, she was going to enjoy every second of her retirement. Except, maybe, for one detail giving her minor qualms. "I'm a little sorry about Richard," she murmured.

"Why waste emotion on such a rude man?"

Arturo was correct. She gave up the qualm and decided to enjoy that aspect of her impending retirement, too. Richard lacked manners, flaunting his flirtation with that set of mammary glands. Right there, in front of everybody, including the glands' husband. What was he implying—that CEOs had droit du seigneur? That executives got to sleep with whomever was attached to somebody lower on the organizational chart?

Power hadn't set well with Richard. He'd been in decline since his first promotion and this shameless, public display was the final straw. She'd declared their marriage contract null and void. Until last night, she hadn't been positive about eliminating Richard, but enough was enough. He'd embarrassed her.

Besides, the fact that he'd been so blatant about it meant that he was planning to end the marriage. Too bad, and very stupid of him. She couldn't wait to see how it would be when they returned home. He'd be on the phone to his accountant—if he hadn't already been—planning to move funds and hide assets. She'd make sure he lived long enough to discover that the money had already been juggled out of sight. And the art. Everything.

Not that she'd needed any of it. She simply wanted to make a point, make him understand her powers, at least a little. As for funds, she was incredibly wealthy, enough of the money carefully laundered by virtue of its supposedly being his money. A perk of being a corporate wife. She had more than enough for herself, for her children, and for all the others she helped through her Shadow Foundation. She'd named it in honor of herself, of how effectively she was ignored at home and outside. Like that radio show she'd heard as a child, about a man who became invisible, but still saw the evil that men did. Through her organization, she funded direct assistance programs for whatever bothered her in the way people treated other people. The Foundation on whose board she sat—nominated because of her husband's position— was run by people who had no idea of its hidden and complex origins. But she'd made sure it was run the way she wanted it to be, and she'd sufficiently endowed it that it could carry on without additional funds, so she'd be retiring from that, too.

Initially, Hannah had moral qualms about running a drug cartel, but given that all the money went for the greater good, she felt she was funneling these profits away from worse hands. Aside from the trusts for her grandchildren and other people who never suspected who their benefactor was, and the art, and the real estate—much of which she rented out to deserving people at below-market rates—and the Foundation, she'd invested a great deal of the enormous revenues in start-up businesses, under the banner of Nonnamus Venture Capital. She liked the play on "Nonna," the grandma, and everybody (except businessmen, apparently) knew that Anonymous was a woman.

Via Nonnamus, the drug money was doing good both for the fledgling companies and for her. Her choices had been sound. A woman had to take care of herself.

It had all worked according to plan. Except for the Richard part. Pity, but he'd forced her hand. Luckily, her business was full of people who knew how to take care of such problems.

Besides, with Richard dead, she'd also be retiring from that most onerous of jobs, being Hannah Hackett, the woman stupid enough to be married to such a wretch of a man. Such a relief to drop that act, shed that skin, come out of the Mrs. CEO closet! Never to drag around photo albums of her grandchildren again. Never to carry pink-flowered bags. Always to talk about interesting things, or to remain silent, or to walk away from the bores.

"You're right," Hanna now said to Arturo. "Richard is a rude man."

Arturo nodded. The skin on his back was tanned to the color of cherrywood. "It is regrettable, but we must attend to the problem of your husband. When do you think?"

"How about the first time he has an assignation with Miss Breast?" Hannah asked. "On the way to his love nest." She'd long known the address of his pied-à-terre, the value of its furnishings, as well as the names of everyone who visited there with him. Nonnamus Real Estate owned the building. She enjoyed secretly being Richard's landlady, and she made sure he paid top dollar.

"On the way there?" Arturo asked. "Not even letting him satisfy his lust one last time?"

She shrugged. "Given the number of times he's already satisfied his lust in that apartment, and given how very rude he was last night—"

"He has had his quota? Enough is enough?"

"More efficient this way. And make sure it's both of them."

"The girl-woman, too?"

The addition of Susie had been spontaneous, but Hannah was a woman who was used to thinking on her feet and she trusted her instincts. "Why not?" she said. "Make it a twofer. Nobody will mourn either one of that set of boobs."

Arturo laughed at her pun. His English was as finely honed as all his other talents.

She lay in the sun, her head resting on a pink-flowered duffel bag filled with photos of her grandchildren and several dozen million dollars' worth of merchandise, her body still imprinted by Arturo's.

Life was good indeed. The future, rich and unburdened, glimmered atop the sea's shining face. Clear sailing ahead.

If You Can't Take the Heat

Sarah Shankman

Sarah Shankman's friends have so many change-of-address cards for her that they elected her president of the international organization "Women Who Move Too Much." She is currently at home in the Bay Area, or Manhattan, or possibly Santa Fe. When she's not on the road, she's writing the comic Samantha Adams crime series as well as other deliciously entertaining novels, including I Still Miss My Man but My Aim Is Getting Better.

Jane Millman stood at her kitchen counter dicing water chestnuts and peanuts. Along with creamy chunks of cooked taro, they would serve as toppings for the tapioca pudding with coconut cream she'd already prepared. The dessert, as popular in Thailand as apple pie was to Americans, was a dish Jane had learned the previous year.

Before. That was how Jane thought of everything back then. *Before.*

Now Jane wiped her chopping board clean and donned a pair of rubber gloves to chop raw taro root. It had been a long time since she'd done much more than microwave a TV dinner or heat a bowl of soup.

As Jane worked her chef's knife up and down, she realized how much she'd missed cooking. The pleasures of kitchen tasks. Pungent flavors. Now she was ready for it all again, especially Thai food, a longtime favorite, with its balance of hot, sour, sweet, bitter, and salt. The cuisine held many surprises for the Western palate, such as the way sugar added to a hot and sour sauce mellowed and married the other ingredients.

Jane thought families were like that too. People combined with the sweetness of love became an entity even better than its individual parts. The Magnificent Millmans were, for sure: Max, her beloved husband, and their precious girls, Frannie and Hope. When she was ten, Frannie had composed a family song.

Max, Jane, Frannie, and Hope
You don't like us, you're a dope
We rock, we roll, we boogie too
Just about nothing we can't do
Magnificent Millmans,
One in a jillions
Boop-boop-e-dope. Boop-boop-e-do.

At that memory, a wave of anguish lapped up and over Jane's shoulders, threatening to knock her to her knees. All grief was terrible, but this past year had been so much harder than anything she'd ever imagined. Her mother's death had been devastating, but this. . .

At first Jane thought she simply couldn't bear it, that surely she would die, that a heart could not continue to beat under the weight of so much pain. Then, one day, she realized that she'd gone an entire hour without despair. Then two. And so it went, but even yet, fifteen months since Before, there were moments like this. Then the tide of anguish would recede; Jane would continue.

And so, Jane finished chopping the raw taro and slid it with the knife's edge into a small bowl of Chinese scarlet, then washed her rubber gloves under the tap. She lined up all the bowls on her kitchen counter: a half-dozen cups of tapioca, three small blue bowls for the other condiments, the scarlet for the raw taro.

Jane was ready for her guest. She settled onto a stool at her kitchen counter. She could hardly wait.

Looking back, Jane thought, it all began that May afternoon, fifteen months earlier, a Saturday, when Natalie stopped by for coffee. Though it was hard to know. Human relationships are so complex, the ribbons of events so intertwined, others' hearts and minds so unknown (even if those hearts once beat beneath your own) that it's difficult to point your finger and say, There, then, that's the place and time my life began to unravel.

But it would do, that coffee.

Natalie, who had long lived across the street and a couple of doors down, had knocked at Jane's back door.

"Come on in!" Jane said. "I was just thinking about you."

"You're sure I'm not interrupting?" Natalie gave a nod to the food spread across the kitchen counter: garlic, green onion, cilantro, lemongrass, and a small bonfire of Thai chillies, tiny *prik kee noo.*

"No, no, I've got plenty of time. Nobody's coming till seven. Did I tell you I was taking a Thai cooking class?"

"Really? I love Thai food. Especially the hot stuff." Natalie plopped on a stool at Jane's counter where Max usually sat. A pair of the reading glasses he bought by the score marked his spot as clearly as a place card. Natalie picked up a bit of chilli along with a sprig of cilantro.

"Watch it!" Jane warned. The tiny peppers were incendiary.

But Natalie had already popped the pepper in her mouth, and a look of bliss transfigured her round face. "Yum. You know I've always been crazy for hot." Then, casually, she asked, "So, who's your company?"

"Max's brother, Ed, and his wife, Jean. The guys have some family business to sort out." Jane heard herself explaining more than she needed to. She felt guilty about not seeing Natalie more often. It had been a while since they'd had her over for dinner.

Not that Jane didn't like Natalie. Her intelligence and quick wit had always amused Jane, though her tongue had grown rather sharper since her divorce. But Natalie was a friend, a buddy, a neighbor she could count on, and Jane's elder daughter, Frannie, and Natalie's daughter, Megan, who was away at college now, had been off-and-on-again chums since they were tots.

Jane knew it was difficult for Natalie, being all alone now— particularly in this neighborhood. Their tree-bowered street in the Rockridge section of Oakland, just south of the Berkeley line, was like a throwback to the fifties. Every old house was large and well-kept, every yard was neat, and everyone was married, with children—and very caught up with their families.

Of course, after the divorce Natalie could have sold her house and moved across the bay to San Francisco. But she hadn't wanted to move in Megan's senior year, and, anyway, she did most of her work from home.

Natalie wrote a column, five days a week, for a San Francisco newspaper, about anything and everything that struck her fancy. Pretty glamorous, thought Jane, who'd been a do-gooder all her life, starting with her rabble-rousing days at Cal Berkeley. She'd become a welfare caseworker, and now she was the chief administrator of Oakland's child care services. An admirable profession, perhaps, but hardly as jazzy as Natalie's.

Natalie nibbled another bit of hot, then reached for a plate of brownies Jane had made for her ever-hungry teenagers. "May I?"

"Help yourself. There's plenty."

Natalie laughed. "Gotta keep up my weight."

Natalie was a wonderful-looking woman, with an impish face and dark curly hair marked with a blaze of white, but she had put on more than a little poundage since Jack's desertion. She was forever nibbling, taking a bite of this or that. More than once Jane had heard Natalie's justification: "You know what Catherine Deneuve said. At a certain age, a woman can have her face or she can have her figure, but not both."

Jane wondered about that. At forty-six, she was only a year younger than Natalie, but so far had refused to give up the good fight against middle-age spread. She liked working out and visited her gym regularly. On the other hand, she did have more wrinkles than Natalie. Maybe there was something to keeping those cheeks plumped.

Also, Jane told herself, Natalie's job kept her young. Researching her column gave her entree to all kinds of worlds.

Jane said, "I loved that series you wrote last week on bumper stickers. It was so funny. *Imagine using your turn signals*. It's just amazing how you can take one little thing like that and spin it and spin it. I don't know how you do that."

"Yep, that's me." Natalie broke a second brownie in half. "Natalie, the Queen of Trivia."

"No, no, I think it's *wonderful*, what you do."

Natalie shrugged. "I guess. You wouldn't believe how hard it is sometimes to come up with something to write about."

"I'm sure. But look at how you get to follow your fancy. You have such freedom."

Natalie frowned. "You know, Jane, sometimes there's such a thing as too *much* freedom. Since Jack left and Megan's off at school, my life has no structure. I feel like I have to invent it all over again every day. You know, make it up? Things just aren't automatic like they used to be."

No, Jane thought, they wouldn't be. One of the things she'd loved about being part of a couple from the very beginning was the framework a relationship gave to life. Having a partner meant you had a schedule, endless things to do, and then with the kids, *too* many things.

"I know it must be hard," Jane said, thinking, not for the first time, how gifted Natalie was at laying on guilt. "On the other hand, you can take classes, travel, do whatever you want." Jane was thinking that if *she* were in Natalie's shoes, she'd be off on that tour of Thailand her cooking teacher, Kasma, was leading.

Natalie didn't seem to hear her. "I've been thinking maybe I ought to sell the house and move into the city after all. Of course, Megan doesn't want me to, but then, how often is she going to be home? Aren't you lucky, you and Max, that you'll have Hope for another year, after Frannie's gone?"

"Yes, we are. Max and I are very lucky." Jane had had difficulty conceiving, and after taking fertility drugs had feared quintuplets, but instead, her daughters had been born, blam-blam, twelve months apart. Healthy, beautiful, and smart. "Very lucky."

"Now, of course," Natalie said, "I wish I'd had more, a houseful of kids. Maybe Jack would have felt guiltier. Maybe he wouldn't have felt the need to run off and *marry* a child." Natalie's mouth twisted with bitterness.

It was that, Jane thought, later, *that* last comment which made her reach into her bag of conversational topics and come up with Frannie. She was feeling sorry for Natalie, and at the same time, guilty about her own happiness, so she offered up Frannie as proof that her life wasn't perfect.

It hadn't felt like sacrifice at the time. Jane had wanted to discuss her concern about the business with Frannie with someone, but not Max, not right then. He was so preoccupied with the way things had been going with his practice, medicine being what it was these days, that Jane didn't want to bother him. And though Natalie had her quirks, she had always been a good sounding board. Wasn't that what women friends were best at: listening to one another puzzling and repuzzling life's everyday vicissitudes? Listening and offering sympathy? And advice, if asked?

Do you think I should get my hair cut?

What should I do if he's seeing her again?

Should I tell her she's really being a bitch, or let it go?

What would women do without their friends? Without girl talk, that safety zone they share with women they trust?

So Jane leapt in. "Double your kids isn't always double your pleasure, Natalie. To tell you the truth, I've been plenty worried about Frannie lately."

"Frannie? You're kidding."

Natalie's skepticism was understandable. After all, blithe, blonde Frannie was a star. She'd be graduating at the top of her class in a couple of weeks. She was a state champion distance runner. And she'd won admission to Yale with a partial scholarship, which had amazed even Jane.

Hope was also a great student, though she was having a rockier passage through adolescence than her older sister. As Max joked, "My younger daughter doesn't speak Adult, though her French is flawless and her Italian's not bad."

"I found something in Frannie's room," Jane blurted, and then, the moment the words left her lips, she wished she could take them back. It was as if she could see a newspaper headline in banner type, blaring out the news that should have been kept in the bosom of the family. But now it was too late. There they were, her words, cast into the wind.

Natalie's gaze was bright, avid, like a bird's. "What kind of thing? Are you talking about drugs?"

"No, no." Jane shook her head emphatically. Though she'd wondered that herself. Of course, she'd imagined a million possibilities, tried out all sorts of scenarios in the past few days. "I feel awful," she said, not exactly answering Natalie's question, not answering it at all, really, "as if I were snooping."

Jane hadn't been snooping, not the first time anyway. Nor the second, really. Okay, the second more than the first, her suspicions having been piqued, but the first time was perfectly innocent.

Jane had been looking for a favorite silver pin, an art deco design with a chubby angel atop it. The pin wasn't valuable, not in monetary terms, but her dear friend Cecilia had given it to her, a parting gift before she and her husband had been transferred back to Cleveland. Frannie had a habit of borrowing her things without asking. Jane had spoken to her about it more than once.

"Sure, sure, Mom," Frannie had said. "But if you're not using something at the time, why *can't* I?"

"Because it's not yours. Because it's *mine*."

"Well, God, I guess."

But Frannie had never really understood, and in a way, Jane was proud of Frannie's lack of concern about material possessions. Frannie and her friends had always shared their belongings and frequently wore one another's clothes. "It's very *Berkeley*," Max had teased Jane. "You raised her to share and share alike, but you forgot to tell her you didn't mean *your* stuff."

Not the stuff I *care* about, Jane had told herself, as she'd stepped into Frannie's room to search for the pin. I just don't want her to lose something I treasure.

Jane had never been great at absorbing loss, and the disproportionate despair she was feeling at the time over misplacing even the smallest item—a paring knife, a sock—she could lay at the recent death of her mother, Frances. Since that, the loss of one thing was the loss of all. She'd wept over a straw hat left behind at a picnic.

Jane knew that there were those (a different breed of cat) who blithely cut their losses and moved on. She'd recently read a magazine piece in which movie mogul Barry Diller talked about his defeat in the battle for control of Paramount. "They won. We lost. Next." Unthinkable. After her mom, Jane didn't want to let go of another single thing in her life. She knew, intellectually, that she was trying to hold back death, and that was impossible. But the knowing didn't make things any better. She wanted her loved ones, Max and the girls and their dog, Bingo, to live forever. She wanted everything—her keys, her gloves, her jewelry, her memory, her life—to stay just where it belonged.

Jane looked up. Natalie was still waiting for an answer. What had she found in Frannie's room when she was looking for her pin?

"So, anyway, I fought my way through the girl debris to search the top of her dresser, but the pin wasn't there. Sometimes Frannie actually puts things in her jewelry box in the top drawer, so I took a quick peek in there." *Going through her daughter's bureau.* It was such a cliché. And such a no-no.

"I used to do it all the time when Megan was still home," Natalie said, matter-of-factly, tapping another pepper onto her tongue. "I mean, you have to know what your kids are up to. It's not like they're going to tell you anything."

Jane was shocked. "No, no, I don't do that. Never. Just, this one time, and . . ."

Natalie shrugged. "So, what was it? Birth control? Frannie's seventeen, Jane. You ought to be glad that she's careful."

Jane shook her head emphatically. She didn't want to even skirt a discussion of Frannie's sex life or lack of it with Natalie. Or with anyone, for that matter. "I didn't find anything in her dresser. I just took the peek in her jewelry box. Then I thought, Maybe she's left the pin on a blouse or a jacket. So I opened her closet."

"Jesus. She didn't have a boy stashed in there, did she?"

Jane had to laugh, and the laughter felt good. The hand of anxiety that had been clutching her gut released its grip and she could breathe more freely. "No, no boy." She laughed again at the idea of the imaginary boy's frightened face, his goofy grin as he tried to explain. But then her mind's eye fastened on the memory of what she'd seen hanging there, and her stomach tightened once more. "It was a skirt."

"A *skirt*?"

"A brand-new skirt. Short. Black. With the sales tag. A hundred and sixty dollars."

"Wow! So, what'd you think?"

Jane shrugged. "I didn't know what to think. It wasn't something that Frannie would have bought. Certainly not without consulting me, not at that price. She doesn't have that kind of money. Her Saturday job at the card store pays peanuts."

"So, did you ask her?"

"Not right away. I guess I was hoping that she'd bring it up."

"Because you didn't want her to know you'd gone in her things?"

Jane nodded. That was it, precisely. She'd felt guilty. Plus she simply hadn't known how to broach the subject.

"How long did you wait?"

"A couple of days."

"And then?"

Jane was about to answer when they heard, "Hi, Mom. Hi, Natalie." It was Hope, her dark curls a tangle, her voluptuous sixteen-year-old body camoflauged by a baggy polo shirt and torn jeans. Hope opened the refrigerator and stuck her head inside.

"Hi, honey!" Jane said brightly. "What's up?"

Hope only shrugged. She obviously felt that she'd already said way too much. But it took her a while to figure out what she wanted for a snack, and then Max called from his Saturday run to the hardware store. He needed Jane's input on choosing a color of paint for his office. Jane had to scoot.

The very next afternoon, Natalie called. "I made this killer apple tart from a recipe I found in a magazine at the doctor's office. If you don't come over and help me, I'm going to eat the whole thing myself."

Jane didn't really have the time, but she still felt bad about not having included Natalie in their dinner the night before. They really had had a wonderful visit with Ed and Jean.

And the tart *was* delicious. "Fabulous," said Jane.

"Thanks." Then Natalie leaned across the table. "So, did Frannie tell you about the skirt?"

It was then that Jane realized that it wasn't her company Natalie was hungry for. Nor was fear of her own gluttony her motivation. It was Natalie's curiosity that needed to be satisfied. But Jane didn't mind. Not really. Now that she'd unburdened half the story, she figured she might as well finish the tale and gain her friend's input.

"No," she said, "Frannie never did mention it. I waited until I couldn't stand it anymore, and then I finally said something." Jane shook her head, remembering. "It was bad."

"Frannie *stole* the skirt?"

"No, no. She said she had no idea where it came from. That it had simply appeared in her closet."

"What!"

"That was my response. Then, too, Frannie was upset because I'd gone into her things. And even more upset that I hadn't broached the subject right away. 'You didn't say anything because you thought I stole it, right, Mom?'"

Natalie said, "But didn't she think it was possible that you'd bought her the skirt? That it was a surprise? That she ought to have *thanked* you?"

"Natalie, when is the day I'm going to spend that kind of money on an article of clothing for a seventeen-year-old girl?"

"Appeared, huh? Just appeared? That's what Frannie said?"

"From thin air."

"Did you talk to Hope? Is it possible this was her idea of a practical joke?"

"I tried. She just gave me The Look and stomped out of the room."

"How about Max?"

"Well, I didn't want to involve him, but last night, I cracked. You know what he said? 'How can a foot of fabric cost that kind of money?'"

Jane and Natalie laughed. Men.

"So what do you think?" Natalie said.

"Not a clue. I've never known Frannie to shoplift. Except once, when she was a little bitty thing, and she walked out of a store with a Barbie. I made her take it back and apologize. You know, she has a pretty strict moral code."

"Megan took a salad spinner from Macy's when she was six. She got as far as the elevator. She said she liked the way it went 'round." Natalie paused. "Now, Jane, do I remember correctly, that you said the skirt was the *first* thing? Does that mean you found something else?"

Jane had been half-hoping that Natalie would forget. But here it was. She nodded. "I'm afraid so. Pearl earrings. Frannie has a pair of her own. Both girls do. But these were black."

"Black pearls. Ooh-la-la. Very sophisticated."

"I know. That's why they stood out in the mess of stuff on top of Frannie's dresser."

"You went back and looked in her room again?"

"Not exactly. It was more like, I don't know, it sounds stupid, but I couldn't stop thinking about the skirt, and it was as if I'd put myself in some sort of trance, and I was thinking, Okay, I'll pretend I'm the person who put the skirt in Frannie's closet. And I was standing there, in the doorway of her room, trying to imagine that, trying to *be* that person, a part of me standing back and trying to *see* that person, when I spied the earrings."

"And?"

Jane shrugged. "Frannie went ballistic. She said she hadn't even noticed them. She said that somebody is trying to make her look like a thief, trying to drive her crazy, and she doesn't know who or why. She's doubly furious that I found the earrings. To tell

you the truth, I'm pretty mad at myself. I shouldn't have been in
her room."

"But you weren't snooping. Not really."

"I'm not sure what the hell I was doing. I want to believe
Frannie, of course. And I do. She's always been such a grand kid.
Then I find myself thinking, Why would she do this now? Why
would she go crazy now?"

"Well, maybe it's a weird form of senioritis. A temporary
thing. Maybe she's freaked about leaving home, going off to Yale.
Everyone's made such a big deal about it. Y-A-L-E. Maybe she
feels like pressured, is afraid she won't do well, and she's just acting out."

"I've thought of that and more. I stay up nights trying one
story, then another. And Hope's gone crazy too. I asked her about
the earrings, and, well, you know this stage she's going through.
'Search me,' she screamed, 'if you think I'm a thief!' Then she
stormed into her room and started pulling out clothes, books . . . .
She threw that pitiful macramé thing she wears sometimes as a
necklace on the floor. 'Look!' she said. 'Go through everything.'
It was awful."

"The sibling rivalry thing doesn't help."

"I know. That's never changed, since they were tots. We
thought because they were so close in age that it wouldn't happen, but it's always been there, in one way or another. That's one
thing, Natalie, to be said for having a single child."

Natalie nodded around a mouthful of her second slice of tart.

"But, on the other hand, in the past few years, Hope's pretty
much screened out Frannie. She doesn't pay much attention to
her sister. She has her own friends, her own life."

"Nonetheless, Frannie's getting into Yale has to have made
some impression on her. Don't you think Hope's jealous? It seems
natural that she would be."

"I don't know," Jane shrugged. "Hope's grades are just as great as Frannie's ever were. Actually, she's been talking about med school, thinking about colleges with good premed programs. Harvard, maybe. I hope she doesn't set her sights too high."

"On the other hand, she might make it."

"Yep. Of course, another option she's considering is bagging college and hitchhiking to New York to earn her keep playing guitar in the subways."

"Oh, God! Please, anything but New York." Natalie's Megan was in school there, but she seemed to be majoring in the bright lights of the big city. "So, what are you going to do?"

"I don't know. Keep our fingers crossed, I guess. Pray that the whole thing goes back to wherever it came from."

It was a couple of days later that the tiny box, glowing with Tiffany's distinctive light blue, showed up on Frannie's bed.

"Look at this!" Frannie shrieked, shoving the box under Jane's nose as if it were poop and Jane the offending pooch. "Where the hell did this come from? Why is this happening to me?"

Jane didn't bother frowning at Frannie's language. She wondered the same thing. Where the hell *had* the box come from? Why *was* this happening?

"What is it?" she asked the furious Frannie. "Show me."

With trembling hands, Frannie opened the box and removed the silver bangle bracelet with the tip of one finger, as if she really didn't want to touch it.

"Jesus," Jane breathed. "Still in the box. You think it's a gift?"

"Precisely." Frannie spit out the words. "A graduation gift. Everybody's been getting this exact bracelet."

"So? Maybe somebody gave you one, too."

"Sure, Mom. One of my best friends thought it would be a really cool idea to give me this bracelet, unwrapped, with no card. To just leave it on my damned bed!" Then Frannie dissolved in tears. She couldn't stop crying, and her sobs ripped at Jane's heart.

"I don't know what to do," Jane now said to Natalie across the table.

"Have you considered calling the police?"

"What could I say to them, Natalie? 'Someone is coming into my house and leaving my elder daughter gifts. And we want them to stop.'"

"I see what you mean. But, on the other hand, maybe they know where the stuff is coming from. I mean, maybe someone's reported it missing."

"Perhaps. I don't know."

"Have you talked with Hope again?"

"I had to. I've been trying to think about this logically. It's hard because, for one thing, you know we've always left our back door open; *anyone* could come in. But I'm trying to zero in on the kids who have regular access to our house. Frannie's circle of friends is small and incredibly tight. It's hard to imagine any of them doing anything to make her look bad. So I sat Hope down and asked about *her* friends, especially Heather, who's been so needy since her parents divorced." Jane caught herself. Damn. She hadn't meant to say that. Megan had gone through a rough time at the beginning of Natalie and Jack's divorce. In fact, she'd run away.

Natalie waved away her apology. "So what about Heather? What did Hope say?"

"That it might make sense if things were being stolen *from* Frannie. But the other way around? Why would her friends, Heather or anyone, want to *give* things to Frannie? And Hope's got a point, you know. This whole thing's so crazy. What does it *mean?*"

"I think that's what you have to figure out, Jane. Either Frannie's taking these things and has made up this whole scenario to cover her tracks, or someone is trying to make it look that way, trying to make Frannie look like a thief. Now, who would want to do *that*? And why?"

Monday evening, Jane called Natalie. "We know who the bracelet belongs to."

"I'm coming right over," said Natalie. Within minutes she was sitting at Jane's counter, watching her chop onions—or trying to. She was so upset, it would be better, she knew, if she put down the knife.

"Lisa Broadhurst. It's her bracelet."

"She's in Frannie's class?"

Jane nodded. "A friend of Frannie's. Not a close friend, but a friend. Frannie said everyone at school is talking about someone having stolen Lisa's bracelet, and Lisa's very distressed, of course."

"How about the skirt and the pearl earrings? Were those hers too?"

"Frannie didn't know. And she couldn't very well ask, could she? I mean, not without incriminating herself. *Incriminating!* Jesus, I sound like Court TV." Jane dropped her head into her hands. "Lisa's parents have called the police."

"Did Frannie tell Lisa that she has the bracelet?"

"No. She couldn't figure out how to do that. 'What am I going to say, Mom? How am I going to tell her? She's going to think I took it, that I went into her house and took it.'"

"Well, she has a point there," said Natalie. "How did you advise her?"

"I told her to try to calm down. To wait. I called Max at the office, and he's coming home early, and we're going to sit down and talk this thing through." Jane paused. "Max thinks we ought to have Ed join us."

"Ed, his brother? The lawyer?"

"He's a criminal attorney." Jane shook her head. "*Criminal.* Can you believe this? It's like some kind of nightmare. Poor Frannie. Oh, God. My poor little girl. I feel so awful for her. I wish it were happening to me. I wish I could step into her shoes."

"We all feel that way," Natalie soothed. "Mothers always feel like that when bad things happen to their kids."

Jane rose early the next morning, before the rest of her family, as she did every day. She liked to have a little quiet time with her coffee and the paper and gain the use of herself before the day's onslaught.

This particular day was one she was not looking forward to, and she was having difficulty focusing on the paper.

They'd decided, in their family powwow the night before, that Frannie, Jane, and Max would go over to the Broadhursts' house early that evening. Jane was to call the Broadhursts and make the appointment for the three of them to try to explain the inexplicable.

"What am I going to say?" Frannie had wailed.

"We'll just tell them what happened, sweetie," said Max. "We'll lay out the facts. We'll tell them the truth."

"No matter what, they're going to think I stole Lisa's bracelet," said Frannie. "What else could they think?"

"We'll take them the bracelet. We'll tell them our story. That's all we can do."

"Everyone at school's going to be whispering about me." Frannie had stopped moaning. Her tone had grown icy. Stoic. This attitude hurt Jane even more than her daughter's distress.

Frannie had always had that capability, to shut down and ignore pain. It had served her well as a long-distance runner. When other girls fell by the wayside, their outer limits met, Frannie could simply shut the door on her fatigue, the screaming in her legs, her lungs, her gut, and soldier on. Jane had wondered from time to time what this toughness, this capacity for insensibility, said about Frannie. But she and Max had decided that Frannie actually felt not too little, but too much, that the thick walls she threw up were for protection. Frannie had a very tender heart.

"I think we're within our rights to ask for the Broadhursts' discretion," said Max. "I remember meeting Pete Broadhurst when we were having that brouhaha with the zoning commission. He seemed like a reasonable man."

"Everyone'll know." Frannie stared straight ahead, her mouth tight, her face stony with resignation. "All Lisa has to do is tell one person, and everyone will know."

"Oh, honey," Jane said, and tried to draw her daughter close, but Frannie could not be comforted. And Jane knew that she was probably right. People would know. People would talk. But maybe they'd be incredibly lucky. . . . Oh, God, she thought, if only she could do this for Frannie. If only she, with her years of perspective, the nonchalance that age and experience bring, could shoulder this burden.

Now Jane stood, poured herself another cup of coffee, then flipped the entertainment section of the paper over to the back page to take a look at Natalie's column. She usually found something there that made her chuckle, and God knows, today she needed a little cheering up.

If Only I Could Step Into Her Shoes, the headlines read.

Jane blinked. Surely not . . .

"If only I could step into her shoes" was also the beginning of the first sentence of Natalie's column. Then the piece laid out the particulars of the Millman family's dilemma. The mysterious appearance of the skirt. The black pearl earrings. The silver bracelet from Tiffany's.

Jane raised one hand to her mouth as she read on with growing horror. "No," she cried through her fingers. "God, please, no."

Natalie hadn't named their names. She hadn't said, "Jane and Max Millman and their two lovely daughters, Frannie, 17, and Hope, 16, of 1212 Pineapple Street, in the Rockridge neighbor-

hood of Oakland . . ." But she might as well have, as far as anyone who knew them was concerned. Frannie's schoolmates would
definitely know. Their parents were reading these very words,
this very moment, calling to their children, "Hey, guys, look at
this."

And she had quoted Jane, word for word. Jane could hear her
own voice as she read, the words swimming there in black and
white before her: *I want to believe (her), of course. And I do. She's
always been such a grand kid. Then I find myself thinking. Why would
she do this now? Why would she go crazy now?*

Word for word.

How did Natalie do that? How could she remember?

*It's like some kind of nightmare. Poor (daughter). Oh, God. My poor
little girl. I feel so awful for her. I wish it were happening to me. I wish
I could step into her shoes.*

Had Natalie tape-recorded their conversation? Had she worn a
wire like that hideous Linda Tripp? Was Natalie the same kind of
traitor as that despicable woman, the same brand of Judas, who
would betray another woman, her *girlfriend*? Would she sell out
Jane and her family, neighbors, people she'd known for years,
whose kitchen table she'd put her feet under, for a goddamned
column, to fill a space, for an easy day's work? But here they were,
Natalie's neatly constructed sentences and paragraphs which
went on to deduce—and this seemed to be the point of the column—that parents of "privileged children" often were blind to
what their kids were up to.

Privileged? Yes, Frannie and Hope were, but no more than
Natalie's Megan. And they weren't thieves.

Then Jane felt her gorge rise, and she thought it possible that
she was going to be sick, that she was going to spew all over this
vile piece of fish wrap.

Jane swallowed hard and forced herself to focus. There had to
be some explanation. More important, there had to be some way

to stop people from reading this. Some way to protect Frannie. Jane felt as if fires were raging all around her, but she was frozen in her chair. She didn't know which way to turn, what to do.

Then the phone rang, and she lurched for it. "Yes?" she gasped.

"Jane? It's Ed." Max's brother. The criminal attorney. The sweet man, the brother-in-law whom she'd always loved, who'd brought his wisdom, his considered advice, his sense of fair play to their kitchen table the night before.

The same kitchen where Natalie had sat and nibbled at her family's very soul.

"Jane," he managed again, then faltered.

"I've seen it."

"Goddamnit!" She could see him, shaking his head. "What about Frannie?"

"No, not yet. I don't think she's up yet."

"Listen, sweetheart, I'm on my way over. That bitch, Natalie. Why would she do this? You know, she makes it sound like Frannie really is a thief. I want you to know she's not going to get away with this, Jane. We're going after her, sweetie. Big time."

"What difference does it make?" Jane heard herself say, her words sounding very far off. "The damage is done. My baby's going to suffer, Ed. She's going to bleed."

"I know, darling. And I'm so sorry. So very sorry. Listen, put my brother on the phone for a minute, will you?"

Jane handed the phone off to Max, who was just then stepping into the kitchen for his coffee. He hadn't seen the column, of course, and Jane stood and watched his face as Ed explained, watched the face she'd loved for so long register puzzlement, then disbelief, then twist with fury.

"I'm going to kill that woman," he said to Jane as he hung up the phone, his words even more frightening for the softness of his voice. And then he reached for Jane and pulled her to his sweet chest.

"Kill who?" said Frannie, stumbling into the kitchen in the boxer shorts and T-shirt she slept in.

Hope was right behind her. "It's *whom*," she said, in her best Little-Sister-Knows-It-All voice. "Kill whom?" And then, making a face at her parents' embrace, "Do you guys have to do that?"

"Let me see it," Frannie said when Jane and Max had finished trying to explain. (As if they could explain.) "Just let me see it."

"Now, darling. . . ," Max said, but Frannie wouldn't be put off. She wouldn't be sidetracked. She was their straight-ahead girl. *Give me the facts, and then I'll deal with it.*

They stood, frozen, as Frannie read Natalie's column, slowly, from top to bottom, taking in every word. Hope read over her sister's shoulder. "Jesus, Frannie," she said.

But Frannie didn't hear Hope. Frannie was already moving.

Frannie the swift, Frannie the fleet, Frannie who had placed first in state in AA girls' long distance, was out the kitchen door.

Jane didn't even pause to think. In her pajamas and the leopard-print driving shoes she wore as slippers, she was hot on her daughter's trail. "Frannie!" she called as her long-limbed daughter sped down the sidewalk, past their neighbors' houses, past white roses and late azaleas and pink rhododendron. "Frannie, wait!"

She's headed for Natalie's, Jane thought. She's going to throttle Natalie.

But her firstborn daughter, as lightning-quick in her bare feet as any Ethiopian runner, her slender legs flashing beneath her red-and-green plaid shorts, ran on past Natalie's house, on down the sidewalk and turned up, toward the hills.

Ah, thought Jane. Then probably she'd turn north toward Tilden Park, where she'd run her whole girlhood. Maybe Frannie would find some salve for her pain on those familiar paths.

That's good, thought Jane. Frannie'll go that way, and then I get to kill Natalie all by myself. With my bare hands. With my teeth. I'll show her how bloody a mother's rage can be. A mama grizzly defending her cubs will have nothing on me.

But still, she wanted Frannie to stop. She wanted to comfort her child, to hold her to her breast, to rock her to and fro. "Frannie!" she called, a half-block behind her daughter now. Jane was keeping up better than she'd have thought, her sweaty hours in the gym paying off. "Frannie, honey, stop!"

But Frannie took no heed. Maybe she didn't hear her mother calling. Frannie ran and she ran, flew faster and faster up the hill toward Broadway.

"Frannie! Please!" Jane cried. Very soon she wouldn't be able to speak. She was running out of breath. Her side hurt. She couldn't keep up this pace.

Ahead, Frannie stretched way out. Even on these broken sidewalks, zigging around old trees, she ran with exquisite form. Her coach would have been proud of her as she ran from the hurt, ran from the pain, tried to escape the humiliation that she knew was barreling down on her. Frannie was in overdrive, full-out, nothing held back, burning gas. Brakes were out of the question. Brakes were a joke. Brakes weren't even a possibility for Frannie Millman on this fine morning in May, two weeks before she was to step up on the stage and deliver her valedictory and leap into the bright and shiny future of the young and blessed.

On Frannie ran, a fresh bay wind at her back, wings on her heels, and fury in her heart. Frannie didn't pull up, she didn't slow, she didn't even acknowledge Broadway, the busy thoroughfare, when she hit it. Frannie, the valedictorian, the golden girl, ran, ignoring that most primary lesson her mother had taught. That cardinal rule: Look both ways before you cross.

The driver of the silver Mercedes never even saw Jane's darling daughter—fleet of feet, keen of mind, and sweet; Jesus, that child had been so loving in her ways—until she tumbled like a crazy gymnast over and up his windshield. He hadn't even had time to register the ka-thunk before Frannie's fatal somersault began. He never had the chance to see how beautiful Frannie was without the scarlet gushing from her mouth, without that terribly wrong angle of her slender neck.

Now, it was September, over a year later. Fifteen interminable months, to be exact. Jane and Max had just returned from getting Hope settled in at Stanford, only an hour south down the Peninsula.

Hope had applied for early admission and had snagged it. Jane and Max were thrilled for her, of course, but they were doubly glad that, in lieu of an East Coast school, she'd chosen to stay so close to home. "I want to, Mom," she'd said, "for all of us."

They'd had such a terrible time. People say that the death of a child is the fiercest loss, and Jane had certainly learned the truth of that. They also say that such a death frequently rips through a marriage like a tornado, that there's so much pain that the center of a union, no matter how strong, simply cannot hold. Max and Jane were also testament to that view.

A psychiatrist friend of Max's said that they should have another child, that a new life to nurture would be their salvation.

"Is she crazy?" Jane said. "I'm much too old. And I wouldn't if I could."

"We could adopt," said Max, late one night when they'd been up, fighting. They hardly ever used to fight. "I want you to seriously consider it, Jane. If you won't, then I'm going to think about leaving you once Hope's off to school."

Since that conversation, Jane had been thinking about it quite a lot. And she was almost there. Not a baby, of course, but a youngster who needed them as much as they needed her. Or him. "What do you think about a little boy?" she'd said to Max just this morning. "You still up for teaching somebody how to play catch?" Max's answering grin was the best thing Jane had seen since that awful morning, Frannie's last morning.

It had been only hours after Frannie's funeral that Bethany Marks had fessed up to the thefts. She was a strange girl, lovely enough to be a model, but badly troubled. Obsessed, it turned out. Bethany seemed incapable of doing anything but hurting herself and those around her. Bethany explained that she shoplifted the skirt and the pearls and then took the bracelet from Lisa Broadhurst and "gave" the things to Frannie, skipping classes and walking in the Millmans' unlocked back door, because she wanted to be part of Frannie's crowd. Actually, she said, she knew in her heart that Frannie was meant to be her best friend. She had thought that Frannie would figure out that the gifts were from her. She had just known that Frannie was going to call her, any day, and tell her that she loved her. She'd waited and waited for the call that never came.

What was there to say to that? You could no more blame Bethany than you could blame the rain.

Natalie, of course, was a different story. Natalie was not a troubled youngster. Natalie, Natalie, was the Judas, the traitor, the user, the murderer who, to Jane's mind, had taken their beloved Frannie as surely as if she'd put a gun to Frannie's head.

Not that Natalie had thought that Frannie would die, of course. But what exactly *had* she thought as she'd sat and typed that column, as she'd pushed the button to *Send*?

Jane didn't know. No one knew. Natalie had packed up and vanished within hours after she heard about Frannie. She had never returned to the Bay Area, as far as they'd heard. An agent had sold Natalie's house, completely furnished, to a nice man from Atlanta.

What Jane did know—what she counted on, what kept her going—was that one day, one day, dear God, Natalie would sit in her kitchen once more. Sooner or later, Jane was certain of it, down to the marrow of her bones, Natalie would come forward.

The guilt which Natalie had been so talented at instilling in others would turn on her and chew her liver until she would have to seek forgiveness.

Her ego would demand forgiveness.

Ah, yes. Natalie would come to Jane on bended knee and pour out the sorrow of her heart. In carefully constructed sentences. In perfect paragraphs. It would be a masterpiece, Natalie's plea for absolution. And Jane would somehow be transformed into a priest, a Father O'Leary, or better yet, an angel of mercy, who would give Natalie her penance, then perhaps lash her about the head and shoulders a few times so she would have the proof. "Look," Natalie could say. "Look at my bruises." Then Natalie could dine on her deliverance, feast on forgiveness, gorge on her pardon.

Yes, Jane knew, someday, one day, Natalie would appear, hungry for Jane's mercy.

Then, this very morning, it had happened. In the fullness of time, Jane's desire had borne fruit.

Jane had been in her office, at her desk, about to make a call, when, suddenly, she was seized by a shudder. *Earthquake!* she thought at first. Then, *Someone's walking on my grave. No, Frannie's.* She stared at her hand for a long moment, poised above the phone.

Then the phone pealed.

And Jane smiled, for then she knew—her blood sang, her very corpuscles shouted Hosannah!—what that frisson had meant.

Natalie.

"Jane, will you please talk with me? Please?"

"Oh, yes." Jane didn't miss a beat. "I will."

They made the arrangement: Natalie, who said she was in town for only one day, was to arrive at the house about five-thirty, before Max got home. "Come to the back door," Jane said. "I'll be in the kitchen."

Jane left the office early and went food shopping in Oakland's Chinatown. She picked up long slender eggplant, ran her fingers through bean sprouts, marveled at the vitality of the fresh produce. What, she wondered, had she and Max and Hope survived on?

Ashes. Bitters. Rue.

She decided on the menu as she shopped. The tapioca pudding was a given; she'd long know what sweet she'd serve. She'd start with the hot and sour shrimp soup that Max so loved. A green curry with chicken. Steamed jasmine rice, of course.

Now the prep was done. Jane sat and waited, the pudding, which she'd made first, cooling on her counter. The water chestnuts, peanuts, taro chopped. The parade of custard cups, blue bowls, the one scarlet.

Here it came. The knock at the back door. Soft, Tentative.

"Come in," Jane called.

And there stood Natalie, the white blaze in her dark curls wider, but otherwise much the same. Natalie was still plump, even chubbier than before. Jane hadn't thought that crow would be so fattening.

"Come in," she said, pulling the door closed behind Natalie, throwing the dead bolt. She seated her old friend at her accustomed stand at the counter. She poured her a cup of coffee.

Natalie's coffee was still steaming when she began her chant of mea culpa. Her words tumbled and rolled. *Sorry. What was I thinking? Seemed at the time. Never make it up to you. Forgiveness. Sleepless nights, Horrible. Wracked with guilt. Dear Frannie . . .*

"Yes," Jane said. "No." She murmured, cooed, made the kind of sounds one might use to soothe a baby. "Go on. Yes, I know."

Finally, it was her precious daughter's name, obscene on this woman's lips, that was Jane's cue. "Yes, yes, well. . . ," she said, then with one hand offered forth the soothing sweet, the comfort of tapioca. Baby food.

"Oh, Jane," Natalie cried. So touched, so grateful.

Jane pushed the tapioca closer, then followed with the four bowls of condiments. Three blue, one the scarlet of danger. "For texture," she said. "Crunch. The raw taro—that's the red bowl—is very hot."

Natalie smiled. Jane remembered.

"Actually," said Jane, "it's probably too hot, now that I think of it." She laid a cautionary hand on the bright bowl. "Here. Let me take it away."

"No, no." Natalie clutched at the raw taro.

"This is *really* hot," Jane insisted. "You won't like it. Just have the peanuts, the cooked taro, and the water chestnuts. They'll be fine."

Jane didn't elaborate any further, though she could have. She'd done quite a bit of research on taro. The tuber, in its cooked form, is a popular starch in Asia, sometimes known as poi. Raw taro, however, is highly poisonous. Jane's Thai cooking teacher had once pointed out the tuber in the market, on a field trip, and casually mentioned its danger. Jane hadn't thought much about it at the time, but later, after Frannie's death, all sorts of things, surprising things, dark things, had floated up.

How dangerous? Jane had wondered. Highly acrid, she'd learned from her library research. The milky juice is used on poison darts and for killing tigers. Almost insipid to the taste at first, the ingested root then produces an intense burning and itching to the mouth and throat. Severe gastroenteritis follows, and a massive inflammation of the mucous membranes, which, if not treated immediately, results in cramps, convulsions, and death.

Natalie grasped the scarlet bowl.

Okay. Jane shrugged as Natalie dumped half the raw taro into her pudding. She stirred twice, then spooned it all down, licking her lips. "Yummy," she said. "And not hot at all. You never developed much tolerance for heat, Jane, but you're still a wonderful cook."

Jane smiled, then watched as a frown crossed Natalie's face. Natalie lifted a hand to her mouth. She blinked rapidly, and the tears began to stream. Her mouth opened and closed convulsively. Before Natalie could manage more than a howl, the phone rang.

"Excuse me," said Jane, picking up the cordless phone and turning toward the door to the dining room. "I won't be but a moment."

She'd asked Max to call her about quarter of six, before he left the office, to see if she needed him to pick up anything on the way home. A roasted chicken. Deli food. The sort of thing they'd been subsisting on since Before.

"Hey!" she said, raising her voice a bit over Natalie's wheezing and thumping. It was time to leave the kitchen now, much as she hated to. "Just a sec," she said to Max as she walked into the dining room, reaching with one hand behind her to shove a dining chair beneath the doorknob. The other door out of the kitchen, she'd secured when Natalie arrived. She patted the key in her pocket, the key to the kitchen door's dead bolt.

Locking the barn door too late—she knew that's what Max thought every time she did it. Too late to keep out Bethany, too late for Frannie, but not this time. No, not this time.

"Guess what?" she said to Max. "I'm making Thai food. Yes! I know! Shrimp soup. Green curry. Tapioca pudding. Yes! No, no wine. But pick up some beer, okay? Yes, that'd be great. And I have something to tell you. You won't believe who called. Stopped by. In fact, she's in the kitchen right this minute. No, that's okay. I have a minute. Go ahead and tell me."

Jane made her way with the phone into the living room, where she settled onto a sofa. Out the window she could see the house where Natalie, her friend, her bosom buddy, had once lived. The sidewalk down which Frannie had taken her last run.

"Unh-huh," she said to Max as the minutes ticked by. The sounds from the kitchen were fainter now. And then they stopped. Finally, she said to Max, "I'll tell you about it later. Let me get back now. Yes. I love you too, sweetheart."

But Jane didn't hurry into the kitchen. She picked up a magazine from her coffee table, a copy of *Saveur*, and flipped through the pages, noting with a smile an article on peppers, turning down the corners of an interesting recipe or two. Then, finally, with a sigh, Jane rose. It was time to go back in the kitchen, to put away a few things, to wash the scarlet bowl, and to see how her old girlfriend was getting along.

Thinking

Marilyn Wallace

Marilyn Wallace, the daughter of a New York City policeman, has ignored the warning about never going home again and returned with her husband to the Big Apple. She finds it juicy. Her most recent novel of psychological suspense is Current Danger, *but she's also the creator of the Jay Goldstein/Carlos Cruz detective series, as well as the editor and founding mother of the five-volume award-winning* Sisters in Crime *anthologies.*

"There's a fine one, over there." Maureen McBride points with an arthritic finger past the white poodle, its red tongue drooping as it pants in the shade of the backyard fence. "You take it, dear. Victory Garden or no, I'll not be eating tomatoes until this indigestion settles down."

Even if she's right about the power of her thoughts, Maggie Donally knows one thing for certain: She hasn't created her mother's stomach problems by thinking the wrong thing. Maureen's digestive tract has plagued her for as long as Maggie can remember. She shakes off a momentary shiver and follows her mother's finger, her glance passing over her son. Michael's sunburned, skinny arms and legs surely are growing as fast as the weeds he's so proud of piling in neat stacks at the perimeter of the garden.

The tomato, hidden among the leaves like a big, juicy sun, fairly leaps into her hand at her touch. She sets it in the gathering basket and gasps. A pencil-thin worm the green of new peas seems to look directly at her, as if daring her to do something about the black-rimmed hole and the mushy, brown tomato flesh beneath.

Maggie stares back at the cheeky wriggler. *You'll not be satisfying Mrs. Ballard's taste for juicy tidbits,* she thinks. Swiftly, she cuts away the spoiled part, and sets it carefully in the old wicker gathering basket, cut side up. Fifi, startled from some doggie dream, springs up and yip-yips until Maureen reaches out to scratch her belly.

"Sit, Fifi. That's a good girl. There's a war on, don't you know," her mother scolds in her singsongy brogue as she turns toward Maggie. Her sundress is bunched discreetly on her knees so it won't get stained as she weeds around the pole beans. Her permed curls glisten a steely gray and sweat trickles down the furrows that line her face. "What's the good of a Victory Garden if you're only throwing out the food? The good Lord gave you sense, Maggie, but since Owen died, it seems to have gone missing. 'Tisn't just for the perfect vegetables we're working in this broiling sun. The boys over there givin' up their lives and you safe in Brooklyn throwin' away a tomato, it's a crime."

Michael has frozen in place at the sound of his father's name. Maggie reaches out to stroke his arm, but abruptly he springs up and makes a show of brushing off his knees.

"Well, then, if it's a crime, I plead not guilty." She holds up the basket to show her mother the half-tomato dripping juice onto the cucumbers. *Give me some credit every once in a while,* Maggie thinks. She leans over to pinch off a tomato sucker, determined not to tempt the gods by thinking angry or even ungenerous thoughts. Her mother's right, after all, about making do with less than perfection. It's a wonder that they've been able to coax anything edible from this pebbly patch of dirt.

And a miracle that she and Michael eat their tomatoes and beans in an apartment they don't have to share with that little white dog, with its funny, stiff curls and its constant yapping. Maggie looks from Fifi to her mother, a sudden giggle nearly escaping.

"I just don't know," her mother says as she stands and taps a clod of dirt from the bottom of her shoes, "what's on your mind these days. What can you be thinking, Maggie?"

A breath of air from the open window plasters a curl of damp hair to Maggie Donally's neck, and she realizes she's been staring at Mrs. Ballard's maple tree across the yard. The leaves have turned a tired green. Tired of the summer heat, as she is, although her list includes rationing and President Roosevelt's speeches, and, ever-present and all-consuming, missing Owen. At least the war effort makes it patriotic not to wear stockings in the summer. The weariness sits so heavily on her chest, she feels she's in danger of forgetting how to breathe.

The Andrews Sisters are trying to sing about "Boogie Woogie Bugle Boy," but a vacuum tube has come loose again. The trio sound like they're drowning. She gives the cracked old Emerson a firm jolt with the flat of her hand, then reaches for a box of macaroni. It's so humid her bare feet leave prints on the green linoleum as she moves toward the stove.

How lovely it would be to lie in a tub of cool water until the weather changes. But it's almost seven o'clock and Michael has been sitting at the table, drawing airplanes and tanks with quiet concentration, for almost an hour. Her heart quickens when he presses his straight white teeth against his lower lip, the way his father did when he was paying bills or working on his model ships.

"No good. It's dirty," he whispers. Michael's lashes brush his cheeks as his dimpled fingers reach for the paper. "Grandma won't like it if it's dirty."

Maggie grabs her son's wrist. "No, it's not. You're old enough to know we can't afford to throw away a perfectly good piece of paper just because of a tiny smudge. Grandma won't mind."

If only he would just—no, she can't think that. No telling what will happen if she allows herself to finish a thought born of anger. She lets go of the boy, smooths the paper, wishes she could take back the impatience that makes her voice snappish and her touch abrupt. He is, after all, six years old. "I didn't mean to yell, sweetie. You finish your picture and I'll make us a nice supper."

Blessedly, Michael's eyes light with pleasure, and he nods and bends again to his work.

Her son baffles her with his desire to do things exactly, precisely, correctly. Since Owen died, anyway. As though he's afraid he'll be punished with another loss if he doesn't follow all the rules.

"It's so hot I think we're going to need ice cream after we do the dishes tonight." She strokes his shoulder, and he smiles up at her.

"With sprinkles?" he asks in his hoarse, little-man voice, so funny coming from a boy all elbows and freckles and unruly brown hair.

"Sure, baby. With sprinkles." Maggie straightens the paper, hands him his pencil, then fills the pot with water and sets it on the stove, glad to have made her child happy with a mere mention of ice cream.

That's better. *You must think positive thoughts, especially about Michael. He's your gift, the only thing left of Owen,* she reminds herself.

She reaches for a match and strikes it as Michael stares at the stove in fascination. "You said I could light it next time."

Laughing, she blows out the flame and hands him the matches. He's bouncing like a jack-in-the-box. "You do this one. But remember, you're never, ever to light the stove unless there's an adult around. Right?"

His chin nearly bangs against his chest as he nods agreement. Reverently, he pulls a wooden stick from the box and scrapes it across the emery paper. A splutter of bright fire erupts and she guides his hand to the gas jet and watches his eyes dance with delight as red and blue flames flicker around the ring.

The spent match hisses as Michael solemnly drops it into a puddle of water in the sink. Satisfied, Maggie waits for the white pool of oleo in the bottom of the saucepan to start bubbling, then stirs in the flour. She's about to pour in the milk when the doorbell rings. Michael runs past her, stands on tiptoes, and shouts, "Who is it?"

"It's Mrs. Ballard, honey. I need to talk to your mommy."

What now? Another rubber drive she's organizing? A request for used baby clothes for her niece? Edna Ballard carries on as if she's a regular one-woman Red Cross, except everyone would be better off if she—

You nip that right in the bud, Maggie warns herself as the milk sloshes into the pan. *Whatever the power of your thoughts, Edna means well.* Impatient, she strides to the door, undoes the lock, and lets her neighbor in.

"It's criminal, how that family throws away perfectly good dish towels with only the teensiest holes in them when the president has told us about shortages and all. It's going to take all of us to win this war." Edna's smile crinkles her round cheeks as she holds up two stained and torn squares of cotton, peers into Maggie's pots, moves to the table, examines Michael's drawings. Finally, she plants herself in the chair.

"Our supper will be ready in eight minutes, Edna. Can I get you some iced tea?" The noodles make sharp little clacking noises as Maggie dumps them into the boiling water. She keeps her back to the table and tosses cubes of orange cheese into the simmering milk.

"I won't be bothering you. Thanks anyway. I just need a little favor."

Maggie turns, hoping the set of her mouth and her crossed arms will deliver a message.

Edna fans herself with her hand. "You know Susan Green down the block? Well, she was supposed to bake an apple pie for the Field Day picnic day after tomorrow, but she's gone, poor thing."

The room grows dim and cold. *It's true, then. All it takes is my angry thought.* Maggie reaches for the counter to steady herself.

"You okay, Maggie? You look pale," Edna says as Maggie shakes the macaroni box.

Serve Susan right if he found a way to keep her from leaving. Maggie remembers her unspoken reaction as clearly as if the words are written in white chalk on her blackout shades.

She can't believe Edna is being so casual about Susan Green. "Susan's gone?"

Eyes wide, Edna claps a hand over her mouth. "Not *that* kind of gone. Gone *away*." She chuckles, her mouth puffing with surprised laughter.

The room stops spinning, and Maggie leans against the cool edge of the sink. "Where to?"

"You know that fella, Arnold, she was keeping company with? Well, he got so sore when he found out she went to a USO dance with someone else that he went to work and—"

"He chained her to the radiator," Maggie says softly.

Edna's head tilts. "To the stove. I thought she said she didn't tell anyone. Anyway, she's gone away, moved, cleared out her apartment and disappeared in the night. I never figured Susan to have enough ginger to do that. So now I need someone to bake that apple pie. Can you do it?"

Maggie doesn't bother to complain about using her precious sugar ration on a pie she'll give away. She's hardly aware of her nod of assent, or of dumping the steaming tubes of limp pasta into the dented old colander or of pouring the cheese sauce on. At least her thoughts hadn't hurt Susan.

Michael's regular breathing in the other room calms her. Maybe the problem is only that she's exhausted.

Just once, she'd like a day off. Weekdays, it's up by six, get Michael to her mother's house, crowd into the stifling subway car, hurry to the doctor's office to file mountains of papers and answer the phones and keep the waiting patients calm even when the doctor is hiding in his office finishing off a bottle of Scotch or whatever it is she smells on his breath every morning. Then back on the subway to pick up her son, fix supper, do the dishes, give him a bath, and tuck him into bed. Saturday and Sunday it's shopping, cleaning, church. And laundry and ironing. Her child will not look raggedy in front of Father Healy just because Owen Donally is dead.

No time at all to play hooky from chores. If only she could, they might take the trolley to Prospect Park. How at peace she would feel amid all that expanse of grass and sky, walking in the dappled shades of the big elm trees with her sweet little boy.

She sits in the dark and stares out the window to the Ballard yard. Susan Green was a lucky one, spared the ill-effects of Maggie's thoughts.

Last month, the woman wouldn't stop, complaining in that high, tight voice that her boyfriend was constantly after her, touching her and kissing her when she was cooking or sewing. Going on and on about how he followed her wherever she went. Never realizing how lucky she was that her man was around to bother her.

The air is still and Maggie reaches for her glass, sips the luke-warm tea. As she wipes her forehead with the back of her hand, she notices a book of matches on the shelf with Michael's toys. Did she put it there in some absentminded moment? She crosses to the other side of the room, slips the matches into her pocket, and stands at the window watching the fireflies blinking in the darkness outside.

Restless, she pulls down her blackout shade, turns on the table lamp, flips through a *Life* magazine until she comes upon a pho-tograph of rubble that was once a Berlin hotel, bricks piled like children's blocks, all tumbled and chaotic.

Greta Heffernan is German, but Maggie's certain that's not why the landlady was the first victim of her angry thoughts. Mrs. Heffernan was a mean old bat, standing at the door the first of each month, soft little hand outstretched for the rent money. And Maggie always on time, except the once. Because she'd forgotten her passbook and the bank was closed by the time she returned with it. Greta Heffernan had folded her arms across her bony chest and said she was changing the locks unless Maggie paid up in full by the next evening.

Do some people good to know what it's like to have money troubles, Maggie had thought as she trudged up the stairs.

Two weeks later, after a moving van drove off with Mrs. Heffernan's heavy mahogany sideboard and table and the uphol-stered chairs she kept covered with sheets except for Christmas, Maggie had rushed downstairs and joined the other tenants on the front stoop.

"Bank foreclosed because Mrs. Heffernan was in arrears," Mr. Vincente had said. "Now we pay rent to Brooklyn Savings. Some landlord, no?"

Maggie looks around the room, glancing at Michael's books and papers and his baseball glove stacked neatly on the shelf. He always remembers to tidy up before bedtime. She sighs. Owen left a mess wherever he went, a whirlwind of laughter and activity. She gazes into his smiling eyes, but the man in the photograph just keeps staring straight ahead.

She longs to ask for help but Maggie doesn't know where to turn. Since Owen died, she's gotten out of the habit of prayer. The God who took him, so young, so sweet, surely can't help her. The God who denied him the chance to see his son grow up is not to be trusted. All she did was think about how it would be if Owen didn't have to go off to the war. That, she admits with a quaking shudder, is really where it started.

"Posh tish, girl," she whispers to the empty room.

It can't really be that she's become dangerous. Susan Green proves that her thoughts have not become weapons, proves that she can't hurt people just by *thinking*.

The doctor she works for insists on paying for her to have a telephone so he can reach her when he needs her, but Maggie's not always sure this is a gift. She holds the receiver away from her ear because the dog's barking grates against her nerves. That little white creature, with its nasty breath, all sharp teeth and sharp toenails, always makes such a racket when her mother talks on the phone.

"You can't do it. Hush up, Fifi." Her mother waits until the poodle is quiet. Her voice is loud, clear, full of censure. "You can't make an apple pie without cinnamon. And do remember, dear: My dentist appointment is early in the morning, so you'll have to drop Mikey off at school yourself tomorrow. And it's Field Day, so make sure he doesn't wear a white shirt."

As though she's likely to forget, having been reminded twice daily for the past week. "Yes, I remember, Mother. We'll see you at the regular time on Friday."

Maggie hangs up the phone, pokes at the sliced apples. She should have known better than to call her mother for a recipe and not expect to have a lecture thrown in for good measure. Cinnamon it is. She kneels beside Michael, who is engrossed in another drawing.

"Let's go, sweetie. We have to go to the store."

Michael frowns, looks at the paper, and adds a burst of flame from the tank's gun. He starts to draw a head poking out of the hatch.

"Michael." Maggie scoops her keys into her hand. "Sweetie."

When he finally glances up, he says softly, "I want to finish my picture."

Olensky's is just down the street. Michael seems so peaceful, so engaged in his drawing that she hates to disturb him. "All right, sweetie. I'll be back in exactly ten minutes." She points to the clock on the kitchen wall. "When the big hand gets to the four, I'll be walking in the door. You sit right here and draw your pictures, okay?"

Michael smiles and nods. Maggie hangs in the doorway watching her son. She's never done this before. As though he knows she's uneasy, he looks up at her, his brown eyes shining. He's old enough, she thinks, and she kisses the top of his head before she leaves.

She races down the stairs onto the sidewalk and half-trots the two blocks to the store. In the cool, comforting gloom, smells of onions and fresh bread greet her, and the paddles of a ceiling fan stir the air. She finds the spice shelf, reaches for the smallest tin of cinnamon, then turns to see that five people have lined up at Mrs. Olensky's cash register.

If Mrs. Olensky takes her customers in order, she'll be gone longer than the ten minutes she promised Michael. "Excuse me," she says, "but I only have this one—"

"You wait your turn," the stout woman at the front snaps. "You think you're the only one in a hurry?"

Fat battle-ax, Maggie thinks. *How would you like it if*—and then she stops herself. With practice, she'll be able to control this impulse. She glances at the clock above the door. She's going to be late, and there's nothing she can do about it.

Mrs. Olensky frowns, gives Maggie an apologetic sideways glance, and rushes through the large woman's order. The store is silent except for the swish of fan blades and the rattle of paper bags as onions and flour and bottles of milk are packed up. The woman peels off her ration stamps and glares at Maggie before she lumbers out the door with her packages.

The next woman in line turns and says, "Come on, dear. You can go ahead of me." Everyone else waves her ahead.

"Oh, thank you. You're all so kind." Maggie smiles gratefully, puts three coins on the counter, and hurries out the door.

The pavement is hot beneath the thin leather of her shoes as she steps off the curb. She'll only be five minutes late. Michael will still be sitting in his chair, drawing, and she'll bake the apple pie. Tomorrow, she'll drop Michael and the pie off and then go in to work a little late. Her son will go to the Field Day picnic and play in the grass with his friends, and—

A fire truck careens around the corner at a tilt, tires screeching. Fumes billow from its exhaust. Maggie stumbles back onto the sidewalk.

"Maggie!" Edna Ballard tugs at her sleeve. "My goodness, you'll get yourself good and killed daydreaming that way."

"I was"—she hesitates to say it aloud—"thinking."

Edna's eyes twinkle with mischief. "About that young man who sits next to you on the trolley?"

Nosey parker. If only— "No. About how much cinnamon I should use." She smiles sweetly as she waves the tin of spice she's just bought at Olensky's. "For the apple pie, for Field Day, you know."

Edna links her arm through Maggie's, keeping stride at a brisk pace. "I told Alice I could count on you. I said—"

But Maggie isn't listening. That's her house. The fire truck and a police car have stopped in front of her building, and a crowd has gathered at the front stoop.

Michael. He's in the apartment alone. Something awful has happened to her little—

He's fine.

She must think positive thoughts. Maggie unhooks Edna's arm and runs down the street toward home.

My boy is all right.

Voices buzz around her, but she can't stop. She pounds up the four flights, a pain stitching into her side, her footing almost lost when her shoe catches on a peeling square of linoleum.

Michael is not hurt. Nothing has happened to him.

The door to her apartment stands open. Three men in black slickers and boots mill around in her kitchen. A patrolman, his blue hat tilted up to reveal kind gray eyes and a mouth that looks like it's trying not to smile, kneels in front of Michael.

Tears trickle down her son's cheeks, little streams of sadness and confusion. He looks frightened.

"I was bad, Mommy." His voice is so soft she can barely make out the words.

Maggie Donally takes a breath and examines her son. He seems to be whole, nothing cut or scratched or torn. Then she senses it, a lingering presence, a burnt smell that's not quite there, like a drop of water that's just evaporated. "What happened?" she says softly.

Michael's pale face floods with color. He swipes at his cheeks, then slumps in the chair and bends his head. "It was a crime. That's why I called them."

Oh, her poor little boy, so confused since Owen's death. "What do you mean, baby?"

"I'm not a baby. I'm old enough to know. The match started burning my fingers and then I dropped it and it fell on the bed."

His eyes grow wide and his little chest heaves. "The blanket . . . the blanket went on fire. I got the teapot and dumped water on it and it went out. It was wrong, what I did. It's a crime. So I looked on the paper by the cupboard by the telephone and found the number for the police. Then I called them so they could come arrest me."

Her heart twists with pain, his and her own, but before she can do anything he takes a shuddering breath and says, "Is the jail far away?"

Maggie lifts her son out of the chair and holds him in her arms. His scalp smells of little-boy sweat and shampoo, and his face is still damp with tears. His breathing slows as she strokes his hair.

"Hush, baby. Now you listen to me. You did something dangerous, something that might have hurt you. But it wasn't a crime and you're not going to jail. You shouldn't play with matches. But you don't go to jail for that. You also shouldn't leave milk out to spoil, but that's not a crime. You understand, Michael?" She wants to get it exactly right, but she knows she'll only confuse him if she talks too much. Later, they can go over the fine distinctions between law and morality.

Why does he feel so guilty? Why does her child think what he's done is so bad it's a crime for which he should go to jail?

Michael is frowning. "But Mrs. Ballard said not saving towels is a crime. And Grandma told you wasting food is a crime. So if they're a crime, then lighting a match and burning a hole in the blanket must be worser."

"I'll tell you what," she says hopefully, "we'll ask the policeman. He should know what's a crime, right?"

His mouth softening, the tears dry now, Michael peers into the hallway. "All right," he says.

She beckons the patrolman into the room, points to the empty chair, and waits until he's seated. "Please answer my son's question. Tell him the truth, Officer . . ."

"Reilly, ma'am." He folds his long fingers together, rests them on his knees, and smiles. "What do you want to know, son?"

With a start, Maggie realizes she's seen the man before. Take away the uniform, put him in a brown sweater worn at the elbows, and he's sitting beside Owen in the bar on the corner a couple of nights after work. If only Owen hadn't died. If only he hadn't listened to her when she asked him to find out why it was so cold in the apartment.

But he had, hadn't he?

When she'd heard his footsteps going downstairs, she'd wrapped her arms around her chest and gone on drinking tea and reading. She'd hardly even noticed the stray thought until later.

I don't want my husband to go off to war.

If Owen were to suffer some minor injury when he checked the furnace, if he were to, say, lose the finger that would pull the trigger on an army rifle, he wouldn't have to serve in the military.

But when the coal furnace he was feeding flared up before he could close the door, the accident did more than take his finger. It had taken his life. And that's how it had started.

Suddenly, she can't hear the policeman's words anymore. Inside her head, it feels as though someone has turned on the sun after a summer thunderstorm. Everything is clean and new, hopeful. She hasn't made all those awful things happen. She only believed she had such power because she felt guilty about Owen.

She never once harbored anger toward old Mr. Kenyon, who slipped on a loose rug and suffered a heart attack. And Alice Berry, who scalded her face when her pressure cooker blew up— she didn't even know the woman. Relieved, she turns to see Tim Reilly explaining to Michael that he's done something bad, but not bad enough to go to jail. That the reason it's bad is that it might hurt him. And then he's inviting Michael to come to see him play handball on Saturday at Tilden High School. Her son, eyes full of questions, looks at her in astonishment.

"I think we can arrange that, Michael. Now you tell Officer Reilly you're sorry for causing him trouble."

As Michael says the words of apology, Maggie holds on to his hand. *People who make others feel guilty should choke,* she thinks as she smooths her skirt.

"Thank you, Officer Reilly. I think we'd best get on with our chores now. We'll try to come to the handball game on Saturday." Maggie walks the patrolman to the door and watches as he signals the fireman that everything's okay. She says softly, so Michael can't hear, "You were kind to my boy. Thank you for that, too."

"Owen was a good man. Your boy must miss him—"

Before he can finish his sentence, the telephone rings. She's glad for an excuse not to be hearing Tim Reilly's sentiment, glad she doesn't have to fight back a flood of tears in front of him. "I'll go get that now. Thanks again."

He smiles, touches the brim of his hat, and walks down the stairs.

When Maggie lifts the receiver, all she hears is a terrible, wheezing cough. The sound is dreadful, and Maggie finds herself clutching her own chest, repeating into the phone, "Hello? Who is it? Hello?"

The awful sputtering sound finally stops. "Maggie, I—"

"Mother? What's wrong?" She can hardly catch her own breath, can barely stand listening to the dog bark while she waits for her mother's answer. As the racking and wheezing begin again, Maggie retreats into blankness, ceasing to let her thoughts become words because she is afraid of them.

"Mommy." Michael squeezes her hand hard, and Maggie realizes she's still holding the telephone.

"I didn't mean it, Mother," she shouts. "I take it back. Talk to me, Mother. Say something."

But the only sound Maggie hears over the telephone line is

Bing Crosby's voice, the crackle of radio static, and the frantic yapping of her mother's little poodle.

A Bus Called Pity

Carolyn Wheat

Attorney, teacher, award-winning writer, Carolyn Wheat is a triple threat and then some. This former Brooklynite now lives in southern California, where she regularly produces award-winning novels and short fiction. Her Edgar-nominated first novel, Dead Man's Thoughts, *introduced Brooklyn attorney Cass Jameson, who has gone on to impress critics and readers alike.*

It's a five-movie bus ride from Laredo, Texas, to San Miguel de Allende, Mexico. Susan slept part of the way and practiced her Spanish by deciphering as much as she could of *El Fugitivo*. It helped that she'd seen the movie twice in English, but it was disconcerting to hear Harrison Ford and Tommy Lee Jones speaking harsh, guttural Spanish.

The bus was more comfortable than she'd expected, but the long trip gave her time to think, and that wasn't good. The movies on the little screens overhead didn't help either, really, since they all involved innocent people shot and killed for no reason that she could see.

She tried to read, but her eyes refused to stay fixed on the page. She tried watching the scenery, but the arid land dotted with run-down tire stores and taco stands depressed her. Why had Jason chosen this country? Why couldn't he stay home, where the grass was green and people spoke English?

It was that Roger, she supposed. Roger wanted to live in Mexico, so Jason wanted to live in Mexico. He'd always been like that, Jason, moving into his lovers' lives as if renting a new apartment, letting their hobbies become his, adopting their attitudes toward movies, food, and even politics.

I'm the perfect wife, he joked. Now that all the women are liberated—and here he'd give Susan his special smile and the wink that went with it—I'm every man's dream, Doris Day in Gap jeans. I'll kiss my man good-bye in the morning and meet him at the door with a cold martini and a hot cassoulet at night.

He was cute when he camped it up, but the kernel of truth in those words was too rock-hard for a smile now. He hadn't written her in three weeks, and that just wasn't Jason, no matter what the girls at work said about sons forgetting to keep in touch with mothers.

He always said he wanted her to visit, to see the town where he and Roger lived in opulent exile. His words. She said, What do you mean, exile? You make it sound like you're a fugitive or something.

He'd laughed and gone into camp mode again, playing a swishy version of *El Fugitivo* over the phone.

What she wouldn't give to hear his voice one more time.

Because that rock-hard place in her stomach was growing bigger and bigger and she knew, without a shadow of doubt, that she wasn't going home with Jason sitting next to her on the bus, making jokes all the way to Laredo. Something was very, very wrong, and if it was the last thing she did in this life, Susan was going to get the truth out of that Roger.

Getting into town was a blur of choices made with insufficient information, of letting herself be managed into a cab in front of the Central de Autobuses and deposited in front of La Villa des Arbolitos on the edge of a dusty-looking park. She gave the driver a fifty-peso bill and waited for change, then handed him an over-sized coin and hoped it was enough.

Her eyes filled with sudden tears as she stepped into the shady entranceway. Jason always said that when she visited she had to stay at Los Arbolitos, which he'd called the friendliest hotel in Mexico's friendliest town. Now she was here, seeing the bougainvillea-draped walls and plant-filled courtyard for herself, only Jason wasn't there to show her to a room he'd picked specially for her and filled with things he knew she'd like.

La Señora Callahan ran Los Arbolitos like an old-fashioned European *pensión.* Breakfast and dinner were included, and all the guests sat at big family-style tables, meeting one another and talking about their day. The older women with the leathery tans spoke of golf up at the country club, while the Canadian couple had shopped for pottery and the American mystery writer had looked up old friends who were really and truly exiled in San Miguel.

It was fascinating company, and under ordinary circumstances Susan would have enjoyed them immensely, but when the Canadian wife asked why she'd come to San Miguel, she burst into tears right over the broccoli soup.

"My son, my son" was all she could say. Sobs prevented her from finishing a sentence. All the guests stopped eating and one of the golf ladies stood up and placed strong arms around her shoulders. La Señora gently but firmly led her away from the table so the others could resume their dinner. Within minutes she found herself in a small but neat room decorated with Mexican fabrics and furniture. She lay on the bed while La Señora placed a cold compress on her forehead and told her to get some sleep, they'd talk in the morning.

* * *

They were on their way to get the bus into town. Manuel and Francisco, the older boys, carried the heavy plastic cooler between them, while Mercedes pushed the wheelbarrow and Conchita hauled the huge grain bag, which wasn't as heavy as it looked. Five other children ran beside them, laughing and chattering, even though they weren't going to ride the bus into San Miguel; they just wanted to be part of something happening instead of hanging around the settlement waiting for their mothers to put them to work.

The children loved the bus ride and the trip to San Miguel and the chance to sit in the shade of Le Jardin, the bustling square at the center of town, selling sodas and bottled water and hand-embroidered cloth to passing tourists. Their grandmother, decked out in her best *huipil* and embroidered white skirt, brought up the rear, her broad face sheltered from the hot sun by a straw hat.

Manuel saw it first. He said this later to anyone who would listen, even though Francisco insisted he was the one who first said, What's that white thing over there?

Manuel said, Okay, maybe Chico said it first, but he was the one who ran over to it and saw it close up. Saw what it was and shouted the word all the way back to the others, who swarmed up like bees attracted by the sight of the incongruous thing in the middle of absolute nowhere.

Finally Abuela Matilda heard the word and made her slow, stately way toward the tree under which the children stood.

"*El baño?*"

"*El baño,*" Manuel replied. "A bathtub."

"We could use a bathtub," his grandmother said with a sage nod of her head.

"We couldn't use this bathtub," Francisco said. "It's all filled with white stuff."

Matilda Anita Maria Guzmán de Rodriguez walked around

the tub and stood next to her oldest grandson. She followed his pointing finger and saw what he meant. The tub was filled to the brim with hard, white plaster.

"Who would do a thing like this?" She murmured the words to herself, knowing the answer as well as any of the children, but not needing to say them.

Mercedes was only ten; she said what everyone else took for granted and had no need to say. "Gringos," she pronounced firmly. "Crazy gringos."

Susan supposed it was a pretty town. Lots and lots of stone, old stone, piled up into huge colonial churches and laid underfoot in the form of cobbled streets and raised sidewalks. It made for awkward walking, but of course she wouldn't have noticed it, would have been charmed by it, had she been promenading the streets on Jason's attentive arm instead of making her way alone down narrow streets whose high walls reminded her of medieval monasteries.

People lived their entire lives behind those walls, Jason had told her. You walk along the streets and think this town is nothing, that it's all hard stone and few windows and what you don't know is that if you open a door, even the most simple and unprepossessing door, you'll see huge spacious houses with courtyards and lush gardens, rooftop views and little casitas in the back that rent out for a song.

That's what he and Roger had done, rented a casita from the owner of a larger house. But the owner was in Venezuela, and Roger never answered the phone anymore, and finally a voice on the other end told her in impatient Spanish that the number was disconnected. So she had an address but no way to get through the door into Roger and Jason's secret world behind the high stone wall.

They couldn't have been the only gay couple in San Miguel,

she told herself. Someone in the foreign community must have known them, must know a way to put her in touch with Roger.

And of course there were the police.

But something held her back from involving them right away. Maybe it was the rumored corruption of the Mexican police, or maybe it was the instinctive enmity between cops and gay men, but she decided she'd save the police for later, try reaching Roger through the English-speaking community instead.

"The Hardeen," the women at Los Arbolitos called it, although it was spelled Le Jardin and she couldn't quite get the French pronunciation out of her head. Susan made her way toward the square and caught sight of La Parroquia, the parish church. For the first time since she'd boarded the bus in Laredo, she smiled.

La Parroquia was a perfect replica of a Gothic cathedral, except for one thing: It had no bottom. The spires pointed to the sky like so many skinny arms, but they didn't rise from a base of heavy Gothic arches and flying buttresses the way they did in Europe. They just started at ground level and rose into the air on their own. It looked as if the underlying church had sunk into the ground, leaving only spires.

Jason had told her the story. A self-taught priest-architect wanted a Gothic cathedral in San Miguel, but he didn't like the way the whole church looked, so he had his builders make the church of spires alone. Just like that. It was a metaphor, Jason said, for the way Mexico dealt with its various conquistadors. Take what you like and ignore the rest. Take the spires, leave the building. Take the pageantry of Christianity, add it to the death worship of Aztec religion, and create the Day of the Dead. Take the tourist dollar but refuse to let them Holiday Inn the place to death by declaring the entire town a historic district.

Tears threatened again. Why wasn't Jason standing next to her, telling her this story in his wonderful light tenor voice, pointing to the spires and adding bits of information about the best place to get a cup of coffee, the best shop for handmade fabrics? Leading her through the town as if she were a queen on inspection tour, making sure she saw everything and enjoyed every minute of her stay?

Jason was the best tour guide in the world, and Susan had seen more than one part of the world through his perceptive eyes. He would have been so glad to have her here, to show her his personal San Miguel instead of the postcard-town everyone saw when they visited.

Enough. She wasn't helping Jason by standing here going all misty; she had work to do. She turned away from the church and focused on the Jardin, with its gazebo-bandstand in the middle and its benches filled with people, some Mexican, most not.

She took a deep breath and walked up to the first bench. The man with the spare tire and his brightly clad wife were obvious newcomers, since they sat poring over a map, so she went up to the man with the beard sitting next to him.

"Excuse me," she said in a voice that sounded too loud. "Do you live here in San Miguel?"

The man looked a little wary, but he answered, "Yes. I've been here a year or so. Why?"

"Do you know Roger White or Jason McClendon, by any chance?" She couldn't believe she'd just said Jason's whole name without even a tremor in her voice, as if he were an acquaintance she'd decided to look up instead of a son she feared dead.

"Heard the names. Don't think I know them." The man looked to his left and called, "Hey, Ed, come here a minute, willya?"

Ed allowed as how he'd met Roger a couple of times at the *biblioteca,* but didn't know him well and hadn't met his lover, and weren't they renting La Casita Amarilla, the yellow house, from Yolanda Beltran, the sculptor?

Señor Ed called six or seven people over to him as they talked, and each one added his or her bit to the information until finally a hefty girl with a long pigtail and paint-splattered overalls said she and Jason had been great friends until he'd gone to Brazil. No matter how many people asked Roger when Jason would be back, she added, he never seemed to have an answer.

Brazil. Jason was not in Brazil, Susan said in such a firm tone that the girl looked taken aback, as if it had never in this world occurred to her that Roger was lying. And it wasn't as if Jason couldn't go to Brazil if he wanted to, it was just that he would have told her, would have shared the experience with her so she could go to Blockbuster and get cassettes of Brazilian music and rent Brazilian movies and eat *feijoada* and think of him in Rio de Janeiro.

"Oh, my God," the girl said, clapping a paint-stained hand to her mouth, "you're Susan."

The tears came in earnest now, and she let the girl place an arm around her and she sobbed out all her fears and doubts and longing for Jason while the others stood around and murmured kind but meaningless words.

He'd somehow thought it would be like watching Marisol get flan out of the pan. She would run a knife around the crusty edges and loosen the custard, then ease it out onto the plate, where it would always land with a nice liquid plop.

But this wasn't custard, it was plaster, and no amount of chipping away at the edges with a chisel was going to loosen the huge hard mass in the middle, and José's vision of baths in a white porcelain tub instead of the old zinc washtub were disappearing rapidly. No matter that he still wouldn't have running water and the tub would be filled, as always, with buckets carried in and heated on the stove—it would still be a real tub and would elevate him in the eyes of the community. He could drop casually into the conversation at the *pulquería,* I was sitting in my tub last night, smoking a cigarette and thinking, and everyone would know that José Maria de Annunciatión Rodriguez-Lobos was a man of substance, a man of stature, a man with a tub.

He needed something bigger. An axe, maybe, or a hammer to pound the chisel into the plaster instead of using only the strength of his hands.

So when he went to the *pulquería* that night, it was with a purpose. He came home with a huge, heavy hammer and a crowbar, after only five trades. His hoe went to Felipe, who needed to weed his garden and who had a hose he could lend to Victor, who in turn lent his wrench to Ricardo, who gave Victor's brother Pedro a length of pipe he'd picked up somewhere, and somehow the whole thing ended up with José placing a crowbar at the chipped-away end of the plaster in the tub and giving a huge heave and knocking out a chunk of plaster with a human hand attached to it.

"I thought Jason went to Brazil three weeks ago," a new arrival said. He was a slight man with thinning hair and wire-rimmed biofocals. "I was in Border Crossings getting my messages, and Bonnie said Jason left that morning for Rio. I said that sounded like fun and I picked up my mail and that was that."

He turned to a middle-aged hippie with a gray-streaked beard, who looked just like Jerry Garcia, only Jewish. "That was three or four days before the Tiger's party, when Roger got so drunk. Mean drunk, Roger."

The Jewish Jerry Garcia nodded and said, "I wouldn't want to be in Roger's way when he's had too much tequila," then realized he was in the presence of Roger's lover's mother and ducked his head like a little boy who'd embarrassed the family by mentioning something adults had all agreed must not be mentioned.

"I heard he threw up in the fountain," one of the women said.

Señor Ed, who seemed to be an unofficial leader of the community, took back the conversation and explained that everyone got their mail at private mailboxes and that Border Crossings was one such message service. He offered to take Susan to see if Jason had a box there. Susan readily agreed and let Ed and the pigtailed girl, whose name was Heidi, lead her along the narrow streets.

Border Crossings was a combination mail service, souvenir shop, and coffeehouse. Ed ordered coffees all around and introduced Susan to Bonnie, the owner. Bonnie's face fell when she realized who Susan was, and she wordlessly reached behind the counter and pulled out a stack of mail.

"Jason hasn't been in for a while," she explained. "I wondered when he was going to be back. I guess if you're his mother, it's okay to give this to you."

Susan placed the bundle into the straw bag that contained her search kit—pictures of Jason and Roger, the address on Avenida Hidalgo where the yellow house stood, a map of the town.

"Someone was just in here talking about Roger," Bonnie went on. "Let me try to—oh, yeah, it was Tyler; he said Roger was coming over to his place to use the shower, since his tub was filled with plaster dust or something from an installation that Jason was working on. So if you want to find Roger, I'd track down Tyler if I were you."

Tyler's place, it turned out, wasn't really his but belonged to his girlfriend, Annie the Poet, who was renting an apartment on Calle Hernández Macías, on the other side of the Jardin. As the little group walked along the sunbaked street, Susan noticed an old bus negotiating the narrow, hilly streets with a bouncy sort of ease. Its destination was La Piedad, which Heidi explained was a little town to the south named after its principal church, Our Lady of Pity.

Susan wasn't Catholic, but she decided a quick prayer to Our Lady of Pity wouldn't be out of place.

When they reached the house—or rather, the brown, mottled wall that concealed the house—Susan lifted the huge bronze knocker in the form of a human hand and brought it down with a loud thud on the weathered wooden door.

Tyler answered and said Roger had been there that very morning.

Susan's heart thumped as loudly as the door knocker. He'd been here, right here, the man she was becoming certain had killed her son.

"Where is he now? Does anyone have a key to his house? I have to see him."

At first José thought it was a statue. *Escultura.* And why not, since sculptors used plaster and there were a lot of artists in town. Then he thought maybe it was a mannequin from a store.

But mannequins don't have bones, and neither do statues, and this hand had bones. And flesh. And a tattoo, a spider tattoo, on the wrist.

José rocked back on his *huaraches* and gave the matter a great deal of thought.

The police should be told.

But the police were not entirely welcome in the settlement, for a myriad of reasons José knew all too well. Someone was always up to something that might not quite pass muster with the law, and while some Mexican police had a way of looking past law-breakers if they had a little money to pay *la mordida,* no one in the settlement had money, and in cases where no money changed hands, the law was an implacable adversary. Questions would be asked and explanations demanded and José didn't like the way it sounded: I found a dead body in a bathtub under a tree on the way to the bus stop.

It was a gringo hand, white as snow under the plaster and without hard calluses. That made it gringo business, and Jose had bad feelings about messing with gringo business, but all the same he didn't see why gringo business ought to bring the police into his quiet little settlement.

There had to be another way.

But Tyler, it turned out, hadn't actually seen Roger that morning, just the evidence of a shower having been taken and towels left in a soaking wet bunch on the floor, no matter how many times Annie the Poet had chewed Roger out for just dumping his stuff like a pig.

Tyler invited her in, offered her a cold soda, and settled her at a gaily painted wooden table whose accompanying chairs had yellow suns painted on their backs. He was naked from the waist up, and she found herself thinking that Jason would have swooned over the well-defined muscles and tanned arms—if he'd finally gotten that Roger out of his system.

"Have you tried the Institute?" Tyler asked, and the others nodded.

"Good idea," Señor Ed said, as if his benediction were required before the next step was taken.

The Instituto Allende was a venerable palace-turned-art school, famous throughout Mexico for its classes and exhibitions. Of course, it was the center of San Miguel life for those engaged in producing art, and Susan had planned on making a trip here. Tyler insisted on taking her; he put on a T-shirt that memorialized a long-ago Eagles concert and walked her to the buildings, which were spread over several blocks of the town. Ed and Heidi followed behind, and from snatches of overheard conversation, Susan learned that they, too, were growing very anxious about Jason, having seen evidence of Roger's dangerous temper.

"A lot of people have messages here," Tyler explained as he led her into building after building, many decorated with murals done by past and present students. Some were obvious Diego

Rivera imitations, others were abstract in nature. In one building, an artist stood on a scaffold, actually producing the mural
before an admiring audience who sat in the shade of the courtyard
sipping fruit juice.

Bulletin boards offered cut-rate art classes or rooms for rent in
"spacious casitas" or promised Spanish or guitar lessons or rides
to Mexico city. They offered a glimpse into town life, but had no
interest for Susan until she came across one that said SUBLET—
DON'T MISS THIS OPPORTUNITY TO STAY IN THE HOME OF AN
ARTIST. CALL ROGER WHITE AT 6549; LA CASITA AMARILLA IS
FOR RENT. ACT NOW!

It was dated the day before. Roger had been here, right here,
posting this notice. Subletting the place he and Jason had rented
from Yolanda Beltran.

She didn't recognize the phone number. Tyler said it was
Annie's and sounded pissed off that Roger hadn't asked permission to use it in the ad.

That did it. Roger was planning to leave town.

She had to find him before he did.

Even if it meant talking to the police.

Knowing was one thing, acting was another. And Nestor
Hinojosa hadn't become *delegado* of such a preeminent tourist
mecca as San Miguel de Allende without being very clear on the
difference between the two.

He knew in his world-weary bones that something had indeed
happened to the missing gringo, the one whose sad-eyed mother
walked around town buttonholing every member of the foreign
community who might have information—but he hadn't yet
been asked to do anything about it, and so he did what seemed
most prudent: nothing.

He also knew there was something afoot in the little settlement where José Rodriguez lived, but he did nothing about that

either, since odd things happened in settlements all the time and there was no point in acting until one had every scrap of evidence already nailed down, so that the entire settlement would know that lying would avail them nothing.

Knowing when to know and when to act upon one's knowing: This was the secret to a long and successful life as a public official in Mexico.

But when the woman with the shapeless brown dress and sad face walked into the Palacio Municipal and found her way to his office, he had no choice. It was time to act. Time to find this Roger and bring him in for questioning.

Nestor Hinojosa was a man of the world; he knew they did things differently in *gringolandia.* There a citizen was presumed innocent until proven guilty.

He was glad he was a policeman in Mexico, where things were logical and a man was considered guilty unless and until he produced sufficient evidence of innocence.

He was beginning to think Roger White wouldn't be able to meet the burden.

It was almost Jason's birthday. Twenty-eight, he'd be on Friday—if he were still alive.

Her heart ached as she thought about all the years they'd celebrated, together or apart. You heard people say their hearts ached, and you thought it was an expression, until it happened to you and the genuine physical pain on the left side of the chest, the very real heaviness of every single breath, made you see that it was nothing more nor less than the absolute concrete truth. Your heart did ache with loss and longing and regret and the sweetness of memory, made all the more precious by the realization that it was over, that things you'd loved would never happen again in this world. She would never again make Jason his "birthday cake" of apple pie, as she had every year for twenty years ever since at age seven he'd first said that apple pie was his favorite food in the whole world and would she please make him one for his birthday instead of a chocolate cake.

The year he was ten, he put in more cinnamon. At twelve, he insisted that four Granny Smith apples be added to the mix for extra tartness. By fifteen, he was experimenting with ginger and allspice. He was seventeen when he made his first *tarte aux pommes,* and the year after that he added a calvados sauce and then a drizzle of pureed kiwi. He served crème frâiche with a hint of cassis along with it for his twenty-second birthday (the Year of Chad, she recalled).

Last year, when he flew home for his twenty-seventh birthday, he'd insisted she make her own apple pie the old-fashioned way. "It's a classic, Mom," he'd said with that special wink he reserved for her. "You can't improve on a classic."

Children talk. Children boast. Children run and play in the Jardin and tell their friends all about the latest events in their village. And José Rodriguez's children, Matilda Guzmán's grandchildren, found it impossible to keep their bathtub to themselves.

"*Un muerto,*" Francisco whispered to his friend Julio. "In the bathtub."

"*Mano de calavera,*" Mercedes said, improving upon her brother's account by linguistically stripping the body of flesh and presenting a skeleton image to her best friend Carmen.

"It got up out of the bathtub and walked around the house all night," Manuel confided to Raul, a bigger boy whose respect he craved. "And you could see the spider tattoo on his hand move and crawl. Like on television, on the *X-Files.*"

Manuel had no television, but he'd seen souvenirs from the *X-Files* and a spider tattoo walking right off a dead man's wrist seemed like exactly the thing you'd see if you did have a television.

Not all the vendors in the Jardin were Mexican. Leather Jim sold hand-tooled wallets and handbags from a card table; his Spanish was colloquial enough to understand the children's prattle.

The mention of the spider tattoo had him listening very attentively, then scratching his head as he considered his next move.

Susan was exhausted when she returned to Los Arbolitos for a nap. She hadn't thought herself capable of sleep, but the walking and the heat and the worry closed her eyes the minute she lay down on the tiny, hard bed. Dreams of Jason filled her head, good dreams and bad, Jason alive and blowing out the candles on his apple pie, or Jason dripping blood from hollow eyes, begging her to avenge his death.

When she woke, she wasn't sure which dream had been the nightmare.

After breakfast, which she ate heartily, having missed all meals the day before, she went back to the Jardin to meet Tyler and Heidi and Señor Ed.

"She needs to see Jim," Ed said firmly.

"Texas Jim or Portland Jim?" Tyler inquired.

"Leather Jim."

"Jason's not into leather," Susan protested, although she realized that if Jason had fallen for a leather man, he'd have converted in a New York minute.

Ed smiled. "Not that kind of leather. Wallets and such. Jim sells things in the Jardin most days."

So they waited, sitting on the benches surrounding the little square, surrounded themselves by a covered courtyard flanking big public buildings. Trees cut in the shape of tuna cans shaded them, and a delicate wrought-iron gazebo-bandstand set in the center of the Jardin. A lovely place, with a cool, scented breeze blowing and bright blue skies overhead. A place she could have spent so many happy hours enjoying, if only Jason—

She closed her eyes and willed the thought away. She had to be strong. Grief could wait until after she'd had justice.

Finally Ed said, "Here he comes. Give him a chance to set up his stall, and then go over and talk to him."

There was something very odd about Ed's insistence on her talking to Leather Jim, even more so in that he appeared to want her to be alone during the conversation. He gave the others meaningful stares, keeping them in their seats, as she stood to make her way across the street to the shaded vending area under the canopy.

Leather Jim's face looked like his wares, dark brown and tanned, skin stretched across bone like a drum. He raised an eyebrow as Susan stepped warily toward his table. "You're Jason's mother?"

She nodded, pushing back tears that wouldn't help her now. "You know my son?"

No matter what her heart told her, she refused to put Jason in the past tense until she absolutely had to.

"He asked me to make you something." Jim reached into a box on the sidewalk and pulled out a wallet with red-dyed apples carved into it and her initials in the center.

A tear fell in spite of herself, followed by a huge rush of suspicion. What did Jim want from her? Would he ask for some outrageous sum of money in return for Jason's last gift—a gift he might have made last night and not for Jason at all?

But then how would he know about the apples?

Words from children's lips also manage to find their way into *la delegación de policía;* the boy Raul in whom Manuel Rodriguez had confided was a third cousin to Nestor Hinojosa's sister's best friend's niece, which meant he had the story by ten o'clock the next morning and was on his way to the village in his jeep by ten-thirty.

A body in a bathtub and a missing gringo. It didn't take Señor Sherlock Holmes to put *dos y dos* together.

"You really ought to go to Chiapas," Leather Jim said, in a tone so conversational it was as if he alone had no idea why she was in San Miguel. As if she were a carefree tourist instead of a mother worried sick.

"There's a ruin there, right on the border with Guatemala, remote as hell—Jason talked about it all the time. I'm sure he'd want you to see it."

"I can't go see ruins," she replied, her voice rising along with her temper. "I didn't come here to—"

"See, everyone knows Bonampak," Jim said, drowning out her protest with his booming baritone, "but this place is even more special. I'm talking jungle. It's called Xaxchilan, and there's a temple there will blow your mind. I mean it, you *have* to go."

"Will you stop talking about—"

"I do really nice work, don't you think? Just look at the stitching on this wallet."

Susan backed away. This man was crazy. Talking about ruins and stitching when all she wanted was to know where Jason was so she could take him home and lay him to rest beside his father—and then find that Roger and make certain he spent the rest of his life in a Mexican prison.

"Just look at it." Obsessed gray eyes bored into hers; she took the wallet with a shaking hand and felt the stitching.

And realized there was something inside the wallet. She pried open the billfold and saw a bus ticket to a town called San Cristobal in the state of Chiapas.

The southernmost state in Mexico, the one that bordered Guatemala.

Why would Jason be there? He loved a good Mayan ruin, but he'd have let her know, he'd have filled letters with joyous antic-

ipation, inviting her to partake of his adventure vicariously. He'd
have sent postcards and presents of local handicrafts and—

"I really think you should go," Leather Jim said once more in
his low, intense tone. "You could get a bus right away from
Querétaro or Mexico City."

"I—I'd hate to miss any news of my son," she whispered. She
wasn't sure why she was whispering, only that this strange conversation with this strange man seemed to call for whispers and
secret codes.

She didn't think it was possible for Jim's voice to get lower,
but it did. "Please don't react, but they've found a body in one of
the villages outside town."

Don't react?

She clamped a shaking hand to her mouth and nodded her
agreement. No sound would emerge. No tears.

"The body they found has a spider tattoo on the arm. I think
you know what that means."

A chill ran through her as if the spider had come to life and
walked across her face.

Jason didn't have a spider tattoo.

Roger did.

"But—people saw Roger. He was at some party where he—"

"Did people see him, or just tell stories about him?" Jim
leaned back in his chair and resumed his conversational tone, raising his voice a bit.

"This town has more rumors in it than *cucarachas,* and that's
saying something. All it takes is someone saying Did you hear
about Roger at the Tiger's party? and the next thing you know
six people are repeating it as if they were next to him, when all
they're doing is embellishing on what someone told them."

Susan remembered the wet towels on Tyler's bathroom floor,
towels anyone could have used, towels Jason would have hung
neatly but Roger would have left where they fell.

She remembered the tales of Roger's temper, and the stories of his drinking, which, however embroidered, had to come from some core of truth. She remembered the mail pickup at Border Crossings that never seemed to happen when Bonnie was on duty. What if Jason picked up Roger's mail and left his own? What if he'd posted the "for rent" sign at the Institute?

Roger, not Jason, was dead.

Jason was in Chiapas, waiting for her to arrive on the bus. Together they'd find sanctuary in a place where he'd be safe from the police, safe from extradition to a country where a plea of self-defense might not be available to a gay man.

As she paid for the wallet and the bus ticket, she sent a prayer of thanks to Our Lady of Pity, who had taken pity on her and her son.

The middle-aged couple emerged from the lime-green taxi looking like survivors of a natural disaster. Well-dressed and well-fed in the florid manner of the gringos, both had an ashen pallor that spoke of some heavy sorrow.

The man helped the woman negotiate the cobblestones. They stood before the door for a moment and the man said, "This looks like the place."

"That's what he called it. Los Arbolitos. It means 'little trees.' The woman's eyes filled with tears. "Roger always said we had to stay here when we came to see him."

"Now, Mother," the man said, but his voice was far from steady. He rang the bell and waited for Señora Callahan to show them to their room.

Along the narrow street flanking the little park rattled an ancient bus bearing the legend LA PIEDAD.

Hello?

Angela Zeman

Angela Zeman, a former advertising executive, is the author of the Mrs. Risk "witch" story series in Alfred Hitchcock's Mystery Magazine. *A full-time writer and sometime panelist at mystery conventions, she has one "witch" novel with her agent and one in progress. A second book, also in progress, is not a "witch" novel. She practices kung fu, tai chi, and yoga, and is a Divemaster scuba diver. She is also well on her way to earning a graduate gemologist degree from the Gemological Institute of America.*

"Hello? Geeze, at last! This is Nancy Wolcott on the Island. I been callin' two weeks already. You ever figure to call me back, or what? I need medical care!"

Vera, taken aback by the venomous tone, answered, "What? I'm—I'm sorry, I didn't catch the name." She hadn't really caught anything. The words had whipped across her sluggish brain like arrows, sharp reminders of her helplessness that left her frightened as they penetrated her carefully constructed mental fog. A shiver made the phone receiver tremble in her one good hand, which was now clammy, despite the heat that roasted the narrow kitchen.

It had to be close to two o'clock. She knew because *The Dating Game* was nearly over. The summer afternoon sun had, as always, brought out the chemical smell of the sticky, peeling linoleum. Vera often hoped that it was lethal, that gassy smell. She spent most of her time in here, a cripple, answering a crippled phone, watching the tiny antiquated crippled TV. Any escape would be a good escape.

"*N-A-N-C-Y W-0-L-C-0-T-T.*" The voice spelled out the name loudly, with exaggerated care. "From the Island."

"The *Island?*"

"Oh, fer—yeah. *Gilligan's* Island. Tell the doc I gotta talk to him!"

Vera's eyes blinked wide, her lips parted. "I, uh, think you have the wrong number."

Click. As easy as that. Vera breathed deeply, struggling to do so within her partially paralyzed upper torso. She swiveled her wheelchair to face the TV on the old wooden table more square- ly. *I should've said wrong number right away,* she thought. *Why should I have to put up with talk like that? Mean voice. Probably a horrible person.* Gradually her shivering ceased and she became reab- sorbed in the TV show, her mind supplying the color, and even some of the faces and shapes when necessary. She'd long ago trained her mind to create her world the way she wanted it, with details she selected. The rest, after years of practice, she ignored.

A voice suddenly intruded on her solitude. "Oh, my dear, why do I always find you in here? The *heat!* And that smell. The very walls are baking, and they're obviously not made of cookie dough," scolded a cheery voice. Into the tiny room, which decades ago had been converted to a kitchen from its former life as a sun porch, trundled Mrs. Benedetto. It was Wednesday. The matronly, rounded figure could only reach Vera by knocking cumbersome wooden chairs aside to make passage. As she advanced, she flicked away grimy paint shards that stuck to her immaculately snowy uniform. Her face revealed poorly disguised disgust at such abundant dirt.

Mrs. Benedetto was a home care practical nurse, paid for three visits a week by an insurance policy the courts forced her ex-husband to provide. And not just to fulfill husbandly duty. On the night his office buddies called Vera, she'd patiently extricated him, stumbling and drunk, from his favorite after-hours bar. On the way home his drunken grabs for control of the steering wheel had aimed the Buick through a brick wall of a boarded-up dry cleaner's. He'd dislocated his shoulder. Vera hadn't done as well. After much hospitalization, the medical staff had rejected any hopes for her return to a normal life. Weaving in and out of drug-induced delusions, she'd keened from grief, her long-pent-up dreams for a family forever shattered. Until the doctors eventually weaned her from the painkillers, her unborn children clustered on her dead lap daily and she clung to their little ghosts. She was relieved when, drug-free, by developing an immense strength of will, she could finally "forget" the reason for the unrelieved despair that now gripped her.

Simultaneous with the healing of her husband's shoulder came divorce papers. Her dependence repelled him, he said. Evidently the insurance company felt the same. The courts found it necessary to force the insurance group to comply, it being anxious to insure only healthy or swiftly terminal clients. Vera wasn't young, but she wasn't old. And she would never get better. Anathema to husbands and insurance companies.

Vera looked up, spotted Mrs. Benedetto's smile, and blushed with wordless gratitude. But behind the motherly figure a shadowy one moved, catching her eye, and the blush paled.

Vera's head gave a quick shake of denial. "I like it in here." Fright made her voice insistent, but the motherly woman clucked as she wheeled her charge back through the gauntlet of sticky furniture into the cooler regions of the boxy two-story house.

Outside, the cracking, gap-toothed shingles had once been green, and the tiny yard and shrubs abundant and flourishing. Just as Vera had once been lithe and athletic. The lean figure followed, strolling leisurely from the overbright kitchen through a small dining nook to the dark relief of the living room.

After positioning Vera in front of a cool breeze coming in from the open front windows, Mrs. Benedetto fanned Vera's face with a newspaper. "You're so flushed and hot. Honey-Ann, dear, would you get your poor sister some water? I'll get to work meantime."

The figure among the shadows vanished toward the kitchen. She came out again and handed Vera a glass filled with ice and water, beaded with moisture. "The glass is slick. Don't drop it now," said Honey-Ann to her, grinning knowingly.

Vera drank, trying not to betray how incredibly delicious the icy water tasted and how much she needed it. Then, miserably, she gazed up over Mrs. Benedetto's round shoulder at Honey-Ann. *I didn't say anything, I swear,* her eyes pleaded.

Honey-Ann slowly shook her head. "She loves it in there, Mrs. B. I can't make her come out—it's maddening. So would you like some iced tea before you get started, Mrs. B.? A hot day." Her voice, friendly and solicitous, clashed with her deadened expression. She shifted from one slim bare leg to the other, buttocks nearly but not quite covered by the cutoff jeans, long bony arms folded in front of her meager torso. Her lips lifted at each corner, but not, to Vera, resembling anything like a smile.

Mrs. Benedetto waved the offer away. "Thank you, no, you dear thing. But we'll need some water in a basin, soap, and small towels, same as always. Ooh, just look at her. Her poor fair skin is nearly purple. You simply cannot let her sit back there for hours, Honey-Ann. It's depressing, never mind the risk of heat stroke. That hole. You're softhearted for your poor sister, I know, but you're going to have to be firm. This isn't good for her!"

Honey-Ann leaned forward, grinning over Mrs. Benedetto's

back at the mesmerized Vera. "Oooh. you mean she might *die*?"

"Yes, indeed, that's just what I mean. You mind now," she warned, shaking her head at Vera. She began stripping off Vera's tunic, pulling it over her head. It was a shift, cut wide and short, shaped to accommodate the chair. Vera sighed and relaxed to the pleasure of being cool. She closed her eyes. Soon she would be clean, from her pale curly hair to her toenails. Her head would clear, and the ache around her eyes would stop. And she would have something nice to eat. Sometimes a hot dog with sauerkraut, her favorite if it had mustard on it. Sometimes pasta with things in it that had never seen a can. It always happened, Monday, Wednesday, and Friday. For two hours at a time.

"Why, Vera!" At the sound of the injured voice, Vera's eyes popped open to see Mrs. Benedetto holding up the tunic. The middle gaped wide, slashed with bold jags that made the garment unrepairable. Vera flushed. She'd forgotten. Mrs. Benedetto had made the tunic. Bright colors in soft cotton, designed to fit Vera's needs, sewn out of kindness and caring on her own time. Mrs. Benedetto caught a whiff from the tunic and recoiled. "My Lord, Vera, that smell! What did you do in it?"

Honey-Ann placed the basin of water near Mrs. Benedetto, on the mahogany coffee table now nearly black with years of grime. "She said she hated it. Sorry. I meant to put it someplace else today. Didn't want to hurt your feelings—you worked so hard on it. But guess she just had to wear it today, hmmm? God, Vera. Do you always think only of yourself? Y'know, Mrs. B., I didn't want to tell you, but she threw your cookies out in the yard two weeks ago. Those vanilla ones you made, with icing?"

A pause.

Two pairs of eyes focused on Vera, one shimmering with puzzled hurt, one bright with glee. She kept hers expressionless, unable to answer, unable to protest. She'd been forced to live in the tunic since it had been given to her Monday, after Honey-

Ann's scissors had turned it into scraps that had barely covered her privacy. Scraps that were hard to control during private necessities, since she had to manage on her own.

Honey-Ann continued, "Guess, in the end, maybe it's not fair for me to hide it from you. Guess it's better you found out. Wasting your time and money on her like that. For what? And it's not just you. It's whoever does anything for her. She's wacko." She shrugged, then slid a cigarette out of the pack left on the big-screen TV and began to scrape a match.

Mrs. Benedetto shook her head sharply at her. "No secondhand smoke around Vera *or* me."

Honey-Ann looked startled, pocketed the cigarette, and smiled her apology. "I was that upset for you, I forgot."

Mrs. Benedetto nodded. "I'm sorry you didn't like the tunic, Vera. It's too bad you ruined it. I could've given it to another patient. Somebody who doesn't have things as good as you, a sister to devote her life to you." Mrs. Benedetto patted a stoic Honey-Ann on the hand, struggled to overcome her disappointment and hurt, and nearly succeeded. But as the bathing and treatments proceeded, it became obvious to Vera that her usual jokes and kind caresses were gone. As was she, at the earliest moment after her work was done.

Through the torn front-door screen, Vera watched Mrs. Benedetto march smartly down the crooked front walk to slide into the small company van she drove—a white Ford with a logo on the door: green script across a pink helping hand extended to the needy. Now Vera was dressed in one of her old hospital gowns. Clean, but faded, it opened awkwardly in the back as hospital gowns do, some areas worn so thin as to hardly hold itself together. A last few gowns were all she had to wear now, but Vera was past caring. It covered the nearly shapeless mass of flesh that she had become after seven years of living in the kitchen. Scorching in summer, freezing in winter. All the same.

Honey-Ann, sprawled on the prickly beet-colored sofa, lit her cigarette and nudged the handle of Vera's chair with her foot. Without protest, Vera maneuvered her chair with her one working hand, meticulously avoiding the massive mahogany furniture, once joyfully treasured, handed down from her mother as a wedding present. The chair easily traversed the carpet, so flattened by age and dirt that it was little different from the linoleum. Into her bright cave she went. Soon she was staring again at the small TV, her lips moving slightly to spell out the words. A Cadillac Seville could be hers if she guessed the clichè.

The next afternoon, Thursday, the phone rang. Vera's hand snaked out, snagged the receiver. "Hello," she said in a voice that hadn't yet lost all its professional crispness. She'd been office manager to the president of the Fellowship of the Police, Brooklyn branch, before her accident, and had impeccable phone skills.

"Hell freezes over 'fore you return calls, izzat it?"

Vera stiffened. That voice. "To whom did you wish to speak?"

"Well, hairy-balled Krishna. Did I call *you* again?"

Click.

Vera exhaled, slowly, deliberately. She'd been braced for it— for something. Whatever it might turn out to be from such a person. A person in need of medical help. She worried about that briefly, then let it go.

Thirty minutes later, in the middle of *Sally Jessy Raphael,* the phone rang again. Again from the motionless chair the arm snaked out, strangely gaunt and muscled in comparison with the formless body it was attached to.

"Hello."

"You hardly even let it ring, d'ya. Ain't you got nothin' better to do all day than answer the phone?"

Silence. Vera wanted to hang up, but as usual couldn't, no matter how badly she longed to rid herself of the voice on the line. Something inside wouldn't let her, no matter how big a waste of time the wrong number, how nasty the prank, or how abusive the anonymous voice.

A connection was a connection. *We must accept what we're given. . . . So now I'm a philosopher?* After dropping the receiver onto the sticky counter, she focused again on the TV.

The voice squawked. "Hey! You there? I said, You got nothin' better to do?"

Silence. Vera couldn't hang up first, but she didn't have to talk.

Click.

That night, the *Eight O'Clock News* projected its jittery logo across Vera's face in the gloom. The phone again rang. A shiver of nerves raced up Vera's good arm as she grabbed the receiver.

"Hello."

"Y'know, I'm here in the women's prison. I mean, I figure, maybe you never heard that we call it the Island. It's 'cause you town folks don't like us being so close. No civilians even drive by if they can help it. You know, stranded? On a desert island? Anyway, I shouldn't be rude to somebody I never met. Notcher fault if I dialed wrong. Hey?"

Vera blinked. Her attention wandered back to the TV, then bounced back again to the black dial phone on the kitchen counter at her shoulder. The whole world was on the other end. That part that didn't live in the little beige box on the kitchen table, that is.

"How do you get to make so many phone calls from a prison?" asked Vera, curious in spite of herself.

"I work in the warden's office. Long as it ain't long distance, no big deal. They trust me. Funny, huh? Answer the phone, keep files in shape—you get the idea. Cheap labor, twelve cents an hour. But I'm *proud* to lend a hand. I keep the New York State penal system runnin' slick and tight. Like a rubber girdle."

Vera snickered, something she'd forgotten she could still do, surprising herself.

"My name's—"

"Nancy Wolcott," supplied Vera.

"You remember! Geeze, wish that doc could remember. I'm just another body to him, toted up at the end of the day to collect his pay. Shove eighteen of us through his office inna hour to make his quota. You know how many minutes that gives each o' us?"

"Three and a third minutes."

"Yah. Softhearted gentlemen, ain't they? The hypocritical oath."

"My doctors always treated me good," protested Vera, unable to let this pass. They had been responsible for the size of the disability pension she got from the police. They, with the police lawyers, had forced the insurance company to send her Mrs. Benedetto and . . .

Silence.

"Whatsamatta?"

"Nothing."

"Anyways. I was a little lonesome. I won't bother you again." A pause. "Unless you want."

"I—I guess I don't mind."

"Hey. Thanks. Talk again, right?"

"Right."

Click.

Vera replaced the receiver in a daze. She forgot to watch the entire next hour of back-to-back *Simpsons* reruns.

The next day, Friday, again during *Sally,* the phone rang. Vera's arm had hardly any distance to go, as she'd been holding the instrument on her lap. "Hello?"

"It's Nancy."

Vera breathed. "Hi."

"Nice day today, ain't it?" asked Nancy after a pause.

Vera glanced outside, not sure. The full sun hadn't hit the kitchen yet, so it was relatively comfortable. "Not so hot, yet."

"You don't like it hot?" asked Nancy.

Vera nearly laughed. "It gets a little too hot here sometimes."

"Know whatcha mean. Y'gotta watch out for yourself. In or outside, don't matter, does it."

Silence at this grim statement.

"You got any hobbies?"

Vera pondered this, turning the word over in her mind, unable to connect with it. *I survive, that's what I do.* "I watch TV."

"Oh. What else? I mean you can't watch TV *all* day, can you?"

Vera frowned. "What kind of medical care do you need?"

"Why, could you get me a better doctor? One o' yours?"

"I don't think I can, but I would if I could."

"Y'would?" Silence, while Nancy thought that over. "That's nice of you. Y'don't even know me, an' here I am in prison, too." She paused. "It was a coughing thing. Bronchitis, or sumthin'. Actually, I'm better now. Without the quack—no medicine, no nothin'. He saw me once when the cough started. Just strolled by me, said, 'Come back if it gets worse.' It got worse, so I did. I checked in at the infirmary like you're supposed to, but they said he was too busy to see me. It's been a couple weeks now, believe that? I got mad, so I been callin' his house. Trying to. Is he worried about me? Hell, no. I bet the quack charged the state for treating me, too. I'm gonna write a letter to the governor, tell him. You think I should?"

"Sure, why not?"

"Who's the governor these days, anyway?"

Vera told her.

Nancy laughed. "I wan't serious. Geeze, one guy we all know inside is who's the governor."

"I'm glad you're okay."

"Sure. What was wrong with you, when you had *your* doctor?"

Vera froze.

Suddenly Nancy's voice hissed, "Hey. Gotta run."

Click.

Vera spent the next few hours thinking furiously. When the phone rang again, she wasn't prepared. In a panic, her voice quavered when she said "Hello," but to her relief, Nancy didn't mention her last question again.

They spoke for some time, even telling each other a few stories from their childhoods before Nancy had to ring off again.

Vera sat thoughtfully for a while, savoring their conversation. Together they had journeyed from peonies to parents, from capital punishment to the men in their lives. Then she heard Honey-Ann's approach. With an uncharacteristic slyness that made her wonder at herself, she slid the phone far back on the kitchen counter. She stared at the TV, but could no longer summon the lack of will with which she had formerly sat there, basted by the sun and the odors.

Honey-Ann's eyes narrowed as she studied Vera, but then she relaxed. Reaching through the paint-crusted cupboard doors, she took out a can of peas, cut open the can with a crank-style opener, and dumped the watery beige-green peas into a cereal bowl. She shoved the bowl, slopping water over the counter, toward Vera.

"Lunch," she announced. Vera eyed the peas in resignation. Most of Honey-Ann's so-called cooking was something dumped, cold, from a can.

Honey-Ann reached into her shorts pocket. "Mail came." She slid an uncapped ballpoint pen and an official FOP check near Vera's good hand on the kitchen table. The disability check. When Vera didn't move, Honey-Ann gave her a vicious slap across the back of her newly shaved (and much-nicked) head—penance for drinking the iced water Wednesday. Vera's hand slowly went toward the pen, moved to the spot she knew well after seven years, and signed. Honey-Ann whipped the check out from under the pen. Put another one in its place.

"And here." The quarterly Social Security disability check—a very large number in printed script on the line. Vera signed. Honey-Ann smiled. She pursed her lips and said, "Aw, don't take it so hard. Think how I'm keeping you out of jail. Seven years of my life I've devoted to a thief, I deserve something for the goodness of my heart. In fact, Randy came up with a new way for you to thank me. This house. Isn't he just the cutest, brightest li'l ol' squeeze?" Randy was Honey-Ann's latest boyfriend. So far, he'd outlasted the others by passing the three-month mark in their relationship.

Vera gazed around incredulously, thinking, *You want this old dump? This place you've let become junk, stinking rotted trash? My home?* "You want my house?"

Honey-Ann nodded and stretched her healthy, slim body, displaying her creamy midriff and long curvy legs to Vera's indifferent gaze. If there was anything Vera'd learned, it was that people were more than just bodies. Honey-Ann yawned. "It's been okay here, but I'm getting bored. Always wanted to try my luck in Vegas. Randy's itchin' to go, too; he's sick of his real estate job, working nights and weekends. So he dug up a buyer, God knows how. Said we should sell this nasty pile, use the dough as a stake, and go DO it."

"And what about me?" blurted Vera.

Honey-Ann shrugged as she turned to leave. "What about you? I'll bet you won't even notice. Yep, I bet you won't know a damn thing about it. I wouldn't worry if I was you." She giggled.

Vera, agony overwhelming fear of reprisal, asked, "Why do you treat me like this, Honey-Ann? Do you hate me so much?"

Honey-Ann swiveled to look at her, amused. "I don't hate you. In fact, when I found out how good you had it—"

"—*good* I had it?" She glanced bitterly down at her lifeless flesh.

"Sure. I was really happy for you. Because now you had more to lose." Honey-Ann glared. "First you get into the FOP—good money, lots of promotions coming at you. . . ."

"For hard work," muttered Vera.

"Then you marry that plummy executive type—he drew down a good income, too. Why you and not me? I'da married him, for hell's sake. Then your accident! Free money just floating in left and right to poor, poor Vera. Who, *unlike her sister*, will never have to piss her life away in slob jobs, pulling down piddly-ass pay until she dies of old age behind some hamburger counter. Money to last the rest of your life. Nobody to split it with, either—the husband's gone! *I* deserved that kinda life, but wouldn't you know, it happened to you. You deserve pain. Lots of it. Teach you to hurt me like that."

Vera knew better than to speak again. She kept silent, but her mind screamed, *It didn't have to be like this. I would have shared with you. You're my baby sister, the only family I have left, and I loved you.*

Honey-Ann had almost left the kitchen before she turned, swiveling on one heel. "You been on the phone a lot, or is that the TV I keep hearing?"

Vera put all the control she'd ever mustered in her life into keeping her expression deadpan and uncaring. "The phone? All I ever get is wrong numbers. And I can't dial out—you fixed it that way. Remember?"

"TV, then." Honey-Ann frowned, took a step closer, reached a manicured finger out to touch the beige plastic casing. The rabbit ears had broken off long ago.

"Take it," suggested Vera, reading her mind. She made her eyes drift toward the window. It *was* a pretty day out there. A nice day for a walk. Or for a bumpy rolling ride down a cracked, weedy sidewalk in a wheelchair. For a split second she could smell the perfume of cut grass, remembering it from a hundred years ago.

"Aw, what the hell." Honey-Ann whirled and left the room, abandoning her impulse to take the TV.

Vera closed her eyes, squeezed them tight. If Honey-Ann looked back in, she'd be damned if she'd let her see her cry.

Mrs. Benedetto had not come today. She'd sent someone else. Someone younger, indifferent, who talked little, but pushed and pulled on Vera's body as if forced to handle a side of spoiled beef. Someone who didn't quite get her head so clean, and forgot her feet entirely. Honey-Ann, using the phone in the living room, had afterward called the service and, full of praises for the woman, requested she be sent from now on instead of Mrs. Benedetto. Vera had gone back to her kitchen without being prodded.

That night, Vera had dreams in which she'd been long dead and now, by some mistake, had awakened in her tomb. And as hard as she fought it, she couldn't help seeing things: her husband's selfish use of her, her sister's greed-fueled hatred, and worst of all her hopeless hunger for a family of her own. Realities she'd spared herself from facing by being dead. She was returning to maggoty, revolting life. Between the dreams, her dead limbs racked with fire and pain, she sobbed. She emerged from her pallet the next morning unable to see, her eyes swollen nearly shut.

It was Saturday now. Vera wondered if Nancy worked on Saturday. When the phone rang, she didn't dare breathe until she heard Nancy's cheery voice on the other end. Evidently, Nancy worked all hours. No unions in jail, Nancy joked when Vera asked.

They talked a long while. Nancy recounted funny stories about a crazy cell-mate and certain aspects of life in the joint. Vera had to smother her laughter, snuffing and snorting into the soft pillow of her bad arm's flesh.

Then suddenly Nancy asked the question. "Why do you

answer the phone so fast, no matter when I call? What do you do all day? Is there something wrong with you?"

Vera gazed outside, silent with fear, the anguish of her dreams tearing at her again. She reviewed Honey-Ann's rules, her punishments—seven years' worth. While Nancy called out to her from the receiver, worried by the sudden stillness, Vera wondered what harm could possibly come if she confided in this disembodied voice. There was no hope for self-protection, that was obvious: Honey-Ann had made it clear she and Randy would soon finish off what was left of Vera's life. And in truth, Vera felt long past ready to die. So her questions converged into one: Could Honey-Ann ever find out Nancy even existed? She puzzled over possible dangers to Nancy, but couldn't see any. It would feel so *relieving* to tell somebody, just one anonymous voice, what was happening to her. To talk, really talk, just once. Before the end.

She decided to answer Nancy's prodding voice, still vibrating over the line, but suddenly hesitated. *What was it about that dream? Where had the pain come from? And why now, after all this time? What had upset her so much last night?*

Vera pulled herself back to the present and found herself gazing outside, her eyes blurred but clearing. She said, "Why are you in jail, Nancy? What crime did you commit?"

"Um. Well. I killed my husband."

Vera gasped, almost laughed at the absurdity of the reply. "Oh, you can't be serious. What did you really do?"

"I killed him," squawked Nancy. "Believe it."

"Why?"

"He treated me like I was a beer can, like he could crush me if he felt like it. He didn't treat me like I was a person who had feelings."

"Did he—beat you?"

"Hell, yes. He did anything his tiny mind could think of, and thought it was so damned fun. Then he decided to trade me in on a new model by gettin' himself a shortcut divorce. I shot the bastard. In other words, if you ain't quite gettin' it, I shot him *first*. But I did it a little too far in advance o' *his* move, so I got a manslaughter instead of self-defense. But they went easy on the sentence."

"Ah." Vera thought it over. "But why did you ever let him treat you that way? Why didn't you leave? Were you handicapped or something?"

Nancy grumped around a bit, making no sense, until Vera realized she was thinking out loud. "You know, I like you, Vera," she concluded abruptly.

Vera's head jolted back as if Nancy had just shot her through the phone receiver. And indeed the pain was throbbing, pulling at her chest, ripping through her mind like lightning, crashing through her dead limbs. The shock of life. That's what it was. Nancy liked her. And Vera liked her back. Warmth. Kindness. Humor. Spending time together. Acceptance. Respect for each other's thoughts, sharing themselves with each other. However, by being a friend, Nancy was torturing her worse than Honey-Ann could ever dream of doing, even after seven long years of practice.

Nancy, oblivious to Vera's painful rebirth, went on. "I didn't get out because I didn't think nobody else would have a slug like me. That I'd die all alone if I left."

Vera's voice throbbed with tears. "What made you think you were such a slug?"

"Dunno. 'Cause he kept sayin' it. Said what a favor he did me by keepin' me around. See, I thought he loved me, a while back, when we got married. I figured, well, he'd just finally gotten to know the real me. So, to my mind, he wasn't the problem, I was. I believed his lies. Until I caught on."

"How'd you catch on?"

"Oh, one day I bumped into an old friend somewhere. And I

suddenly remembered how I used to have friends before he scared 'em off. They sure knew me, and they liked me. It started me thinkin'. I tried to see myself like other people would. Not easy, babe. I decided maybe I wasn't so bad, just mixed up. But before I could up and go, he told me his plan for the 'no-pay' divorce, and blam."

"Blam." Was that her destiny, too? A bullet? No, Honey-Ann wouldn't know what to do with a gun. Probably food poisoning. Pretty easy—on Honey-Ann.

"So I got sent up. I get on here okay, though. Really."

"It's not so bad?"

"Well, I make the best of it—'at's my nature. You learn, you get on. And I learned to respect myself here, too. You can do time and profit from it."

Vera smiled. Then she thought a minute. "What about thieves?"

"Whaddabout 'em?"

"Well, what's it like there, for people who stole?" She cleared her throat self-consciously. "I, uh, stole some money from my employers once. Years ago," she added hastily. "When I was really young. I found out they were paying guys doing my job a *lot* more than me, and I did the same work exactly. So I asked them to make it even, and they said no. Because I was female. There weren't laws about discrimination then, so that was that. I got so mad, I added little bits to my expense account for a while to even things out. Not that it did, such small sums of money. Four times I did it, five—I don't remember now. I didn't like the way it made me feel, though, so I stopped, then put it all back, doing it in reverse, see? A few years later, laws passed that fixed the problem, and I really did love my job, so I stayed. Then when everything went bad, the FOP supported me. They were my friends when I needed them most. If they ever found out I stole from them . . . ! Nancy, I couldn't stand it. But my sister Honey-Ann got hold of my expense records." *Oops.* She hadn't meant to say that.

"Honey-Ann? *Honey-Ann?*" Nancy paused, a long silence. Then, distractedly, "Listen, Vera, I hate to stop you there, but I gotta go."

Click.

The rest of Saturday dragged, and Sunday was worse. The ache inside the parts of her that were supposedly dead grew and grew. Once, she caught herself lying against the kitchen counter, the aluminum edge cutting into her cheek, her good arm stretched to touch the phone, tears rolling down her cheeks. Abruptly, she stopped. She pulled herself upright and cleaned her face, fearing detection by Honey-Ann. Sunday night she stayed in the kitchen all night, not even pretending to sleep. And she watched TV.

Monday. During *Sally,* the phone rang again. "Vera, you there?"

Relief bloomed in Vera's chest, and she had to try twice to croak, "*Yes.*"

"Sorry I didn't call you back Saturday, but I had things to do. Vera," Nancy shrilled, her words rapid, "why didn't you tell me you were a cripple held prisoner in a house all damn day and night? I'm so mad at you for not tellin' me! Ain't we friends? Don't I mean nothin' to you?"

Vera's mouth parted, but no sounds came out.

"Honey-Ann Porter. That's your sister, ain't it? You shoulda done a little homework before you let a worm like her push you into such a hole. First off, the piddly sums you stole don't even add up to a traffic fine. And you paid it back! Hell, time's up on it too. Everything's got time limits on it but murder. She ain't got records, she's got stiff toilet paper with writing on it."

Vera laid her head on the warped cabinet top and tried to stifle her sobbing. "How do *you* know all this?"

"I know *lots* about Honey-Ann Porter. My brother used to go out with her—like dating a sewer rat, he said. You don't even gotta *hint* what you been suffering. And don't even consider bein' loyal, 'cause that skank ain't *sister* to *nobody*! Family is as family does. Me and my brother, we can tell you plenty about family that ain't family. So we look out for each other's backs true blue. *That's* family. Anyhow, I got my brother to visit me Saturday afternoon, and he coughed up lots of info. For one, that she used to *brag* about what she was doin' to you. *Brag,* Vera. Think about how disgusting that is, not to mention stupid! My brother thought she made the whole thing up. Well. You didn't have family before. Now you do. *Me.* Now get off this damn phone before she hears you blubbering. Watch TV. It's a nice day out, ain't it? I'm tellin' you, watch TV. Do your hobby."

Click.

Vera knew she wouldn't hear from Nancy again. She didn't blame her for being disgusted—truly, she hadn't put up much fight. Not like Nancy had with her husband. She'd been too devastated, at first by her situation, and then by Honey-Ann's betrayal. But she felt the comfort of Nancy's claiming her for family anyway. Tears blurred her vision, ruining her chances to win an entertainment center by guessing its price.

Later, when the woman came from home services, and Vera was enduring her ministrations, she overheard a phone call Honey-Ann took, perched on the stairs landing, all curled up and purring, like a cat full of cream. *Randy, no doubt. He must be some sweet-talker,* thought Vera, uncaring. When the woman left, Vera rolled herself off to the kitchen again, eager to escape Honey-Ann's long syrupy phone conversation. She spent her afternoon trying to resign herself to the notion that at least if her life was not tolerable, it would be short. And somebody, Nancy Wolcott, had volunteered to be her real family. More than she'd ever hoped for after the accident, it would have to be enough.

She turned on the TV and tried to focus on the game shows,

fretfully anticipating her death. When dinnertime came, Honey-Ann arrived, carrying an empty grocery sack. Ignoring Vera's puzzled glances, she whistled tunelessly while filling the sack with the scant food stored in the kitchen, leaving only the canned items. The can opener she laid within Vera's reach. Then she left.

Vera's stomach growled as she stared at the rows of unopened canned peas and corn and beans. They were all within reach, but they might as well have been a hundred miles away—she couldn't work the can opener with one hand. Vera suddenly understood. Honey-Ann would probably restock the shelves before the coroner came. When they found her starved body, the assumption would be she'd purposely deprived herself. After all, Honey-Ann would say, look at the perverse way she'd acted for weeks, even months; Mrs. Benedetto's testimony would corroborate her. Honey-Ann had left the cans here to lighten her chore of refilling the cupboards, and for Vera to look at . . .while she died.

The next night, the police had to break down the front door to reach Vera where she slept—fairly peacefully, although it might only have been inertia from twenty-four hours of fasting. She lay, as usual, in a shelf-stripped pantry off the kitchen, her bed a pad of seven years' worth of rags. It took them some time to find her, but when they did, she blinked like a cornered raccoon at all the men and lights. Among the curious faces, she recognized one and called to him for help. After several puzzled minutes, he suddenly recalled her and her circumstances. He looked oddly embarrassed. She'd changed so completely he hadn't known her. And it was true—she had become another person altogether since seven years ago. She was even a different person than she was yesterday, she decided.

But it wasn't until the fuss died down that she came to understand the reason they were there. Someone had killed Honey-Ann in a bar fight. A man. "Randy," she wondered aloud, remembering his part in the plot to kill her. They wrote down his name. Nobody expected much of her, so she said little. Over the next few days, people came in and took statements, cleaned her decently, brought her clothes and food. She wondered who to ask about all the money stolen from her over the years, but was ashamed to expose Honey-Ann's true nature and her own spiritless submission, so she let it pass. Quickly the murder drifted into the back pages of the newspaper, out of people's minds, and then was forgotten altogether. Dust to dust, Vera mused, a little shocked by the ease with which Honey-Ann had faded from the world's notice. As if she hadn't existed at all.

And then one afternoon, Tuesday, two weeks after Honey-Ann's murder, the doorbell rang. Without waiting for Vera to answer it, a tall, nice-looking young man strode in. From the perspective of her chair she saw a giant with bulging muscles, dark-haired but fair-skinned. Smallish eyes, decided Vera, but a big mouth used to smiling. He brought with him an armload of groceries, which he dumped onto the newly scrubbed kitchen table; then he inspected inside the cabinets and nodded. On the way out, he introduced himself as Nancy Wolcott's brother, Mickey. Named by his dead mother for St. Michael, the archangel, he said solemnly, as if this was a routine part of his self-introduction. The screen door banged shut on his heel as he left.

Vera sat in shock for a while, mulling over this intrusion. Mickey Wolcott. Mickey. Memory played one of its little tricks and the name dropped into place from Honey-Ann's sugary telephone conversation the day before she'd died. Was it Randy or was it a *Mickey* she'd been talking to? The police said only that she'd been killed in a bar brawl. If they'd dug up any suspects or new facts about that night, they had never told her. Euphoric over her sudden release from tyranny and imminent death, she hadn't asked. If Mickey had taken Honey-Ann out that night . . . then was he her murderer? Nancy had said they'd used to go out.

Vera's lips moved in protest, but her thoughts rejected doubt: *He killed her. The man who just left my house killed Honey-Ann.* Nancy freely admitted she'd killed her husband to save herself—she must have ordered Honey-Ann's murder to save Vera. Her friend. Her friend?

Investigation of the bags revealed jars of tomato paste, fresh basil, olive oil, and other ingredients that would make a wonderful pasta dinner—if someone could cook it.

Nancy showed up at seven with Mickey. She burst through the door, shrieking, dancing in circles, "I'm out! I'm out!" Mickey was again loaded down, this time with cutlery and pans. Nancy shoved him and the bags off into the kitchen as if to move him out of the way. But by now, Vera had been expecting her. Had steeled herself to it, actually.

Nancy was short, mid-twenties, small-boned, and wiry. Darker-skinned than her brother, but the hair was the same, glistening black and abundant. High over her right eyebrow began a jagged scar that trailed down between her eyes to end at the bridge of her nose. She circled the chair at first, as if taking inventory, then she whooped and gave Vera a cautious hug. "Don't wanna hurt you, hon," she explained. In big strides, like the queen of the world, she paced off the house. She went upstairs, came tripping down, shouting at Mickey how much space there was, what they could do to fix it up. All the while, Vera sat and watched. Her eyes were steady and wary beneath lowered brows, and she said nothing. What could she say to killers?

Dinner was served around nine. Sister and brother ate with voracious appetites. Nancy rattled on crazily about the thrill of being on the outside again. Good behavior, she insisted repeatedly to Vera, pointing her fork for emphasis. Nodding politely, Vera watched them eat, trying not to flinch each time the fork stabbed at her. Waiting. Killers both, taking over where Honey-Ann left off, but she wouldn't give them the satisfaction of showing fear. When Honey-Ann had begun her reign of terror, Vera's shock had betrayed the depth of her pain, the agony she felt at such complete rejection by her own sister. And Honey-Ann had fed on that agony, enjoyed it.

Okay, now the stakes were far higher. Jail, certainly. Life or capital punishment, she had no idea. No time limit for murder, Nancy had said. No denying that Vera was grateful it happened, too, so fairly enough she was an accessory. But these two would find only a shell to tyrannize. Not the person she really was, had lately become. The person awakened to forgotten self-respect by Nancy's warm humanity during a telephone call to a wrong number.

Wrong number. At this thought, tears nearly started, but she controlled herself.

After dinner, the two cleaned up, then played cards. Vera brooded in the background. *What were they waiting for?* She longed to die now, to get it over with before her fear broke her. Tantalizing baked bread smells lingered in the kitchen, giving the room a cozy aura it had never had before, driving Vera even wilder with the suspense.

It wasn't long before a yawning Mickey had moved in enough bags to make Vera certain they were in her home to stay. While they sorted things out and fussed, she turned her chair to roll in the direction of the kitchen pantry, full of despair despite her best intentions.

"Where you goin', Vera?" asked Nancy, puzzled. "You don't *miss* that hole she made you sleep in, do ya? I made up your *real* bed. You ain't been upstairs in dogs' years, have you?"

Vera turned her chair around to face her. *What did Nancy have in mind? Shoot me now. Please!* Her nerves screamed, but the muscles in her face never moved. "No," she mumbled. "Not since the accident."

Mickey, muscles bulging, leaned over and scooped her up out of the chair, pulling an involuntary shriek from Vera's grim lips. "You're goin' on a diet, m'girl," he panted. "And the gym for us both. Yer nothin' but a blob of fat, and I don't care to bust my springs hauling you up to bed every night."

Vera paled. Every night. *They were going to keep her alive to sign the checks. Just like Honey-Ann. Unfair,* she cried to Nancy in her mind. *I want to die in dignity. No crying or begging. If you don't hurry up, you'll wear me down and cheat me of my only victory.* Already Vera felt the waning of her fragile strength. It wouldn't be long, she knew, before she would crumble before them.

Nancy smacked her brother's bulging bicep. "The gym'll come when she's ready, dolt. She had a shock. Seven years bad luck— gotta have time to get over it. Everything in time."

Clinging dazedly to Mickey's rock-hard shoulder while he slowly mounted the stairs, Vera listened as the siblings argued over possible health routines for her, the cleanliness of her furniture, and various other domestic aspects of the situation. *Is this what murderers talk about?* she wondered, confused. Not on any of her TV shows. It was only when Nancy burst out laughing at Mickey's suggestions for Vera's workout clothes that Vera sobbed—no, actually howled, overcome by her terrors. All movement stopped.

They gaped at her as she lay helpless in Mickey's arms, sobbing wildly. *I'm humiliating myself,* she thought. *A spectacle for them to laugh over, like Honey-Ann had.* Yet a part of her mind registered their bewilderment. It hovered in her consciousness, like a tiny star in the corner of a dark sky. Gradually she controlled herself. She couldn't remember the last time she'd made such a loud noise, and they hadn't punished her for it. Yet.

"Drop me," she cried to Mickey, an impulse.

"Huh? But if I do, you'll hurt yourself on the stairs."

That's what I had in mind—hopefully, a quick broken neck. Then she noticed his aghast expression. Studied it. She finally said, "But if we were somewhere I could rest safely, you'd put me down?"

"Hell, sure. Why not? Cripes, you're a lot of gut."

"Mick! Don't you get it? Look at her face!" Nancy's fists rammed onto her hips. "Before you dropped stuff off this afternoon, or sometime in the last week, did you do what I told you? Did you ask Vera if it was okay for us to move in here?" She got her answer from his lack of an answer.

Clearly controlling herself, she faced Vera squarely. "This is my fault. I asked Mick to drop the dime on you because after Honey-Ann's kickoff, I was in a rush and chokin' on paperwork. See, I applied for early parole. They like it if you can prove you got a good place to go after you get out, like someplace better than the projects. I, uh, kind of invented a letter from you saying we was friends and you needed me. That it was you, the one the FOP liked, who was offern' me this great place. I had Mickey mail it to me from your neighborhood post office—they look for details like that. It knocked four months off my sentence, the letter bein' from you, you know that? They really like you, the cops. The parole board, uh, 'understood' why you didn't come to the hearing."

Vera blinked. "You signed my name? Forgery?" *Then they don't need me alive. They could just stash my body somewhere. Killers and now forgers. Who would even miss me?* She frowned, remembering why she was on the stairs. "What?" But the question was to herself, not Nancy.

Nancy reddened. "Yeah. I used their computer, came up with some old FOP clerical work you did before the accident, printed out your signature." She tilted her head at her brother. "'At's what I had helpin' me, though. And as you now understand, or I *hope* you understand, some types of jobs ain't his strong point, y'know? 'Cause o' that, I figured I oughta handle the paperwork alone. I shoulda realized he'd muff this job, too, though. At least he mailed the letter okay. I'm sorry."

Dazed, Vera nodded. "No problem."

Nancy brightened. "Yeah? Well, thanks. Thanks."

Reaching up to his great height, she gave her brother's shoulder a shove with the butt of her palm. "I thought she was just shy, and all along she's been petrified what she got herself into! Her very first time with us, the first I ever saw her *face*! And it stunk for her because of your fault! Mick, take her up to her room and put her down and then you better run for your life, you scumsucking frozen pizza! You scared hell outta her, and you're gonna pay."

"Women," complained Mickey as he trundled Vera up the remaining steps. "I thought it was pretty clear. Why else bring so much food in, if we wasn't staying? What, *she's* gonna eat it all? Not on *her* new diet. And self-defense. Street defense, Vera. Gotta learn to stick up for yourself. Your problem's tough, sure, but everybody's got some kind of thing, y'know? Can't let that stop you."

Nancy patted Vera's lifeless leg consolingly. "He won't be too hard on you, don't worry. And don't forget, you got me. You really been messed with, and this poor house, too. Mick and me learned all kinds of useful stuff in the joint. You won't be sorry you took us in."

Vera, her eyes still wet from the earlier tears, grinned. Killers? Maybe, but they were *her* killers.

Pleased, she went to bed.

Fall came, then the best winter she ever had, and then glorious spring. Today was one of those bright mornings, tiny fresh green things budding all around. Of course, these days, she treasured every minute, no matter the season or weather. Bumping and careening joyfully down the cracked and tilty sidewalk that fronted her freshly reshingled house (now robin's-egg blue), she approached the corner and prepared for a two-wheeled whirling stop at the traffic light, a highly entertaining move that Mick had taught her. Another wheelchair woman, slightly older than Vera, was already at the corner, and Vera thought it would be fun to impress her.

As Vera advanced, the woman stretched forward, fumbling to push the button for "Walk." At that moment, a youth wearing a faded red baseball cap turned backward darted by and, in a flash, snatched the old-fashioned black leather handbag from the woman's blanketed lap.

Vera wheeled instantly into a sliding 180-degree stop that put her in the boy's path. She whipped hard at his knees, backhanded, with a retractable steel pole as he ran past her. He shrieked and stopped to grab both knees. With the pole, Vera calmly fished the bag by its handle from his loosened grip and slid it back to tuck it safely beneath her other arm's lifeless elbow. He snarled and turned on her, but something—maybe the muscular trim body he saw clad in a martial arts sweatsuit, maybe the no-nonsense cropped curly hair, or maybe the pleasurable anticipation in her expression—seemed to change his ideas, and he ran hard across the street, headed for the next block.

She watched him run. Young and whole. Strong legs. Straight back. And so many problems in his life already. She turned to the stupefied older woman and handed her purse to her. The woman's arms, though trembling, were both working well, Vera noted. The woman looked ready to cry.

"My name is Vera," she said. "You're the widow who lives in that brick house on Harding Street, aren't you? I've been hoping to meet you." She reached over with her good hand and patted the woman's upper arm. Not a muscle to be found. She smiled consolingly into the rounded anxious eyes. "You've had quite a shock. See that little blue house behind us? That's where I live.

Would you like some coffee while you recover? My son, Mick, is the world's greatest cook. And my daughter's home. I'd love you to meet my family. You must get lonely all by yourself. I know I did before my kids came to live with me."

The woman slowly nodded. As they turned their chairs, each politely making room for the other, Vera said, "My son says we all need to learn to stick up for ourselves, even people like you and me. Our problems are tough, sure, but everybody's got some kind of battle to fight. I'll let my son explain it. Did you see my sliding wheelie? Would you like to try one yourself?"

The older woman looked dubiously at Vera, who laughed. "Same reaction I had! Oh, you're going to love my family!"

A Mysterious Collection of **Apple** Recipes

Evelyn's Apple Rhubarb Pie

PASTRY FOR 9-INCH PAN:
   2 cups sifted flour
   ½ tsp. salt
   1 cup shortening
   6 tbsp. very cold water

Mix salt into flour, cut in shortening; gradually add water till you've got a workable paste. Too little will leave it like dry dog food. Divide in half. Form into ball. Chill thoroughly. Roll out, ⅛th inch thick, and line pan. Reserve other half for top crust.

FILLING:
   ¼ cup brown sugar
   2 apples, sliced thin
   2 lb. rhubarb, cut in small pieces

Spread rhubarb on pie crust (already in pie pan) as bottom layer. Spread apples as next layer. Sprinkle sugar over apples. Place reserved crust on top. Bake at 450 degrees for 10 minutes, then 350 degrees for 40 minutes. Find snake to serve it.

Contributed by Susan Dunlap

Aunt Paully's Naked Apple Pie

⅔ cup all-purpose flour
½ tsp. baking powder
¼ tsp. salt
1 egg
⅓ cup ginger brandy
½ cup brown sugar
½ cup granulated sugar
2 medium apples, pared, diced
½ cup chopped nuts

Stir together flour, baking power, and salt. Beat egg; add brandy, sugars, and the flour mixture. Stir well to blend. Add apples and nuts. Spread in a 9-inch greased pie pan and bake in a preheated 350-degree oven, 30–35 minutes. Serve warm or cold with whipped topping or ice cream. Yield: 6 to 8 servings.

Contributed by Pamela J. Fesler

German Apple Cake

I am not permitted to make pies, apple or otherwise. My family won't put up with pastry-failure tantrums. So, I make apple cake. I found this recipe in a Cuisinart cookbook, credited to Sue Weinstein. It can be made without a food processor, but it's a whole lot easier with one.

CAKE:

1 cup sugar
1 cup unsifted, unbleached flour
4 tbsp. butter, cut into pieces
1 tsp. baking powder

1 tsp. vanilla extract
1 large egg
4 large pippin or Granny Smith apples

TOPPING:

3 tbsp. sugar
3 tbsp. melted butter
1 tsp. cinnamon
1 large egg

If you're using a food processor, put all the cake ingredients except the apples into the bowl, and process until the mixture is the consistency of cornmeal. Spread the mixture in the bottom of a well-buttered 9-inch springform pan. (If you don't have a food processor, mix the dry ingredients together, then cut in the butter, and when the mixture is like cornmeal, add the vanilla and egg.)

Peel the apples and remove the cores, then slice them.

Arrange the apples in layers on top of the crumb mixture. Bake in a preheated 350-degree oven for 45 minutes.

Meanwhile, mix together the topping ingredients. Spoon the mixture over the apples and bake 25 to 30 minutes more or until the top is firm.

Contributed by Linda Grant

Recipe for Fall

Drive out into the country and buy a bag of crisp, tart local apples—McIntosh, maybe, or if you're lucky, Jonathans.

Scrub, core, and slice (but do not peel) several apples. Fan slices out nicely on a large plate. Put a big chunk of sharp cheddar cheese on a board. Slice a bit of cheddar, put it atop a slice of apple, and enjoy, perhaps with a glass of Riesling or Gewürztraminer.

When only a couple of apples remain, use them to flavor the following:

Bread Pudding

3 cups milk
3 cups bread, cubed and somewhat dry (preferably French bread with most of its crust removed)
2 tbsp. butter
½ cup brown sugar
3 eggs, slightly beaten
¾ tsp. salt
1 tsp. vanilla
1+ tsp. cinnamon, ¼–½ tsp. each nutmeg, mace (to taste)
1–1½ cups coarsely chopped apples (peeled)
¼ cup sherry

Preheat oven to moderate (350 degrees). Pour sherry over chopped apple and set aside. Scald the milk, add the 2 tbsp. butter, and pour the hot liquid over the bread cubes. Soak for 5 minutes. Stir in sugar, eggs, and spices. Add apples, including liquid. Pour into buttered baking dish; a 2-quart Pyrex casserole dish works well. Set dish in pan of hot water and bake approximately 1 hour or until inserted knife blade comes out clean.

Contributed by Janet LaPierre

Sweet Potatoes and Apples
(A side dish for turkey, ham, or pork roast)

4–5 sweet potatoes, baked, then peeled (or 1 can, drained and sliced)
4 large cooking apples, peeled and sliced
¼ cup brown sugar
cinnamon to taste
maple syrup to taste
2 tbsp. butter or margarine

Butter a casserole dish. Layer slices of sweet potatoes and apples. Sprinkle brown sugar and cinnamon over all. Drizzle with maple syrup. Dot with butter. Cover and bake at 350 degrees 30–35 minutes or until the mixture bubbles and the apples are soft and translucent. Uncover, raise temperature to 450 degrees and bake another 5 minutes till top is brown and edges crusty. Serves 4–6.

Re the recipe: I've never in my life measured these ingredients, since it's never mattered. I try for two parts yams to one part apples in the finished dish. The rest is by guess and by golly. This will be plenty for eight people if you use it in the place of cranberry sauce, and assuming you have the table full of six or seven other bowls of vegetables. Feel free to tinker with the measurements.

Contributed by Margaret Maron

Raw Apple Cake

1 cup sugar
¼ cup shortening
1 egg
1 cup flour
1 tsp. soda
1 tsp. cinnamon
¼ tsp. nutmeg
¼ tsp. salt
2 cups raw, chopped, pared apples
½ cup raisins
1 cup nutmeats

Cream shortening and sugar; add beaten egg; sift dry ingredients together; add dry ingredients, fruit, and nuts; mix well; bake 45 minutes in greased pan (9x9) at 350 degrees.

Contributed by Nancy Pickard, from the kitchen of
Dorothy Arlene Bates Kirk

Tarte aux Pommes à l'Alsacienne

PÂTE BRISÉE:

   1 ¼ cups all-purpose flour

   6 tbsp. (¾ stick) sweet butter, cut into bits

   2 tbsp. lard or white shortening

   ⅛ tsp. salt

   ¼ tsp. sugar

   3 tbsp. cold water

FILLING:

   3–4 Granny Smith apples, peeled, cored, cut into slices

   ½ cup sugar

   ½ cup cream

   1 egg

   1 tsp. kirsch (cherry brandy)

Place all ingredients for *pâte brisée*, except the water, into a large bowl. With both hands, start mashing the mixture until it is uniform in color and lumpy. Add the water and mix rapidly with your fingers, just enough to mold all ingredients into a solid, smooth mass. Wrap in plastic wrap or use immediately.

Preheat oven to 375 degrees. Roll out and line a 9-inch pie pan with the *pâte brisée*. Arrange apple slices on top, and bake for 15 minutes.

Meanwhile, mix together sugar, cream, egg, and kirsch. Pour over the half-baked pie, return to oven, and bake an additional 25 minutes, or until custard is set and golden brown. Serves 6.

Contributed by Sarah Shankman

Apple Custard Pie

1 ⅓ cups flour

3 tbsp. sugar

2 tsp. baking powder

6 tbsp. butter

6–8 large apples

½ cup sugar

1 tsp. cinnamon

½ tsp. nutmeg

1 ½ cups cream

2 egg yolks

Preheat oven to 350 degrees. Sift first three ingredients. Cut butter into flour mixture using two knives until butter is coated and the size of small peas. Press into deep pie pan until crust is uniform and thin. Refrigerate.

Peel and slice apples. Arrange in layers on crust. Mix spices into sugar, then dust apples with mixture. Bake 15 minutes.

Gently beat yolks into cream. Pour on pie and bake for an additional 30 minutes.

Contributed by Marilyn Wallace

Apple Chutney

4 large, tart apples, peeled, cored, and diced
2 large pears, peeled, cored, and diced
1 orange, peeled (reserve large pieces) and diced
1 lemon, peeled (reserve large pieces) and diced
2 large onions, diced
2 cloves garlic, chopped
1½ cups raisins
1 cup vinegar
1 cup apple juice
½ cup sugar
2 tbsp. grated ginger
1 tsp. tumeric
½ tsp. crushed red pepper flakes
1 tsp. salt
½ tsp. cloves

Bring all ingredients except fruit to a boil. Add fruit, including reserved citrus peel. Simmer 30–40 minutes, until fruit is tender. Remove peel. Makes about 5 pints.

Contributed by Marilyn Wallace

Mom's Brandied Apple Babies

Filling: In saucepan combine ¼ cup sugar and 1 tbsp. cornstarch (already dissolved in ⅓ cup cold water). Stir in 1 loosely packed cup of small (peeled) apple chunks, plus ½ cup all-natural applesauce. Cook, stirring constantly, till thickened and bubbly and apples are soft. Tart apples give best results. Stir in brandy to taste, not to exceed ¼ cup.

To assemble: Using 24 mini-crepes (see below), spread 1 tbsp. filling on unbrowned side of each crepe, leaving ¼-inch rim around edge. Roll up as for jelly roll. Place seam side down in greased 15½ x 10½ x 1-inch baking pan. Bake, covered, at 350 degrees for 10 minutes. Mix ¼ cup sugar and 1 teaspoon ground cinnamon; sprinkle over crepes. Makes 24.

Whipped cream, ice cream, and/or toasted sliced almonds are optional garnishes.

Baby Crepes:

½ cup unbleached flour
½ cup milk
3 eggs, separated
¼ cup sugar
3 tbsp. butter, melted
¼ tsp. vanilla

In a bowl combine flour, milk, egg yolks, sugar, butter, and vanilla; beat with rotary beater till blended. In large bowl beat egg whites till stiff peaks form. Fold batter into egg whites. Heat a lightly greased 6-inch skillet; remove from heat. Spoon in 1 tbsp. batter; spread with back of spoon to 4-inch circle. Return to heat. Brown on one side only. Invert over paper toweling; remove crepe. Repeat with remaining batter to make 24 crepes, greasing pan occasionally.

Contributed by Angela Zeman